P9-DTB-057

JUL 2 1 2022

Magnolia Library

the SEED of
CAIN

NO LONGER PROPERTY OF
SEATTLE PUBLIC LIBRARY

ALSO BY AGNES GOMILLION
AND AVAILABLE FROM TITAN BOOKS

The Record Keeper

the SEED of CAIN

AGNES GOMILLION

TITAN BOOKS

The Seed of Cain
Print edition ISBN: 9781789091182
E-book edition ISBN: 9781789091199

Published by Titan Books
A division of Titan Publishing Group Ltd
144 Southwark Street, London SE1 0UP
www.titanbooks.com

First edition: June 2022
10 9 8 7 6 5 4 3 2 1

This is a work of fiction. Names, places and incidents are either products of the author's imagination or used fictitiously. Any resemblance to actual persons, living or dead (except for satirical purposes), is entirely coincidental.

© 2022 Agnes Gomillion

No part of this publication may be reproduced, stored in a retrieval system, or transmitted, in any form or by any means without the prior written permission of the publisher, nor be otherwise circulated in any form of binding or cover other than that in which it is published and without a similar condition being imposed on the subsequent purchaser.

A CIP catalogue record for this title is available from the British Library.

Printed and bound by CPI Group (UK) Ltd, Croydon, CR0 4YY.

For Black women and girls,
namely the Queen Mother, Connie

TABLE OF CONTENTS

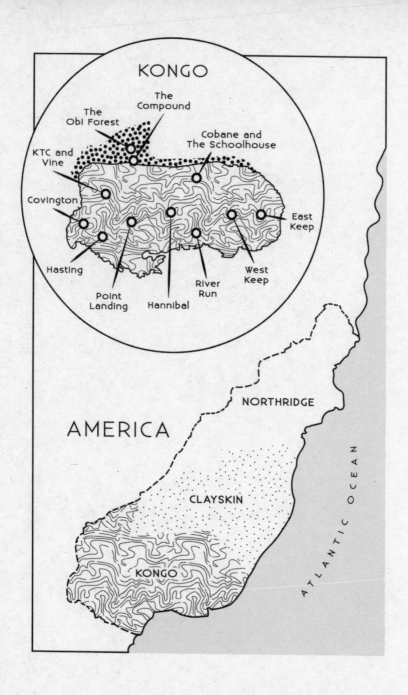

PART FOUR

THE
ARENA

THE RAID OF COBANE

We came like a tide. All at once, at night. A surge of swinging sickles. The English diplomats, at first, resisted. They didn't understand what had changed and, perhaps, neither did we. But the drums knew. The hollow horns we filled with beans and tied to our feet that hissed as we waged like locusts accosting the foliage. They knew. And so, we came. Swinging the sickle, swinging the sickle. Slaughtering anything that stood. And when the English understood that nothing would be left standing—and that *that* was the point—not to win, but to reckon—they ran. And, still, we came. Sweeping. Shrieking. Swinging the sickle.

On day ninety-six we shattered their defense, scattering the Kongo Guard. And the diplomats, with a handful of their army, fled to Hasting where they applied to the American Assembly for aid.

We are under siege.

Out of resources.

Please advise!

Each missive went unanswered. Later we learned that, during this time, America was on its knees. A tribe of female activists, the Sisters to the North, led riots in every major northern city. They aggravated the food shortage that already plagued the Northridge, so famine spread, killing thousands.

The chaos depleted national resources, forcing the Assembly to abandon the southern diplomats.

Dana Kumar, their leader, forsook them too. *Before* the fighting started, he vacated his commission, fleeing north to a base in the Obi Forest, which was rumored to be impenetrable. Behind, he left a stockpile at the Kongo Technology Center, and the worker militia, with me at the helm, seized it. Armor, communication equipment, medicine and, notably, ten thousand Double Helix swords.

And so, in a twist of fate, the old southern masters were left to the grace of those they'd abused for years. We treated them fairly, ending the siege and allowing food and water. They could stay, interned at Hasting, with the understanding that the rest of the Kongo was ours.

They accepted our generosity then plagued us at every turn. They stalled peace negotiations for weeks, then months, obstructing a final agreement. When we held truth talks, to account for our suffering, they registered counter-complaints and made demands. At great length, they issued a public apology. But their guilt, once acknowledged, became insufferable. It manifested in fevered religiosity that, strangely, made them less generous. And more paranoid.

They dug a moat around Hasting and filled it with salt and water. They sealed every entrance and built a drawbridge with massive ropes wound on a giant spool. They installed turrets on every side and kept watch, day and night.

In arrogant English style, they made way for these *improvements* by destroying what they didn't understand. Countless treasures and 200 years of Black history, gone in a month. The library, and the stories of the people inside, were put to fire. Only Obi's mausoleum, a clay watchtower, mysteriously resisted the flame. Though they burned it seven times, six times it refused to light. In their last attempt, they doused it in accelerant, so the fire raged—*gold*—with gilded smoke. And still the watchtower, in defiance of physical laws, remained. A ten-story pillar, with a domed cap, against the Kongo sky. Seeing it, the diplomats' terror compounded. They huddled together, murmuring.

Sorcery.

Devils, magic.

Judgement?

They kept a distance from the flames and prayed the rosary. For twenty-four days the watchtower burned, like a beacon for the Kongo people, a symbol of the bright dawn of democracy.

Hailing it, the people formed a line that spiraled around the voting polls and swirled into the countryside for miles. As they waited, the electors clutched talismans, clay towers speckled with gold to represent the flames. And as they cast their votes, a black stone for General Cobane, white for Senator Osprey, brown for the Rebel Voltaire—they felt the watchtower looking over them, like a sentry.

We established a council of nine with one head—Hosea Khan, the Kha. They elected him over his objection and despite his absence from the battlefield. During the fight, he founded a clinic, tending the wounded and healing the fever that plagued the Kongo before the rebellion. His image was suffused in lore, which he ignored.

After the war, he closed his clinic and abandoned his Council seat. He camped on unclaimed land and passed his time studying earth science. When we held an election to fill his seat, the people refused to replace him. They rebuffed the other candidates and wrote in his name on their ballots. After that, the Council carried on; one vote short on every matter, and with me as the uncrowned head.

I performed the role with zeal. Drawing on my study of world history, and my dream of a Black utopia, I saw to the ratification of sweeping legislation. Marriage and probate, trade and free speech, farming and land-use law. No aspect of Kongo life was beneath my concern. And because of the Kongo's faith in me, and in my love for them, I had free rein—in the early days.

•

I don't know which came first—my public decline, or my personal. But the fall began in the Schoolhouse. It was there that I, at seven, discovered shame. And there again, in the anemic light of the Schoolhouse library, I discovered my grail: the incriminating photo of Obi Solomon dressed in English clothing before the end of the Last War.

Obi was my political forefather, my only counterpart, the people's first general. That he, after leading them to victory in the Last War, would precipitate their demise was incredible to me. *What had happened?*

The question consumed me. In the days before the rebellion, the people shared my obsession. The photograph circulated as White-Face soldiers, Rebels, Keepers and Workers alike analyzed the roots of our oppression.

Obi, his motives and limitations were the subject of debates and rambling pamphlets, all ending inconclusively, since the reasons behind Obi's betrayal remained a mystery. Months of research from every camp produced only more questions as, perplexingly, none of Obi's writings—not a single letter or note—had survived.

Following our victory, I sought to revive the discussion. I demanded entry to the library at Hasting to scour the records there. But, as the Kongo bathed in the prospect of a prosperous future, the nuances of history became unimportant to the people.

Nevertheless, I agitated the matter, relentlessly. *No truth, no peace.* I proposed to reinstate the siege until the diplomats allowed us access to our history. *We would know it, or repeat it*, I warned again and again—until, eventually, the Kongo splintered.

The military proved loyal to me, ready to follow my command. The business sector, with an eye on their purses, balked at the thought of another war. Tension mounted, but the fight never came to a head. When the diplomats burned the library, it ended—superficially.

In truth, nothing was settled. The mystery surrounding Obi's treachery remained with us, towering like the tomb guarding his remains. The stories, and the rumors surrounding them, were a slick of oil that, eventually, separated me from my people. Their faith slipped a fraction, then another. And their doubt planted fear deep inside me, so an old shame festered.

Months later, word came: Nicky McCormick, the leader of the Sisters to the North, was detained. Her disciples were scattered and the northern skirmish was winding down. America was, once again, standing. Soon, it would turn its attention south.

The news revived the diplomats at Hasting. They set aside their prayer beads, lowered the drawbridge and dispatched their final offer—the Accord.

Preamble—

A new world re-union, if you will. A revival of the old American way. Open borders, equal opportunity, meritocracy and, above all, peace. A tri-territory, voluntary surrender of arms.

On the day their ultimatum arrived, the Kongo Council held a public debate—would we allow America to confiscate our weaponry, as the Accord required? Or take up the sword and solidify our secession from the union?

For hours, I urged the people to reject the Accord outright. "We must fight!" I said. "The so-called 'Accord' is nothing less than old bondage in new clothing—a neo-captivity. *Stand up* with the Kongo militia and me, your general. No compromise, no Accord!"

Looking back, it's clear I was terrified. Rejoining the American union without our Helix swords was, to me, the height of naïveté. I was determined to see the Council reject the measure, no matter the personal cost. And, in the end, dear reader, it cost everything—including my life.

The page you are reading—whoever you are—is not the first page of this journal. The first ten sheets are crumpled around me like failures, discarded after one line.

It seems the first line of a story is most important. The teller's whole soul. The crux from which everything flows. I know the first line here. And, for months, I've wrestled with it, knowing too its trajectory. The story it tells is the arc of a grave mistake. And all along the bend is rage and hope. Tears that demand justification or, at least, a destination. And there isn't one. In the end, there is only the bend of another story, sad but true. And good—if your faith allows. So, you ask me, would I have left the arena that night had I known the toll?

I would.

THE LIBRARY

The arena door slid closed behind me. I kept my head low and walked, forcing a casual pace. In a secluded alcove off the corridor, I flipped open my comm-unit.

"Jetson, are you there?" I said. "It's time."

A holograph of Jetson, clad in sleek black leggings, appeared, floating above my palm. He was in the Schoolhouse, two miles south of the newly constructed arena.

His deep voice clipped in my earpiece. "Arika, I didn't expect a call. I—oh—hey, are you okay?" he said, his gaze narrowed on my face. "You look ill."

I ignored his concern. "Are you in her room?"

"I'm down the hall," he said. "When you didn't message, I left. I thought—well, I hoped—you'd called it off."

I stiffened at the sound of footsteps; someone was rounding the hall towards me. I hid Jetson's visual in my cupped hand and continued down the corridor that skirted the arena floor, staying just out of sight.

When the steps faded, I bent my head to my palm. "I'm late because the debate ran long," I whispered. "Kira Swan took an extra twenty minutes, and no one stopped her! Cowards, all of them!"

"Well, how did it go?" he asked. "Do we still need this?" His moss-green eyes darted to the bag he held which, I knew, contained the equipment to break into Kira Swan's safe and photograph its contents.

"Oh, Jetson, yes," I said. "We need it now more than ever."

"Dammit, Arika!"

I held up my empty palm, stifling his outburst. "Blame Kira!" I hissed. "She used the extra time to demand a formal inquiry into Jones's injury."

Jetson gaped. My fight with Jones in the testing room had dogged me for months, but this was an ominous turn. My vengeance, while morally gratifying, was legally questionable, since Jones had been unconscious and disarmed when I'd taken her eye. The diplomats continually pressured the Council to charge me with attempted murder. Now Kira Swan, my political rival, had taken their side.

"Surely the Council denied her!" Jetson said. He sounded afraid.

"They didn't deny her," I said. "They didn't even deliberate. They approved her motion unanimously."

"Even Osprey?"

I swallowed. Osprey's vote had hurt most. In the Schoolhouse, when I'd watched her stand up to Jones, she'd become my idol. Then, during the rebellion, she was the first to read the tenor of the moment. She'd joined the Rebels, and after the fight, floated to the top of society with unmatched savvy. She represented the height of political acumen and the fact that she'd taken Kira's side meant she sensed I was no longer favored to win the Accord vote.

"Osprey's an opportunist. I'll win her back," I said. "Only now, I'm on probation while they investigate. After my closing argument, I'm to clear my docket while they choose an inquisitor."

"Slow down," Jetson said. "An inquiry isn't an indictment."

"It's close enough," I said. "This mission is more than politics now. I need to get into that safe."

Jetson hesitated, but he knew I was right. "She *is* attacking you, and we know she's hiding something," he said, acknowledging why I'd designed the mission in the first place. A maid that fancied Jetson had stumbled upon a safe in a false bottom of Kira's wardrobe last week. The maid gave him the tip, which he'd passed on to me. I despised intrigue, but Kira's scheme had left me no choice. If she had a shameful secret, I would exploit it, just as she'd exploited mine. I had to outmaneuver her or lose control of the Council.

"So, you'll do it," I prodded.

Inside the arena, Senator Osprey, the debate moderator, slammed her gavel, initiating the closing arguments.

Jetson ran a hand over his low-cut hair. "I'll do it," he said.

Gratified, I gave him a reassuring nod and closed my palm on his image.

I circled my finger in the air, raising the volume on my earpiece. "Jetson?" I asked, speaking under my breath.

"Copy," he said.

I moved to the closest entrance to the arena floor. "And the image?" With a flick of my wrist, I turned the scope.

"Crystal clear, General," Jetson said. "The stadium is packed. You're through the double doors now. Walking to the platform, towards Osprey, and there's Swan at the high table, left of center."

My skirted robe swept behind me as I crossed the stadium, mentally thumbing through my argument. Kira advanced her position brilliantly, framing the Accord, and the confiscation of arms, as a path to prosperity. She'd won the business sector, handily. Wooing them with a temperate tone and smile that never wavered, even as she decimated my character. I had command of the militia; they'd follow me, even against the Council. But everything in me resisted that path. The people together was the strongest sword. I wouldn't stop until they united behind me.

I mounted the stage steps as Osprey outlined the structure of the closing arguments. "General Cobane will speak first," she said, "followed by Senator Swan. Agreed?"

I lifted my chin and rested one hand at the small of my back, where I holstered my Apex. I nodded, acknowledging the rules.

Osprey looked to the high table. "And you, Swan? You agree to adhere?"

"I will," Kira said, softly.

The audience roared their approval. As Osprey backed away, giving me the podium, my supporters chanted their devotion.

Ber-seeer-ker, Ber-seeer-ker. Berserker—it was the name the soldiers gave me on account of my battle style. *Ber-seeer-ker, Ber-seeer-ker.*

I acknowledged their praise but, as I stepped forward, weakness buckled my knees and I grabbed the podium. I hated to admit it, but Jetson's observation had been on point. I didn't just look ill, I *felt* it. Insomnia and bouts of vertigo plagued me. More, my memory—sharp from birth—was failing. Last week, I accepted a medal of valor for my leadership in the Raid of Cobane, the first battle of the rebellion. They said I fought on the frontline for forty-two hours, earning the name 'Berserker.' At the award ceremony, I nodded along as soldiers recounted the battle. But, during my acceptance speech, I realized I couldn't remember details of the Raid or the war, just vague impressions and, at times, disturbing echoes—

Find them! Find their hiding places and leave nothing alive. Advance!

A chair screeched against the floor as Osprey resumed her seat at the high table. The cheers from the tiered seating lulled. It was time. Setting my jaw, I punched down the weakness billowing inside me. I took a breath and mentally started the mission clock.

"People of the Kongo," I said. "We have a grave decision before us."

Through my earpiece, Jetson narrated his progress. "I'm in her room," he said. "Moving towards the wardrobe."

I went on. "If we accept the diplomats' Accord, dark people will no longer control the Kongo. If we reject it, we will remain at war with America. Many of you have seen battle, and so have I. I have the scars to prove it." I untied my crimson Council robe and let the wide neck slide down my shoulders. Half-inch *haute* ink tattoos lined my naked back. In the evening light of the arena, they glowed like matchsticks.

"I bear five hundred and twelve marks," I said. "One for each person who died in the first battle." I held the drape of the embroidered robe to my chest and turned a circle. The soldiers in the auditorium followed my lead, recalling the fallen. Howling, they ripped their shirts to display neck-to-waist *haute* tattoos. They lifted their faces, showing off florescent designs the breadth of the neon rainbow.

In my ear, Jetson buzzed. "I've removed the false bottom of the wardrobe. Initiating radio silence in three, two, one." A scuff sounded in my ear as Jetson removed his earpiece to work the dial of the safe.

I gripped the podium as sweat beaded on my back. The safe would lock for an hour if we entered the wrong combination. We had one shot to get it right.

"There's only one path forward," I said, launching the next segment of my speech. "We've got to—"

Jetson cursed. I jerked and my earpiece slid sideways. I worked to maintain my composure before the crowd. "We—We've got to—"

From my dislodged earpiece, Jetson shouted, "Arika, there's a time stamp. She's been alerted."

"We—uh," I stuttered.

At the head table Kira Swan frowned as the alert came to her comm-unit. She rose.

"Stall her!" Jetson said.

Panicked, I shouted, "Senator Swan!"

Kira froze beside her chair. She had her comm-unit displayed in her hand. Her face tense, she scanned her palm for information. Every head in the arena swiveled her way, then back to me. Kira looked up and glared at me as if I'd lost my mind.

"Senator, you—can't leave," I said, improvising.

Osprey sat taller. Her hair, in bonsai style, was shaped like a bird in flight. It lifted from her head, adding clout to her already prominent stature. "General," she said. "Explain yourself."

My mind raced. "It's Senator Swan's turn," I said. Moisture pooled at my temples and my headdress, a horned antelope skull, slipped on my ears. I removed it, resting it on the podium, and hedged on. "We've been here all day; the Council needs rest," I said. "So, I've decided to relinquish my time."

Senator Osprey studied me, her glare calculating. "We *are* running late," she said. Other Council members nodded. "Okay, General, you'll finish this one remaining minute."

Kira Swan's gaze narrowed on me. Her expression darkened as she determined I was responsible for invading her privacy. Her eye skirted the room, looking for a way out.

"Senator Swan?" Osprey said, expectantly. "You're up next. Please take your seat."

Trapped, Swan swallowed. She was still young, only ten years my senior, but her deep bosom and thick waist aged her. With a sweet smile that, for some reason, looked wrong on her broad-chinned, thin-lipped face, she sat.

Filtering through my remaining speech, I picked the most important line. "The first lesson they taught us," I said, "was assimilation for the greater good. Brothers and sisters, Councilors, after years of appeasement, it's time to demand our terms on our land. We will not assimilate! No compromise—"

"No Accord!" the crowd shouted.

I performed the workers' salute, crossing a hand over my heart and lifting it to form a fist, elbow bent, in the air. The room roared to life, joining the cheers of Kongos who watched the debate via live holograph around the territory.

"Council," I said, over the noise, "I concede the remainder of my time to Senator Swan."

I descended the stage and readied to leave the arena. With my pack on my back, I turned at the exit door to look at the stage.

Kira stood at the podium, her jet-black eyes wide with false humility. As she waved, absorbing the shouts of her constituency, I was struck with a moment of clarity. I envisioned the whites of her eyes liquifying. They bled down over her face—erasing dark skin to reveal the pallor beneath. Kongo in flesh, but white at the root.

With a burst of adrenaline, I jogged from the arena floor. In a twist, Kira's inquiry had provided an opportunity. Clearing the docket I kept at my bench in the Schoolhouse was just the excuse I needed to leave early and fix whatever had gone wrong with the mission. As soon as it was safe, I spoke.

"Jetson, are you out?" I said. "Are you in the study room?"

He didn't respond.

I checked to see that the call was still connected. "Jetson?" I said, securing my earpiece.

"I'm here," he said, finally. He sounded faint.

Alarmed, I pulled up his image. He wasn't in the library as we'd planned. He was in his quarters, a Council-issued space in the renovated Schoolhouse. He sat on his unmade bed, looking sick. "What is it?" I asked. I flipped the scope, showing him my face.

His throat pulsed. "The contents of the safe," he said. "There wasn't just one thing to photograph."

"Okay?" I slowed to a walk.

He went on. "There was a folder of papers. I didn't know what was important. And it was dark so—"

My heart sank. "You didn't get photos."

"No," he said, quickly. "I took the folder."

I tripped, caught myself. "*Obi.*"

He swallowed. "If I hurry, I can put it back. Yes, that's what I'll do." He stood.

"Are you mad?" I hissed. "You can't go back to her room. She'll send someone there to check the breach."

"You have to stop her," Jetson said, his face grey.

I shook my head. "Impossible. You saw the look she gave me. She knows I'm involved. And with the time stamp, she'll know someone helped me."

Our eyes locked. Everyone knew he cared for me still. He was the first person she'd suspect.

"We have to destroy the evidence," Jetson said, a thick folder in his hand. He carried it to his fireplace.

I bit my lip as he bent to light the hearth. He removed a long match and flicked his wrist. A flame puffed to life. As it wobbled toward the folder in slow motion, a handful of facts coalesced.

I'd spent months searching for a crack in Kira's perfect image, but the details of her life remained obscure. She graduated from the Schoolhouse, but her records were redacted, something only the headmistress—Jones, at the time—could have approved. She had no verifiable house, heritage or name. And yet, as valedictorian, she received a recommendation, again, from Headmistress Jones. All that was damning enough, and now, this last piece—her demand for an inquiry. *Everything pointed to Jones.*

"Wait!" I said.

Jetson hesitated.

I bit my lip, wanting to give the order to put out the light, but needing to be sure. "Is that what you're hiding, Swan? Are you Teacher's pet?" I whispered.

"What's that?" Jetson asked.

"Put out the light," I said, finally.

Jetson complied as I spoke slowly, tracing the logic.

"Jones favored Kira Swan. We know that from her records. Jones's recommendation buoyed Kira to the top of the Kongo political scene. In the Council election, only Hosea Khan and I earned more votes."

Jetson frowned. "What are you getting at?"

I leaned forward, gaining conviction. "Attacking me, backing the Accord," I said. "What if she's returning Jones's favor?" Jones had been silent for months, lying low at Hasting, and now I knew why. Kira Swan was doing the work for her. My mind narrowed on the memory of Kira's face when she realized I'd opened her safe. She'd been terrified. "There's something in those papers," I said. "Something big. If it proves Kira is working for the North, it won't matter how we found it."

"But, if you're wrong, we'll be charged with treason," Jetson said. He lit another match.

I stared into its glow. He was right. The Council demanded impeccable fealty. We were always on the lookout for the next Obi Solomon, the next leader who would betray the Kongo. Most suspected Voltaire, who disappeared a week ago after months of odd behavior. But now, I felt sure Kira Swan was not just *a* traitor; she was eerily similar to *the* traitor—Obi Solomon.

I mentally counted the parallels: both charismatic leaders with obscure records. Both ostensibly seeking peace. Both intent on surrendering arms and trusting the English.

"History is repeating," I said.

My gaze lifted to Jetson's. I didn't issue an order; I didn't have to. He extinguished the second flame.

"Start reading. I'm on my way," I said. I tapped my ear, disconnecting the call.

The grounds people who conducted traffic at the arena met me at the exit door. "General!"

I nodded curtly. They held the crowd of local spectators at bay as I passed through and mounted the ramp to the newly installed crystalrail station.

With the debate in progress, the station was mostly deserted. I passed a handful of people waiting for the rail and ducked into the bathhouse. Inside, I entered a stall and changed my clothes, rolling my cloak into a ball and stuffing it into my pack. Outside of the stall, I splashed water on my face and huffed, revving the dredges of my adrenaline stores. I dried my face and glanced at the time. Kira was allotted twenty minutes to close her argument. She would cut herself short and follow me, but the audience would be dismissed at the same time. The crowd would clog the rail which, in regular traffic, curved lazily around the city on its way to the Schoolhouse. We had forty-five minutes, at least, to complete the mission.

I moved to the only window in the bathhouse. With a grunt, I jumped for the wide ledge, and pulled myself up to look out at the early evening. Below and to my right were the golden gates of the first Kongo metropolis—City One. They'd built the newer additions around the old Cobane village, and the result was a hodgepodge—juts of modernity imposed on the old, familiar ways. Out past the city skyline was the steepled center of my destination, the Schoolhouse. The most direct route was an overgrown trail I knew from my days as a student. It was the path we'd used to sneak to the village.

Minutes later, I hugged the limits of the secluded path, ducking in the tall grass, like a thief. My heavy pack and a creeping dizziness slowed me down, but I got into a steady rhythm, keeping aware of my surroundings.

I came to a familiar stretch and, out of habit, I squinted to my right. Past the overgrown pasture that buttressed the foot trail was a fenced-in hill of metallic waste. And, beyond that, just visible in the fading daylight, was Hosea Khan's camp. I could see the front flap of his tent was open. I craned my neck, hoping to catch a glimpse of him, but I didn't slow down. The north gate of the Schoolhouse was just ahead.

Breathing heavily, I slipped through the entrance to the green lawn of the sparsely populated yard. I slowed to ensure I wasn't detected as I moved, flitting between fountains, pieces of art and manicured bushes. My aim was a library window that I knew had a faulty latch. The pane was in sight when a woman, talking on a comm-unit, came into view. I ducked into a shadow.

When she passed, I darted into the open to crouch at the window. I looked back to check that I hadn't been followed. I scanned left and right, then my eye caught on a statue across the way, and I froze.

The statue was new to the yard. It must have been placed overnight. Seven feet tall and wrought of solid lava rock, it depicted a warrior and mount in battle. When I saw the warrior's face, I rose from my crouched position. I didn't think of the woman who'd passed or whether another was coming. I'd forgotten the mission entirely. Unblinking, I crossed back over the walkway, as stiff as a statue myself.

I stopped at the base and gazed up at the face, trying to make sense of it. As I stared, a foghorn sounded in the distance and the twilight darkened around me, as if some heavenly creature had closed a curtain on the moon. I looked up through the veil to the stars and the foghorn sounded again, closer—louder. It startled me, but, when I tried to move—I *couldn't*.

Come quick, a soft voice said. *She needs you.*

•

My body jerked back to life. I gasped and blinked, checking the time. Fifteen minutes had passed. I was in the Schoolhouse yard on my back. *When had I fallen? How?* I bent my elbows and rolled my neck, assuring myself that I could, indeed, move. The terrifying rigidity was gone.

However, the sound of that soft voice haunted me still— *Come quick.* I winced. Behind my lids, I could still see her eyes, the color and shape of whole almonds. They belonged to the little kitchen maid who'd brought the news of Robin's illness and, later, of her death.

Footsteps sounded to my right, and I jolted, recalling the mission. The steps were coming closer. I scrambled to my hands and knees and launched myself over the path to the window. I opened the left pane and climbed inside just in time.

I leaned back against the wall to regroup. Placing a hand on my spinning head, I tentatively closed my eyes. They flew open again. The maid and the warrior were still there, in the dark—lurking. I pushed from the wall and hurried into the stacks.

•

I found Jetson in a private study room. He stood on a chair with an instant print solar-pixel camera in his hand. Documents, some tattered and yellow with age, were spread across the study table below him.

"Arika!" he said, looking down at me. "Where have you been?"

"I—I'm sorry. I—"

"Close the door!"

I closed the door and then stared up at him. His bright complexion demanded an answer—*Where had I been?*

I opened my mouth to speak but no words came out. There was no explanation for what had happened at the statue. Fifteen precious minutes had passed without my knowledge. I closed my eyes, willing the world to stop spinning.

Jetson's face softened. "Well, you're here now," he said. He adjusted the lens of his camera and gestured to the table of documents. "We'll take condensed pictures and destroy the originals," he explained. "The pictures will be easier to hide."

"Good thinking," I said, softly.

Jetson eyed me. "You should sit down." He nodded to a chair pulled away from the table. On the seat were two photographs and a small sheet of paper.

Feeling shaky, I sat on the ground by the chair and picked up the paper. "Department of Vital Records," I read.

"It's Kira's birth certificate," Jetson said. "Rare in the south, I thought. And the pertinent information is redacted. I set it aside to examine."

I checked the time. "Anything else? Anything about Jones? We need more, now." If my estimation was correct, Kira Swan was on her way back to the Schoolhouse.

"There's nothing incriminating," Jetson said. "It's memorabilia. Pictures, handwritten letters, newspaper clippings." He snapped an image of the table. "The prints are tiny, but we can magnify them later. Ten snapshots should do it." The print slid from the camera. "Nine down," he said.

He jumped down, placed the print with the other aerial photos on the chair and moved back to the table. "How will we destroy the originals?" he asked, angling the camera over a new layer of papers.

"Purnell's office sits above the old furnace. We can burn it all there," I said.

Jetson nodded. As he snapped a picture, a photo fluttered from the table. I picked it up and froze. The woman pictured was familiar.

She was English. Her white-blonde hair was slicked back in a style that reminded me of the Teachers at the Schoolhouse. She posed with her left shoulder turned out. Her blue eyes focused over the photographer's head.

"Who is this woman?" I asked. My spine tingled as I got to my feet, holding the picture up for Jetson's inspection.

"No clue," he said. Moving quickly, he packed up the contraband and secured the bag against his chest. "Let's move."

I collected the aerial photos and slipped them into my breast pocket with the picture of the woman.

We moved through rows of bookshelves on our way to Purnell's office. As we reached the newly renovated wing of the library, my Apex buzzed, and a chill of premonition grazed my neck. I stopped behind a stack of books and reached for Jetson's shoulder—too late. He stepped into the open.

Kira Swan saw him immediately. "Captain!" she said.

Through the space between the books and the top of the shelf, I saw Jetson jerk to a halt.

"Where is she?" Swan growled. She stood as tall and broad as the armed men flanking her. Her thick bonsai rose like a crown and her laid edges blended into the black skin of her forehead. A thin gold chain hung between her regal brows.

She looked down on Jetson as she reached out a meaty fist and lifted the bag of contraband over his stiff neck. She confirmed its contents. "These came from my private safe. The safe of an elected Kongo official," she said. "And we thought the traitor would come from the Council."

I watched as Jetson squared his shoulders and set his jaw.

"Where is General Cobane? She's wanted for questioning," Swan said.

Jetson shrugged. "I acted alone."

Swan glowered. "Seize him."

"No!" The word burst from my lips. I stepped into the open. "Leave him be."

Kira pointed a thick finger at me. "General, you're under arrest."

I placed a hand on my Apex, daring the soldiers to try. There were six in all, and they were used to following my commands.

Jetson deepened his stance as I turned my head, my mouth in my shoulder. "On my command," I whispered.

"Get her!" Kira ordered.

"Run!" I shouted.

I leapt into the stacks as the soldiers darted towards us. They were fast, but I knew the library. I pushed over a shelf of books and hurdled over a desk and chair. At the old section, I ran left and shoved Jetson right, splitting the chase. I raced in and out and, finally, lost them.

I wove my way to the old librarian's office and found Jetson waiting in the shadow of a bookcase close by. I beckoned him forward and we ducked inside.

"Under here," I said.

We crouched beneath Teacher Purnell's abandoned desk. Shoving Jetson's leg aside, I felt for the latch of a door that I knew led to the basement. I lifted it, revealing a metal ladder and a switch that ignited the furnace. I scrambled down, then looked up.

Jetson wasn't following.

"Hurry," I hissed.

In the dark of the open trap door, he shook his head. "This is my fault," he said. "I took the folder."

I climbed up, impatient. I heard the soldiers coming in our direction. "Come down; we'll talk. I have the pictures here in my pocket." I tapped the breast of my tunic, where I'd hidden the aerial photos. "We can still stop the Accord vote."

"That's days away," Jetson said. "Kira won't stop hunting until she finds me. But, if I turn myself in, you'll get time to find what she's hiding and use it to free me."

"Then let's stay together and work twice as fast," I said.

"And what if we don't find anything?" Jetson whispered.

I shook my head, resisting the possibility.

Jetson went on. "If nothing turns up, I'll insist I did it alone, that you only helped me escape. If we stay together, we'll both go down," Jetson said.

"Then *I'll* take the blame—"

He brushed his lips against mine, cutting me off. "I've already confessed," he said. "And even if you beat the charge, a new accusation on top of Jones' claim..." his voice trailed off. "You'll lose your Council seat, and the Kongo needs you. Now more than ever."

He was right.

I lifted a hand to the pale speckles on his cheek. Only the students who'd endured Jones knew they weren't freckles, but scars. Tiny ghosts reminding me of the one thing that echoed in my gut—that I should have killed Jones in the testing room suite when I had the chance. Now she was hunting me—and, in Kira Swan, she had a talented hound.

"I won't sleep until you're free," I said, passionately.

But, when he bent his head again, I drew back, avoiding his mouth.

He sighed. "And the Vine Keeper wins," he whispered.

"Don't say that. It's—not him," I lied.

Jetson sat back. "When you find something that will save us both, come back for me. Until then—" He offered a graceful salute, touching his hand to his heart and raising a fist.

I responded in turn, I tapped my forehead and wrapped my hand around his, forming an apex. Our fists tightened together, locking in place. He stepped back and closed the trap door.

I never saw Jetson again.

THE BERSERKER

I spent that night in the basement of the Schoolhouse. From the top of the ladder, I heard Jetson walk out and close the door behind him. Minutes later, Kira Swan's unique voice, like a muzzled dog, directed the soldiers, "Arrest him!"

They treated him roughly. Our connection was such that I didn't only hear shouts, I was with him in spirit. My grip tightened on the ladder rung in my hand, and I ground my teeth, tasting blood.

As their steps faded, a slow *drip* sounded, and something tickled my cheeks. I lifted a hand to feel tears. They streamed down my face to swell beneath my chin and *drip*—mournfully. I swiped the wetness away and climbed down into the basement.

The room beneath the office was bare except for the ancient furnace that heated the old section of the library. I moved stiffly from the base of the ladder toward the belching blaze. Its dry heat was treacherous, but the flames were the only light in my hiding place. I fell to my knees, setting the ten photos and a half-empty water skin before me in a line.

Our scheme had rendered the content of the documents nearly illegible. Without a magnifying glass, I squinted over the tiny words as I tried to make out a case against Kira Swan. I needed evidence: proof of treachery that explained why I'd broken the law to expose her.

As the hours passed, the furnace roared, and I dried in its fervor. My cheeks and forehead tightened and peeled, exposing the tender skin beneath. When I lowered my head to shield my face, my eyebrows singed, and moisture steamed from my sockets. The thought of Jetson in the Pit drove me forward. I pulled in a burning lungful of air and pressed on. Even so, my strength waned.

With no food and only a little water, my tongue puckered, and my lips stuck to my teeth. Exhaustion set in and I grew disoriented. Scarlet images seared my mind and circled the room. They twittered, divulging secrets, then puffed into smoke as I chased them.

Most insidious was the portrait of the blonde woman with her severely styled hair. Her fine features, her blue eyes, her gleaming head— the combination disturbed me. I glared at her serene face and, in my mind, her pink lips peeled back and her white teeth crumbled, revealing a silver tongue. I snatched up the picture and rushed to the furnace. I pulled back to throw it in then froze, sniffed. A singed smell—like burning hair—stung my nose! I lifted a hand to my bonsai as it crackled—on the brink of flames! *Obi!*

Covering my head, I stumbled to the room's only window to smother the heat against the cool glass. At length, I straightened and ran shaking fingers over my hair. I had to get help!

I flipped open my comm-unit and entered the number for the Sky Valet. The service delivered hovercrafts to any address in the Kongo. If I ordered a craft, I could take it to Covington's flat on the far side of the city. Covington would help. Crafts were in short supply but, like all Council members, the Valet reserved a vehicle for my exclusive use.

A voice answered. "Sky Valet, registration number, please."

I snapped my palm shut, cutting off the call as I realized my mistake.

Registration was required to reserve the vehicle, so it could be tracked. I would have to get to Covington's place on foot.

I collected the aerial photos and secured them in my breast pocket. I moved to the window, shifted the lock and shoved upward. Moist air splashed across my face. I opened my parched mouth and lowered the crown of my head, so wetness settled on my nape like a washcloth.

I boosted my bag through the opening then, with trembling muscles, I heaved my upper half onto the window ledge and scrambled into the Schoolhouse yard. I pulled the cloak from my pack and got my bearings. I moved right, across the deserted yard, toward the north gate.

As I walked, I wondered what had transpired in my absence. Did the Council believe Jetson had acted alone? Were they hunting for an accomplice? Perhaps they assumed I, like Voltaire, had succumbed to the pressure of leadership and absconded. To be cautious, I kept to the early morning shadows.

Close to the high northern gate, I passed a pole where a freshly printed poster caught my eye. My name, in bold lettering, jumped out from the page. WANTED: GENERAL ARIKA COBANE, ATTEMPTED MURDER, FAIR TRIAL. I glared. The investigation had taken less than a day! I ripped down the poster, stowed it away and hurried on, slowing only when the statue that had transfixed me earlier came into view.

Beside the warrior replica was a model of Obi's mausoleum. I moved between the pair of statues, keeping my head down to avoid seeing the warrior's face. I was nearly past when the urge took hold of me to look up. I shook my head, trying to loosen the craving. It was senseless. The statue was grotesque; I wanted nothing to do with it. I was here, a fugitive, on account of the time I'd wasted, horrified by its visage. And yet, still, like a rotting tooth, hanging on by a root, I felt the need on the tip of my tongue to probe it.

Tentatively, I read the title plate: *The Berserker.* I took a breath and looked up.

It depicted me, ferocious during the Battle of Cobane. I was astride Mary's back, straining, standing in the stirrups. Aside from her dark form, the only familiar part of the work was the bauble around my neck. Dark red, tear-shaped, set in gold. I'd stolen it from Jones on the day of the final exam. The day I'd watched my papa die. It served as a reminder, decorating my chest, like a tiny mausoleum. The rest of the statue was barely human. Sharpened incisors, raised veins, spare fingers bent on a dripping sickle.

Find them! Find their hiding places and leave nothing alive. Advance!

I woke, seconds later, on my back. I stumbled to my feet and crouched defensively. Pivoting left, right. Surveying the yard. I knew, even as I searched, that it was still deserted. There was no enemy, only the echo of one in my head. The foghorn and the kitchen maid, the veil that had darkened my vision—all in my head.

I swallowed, backing away from the Berserker. I wasn't just sick. Something was terribly wrong. I turned and ran.

THE FUGITIVE

I stopped on the trail close to Hosea's tent, pushed my hood back and looked left across the overgrown pasture. From this angle, the fenced-in waste adjacent to his camp took on the sheen of tarnished copper. The metal shone in the early dawn so I couldn't tell if his light was on or not. As I left the foot trail, I wondered if he would welcome me.

During our frequent visits, he'd been clear he wanted nothing to do with my government work. He'd listen as I detailed my fight for control over the Council, but he never opined. This time would be different, I told myself.

I carved a direct path through the tall grass towards his tent. He would care because I was *sick*. More, Jetson was in danger. Hosea held sway over the Council; surely for Jetson he would intercede. For *me*.

I stopped at the pile of copper slates and pieces, remnants of the giant fans that once tempered the soil for farming. The fans had become obsolete after the rebellion, when most everyone began planting the new seed, which nurtured and harvested itself. To grow a potato one merely planted, waited a bit, and brushed off the dirt. Wheat sprouted in a day and, in ten, grew so high and heavy it toppled over, pulling the roots from the ground.

When the fans began tilting months ago, the Council ordered them hauled to the waste yard. Hosea Khan had objected to the demolition, then spent weeks scrubbing the pieces for sediment. After, he'd explained why the fans had tilted in the first place: *tectonic slip.* The fans had fallen prey to a fault line created by movement in the lithosphere layer of Earth.

He advised the area around the line remain off-limits for farming, and the Council had agreed. Despite its value, the land just west of City One remained unsettled, except for Hosea's camp, where he studied the fault.

I squinted ahead to see there was, indeed, a light on in Hosea's tent. I threw my bag over the picket fence, climbed up and jumped down. My vision blurred, and I reached for a mound of copper to steady myself.

When I could stand again, I slowly skirted the mound of metal to climb carefully over the fence on the opposite side of the yard. I let myself down, landing in Hosea's small medicinal garden.

At the flap of his tent, I called his name. The sound croaked from my dry throat. I swallowed and called again. "Hosea Khan!" No answer.

I surveyed the area, but saw no sign of him in his garden or in the off-limits field beyond. I pushed inside the tent.

In the middle of the canvas room, I turned in a circle. His bed roll was flat and clean and his chair was pushed neatly beneath his desk. Two crystalights floated near the back wall, illuminating the maps and diagrams that hung there. It looked as if he'd just been studying the information, but the space was empty.

I moved to his desk. Beside an open book was a chart documenting the growth of the fault line he'd identified. He'd gone last week to gauge the line's descent south, but by now he should have returned. And, indeed, an uncapped pen rested by the chart, as if he'd just notated. *Strange.*

I turned, feeling his presence in every angle of the room but, as I looked around, I assured myself that I was alone. With a sigh, I checked the time: City One would awaken soon.

I found pen and paper and jotted a note for Hosea. I read it back and looked around for a place to leave it. Beside his desk was a seismograph; he used its rolling pin and needle to track tectonic vibrations in the earth. I moved around it to his sleeping place, knelt and removed my pack. I lifted his pillow. His clean mint smell wafted and I paused, inhaling. I placed the note on the ground and adjusted the pillow, so one corner of my handwriting was visible.

As I stood again, I swayed. I shook my head to clear it and thought about searching his tent for water. Before I could, an image of Jetson, suffering in the Pit, crossed my mind and I knew there wasn't time. Swallowing my discomfort, I shouldered my pack, and left.

In minutes, I was inside the perimeter of City One, avoiding crowds of late-night revelers and early risers. Exhausting the last of my strength, I aimed for Covington's flat.

She yanked me inside. "Arika! You're alive!"

"Water," I rasped, collapsing onto her.

"Yes, General." She removed my pack and helped me to her bed. As I laid back, she picked up a yellow *bambi* robe and wrapped it around her sleeping gown.

Suddenly, a dark figure rose from the other side of her bed. I rolled, on high alert. Then I recognized the face. "Martin?" I said. As I stared, Martin's form took shape. He'd been a respected captain in battle, but he'd receded from political life soon after the fighting ended. He'd grown a thick beard to obscure his identity and rarely left his flat, which was across the way from Covington's.

"It's me, General," Martin confirmed. He stood and slipped into a printed wax cloth shirt. At the base of the bed, he intercepted Covington, took the glass of water and handed it to me. "The whole of the Kongo is looking for you," he said.

"I know," I croaked, sitting up.

When he slid a palm over his belly, tucking his shirt into his trousers, I dropped my eyes. Our military work brought the three of us together often. But now, I realized, Covington and Martin spent significant time without me. The idea of it tightened unpleasantly in my throat.

Quickly, I gulped the glass of water and took the wanted poster from my sack. I smoothed it out. "I found this on my way here," I said. "Do either of you still have access to the Catalogue?"

Martin glanced at Covington then nodded. "Yes, but—"

"Good," I said, cutting him off. "Bring up the file on Obi Solomon."

Martin sighed, but complied, palming his comm-unit.

The Catalogue was a virtual public document begun in the days before the revolution, when access to information was limited and unauthorized scholarship was policed. Anyone with credentials had entree to the Catalogue, but the goldmine of information had come from a contingent of Rebels posing as Keepers. They'd infiltrated the library at Hasting and had virtualized nearly seventy percent of the records there before their work was discovered and cut short. At its height, twenty thousand notes were added daily as the search for the truth of our history captured the public eye.

Martin scanned the opening page of the subfile on Obi and looked up at me, bewildered. "It's what I thought," he said. "Nothing's been added for months."

"We're not adding," I said. "We're cross-referencing." I leaned over and tapped his palm, pulling up a search function. "Covington, make coffee. It's going to be a long day. I think I've got a new angle on—"

Covington took my shoulders. I looked up, meeting her concerned gaze.

"Arika," she said. She spoke slowly, as if afraid her words would trigger a landmine. "You're wanted for murder."

"Attempted murder," I corrected.

"We need to organize your defense."

"And we will," I said. "But first, I've got to free Jetson." Speaking quickly, I explained the botched plan.

"Slow down, General," Martin said. "Jetson confessed, but Swan claims you used him as a cover, then abandoned him when you were caught."

"That's not what happened!" I said, defensively. "Look, just help me search!"

"What are we searching for?" Martin said impatiently.

"A connection between Kira and Obi!" I snapped. "Kira's a traitor. He was a traitor. You see? Kira's in league with Jones and the English, just like Obi Solomon. They're plotting!"

"Plotting what?" Martin asked, adjusting his round spectacles.

"I'm not sure, but the proof is here." I fumbled as I pulled the aerial photos Jetson had taken and the picture of the blonde woman from my pocket. They scattered across my lap. "These were all taken from Swan's safe," I said, scrambling to collect the pictures.

Covington and Martin looked from the contraband to each other.

"Oh, Arika, how did you get those?" Covington said. "Is Kira right? Did you really order Jetson to betray the Kongo?"

"No! Jetson would never betray us. We broke into the safe to protect the Kongo. Just, just look at the pictures."

Martin let me shove the messy pile into his hands. He knelt reluctantly and flipped through the pictures, pausing on the woman with blonde hair.

"She looks familiar, right?" I said, rubbing my temple.

Covington looked over Martin's shoulder, tilting her head. "Well, she's English. She may look a bit like a Teacher," she said, "but not one I recall."

"Me either!" My voice was shrill. My eyes wide.

Martin flipped to the last photo. "Most of these are illegible," he said. He looked over at me. "So, what's here—what's the proof?"

I scratched my throat, where the ruby necklace lay against my skin. "I—I don't know," I admitted.

Covington deflated.

"General," Martin said, gently. "When was the last time you slept?"

"Who cares! Jetson's in the Pit," I snapped. "We'll enlarge the pictures. Identify the woman. Then we'll match the information with what we know about Obi and—and—" My train of thought slowed to a stop.

Martin looked grim. "Maybe later," he said.

"Captain!" I shouted. "We can free him if you help me!" My Apex flew into the air, responding to my distress.

Martin stood and shielded Covington with his body. "General," he warned. He put out both hands.

I growled and my Apex circled my head. I heaved myself up.

Martin lunged to restrain my arms. Covington got a hand over my mouth. "Arika, hush!" she hissed. "This obsession with Obi is madness. If they find us here with those pictures, we're all done. They'll do us like they did Jetson."

I froze, looking into her eyes. She was terrified. Martin, still holding my arms, looked gray beneath his trimmed beard.

I freed my mouth. "What are you talking about?" I whispered. "What did they do to Jetson?"

Covington shook her head, her mouth sealed. But I knew. Somehow, I knew. A bolt of sorrow electrified my neck and zapped from temple to temple. My heart broke and a foghorn sounded as a veil dropped over the dawn.

THE VEIL

My time behind the veil is always the same. It starts with a foghorn. A curtain comes to eclipse the celestial lights. Then comes the maid, her eyes the shape and color of whole almonds. She beckons me as she did in our real-life encounter in the Schoolhouse.

Come quick, she says. *She needs you.*

I know the maid is not actually there. She's an apparition. But she looks and sounds so lifelike, I can't help but speak back, "You!"

I didn't know her name, back then. I wouldn't learn it for months, but I've always sensed the impact of our encounter. Our meeting changed the course of my life. At her urging, I broke a Schoolhouse rule as I hadn't done in ten years. Jones caught me and forced me to spy on Hosea, which led me away from the Schoolhouse and into the village, where I fell in love with my people again. Our meeting started it all.

Come quick, miss, she says, again. *She needs you.*

The Schoolhouse wall appears at her back, and she gestures to it. As had happened in our real-life encounter, the wall slides open, revealing a passage. In the real past, the passage held stairs that spiraled to the Schoolhouse kitchen where Robin waited, sick and suicidal. Behind the veil, however, the passage is a mystical flume; a crack that ostensibly winds back through time.

I'm conscious of the veil but the temptation to follow the maid and relive that pivotal moment, with more courage than I had the first time around, is irresistible. One time, in the Seekers' camp, I gave in. The horn faded, the veil fell, the maid beckoned, and I followed.

Inside, I look around for the little maid. In the moment I realize I am alone, the door shuts, snuffing the ambient light from the Schoolhouse hall, and I jump—*crack!*—hitting my head on a ceiling I can't see. On my knees, I touch my crown and feel warm stickiness. I look down at my hand to gauge the extent of the blood and see—nothing. The tunnel is dark like I've never known before or since, like the Devil's pocket, like the throat of a wolf. So dark, my mind demands I open my eyes, and I try, *again and again*—but my eyes are already open. I press my lids back so the dark soaks in and expands inside me. It fills my ear canals with pressure, so I feel I'm underwater.

On my hands and knees, I crawl back to the passage door. I lift a hand to pull the latch, but I can't find it. It's gone. I push the door, willing it to open. I stretch my arms wide and high, looking for a hinge. There is no hinge, no seam, no door. I crane my neck—*crack!*—my head hits the ceiling an *inch* away. I know, now, I have to move. The passage is shrinking.

I curl in a ball and unfurl in the opposite direction. On my hands and knees, again, I crawl into the fissure. The floor is like ground glass on the pads of my palms and the bones of my knees. Each grit is a tiny needle, and my flesh gives way, popping open, beading blood. My thoughts circle like an undertow, whispering what I don't know—*Where does the tunnel end and when? What if it doesn't end?* I lift my head and—*crack!*—it hits immediately. A scream builds inside my chest, and I seize up, shriveling like a petrified insect. A puff of air would blow me away—*unless the tunnel runs out of air.*

When I can move again I, for the first time, appreciate pain. It's real and familiar, something to cling to. I grab hold and trudge on, slicing my forearms along the tunnel floor.

The shrinking fissure forces my head down, rips hair from the root, wedges my chin to my chest, so I feel I'm being strangled. I make myself smaller, laying my arms over my torso, crossed at the wrist, like a posed corpse.

I roll my ankles and dig my toes, driving my head into the crack. *Dig, slide, dig, slide.* The rock contracts like a jacket. *Dig, slide, dig, slide.* I'm raw and skinless. A worm of the earth. *Dig, slide.* The world must give. It doesn't. *Crack.* The crown of my skull meets the other end of the tunnel. And the tunnel is not a tunnel, but a cage.

In the end, I seal my open mouth around the closest wall and a scream rips my throat. With nowhere to go, the scream shouts back immediately, filling my lungs. So, when I scream again, and again, the sound is condensed, compacting exponentially until it is the *most. Potent. Scream.* And, still, nobody cares. No one sees. And I don't blame them. In this dark, I can't even see myself. I only imagine, visualize, hope I exist.

And sometimes, dear reader, I doubt it.

PART FIVE

THE OBI FOREST

*It takes enormous trust and courage to allow
yourself to remember.*
BESSEL VAN DER KOLK, THE BODY KEEPS THE SCORE:
BRAIN, MIND, AND BODY IN THE HEALING OF TRAUMA

THE COMPOUND

"Gaap!"

The shout rang out across the encampment. I kicked the drape of my robe aside and mounted my horse, merging with the stampede north toward the Obi Forest. Flanking me, a party of Seekers, zealots who spent their time theorizing about the firewall that blocked traffic into the forest, took up the cry.

"Gaaap!"

"Chernobyl!"

"GAP!"

The randomized location of the Chernobyl Gap, the only safe way through the firewall, was controlled by an algorithm designed by the original scientists. Director Kumar alone could bypass the equation. He guarded the entrance jealously, inviting in who he pleased. The rest of us, Seekers, watched and waited, chasing the traveling Gap with religious vigilance.

"Gaaap!"

"Chernobyl!"

"GAP!"

I maneuvered my mount beside the zealot who'd sounded the alarm, squinting to follow his line of sight. Rumor had it the Gap appeared only to the pure of heart.

After Jetson's execution, I was formally indicted on the allegations Jones had leveled against me—mayhem and attempted murder. Kira Swan, picked to prosecute, would present Jones' testimony. And Covington would put on my defense. In the meantime, I'd submerged myself in the heavy robes of a Seeker, looking for atonement.

A cry went up as the nose of the zealot's mount crossed the barrier—this was it! Gathering my strength, I spurred my horse and—

Zap!

The firewall sparked a foot from my mount. I yanked the reigns. Horses screamed and people toppled. The zealot, spread-eagled against the wall, sizzled. In death, he emitted a stench like game meat, broiled bone and char. Gagging, I swayed in the saddle.

"Easy, General!" a voice called. It came from beyond the wall.

"Get her out of there!" Another voice, again from the other side of the firewall.

I squinted at the wall. It wrinkled before me, then split as a finger poked through. The finger sliced down, tearing the wall like a sheet. A hand broke through the tear and swiped my shoulder, scraping a brown medicinal patch from my skin. The patch fluttered to the desert sand.

The wall burst open, and a man stepped through. He was built like a slender warrior. His sculpted deltoids gave way to a muscular chest. His skin was white, but he wasn't English. He had fuzzy blond hair, thick pink lips, a wide nose and eyes the color of dried blood.

"Who are you?" I asked. Though something told me I already knew.

He chuckled, flashing white eye teeth.

A narrow canister was in his hand. He steadied it an inch from my nose and flicked a lever on the side. A piece of the can receded, leaving a cone-shaped hollow. He depressed the top of the can and a mist sprayed from the cone.

I inhaled and toppled from my horse. I hit the ground hard, then sat up clenching a mound of sand. It was as fine as powder— different from the coarse terrain of the Kongo. The sand jerked robotically in my palm. After a moment of hyper-pigmentation, the solar mimesis algorithm recalibrated, and the image settled. From every angle I was, again, holding a fist of sand. And there, on top, was the medicinal patch that had peeled from my shoulder.

I touched the helmet on my head as the truth hit me, breaking the hold the *pagote* root had on my mind. I was not in the Kongo desert. I dropped the sand, and my nails scraped the flooring that tiled the advanced training room of the Director's Compound.

The illusion broke down rapidly. The bright sun was inconsistent with the cool temperature. The artificial horses and most of the Seekers were identical holographs. A handful of flesh-and-blood people dressed in programmed simulation suits added variety to the farce.

Hosea's concerned face came into view. "Are you back?" he asked, holding out a hand. He gave a signal, dismissing the extras. When they'd gone, he looked me over, searching for injuries.

The white man bent to retrieve the brown patch that administered the *pagote* root, a hallucinogen that lowered inhibition and made it hard to discern reality from fiction. Under its influence, nuances—hyperpigmentation, logical inconsistencies—went unnoticed. When he stood again, I remembered who he was. My time with the Seekers had taken place before he and I met, which is why I hadn't recognized him in the simulation.

He was not a warrior—far from it. He was a brilliant scientist. A savant. He understood the inner workings of the simulation technology better than anyone. As he inspected the patch he'd attached to my skin before the simulation, the last of the *pagote* cleared from my head and my memories repopulated.

I'd first met Lee Ford on the day I'd come to the Compound.

•

"Lee Ford, say hello," Director Kumar ordered.

Obediently, the white man inclined his head. Hosea Khan stood at my side, but Lee Ford ignored him. We were in a desert clearing south of the firewall, not far from the Seekers' camp. It was late afternoon, but the hot Kongo sun beamed relentlessly. I shielded my eyes to study the Director as he introduced his companion.

"Lee is my most trusted researcher," Kumar explained, gesturing to the man with skin like limestone. "I've brought him along to observe."

Kumar held his head at a forward angle, enhancing the prominence of his forehead as he peered at me over rectangular glasses perched halfway down his heavy nose. Straggly eyebrows partially concealed his gaze, which commanded attention.

Still, I struggled to keep my eyes from his physique. The photographs I'd seen of him had hidden a critical aspect: instead of flesh and blood, his thighs perched upon a pair of bionic legs. They bulged with thick wrought-iron bones, then tapered into sleek metallic shins. At the end, his ankles streamlined then curved out like a saber.

He adjusted the angle of the hooked cane he leaned on and went on. "I know the details of your illness, but I can't credit it," he said. "The infamous General Cobane, the Berserker, has become the Mute?" he lifted an eyebrow, seeking confirmation.

I nodded. The Seekers had dubbed me 'the Mute' when I fell ill in their camp. When Hosea found me, a month after Jetson's execution, I'd been silent and stiff for a week. The catatonic *episode*, as he called it, was a malfunction of my physiological fight or flight response to stress.

"Hosea revived me," I said. "But I want answers. Hosea says you have the equipment to study the root of my illness."

"Study and *cure* it," Kumar said. "*If* you're willing."

Hosea cleared his throat pointedly.

Kumar chuckled. "And if you can convince my son to trust me."

"A cure?" I asked. "You've encountered this—problem—before?"

"I study primordial neuronal pathways, particularly the parasympathetic fight or flight response," Kumar said. "Your symptoms present a fascinating case study—the Raid of Cobane, for example—"

I dropped my gaze, intentionally tuning him out. From experience, I knew that speaking of the raid would bring on an episode. I still had no personal recollection of the battle and yet, a particular echo from the fight plagued me nightly.

Find them! Find their hiding places and leave nothing alive. Advance!

I refocused on the conversation as Hosea explained his treatment plan. "We'll make use of Father's technology, but nothing invasive. No unnecessary medicine and no taking blood," he said. "We've agreed that I'll be present for every test."

"But Lee Ford will oversee the technology," Kumar injected. "Lee runs all of my labs at the Compound."

"He's also my brother," Hosea added.

"We share no blood," Lee said, speaking for the first time. He shifted his weight and turned his face away, surveying the horizon.

Hosea didn't deny Lee's assertion, but a cold silence fell.

The Director clapped, flashing an emerald ring. "Well then, what say we get on our way." He jabbed a finger at Lee Ford. "Bring the draught," he ordered.

Lee moved to the vehicle they'd arrived in, a late-model hovercraft with a windowless trailer attached to its back. I watched as he retrieved a metal case from the passenger seat of the craft, opened it and took out a vial of gold liquid. Lee returned to address us. "You'll both take a dose of this," he said, swirling the liquid in the vial. "Then you'll ride in the trailer with me. Once we're in the Compound, Father will let us out."

Hosea eyed the trailer. It looked like a holding cell. His gaze shifted to the older man's bionic legs. "If the three of us are in the trailer, who's operating the craft?" he asked.

Kumar smoothed his oiled beard. "It's manned by the armed courier you see there: a prototype. If it works as planned, I won't have to escort visitors to or from the Compound. It's coded with the firewall algorithm and designed to execute anyone who exits before the destination is reached. Except me, of course." He chuckled.

Hosea's brown eyes flashed a gold color as he gazed at the apple-shaped courier robot in the driver's seat of the craft.

"If you leave with a courier, you can come and go as you please," Lee said. "But Father doesn't let anyone know how he gets through the firewall or the exact location of the Compound once inside. Not even his precious son." He said the last bit under his breath, spitting the word 'son' like poison. "With the draught you'll sleep most of the way."

"Don't fight this, my boy," the Director said to Hosea. "And be grateful! I could insist you go through erasure and quarantine, which is my usual protocol. The medication is harmless! Lee, show him."

Lee uncorked the vial and spilled a measured amount on a small bandage. He rested the bandage on his inner wrist and waited ten beats. He lifted the bandage just as the last trace of gold disappeared into his ashen skin. He held the vial out to Hosea Khan and smiled, a diagonal hitch of his full mouth. Hosea pushed it away.

The Director inclined his head deferentially, but his tone was final. "If you don't take the medicine, I'll leave her here." He nodded toward us then ambled to the passenger seat of the hovercraft, leaving Lee to stand guard. Lee spread his legs and folded his hands at the base of his spine.

Hosea looked down at me. "I don't like this," he said. "But we need shelter and the Compound *is* secure."

The Compound was a military technology base, built by the original scientists after the old governing document, the Compromise, was signed. The Director repurposed the base and

Hosea had petitioned his father for sanctuary on my behalf—away from the dark memories and relentless responsibilities of the Kongo. Away from what he called my 'fixation' on Kira Swan.

"We don't have a choice, Hosea," I said, softly. "I've got nine months before the trial and nowhere else to go."

Hosea nodded, mulling over the facts. To gain time to investigate Kira, I'd convinced the Council to let me heal before I defended the allegations against me. With my seat in limbo, they also agreed to wait for a final vote on the Accord. In exchange, I would hold the Kongo militia, who backed me implicitly, to the lucrative temporary ceasefire the Council had penned with the American Assembly.

"I believe you're right," Hosea said.

Lee Ford had been listening in. He moved forward and offered the vial again. Hosea took it, removed the cap, and sniffed the liquid. He wet his finger with the medicine and walked away, touching it to his tongue. I watched his back as he continued, monitoring the potion's effect on his senses.

When he was a distance away Lee Ford spoke. "You're wrong, you know," he said.

I jumped, unnerved. He'd stood so perfectly still – like a blank white wall.

He went on, his tone analytical. "You said *we* don't have a choice—and *you* don't. But Hosea Khan does. Be warned, Hosea always chooses what *he* wants."

His hostility was off-putting, but I was curious. "What are you talking about?" I asked.

Lee repeated Director Kumar's threat—*I'll leave her here.* "That means his dear boy is welcome regardless. He's your ticket. You're just the bait. Get my meaning?"

He had a rapid speech pattern that was difficult to follow, but I nodded, understanding. Kumar wanted Hosea at the Compound, and he was using Hosea's desire to help me as a lure.

"Hosea was born with options," Lee said. "So, the question is always what does he want? Care to guess?"

"He wants what's right," I said, confidently.

"And what do you want?" Lee asked.

"Freedom for the Kongo," I answered instantly.

Lee Ford's mouth curled. He was lean and sleek, like a garter snake. His pale skin shone in the ripe sun. "Hosea's too afraid of Father's science to care for the Kongo—or its freedom," he said. "*But* it was a trick question." He winked. "Even he doesn't know what he wants. He'll come for a bit, then he'll go—you'll see."

I frowned. I didn't see the connection between science and Hosea's loyalty to the Kongo. But, before I could ask, Lee went on.

"And when Hosea breaks with Father—and they *will* break—what will you do? Will you align yourself with Father for your *own* good—or concede all to the blessed son? Now, there's the question. That's the dilemma." Lee sighed. "I've been there."

I leaned in. "And what did you choose, your father or your brother?"

"Choose?" He laughed without smiling. "You're mistaken, General. I don't have choices either."

"But you said—"

"A dilemma, not a choice," he said.

"Then why are you telling me this?" I asked, annoyed. He knew I'd come here with his brother and he knew I'd come for a cure. And yet, according to him, I couldn't leave with both.

His eyes shifted. They peered over my shoulder and thinned to slits. I followed his gaze. Hosea was moving back to us.

I faced Lee. "If I can't have both, and I can't choose," I said. "What's the solution?"

Hosea arrived before Lee could answer. "Leave her alone, Lee," he said.

Lee saluted with one sarcastic finger. Then, slowly, staring at Hosea, he bent and pressed his mouth high on my cheek. "Ask me again, later," he said.

Hosea reached over my shoulder and forced Lee back several inches.

Lee Ford growled, then smiled with dislike in his eyes. "Easy, Kha. I'm only trying to help."

"She doesn't need that kind of help," Hosea said.

Lee ignored him and spoke to me. "Did you hear it, General—*that kind*? See how he turns his nose up? He takes such pride in his clean hands. The truth is his hands are clean only because he runs from every battle and leaves the rest of us to survive. But—" His eyes found mine. "But something tells me you're a survivor."

I wet my mouth. His insight was crass, but keen. Covington, I knew, felt much the same way. Hosea had left the Council to study the fault just when we'd needed him most. At that moment, I decided to befriend Lee. I sensed I'd need his help at the Compound.

I turned to Hosea. "Lee says you're my ticket. That Kumar's labs are off-limits without you. Is that true?"

"Leave Father out of it," Hosea said. He put a hand on my shoulder. "Trust me, his technology is dangerous. We need the Compound for shelter but we'll avoid his science, and him, wherever possible."

Lee snorted knowingly and I wondered again about Kumar's science. What made it *dangerous*? My eyes moved slowly from Hosea Khan to Lee Ford and, in the distance, to their father, Kumar. Hosea hadn't answered my question but, seeing the possessive stare Kumar leveled on him, I determined Lee was right. If I wanted the Director's help, I had to please his son.

"We can leave Kumar out of it," I said. "But I'll decide for myself who I talk to and when."

Lee Ford gave a shout of laughter. "I think she means it, *brother*." Hosea's mouth tightened as Lee went on, delighted. "Now, don't be alarmed; this is how it feels to encounter a disappointment."

Hosea turned a shoulder to Lee Ford and looked down at me. "I'll need your weapon now," he said.

I nodded. We'd discussed it at length before he'd summoned Kumar. The nature of my illness made my Helix, stronger than any danomite sword, intolerably dangerous. Hosea had agreed to help me only if, for the time being, I disarmed.

I palmed my Helix as he produced a cloth sheath that, he'd explained, would make it impossible for me to control my weapon from a distance.

I took the sheath and, reluctantly, slid my Apex inside. I handed the weapon to Hosea Khan then touched the empty holster around my waist. It dangled awkwardly, like a limb that had inexplicably gone numb. "Let's get out of here," I said.

Lee administered the draught under Director Kumar's watchful eye. After, he took my arm and marched me to the trailer. "Ready or dead," he whispered.

I looked over my shoulder, up into his weird red eyes. "I'm ready," I said.

His white fingers tightened under my armpits, curving over the top of my breasts. He boosted me up and climbed in. Hosea followed, wedging himself between us.

•

I loosened the chinstrap of the radiological helmet and stared up at the white planes of Lee Ford's face. His eyes were deep set and framed with ash-blond lashes. The irises weren't only red, as I'd first imagined, but a fiery brown, like cinnamon. He had a caustic sense of humor, but over the months I had been here I'd gotten used to it.

"Lee Ford, the albino," I said.

Lee gave a mock salute. "Welcome back, General."

I removed the helmet and another level of the simulation dissolved. The altered events of the test blurred in my mind, leaving only the real memories that had seeded them.

Hosea reached for my hand but I brushed him aside and stood to interrogate Lee. "Did I pass? What happened?"

When I demonstrated my return to strength tomorrow, working out in front of the Kongo people, it would be Lee who would calculate the score.

Lee nodded to Hosea. "Ask *him*. He's the one who pulled you."

Pulled? I whipped around to confront Hosea. "You pulled me out of the simulation before the end—why?"

"You weren't responding well," Hosea said. "Show her, Lee."

Lee Ford walked into what looked like the sun rising on the peaks of the Kongo. He stopped in a patch of prickly pears. The spikes, thin and stiff as needles, should have torn through his shoes. Instead, he adjusted some invisible dials, and a second later, the desert scene was replaced with an expansive white room.

Returning to where Hosea and I waited, Lee retrieved a file from his comm-unit. He projected a visual of the simulation and waved an index finger to advance the scene to before the zealot's body burned. I'd had the same encounter in real life, but the simulation, designed to test my response to stress, altered aspects of the memory to gauge my strength. I watched through my own eyes as the smell of charred flesh, one of my triggers, hit like a monsoon.

"Stop here," Hosea said, pointing at the projection. "Your heart rate dropped, then careened. Your blood pressure peaked, and your hormones reached a dangerous level. I pulled you out to avoid another episode."

I cursed. "Replay it," I ordered. Lee Ford complied.

I watched as, in the simulation, Lee sprayed the *pagote* antidote. At the bottom of the projection, the heart icon blinked red, indicating tachycardia. I looked away.

"Turn it off," I said, snatching up the canister Lee Ford had discarded. "How many minutes into the scene did I make it?"

"Not even ten," Lee said, minimizing the visual with a swipe of his hand.

My fist tightened on the can. A return to health wasn't enough. To convince the people to reject the Accord, and Kira Swan, I needed to restore the Kongo's faith in me to its height, just after the rebellion, when there was no doubt of my prowess.

"Let me do it again," I said. "Right now."

Hosea retrieved the data chip from my abandoned radiological helmet and slipped it into his pocket. "It's too risky," he said, finally, his face grim. "You're getting worse, not better."

"Which is why I need the practice!" I reasoned. "Lee? You know the equipment better than anyone. Can we run it again?"

Hosea's jaw tightened.

Lee looked narrowly at his brother. "If we start from a different place in the timeline, we can rerun the test. But I *may* have to increase her *pagote* level for believability."

Hosea and I spoke at the same time.

"I'll do it!" I said.

"Medically unsound," he countered.

Lee glanced from Hosea to me, amused.

"Arika, a word in private," Hosea said. Without waiting for an answer, he strode towards a storage room across the training site.

I followed him into the room and slammed the door. We often spoke in private, but never on his command. Hosea pointed a finger. I swatted it aside.

"The workout is tomorrow. Tomorrow!" I closed my eyes and took a deep breath. "I want another test, now."

"Increasing your *pagote* is not the Way," Hosea said.

I groaned, rubbing my throat where the ruby necklace chafed. 'The Way' was Hosea's prescription for my illness. He'd synthesized the ancient combat arts to create seventy-seven Master Ways, and I practiced the first seventy-six daily. Way Seventy-Seven—the most powerful Way—was a divine mystery. According to Hosea, I couldn't see it as it was beyond my current level of training.

After months, I'd improved significantly in form and longevity, but the most advanced Ways still left me gasping, and controlled breathing was key. Each Way—a choreographed series of movements—existed merely to accompany the breath which, Hosea believed, was the conduit between the finite material of our bodies and the infinite power of the invisible. In the final Way, the mind quieted and the body transcended, aligning perfectly with the Will of the ultimate universal power. It was this transcendence that, he claimed, gave him his extraordinary physical abilities: speed, endurance and strength. After nine months, the transcendence still eluded me.

"I've tried it your way, Hosea. I'm out of time," I said.

"It's not my way," he corrected. "It's *the* Way, the *only* way."

I shook my head, dismissing his philosophical talk. Time was of the essence. After years of struggle, the people wanted ease and prosperity. They'd gotten a taste of it with the temporary ceasefire agreement. Trade with the north, unhindered by treaties and strife. If I had any chance at swaying them to secede, I had to show them a better way *now*.

I met Hosea's gaze. "To be free we need land and the means to defend it," I said. "You know this as well as I. The workout has to be perfect! The people will unite behind the Berserker, but not unless I've conquered the Mute."

"But you're better than the Berserker," Hosea said, gently. "And you haven't conquered the Mute."

I looked away.

He stepped forward and took my shoulders. "You're ignoring every sign that something is wrong. Something in here," he said. He tapped my chest where my heart beat. "And something here." He touched my temple, so his palm caressed my jaw. "You were almost there today," he said, softly. "Then *something* changed. Did you *know* the Seeker who died on the wall?"

As he studied me, his eyes flashed like brass and the fine hairs on my neck rippled. That gleam unnerved me. I'd seen it often enough to know it wasn't a trick of the light. It was... strange. Beneath its weight, I felt he could see inside me. More, his insight was *supernatural*.

My memory was healing and I recalled the Raid of Cobane. A shameful detail of the battle had resurfaced and the pain of remembering it was sapping my strength. Hosea's digging and analyzing had to stop before I, again, lost my grip on reality.

I fidgeted with the canister that was still in my hand, then stuffed it into the empty holster around my waist. "I'm taking the higher dose of *pagote* and redoing the test," I said. I spoke firmly, but with a civil tone. Hosea honored my decisions, but we knew—deep down—he'd been my ticket to the Compound. I was here with his permission and at any time, he could withdraw it just by leaving—something I sensed he was eager to do.

He opened his mouth to argue, but I spoke over him. "More," I said. "I want the Director to review the scans taken during the next test."

His eyes flashed.

"Please, don't argue," I said quietly. "It's time for the cure."

His concern was palpable and I understood his position. I was charged with attempted murder, a capital crime, and his focus was the trial. He didn't understand that the people's faith, for me, loomed larger than death. I made to leave, then stopped, one hand on the door. I turned back.

"We can still meet in the gazebo this evening—if you want," I whispered.

He dropped his head, slipping his hands into his pockets. "I don't know," he said, finally. "I think, perhaps, I made a mistake."

The words landed like a honed blade, and I jerked involuntarily.

Hosea started towards me. "Arika—"

I left, before he could say more.

•

Outside the storage room, I spun away from the door and sagged back against it. *A mistake.* I squeezed my eyes shut, pushing back the sting of emotion. *A mistake?* I gulped as the air whooshed out of the room. *A mis—No, no.* No. I shook my head. I couldn't think about it now. I pushed away from the door.

Lee saw me coming and closed the sketch pad he filled in his spare time. "So we're on?" he said, crossing the room and putting the pad into his sack.

I cleared my throat. "We're on. And, in this next test, we'll be taking scans, in preparation for the cure. Alert the Director and use whatever *pagote* you need."

I heard Hosea come up behind me. He stopped, his chest squared with Lee Ford's. "Are you mixing the medication yourself or using one of Father's couriers?" he demanded.

"I'll do it," Lee said.

Hosea nodded. "And you're reducing from high-grade, old-seed plant, diluted with purified water to a concentration of—"

"Twenty-four point two percent," Lee said. He turned his back on Hosea so only I could see his rolled eyes.

I stepped between them. "How long will it take to reset the test?" I asked.

Lee's eyes slid away. "An hour. We'll work in the big lab to accommodate the scans."

"I can't meet until after noon," Hosea said. He turned to me. "My patient has shown signs of waking; I have to be there when she opens her eyes."

I sighed. Hosea was still measuring the growth of the fault he'd identified months ago. The line had stretched south and north, to the Obi Forest. Then, last week, after a dozen minor tremors, a sizable earthquake had shaken the sinkhole in the predawn hours. At daybreak, Hosea Khan, always the first to awaken, had discovered an unconscious woman in the north yard. Since then, he'd nursed her, certain she had information about the quake, the fault and the forest where, he believed, the quake had originated.

"She can't wait one day?" I asked. "The demonstration is tomorrow."

Hosea shook his head. "She can't wait. I need to find out what she knows while it's fresh in her mind, and Father's keen to enforce his protocol. I can't hold him off much longer."

It was on the tip of my tongue to call him a liar. His passion for medicine and medicinal plants had found perches in the fertile, quaking ground of the Obi Forest and in this patient; but nothing was as pressing as securing my position in the Kongo.

"Father and I can always run the simulation without you," Lee suggested.

Hosea's lips thinned and a pulse kicked in his temple. "You'll do nothing without me present," he said, eyeing Lee Ford. "Right, General?" He turned to me for confirmation.

I looked between them.

"Arika?" Hosea prompted.

"We'll wait for the Kha," I said, finally.

Hosea squeezed my shoulder and left.

THE BROTHER, LEE

The door shut behind Hosea Khan, leaving me alone with Lee Ford. Longing for my Apex, I whipped the canister from my holster and clenched its girth. It was technically called an aerator and it was another of the Director's inventions. It turned liquid into breathable mist, the perfect vehicle for mind-altering substances since the nose, as Lee explained, connected directly to the brain through a specialized nerve.

The nose-brain connection was also why a stench, like the smell of burning bodies, triggered emotions in me that were impossible to escape—no matter how fast I ran. I spun and launched the canister at the wall.

Lee Ford clicked his tongue. "Now, General, is that *medically sound*?" he said. He assumed an exaggerated posture as he retrieved a discarded simulation suit, mocking Hosea's upright walk.

I disapproved of his cattiness but, in the past week, as my symptoms increased, so had my complicated feelings towards the Kumar men. More and more, Lee's gripes about his brother rang true. Hosea was unusually bothered by his father's scientific work and his agitation was growing every day. During our early session yesterday morning, a mere mention of it had triggered an angry response. We'd been in the gazebo, hours before dawn.

"Way Seven," he announced. We moved as one. Squatting, plunging, rising and lunging—exchanging air. Pivoting in and out. Hard and soft, slow, then darting. Inhale, exhale. In the end, we faced each other and bent at the waist, finishing the series.

"It's not working, Hosea," I said, feeling winded. "I don't feel powerful. I can barely keep up."

Hosea set. "Fourth Way," he announced. "And this time, focus on breathing."

I huffed. "I do focus. The problem is I don't understand! And I know what you're going to say," I said, quickly. *"Control your breath, and you'll understand the final Way, and then you'll see it.* But that doesn't make sense! How can I understand a Way I can't see?"

Instead of answering, he began to move.

I stepped away, resisting. "It's not working," I said again. "I don't see it. I don't even know what I'm looking for!"

He reset his position. "Fourth Way," he repeated.

Biting my tongue, I stood and mirrored him.

When the series ended, I was gasping. I tried again. "Hosea, the Director says—"

"No," he said, firmly.

"But if there's a cure then—"

"No!" he said again. He moved to tower over me. "Stop listening to my father; nothing he puts in your head is going to help you. Now, *focus.* I'll explain again."

Lee circled his arms. He stood on one leg, as Hosea did for hours during his daily exercise. He lifted a brow and looked down his nose at me. "Take a breath, Cobane."

It was a perfect imitation of the Kha. I bit back a smile and sat to unlace my simulation shoes. My body buzzed with adrenaline, and I needed the release of my regular morning jog to prepare for a difficult day.

Hosea Khan and I had always balanced two relationships. On one hand we were trainee and guide. On the other, friends… and recently more. Ordinarily we passed seamlessly between the two. But, as our training relationship strained, I couldn't shake the feeling that the next few hours could destroy our friendship as well.

Lee dropped the pose and threw up a hand. "You heard him— right?" he said, scornfully. "Am *I* mixing the *pagote*? I *always* mix the *pagote*. Father and I designed the chemistry together. And where was he?" He pointed after Hosea Khan. "He was off playing superhero in the village. But he lectures me on how it works."

"He's double-checking, Lee," I said, mildly. "And the fever was dreadful. Thousands more would have died if Hosea hadn't found a cure. So, he wasn't playing superhero." I pulled on my running moccasins. "He actually *is* a hero."

Lee scoffed. "You give him all the credit. If you knew what I knew about the fever, you'd spread some of that praise around."

I pursed my lips. "Then tell me what you know," I said.

He opened his mouth to say something, then seemed to think better of it. He retrieved the aerator I'd thrown and sat down beside me checking the canister for dents. "I just don't want to be questioned," he said, finally. "Not by him and not about science. Science, I *know*. You know?"

I lowered my gaze, understanding perfectly. Lee could be cruel, but never without provocation, and when we weren't at odds I enjoyed his company. I looked around. The room was empty except for the two of us, but in the Compound the air could have ears. I took a mirror from my pack and angled it towards the ceiling. It caught the crystalights overhead, but I wiggled it back and forth, looking for patrols, tiny flecks of metal that vibrated at specific frequencies and transmitted sound in real time. Patrols were undetectable to the naked eye but, in intensified light, they flashed like embers escaping a fire. They could be assigned to a room or, using the unique radio frequencies emitted by individual comm-units, they could follow a person. I had a pack of patrols surveying Kira Swan for months, but nothing had come of it—yet.

I put my mirror away and looked at Lee. "I *do* know," I confessed. "I don't like to be doubted either." I fumbled as I tied my laces, feeling as if I'd betrayed Hosea Khan.

"Well, I believe in you," Lee said after a while. He leaned over and tapped the toe of my running shoe. "Can I join you?"

I looked up sharply. "Don't you have to reset the simulation?"

"As it turns out," he said, his tone mocking, "resetting the simulation only takes a minute." He smiled mischievously.

I sighed. "So, you *lied*."

Lee chuckled and stood. "*At ease*, General. On this, the dear boy and I actually agree." He sobered and held out a hand to help me up. "You needed a break."

I took his hand and looped my pack over my shoulder.

•

The original scientists built the Compound into the rock sides of a natural sinkhole in the west mountains of the Obi Forest. Director Kumar had spent years improving upon the design and the resulting fortress was sturdy, but poorly planned.

So many had a hand in shaping it that no one knew its exact layout. It was a maze of tunnels, loops and dead ends, carved of the same grey sediment. It was easy to get lost and given the recent quaking, dangerous to take the unrenovated routes that hadn't been reinforced in two hundred years.

From the training room, we entered a well-lit corridor that quickly emptied into a tunnel with a low ceiling. The way was narrow and dark, but it provided the most direct path to the barracks in the east wing.

We stopped by my room, and I offloaded my pack before we continued to Lee Ford's assigned living space. Once there, he activated a crystalight, tossing it into the air near his wardrobe.

As he retrieved his running gear, I wandered past him to the window that dominated the west wall of the room. The window, made of specially engineered glass, overlooked the courtyard square at the base of the twenty-five-level Compound.

I squinted out at the grand stone staircase that ran the length of the sinkhole opposite Lee's room. The early morning fog was thick, obscuring the base of the hole, where the staircase began. But I had a picture of the base in my mind.

There were fruit trees all around and a thriving vegetable garden, split by a winding path. A subterranean piping system continually drained the base of the hole, and the drained water collected in a cistern situated at the north bend of the yard. The cistern's peak was the highest point in the Compound and its contents met most of our water needs.

In the center of the base was a grassy knoll, the Courtyard Square, where the Compound's two hundred and twelve inhabitants gathered from time to time. Some of my loyal soldiers had braved the Director's protocol and followed me to the Compound. But, as time passed, and my illness lingered, the lure of wealth had pulled them away. They'd returned to the Kongo to enjoy the booming economy, fueled by the new seed. Only a handful of my people—the bandits, Covington and Martin—remained. The rest of the Compound's inhabitants were the Director's scientists, staff and personal guard.

Steeling myself, I looked directly at the gazebo at the summit of the grand staircase. Its tin roof was held up by four concrete pillars wrapped in succulent vines. They wound down to anchor beneath the wooden platform where Hosea and I trained each night.

My view of the platform's waxed planks was obstructed by a line of bramble bushes. Still, I could picture it. My heart clenched as I thought of our last few sessions there.

Hosea had finally kissed me three nights ago. He'd kissed me again the next night and, last night, we'd nearly made love. I'd hoped that tonight would be *the* night. The first time there were no walls or secrets between us. For days, I'd struggled to sleep, reliving that first kiss—the kiss he now called *a mistake*.

"Ready or dead?" Lee said, morosely. He'd come up behind me, dressed to go.

I tore my eyes from the gazebo. "Ready," I said and followed him from the room.

•

The east wing exit opened automatically, and the fresh dawn swept over us. The morning was cool and the moon, still visible, was a silver coin in the sky.

By silent agreement, I set our pace as we began to jog along the stone walkway. The passage curved in a circle, following the natural shape of the sinkhole, a large, round bottom that narrowed slightly at the top. A safety rail of rope and wood lined the bend. Beyond the rail, the path dropped off into a freefall down to the courtyard.

I stayed away from the treacherous rail and close to the row of top-level rooms identical to Lee Ford's: dome-like, with three rock sides closed in by a floor-to-ceiling window. From the outside, where we jogged, the windows were opaque, maintaining the occupants' privacy.

I increased my pace, leaving the east wing behind as we climbed to the southern crest of the sinkhole. Here, the path widened into a plateau, which butted against a mountain valley uniformly packed with a brawny species of tree. Their dense green foliage and muscly vines, as thick as a man's wrist, formed an impenetrable parliament that obscured the forest floor.

As we passed the valley, a cool wind blew and I slowed, thinking of Hosea Khan. I'd watched him from my window as he meditated here for hours, gazing at the trees. He spent more time with the forest vegetation than with any other living thing. Did the trees know the Way? Could they see it? I craned my neck towards the forest and closed my eyes for a moment, seeking their counsel.

Run, they whispered.

I opened my eyes and stared out across the canopy, certain I'd heard something.

Run away, they said again.

My heart skipped. In fact, it would be my pleasure to jump into their dark arms. The leafy limbs would make a soft landing. I'd brush off and run home to the Kongo.

I refocused on the walkway and increased my pace again. Lee kept up, his breath synching with mine. We pushed each other hard, then harder, until my lungs ached and my body's demand for oxygen outpaced my anxiety. When we sprinted, flat out, my thoughts paused. The silence lasted only a moment, but I relished it, tilting my chin and exposing my throat to the sky.

Lee Ford brushed my arm. I glanced over and he signaled for me to follow.

"You go," I huffed, slowing to a walk.

He eased his pace and looked back at me. "We only just started," he said.

"I have to eat before the next test," I explained, waving him on.

Lee rolled his eyes. Regimented eating and hydrating was one of Hosea's health conventions. "Are you even hungry?" he asked.

I stared, refusing to answer. I wouldn't weigh in on Lee's side of their rivalry twice in one morning.

"Just what I thought." He turned and walked back toward me.

"Hosea's studied this illness," I said, defensively. "He revived me when I was catatonic for a week."

"Of *course* he did, he's a medic!"

When I turned away, Lee grabbed my arm. "Okay—okay! Easy, General. All I'm saying is you have *other* options."

I pulled my arm from his grip, but I didn't move away. He'd mentioned *options* before, two days ago when I confessed my concern about the weapon that had brought down the leader of the Sisters to the North, Nicky McCormick.

New reports verified the triple-point sword was made of danomite, a synthetic magma developed in the end days of the old world. Danomite arms had been key to the Kongo Army's success in the last war, but only in alloyed form, as the pure substance was notoriously unstable, equally likely to explode in your hand as it was to incinerate your enemy. Using advanced thermodynamics, the English had created an undiluted weapon. A pressurized magma sword that was at once gaseous, liquid, solid—and stable. The Dark Guard of the north had paraded Nicky McCormick, known as The Red, in chains, between towns, showing off the sword's capability. Eyewitnesses said she'd looked small without her red afro. Scorched, charred, blistered from the inside out.

I'd read about the triple point's schematics and wondered, anxiously, whether the Helix could match it. I knew the Kongo militia would be wondering the same. When I asked Lee his opinion, he'd mentioned my *options*.

Father spent years compiling Double Helix swords, he'd said. *Why do you think he left them in the south to be captured by the workers?*

I analyzed Kumar's motives for several minutes, before Lee supplied the answer. Kumar had set aside the Helix swords to reach for an even greater weapon.

It's more powerful than the Helix and triple-point swords combined, and we're near a prototype. So, now you have options, he'd said, lifting a brow. Then he'd offered himself up as a viable ally.

At the time, I'd determined to share the information with Hosea Khan. But, in two days, I hadn't found the right moment to speak with him. In my gut, I knew that moment had passed.

"I can show you, if you want?" Lee said, regaining my attention. I pulled in my bottom lip, uncertain.

Lee bent down, catching my eye. "Would it help if I showed you what Hosea is doing right now? You can see exactly why he put off redoing the test."

"You can do that?" I said, skeptically.

The corner of Lee's mouth lifted. He led me back to the west wing. Inside, we made several turns as the passages got smaller and darker. We passed two of Director Kumar's *No Trespass* signs, and finally stopped in a damp, unrenovated corridor.

Lee tapped his comm-unit and projected an image. "Take a look," he said. Floating above his hand was a visual of Hosea Khan, standing over a medical bed he'd set up in his infirmary office.

"How are you doing that?" I said. Patrols only made audio recordings. This technology gathered visual data as well. "Does Hosea know?"

Lee shook his head. "I set it up last night. Now, look! See what he's doing."

I leaned in to get a good look at Hosea's patient. "She's English!" I said. She was thin with red hair. Lacerations crossed her face and neck, and she lay under the covers like stone. There were no signs of waking. Instead of tending to her, Hosea moved to sit at his desk. He took up a pen and bent over his work, making marks.

"He's charting," I said, confident in my assessment. I'd watched him pore over various maps for months. When asked about them, he changed the subject. When I insisted, he withdrew. And now here he was, charting in private, instead of supporting me.

The back of Hosea's hand blinked blue, signifying a comm-unit call. Director Kumar's name flashed. Moving quickly, Hosea stacked the papers before him and placed them in the drawer of his desk. Then he answered the call.

Kumar spoke immediately. "Bring the white girl here, now!" he demanded.

Hosea stood and moved back to the English woman. He turned a knob, adjusting a machine beside her bed. He untwisted a tube running from an IV pole. He lifted her right lid and shined a pin light into her pupil.

"She's sleeping soundly, Father," Hosea said calmly. "Once she wakes—"

Kumar cut him off, reading from a sheet of paper. "Report," he said. "Five-thirty a.m.—Hosea says the English woman is, quote, 'waking'. That was fifty-three minutes ago, my boy. Plenty of time to ask her about some plants. Now, bring her here."

"She's sleeping," Hosea said again. "I *said* she's showing *signs* of waking. Tell Lee to check his quotes before sending them. An inaccurate spy is nothing more than a nuisance."

"Hosea Vine Kumar, you agreed to inform me the minute she awakens."

"She's not awake!" Hosea said, exasperated. "I'll tell you when she is."

Kumar waved a hand. "It's too late. I've changed my mind. I'm instructing Lee to perform a complete wipe this evening."

Hosea shook his head. "Father, that's—"

Kumar cut him off. "Don't tell me what it is, boy. I know what it is. I invented it. And I'm done waiting. A complete wipe, that's my protocol."

"She's *my* patient," Hosea said.

"And this is my Compound," Kumar countered. "Mine. You know I care for you but you're taking advantage. I can't risk the white girl's knowledge getting out. You have until supper to get her awake and get the information you're after."

Hosea disconnected. He returned to his desk and removed his chart from the desk drawer. He bent over it, working quickly.

"Interesting," Lee said, a smile in his voice. "Whatever that is, he's hiding it from Father. Or so he thinks." Lee peered at the projection, trying to make out the fine lines of Hosea's work.

He went on. "Our intention was to keep a closer eye on the English woman. But Father will want a look at whatever he's drawing. He's always after Hosea Khan's secrets."

I studied Hosea's spread of papers. The geological map he'd drawn wasn't familiar. Quickly, I committed the details to memory.

"Any luck?" Lee asked, noting my examination, testing me. *Would I betray Hosea Khan?*

"I have no idea where he's drawing," I said, honestly. I couldn't disguise my annoyance. Lee was right: Hosea was full of secrets. It was all for my good, he said, to shield me. But he didn't understand that the time for shields had passed. We needed to attack.

Lee made a series of gestures then tapped his palm and tossed his hand, sending out a message. "Father will figure it out," he said. He closed the live feed with a swipe of his hand.

"So, now you know what he chose over you."

"A map," I said, bitterly.

Lee's brow arched sympathetically. "I used to believe in him, too," he said. He placed a hand on the sinkhole wall behind me and leaned in, breathing on my face.

82

Before I could duck away, the wall behind me moved. I pivoted, hiding my surprise as an opening appeared and widened, revealing a room the size of a large broom closet. An ascending staircase angled from the space and disappeared into jagged rock.

Lee snaked around me, through the opening. He mounted the first step and turned his head, speaking over his shoulder. "Are you coming?"

THE OTHER LAB

The opening shut behind me, completing the darkness, and a draft crawled across my cheek. From the staircase, Lee tossed a crystalight.

I moved deeper inside to test the first step. "It's original stone," I said. "Does Hosea—"

"No, he doesn't know," Lee snapped. "He doesn't know everything! Father only shares the blueprints with me." He started up the steps. "Come on."

At the top of the stairs, he turned left and continued, making quick turns down narrow halls. Behind him, I began to feel claustrophobic and hot, despite the cool sheet rock.

"What's a 'complete wipe'?" I asked, trying to distract myself.

Lee spoke over his shoulder. "It's a scramble that doesn't require the recipient be awake. So, it's less precise."

I grimaced. "Obi, she won't remember anything at all."

Lee glanced back. "General! Are you feeling bad for an English girl?"

"No," I said. But I didn't like the idea of complete non-consensual erasure. The technology was dangerous.

The ceiling dipped and I hunched down, my heart thudding. "Are we there yet?"

"Almost," Lee said.

Sweat trickled into my ears. I swiped it out and—*Hoooonk!*
I stopped. "Lee," I whispered, nervously.

He pivoted down another hall. "Not much farther. Come on."

I took a shaky step. *Hooonk!* "Lee! Lee!" I shouted.

He turned back. "General? General, can you hear me? Arika—"
Hooonk! Hooonk! Hoooonk!

Come quick. She needs you.

For nine months I'd studied my illness. So I knew, when threatened, a normal person responds with a surge of energy to fight the threat or escape it. The process, prehistoric and physiological, is controlled by two chestnut-shaped areas in the temporal lobe. I knew the exact anatomy of the two chestnuts, called amygdala. Mine were, inexplicably, broken. When afraid, I couldn't fight or fly. In the moments that mattered most, I hid, frozen behind the veil.

Come quick, miss. She needs you.

I kept my chin up and my teeth clamped. If I didn't respond, I knew I had a chance. I focused on the veiled wall where Lee had disappeared. I shouted at it. "Lee!"

"Arika," he called.

I gasped, hoping I'd heard right.

He called again. "Arika!"

His voice was faint and I couldn't see him, but I didn't care. I took a breath and threw myself forward, into the veil.

•

I woke on my back. I looked down. I lay on a polished metal table upon what looked like a pile of lab coats. One folded coat supported my head.

"Are you here?" Lee said, urgently.

Conscious of Lee's assessing gaze, I sat up slowly. The dizziness and fog had abated. The veil, once pierced, released completely. If the spells weren't episodic, I could imagine they were dreams. "I'm back," I said, firmly.

"If you need to rest, we can wait," Lee said, sounding unconvinced. There was a rare softness in his face as he eyed me.

"Where are we?" I said, avoiding his pity.

He'd carried me down the narrowed tunnel and into a laboratory I'd not seen before. There were slate gray walls and a lower ceiling than in the renovated labs. Metal tables stretched from wall to wall, and tiered cabinets rose from the floor to the ceiling. There were no windows. No access to the outside world.

"This is the Empire Lab," Lee said. "And *no*, Hosea doesn't know. This is where we develop prototypes the Assembly would frown upon. Gossip is impossible to control in the other labs. Here, everything is top secret, so we explore without restraint. Of course, we won't have to hide once we're independently run and funded."

My gaze landed on the most prominent object in the room, a clear prism as large as a full-grown man. I hopped down from the table.

"General, maybe you should lie down," Lee said. "I can take you to the infirmary."

Ignoring him, I moved to inspect the interior of the prism. Lee followed at my elbow, like a nursemaid. "Is this the weapon?" I asked. Lee stared at me, his brow furrowed. "Lee, I'm fine!" I snapped. I repeated myself. "What is this?"

"It's a thought MRI," he said, reluctantly. He ran a possessive hand down a sleek side of the prism.

I hid my surprise. I used a thought MRI daily to seed my simulation exercises. It consisted of a heavy helmet and metallic tiled gloves attached to each other by thick wires. I walked around the exterior of the prism. It was nothing like the machine I used. "Tell me more," I said.

"The artifact you're used to produces twelve hundred frames of thought a minute," Lee said. His concern for me seemed to subside as he warmed to his subject. "This later model produces twice that, as well as the subject's musculoskeletal and neurological responses to the frames. The seed files produced are spectacular." He gestured to a lab table a few feet away.

I walked over and peered down at three stacks of seed files. One stack of the one-inch squares was neatly labeled, another wasn't. The third stack was small and set to the side.

"Once the memories are labeled, I store them here," he said. He rested a hand on the organized storage unit beside the stacks.

"And what's this?" I said, gesturing to a journal open beside the unit. He closed it quickly. "Those are my notes," he said.

"Notes," I lifted a brow. "You take notes on your own memories?"

"It's how I research," Lee said. "Every second, the brain collects thousands of pieces of information. We're conscious of only a fraction. So, often, an idea looks different when you go back fresh and study it."

I frowned, considering. "So," I said, slowly, "you go back in time to research your own brain."

He nodded. "Something like that." He grinned. "Speaking of superpowers," he pointed to the smallest stack and rolled his eyes, "those files belong to the son himself. He sent them a few months ago, hoping I'd see *him* differently."

"But you never will," I said, guessing.

"I haven't even watched them," he said. He stopped smiling.

I reached past him to pick up a file from the middle of the storage unit.

He snatched it from my hand as I read the label—*Mother*.

"Your mother then?" I said, watching him closely.

Lee started to answer then hesitated, his brow wrinkled, then he shrugged. "Yes, my mother," he said.

And Hosea's, I thought. My comm-unit buzzed. A message from Covington. *Reminder: You're to meet Martin in the Mess Hall in five.* I replied. *Change of plans. New project. Both of you go to the library. I'll meet you soon.*

As I typed, I watched Lee Ford from the corner of my eye. I was curious about Weka Vine, the brothers' mother, and Kumar's mistress.

Lee Ford replaced the *Mother* seed file, picked up the storage unit and put it into a drawer. I noted the drawer's placement and moved away. "So why don't we use the advanced TMRI?" I asked.

"Hosea would never allow it," Lee said. He chuckled, showing sharp teeth. "The advanced machine produces seeds as immersive as old-world cinematography. Too immersive. For all your exercises he has me build in levels of *unreality*, so as not to fully immerse you. He thinks you'll follow what you see in the darkness, and you won't come back. Whatever it is you see." His eyes narrowed and softened again, searching me for answers.

I turned aside. *The veil*, *double consciousness*—those were words I developed to wrap my own mind around my illness, but they were inadequate. Stuck in a world that isn't the world. Aware of myself apart from reality. If I had the words, I'd explain myself to Lee, just to not be alone. But that was part of the abyss.

The entire experience fell in a crack between words. So, even if I told him honestly, he would never truly understand. A bleak feeling washed over me and settled bitterly on my tongue.

"Just leave it alone, Lee," I said coldly. "You'll never understand."

Lee's lips flattened on his teeth. "But young Master Kha will, of course."

I whirled on him. "You say *we*—we do this and that, we make power—but isn't this your father's lab?"

"He trusts me," Lee said.

"Of course he does. You do whatever he wants. Doesn't that make him *your* master?"

Lee stiffened. "It's different. I'm his son."

"Well, he doesn't call you son." Instantly ashamed, I bit my tongue, then stuttered. "Oh no—no, Lee, I shouldn't have said that."

He looked away, but the arrow had landed squarely. I can still see his face, even now—twisted and crimson. He moved to the TMRI machine and rested a fist on its side. When he looked at me again, the soft expression was gone.

"Should we get to the weapon?" I said eventually.

He nodded and moved across the room to a high cabinet, opening it to reveal a keypad inside. He pressed seventeen buttons and the top shelf of the cabinet adjusted and clicked. He reached up and removed an object from a charging station unlike anything I'd seen before. It had a cord like an old-world electric appliance, *but such appliances were banned in the new world*. I stretched to my toes, but he closed the cabinet before I could get a better look.

With the object flat in his palms, like an offering, he nodded for me to join him at a metal table.

I bent as he rested the trinket between us. It looked like an arm bracelet. "What is it?" I said.

"You asked me for a solution once," Lee whispered. "*This* is proximity to power."

I straightened, waiting for him to explain.

"Power is good," he said. "But, in the end, proximity to power is better."

I opened my mouth to argue.

He held up a hand. "Hear me out, Arika," he said. "No one aims for the lackey. No one targets the page. I live in my brother's shadow, but the dark is ripe with opportunity. Understand?"

I considered him, propping my elbows on the table. "Opportunity," I said, slowly, turning the word over in my mouth. "To what? Betray your father and steal that *bracelet*?"

"No, General," Lee said. His tone called me obtuse. "I won't steal it because I don't have to. Father will give it to me. He's a private man but I run this lab—all his labs—and I know his safes and secrets. I'm the only one who knows, and that is the value of a powerful man's trust. You mock my subservience now but wait and see. I'm not my father's favorite son, but I am his heir—and that, in the end, is more valuable."

I nodded, understanding him perfectly. In the Schoolhouse I too had settled for proximity to power. My source had been Teacher Alice Jones. And, like Lee with Kumar, I'd done everything to please her. I'd obeyed, without question, the most despicable orders. Deceit went hand in hand with oppression. When every fair means of ascension was blocked, intelligent people—survivors—turned to the foul.

Like me in my senior year, Lee was overlooked and undervalued. He'd dedicated his life to his father and he awaited his payout, like a fuse. On the day I'd finally deployed, with my back to the wall in the testing room suite, I'd ignited a revolution. What would come of Lee Ford's fury?

I picked up the bracelet and ran my fingers along the tangled snake design. Each of the snakes had a prominent pair of eyes that unnerved me, reminding me of something I'd seen before. I looked at Lee. "I assume it's not just a bracelet?"

Lee arched both brows as he came around the table and took the trinket from my hands. He slid it onto his bicep and moved his fingers across the design. The bracelet cinched. Then, it disappeared.

I blinked. "Obi, where did it go?!"

"It's still here," Lee said. He tapped a finger on his bicep and a *click*, the sound of his nail hitting the bracelet, reached my ears. He adjusted the position of his hand and tapped an intricate pattern with his fingertips. A second later, *he* disappeared.

THE BRACELET

"Lee?" I said, my heart jutting in my chest.

He reappeared and caught my shoulders. "Ah-ha!"

I twisted loose and glared at him.

"Scared?" he said, drawing the word out.

"Just do it again," I ordered.

With a grin, he tapped a pattern on the bracelet, still invisible on his arm, and vanished.

"Is it a simulation suit?" I said, speaking into what looked like thin air.

Lee reappeared. "Not a suit. Suits are based on mimicry."

"Then a holograph?"

"Negative. The bracelet is more advanced than anything either of us have encountered. I believe it's based on the principles that govern the movement of light, but *I* didn't make it."

"Who did—Kumar?" I asked.

Lee waggled a brow, but declined to answer. Taking my wrist, he disappeared again. He moved my hand along his muscular chest.

"My guess," he said, softly, "is that the bracelet creates a force field that changes the speed of light deflecting from anything inside, rendering it unseeable. If I'm right, then the bracelet defies the laws of physics. And if one law can be broken—why not two? Or—*seven*?"

"Seven," I repeated. It was an odd number to skip to. "Why seven?"

Lee's fingertips pressed the pulse in my wrist. "Why not?" he whispered, letting the idea float in the air between us. He reappeared and slipped the hoop onto my bicep. He tapped a pattern and I vanished.

I felt the cool fan blowing the hairs on my arm. I felt the rock floor beneath my feet. But I couldn't see my body. A bizarre sensation not unlike the feeling in the crack behind the veil flittered inside me. Only, I wasn't afraid. I felt *strong*. I waved a hand and pictured my palm moving an inch from my nose and, just like in the dark, my mind acknowledged the movement as if my eyes had confirmed it. I inched my fingers along my arm until I felt the bracelet. I pushed it down my arm, over my wrist and took it off. When I reappeared, I ran my hands over my stomach and thighs, the soft wool of my hair, my neck—solid and real.

Lee grinned. "Did you feel it?" he said. "The power?"

I nodded.

"Well, that's just a taste," Lee said. "There's more on the horizon for anyone bold enough to pursue it. Father studied the bracelet for years. He finally entrusted me with the project and I'm close to understanding its mechanics. Once I do, we'll duplicate the bracelet and make more that break other laws. I've presented him with plans for an empire, independent of America, here in the Obi Forest. We'll govern ourselves, protect ourselves and change the world with science—no limits."

"No limits?" The phrase felt like a lion yawning before me.

Lee slipped the brown-toned bracelet back onto my arm and activated it, so its strangeness flowed through me. His queer take on darkness subverted the fear that consumed me behind the veil. And, in a way, he was right: invisibility *was* ripe with opportunity. Behind the veil, I felt hidden and alone, but I was also *free* to be whatever I imagined. A shape-shifter endowed with superior knowledge of my own existence; not just aligned with the will of the universe, but perhaps, a power unto myself.

The possibilities filled me with a dangerous excitement. I took the bracelet from my arm again and shoved it in Lee's direction.

He smiled, knowingly. "So, you ken what I'm offering," he said. "Not just freedom, but the Kongo itself. Father is an old man. When the empire passes to me, *I'll* be the Kumar of influence." He thumped his chest. "If we're allied, I'll give you whatever piece of the Kongo you want. Order the Council to reject the Accord. Or do away with the Council entirely."

"Impossible," I said.

"Like magic," Lee agreed. He winked, twirling the bracelet so the tangled snakes, still strangely familiar, swirled in the laboratory lights.

I stared, considering. An empire with the ability to bend physical laws would quake the depths of the American power structure. But, according to Lee, neither he nor Kumar had the ability, as they couldn't yet replicate the science and bend other laws—of gravity and matter, energy and space. Until they could, the bracelet was nothing more than a party trick. Certainly not a match against the triple-point sword.

At length, I met Lee's gaze and shook my head. "I've seen what you had to show me, Lee, but I'm going to go now," I said, firmly.

Lee slipped the bracelet on his arm and tapped, so it disappeared but he remained in view. He pointed to a segment of the wall. "The way back is through there, General. Just press and hold."

Slowly, I moved in that direction. I expected Lee to stop me. He'd been after me for months, pressing his case and encouraging me to break with Hosea Khan. I was used to his coercion, but today's bid had an air of desperation. As I reached the exit, Lee's footsteps came behind me. He extended a hand and I watched its shadow, like a spider moving along the wall.

Just when I thought he'd grab my shoulder, he rested his hand on the secret door, blocking my way. "It's no secret I want you as an ally. What can I do to change your mind? Name anything."

I nodded to where the invisible bracelet clasped his arm. "When will the technology be ready?"

"I'm close," he said, his voice pitched with excitement. "More so than even Father knows. I'll present my most recent findings to him later today. Then I'll make more and practice using them in combination."

I frowned. "What do you mean?"

"Physical laws are more powerful in combination, right? There are rules of space and rules of time. Then there are laws that govern the spacetime continuum."

"Wait—space *and* time—like, time travel?" I said. I was more than skeptical.

Lee nodded, his eyes bright. "That's where the power of the bracelets lies, in combination. Wielding them together requires knowledge *and* skill. Not just tapping in sequence, complicated strokes and mental prowess. Once I have more bracelets, I'll focus on utilizing their potential."

I nodded. "Well, let me know when you're more than close," I said. "If you can weaponize the physical world, it will change everything."

"Aye-aye, General." He touched a finger to his brow and slanted it up into the air.

•

Back in my room in the east wing, I removed a handful of seed files from my wrapped vest. I'd had time to blindly reach into the drawer twice, snagging the file marked *Mother* before Lee had returned his attention to me. Martin and Covington were expert researchers, uprooting secrets that could, theoretically, be used to coerce. The files would be a mine of useful information. Information I needed to hold my own against Kumar as I pressed to acquire the cure.

Even so, guilt gnawed at me as I scooped out another handful of files. Out of respect for Hosea, I'd limited our research into the Kumar family. That courtesy had ended this morning, when Hosea withdrew his support. Without him, I would need every missile at my disposal.

I put the seed files in an envelope and pulled a red accordion folder from a stack. We had files on everyone of interest to the Kongo. The name written across this one was *Kumar*. I opened the folder and read Martin's summary.

Dana Alexandra Kumar was the son of English heiress Elizabeth Glosser and her gardener. When Elizabeth died, she left her fortune to her husband, Marion Glosser, called the Duke of the North. Marion disowned Kumar when he was thirteen years of age. Undeterred, Kumar took a low position at the smallest Glosser lab and spent the next fifteen years earning his stepfather's approval. He outshined his brother Dorian, the couple's legitimate son, in every way, working his way up to eventually transform the minor lab into the biggest megatech lab in the north. Nevertheless, when Marion died, he specifically disinherited Kumar. He left his entire empire to Dorian on one condition: his brother Dana could never work in a Glosser lab again. Dana Kumar took charge of the Kongo that year, but Hosea Khan and Lee Ford were only introduced as his sons after the Compromise restrictions loosened, after the Rebellion.

Setting the folder aside, I undressed and wiped the sweat from my body with a moist rag. I air dried and went to dress. I ignored the built-in wardrobe assigned to me: there hadn't been clean clothes in it for a week, since Covington had last had my things washed and hung.

Stepping over a stack of books, I lowered myself to the floor and pulled a pair of leggings from under the bed. A shirt came with them and, sniffing it, I pulled it over my head. I added a vest and pressed my bare feet into a pair of moccasins.

Back at my desk, I added the envelope of seed files to the red folder and secured the folder in my pack. Finally, for the first time in nine months, I knelt near the lower left drawer of the desk. I gripped the handle and, taking a fortifying breath, slid open the drawer. Inside were items from the past that I couldn't throw away. Pictures, old school notes, and the journal I meant to write William's story in—before his death.

Just the sight of the memories brought tears to my eyes, blurring my vision. Moving quickly, I shifted items aside until the boomerang William had whittled for me in the oasis came into view. I snatched it up and stood, trembling.

The irony of my inability to confront William's memory was not lost on me. In two days, I would give a speech insisting on an honest look at the Kongo's dark past. *We would know it, or repeat it.* As proof, I would point to the similarities between Obi Solomon and Kira Swan.

My quest for historical integrity had always set me apart. And yet, here I was, terrified by the ghosts that haunted my own heart.

The open drawer stared up at me with judgement—*No truth, no peace?* I kicked the drawer shut. Taking a breath, I forced myself to look down at William's boomerang. It wouldn't hold off an attack for long. But, if I had to face Kumar alone, its weight was better than nothing. I slid it into the holster at my back. It was time to meet Martin and Covington.

THE LIBRARY WEST

"Surprise!"

I jumped as I rounded the corner to find Covington and Martin stood, side by side, at the front of a pack of my well-wishers. Pidge and Finch stood behind them. Further back were dozens of the Director's people who had supported me for months. Most were Kongo, Vine workers loyal to the Director since before the rebellion. But some were Clayskin—maids and mechanics who worked at the Compound for pay. They stood in front of the four glass doors that separated the temperature-controlled Library West from the rest of the Compound.

I forced a smile as someone counted down from three, then the group launched into a song of congratulations. As the last note lingered, I moved forward. The group parted and Walker strode through the opening with my breakfast fried egg, buttered paw-paw and a small pound cake finished with lemon glaze, a luxury.

Walker placed the tray in my hands. "Congratulations, General," he said in his slow drawl, speaking for the group. "We're all downright excited to root for you tomorrow."

I nodded, graciously. As they crowded closer, however, their bright eyes baked my skin, so it felt tight.

Pidge spoke from my right. "Finch and I have been telling them to clear their schedule. The General's return isn't a show they'll want to miss. Right, Finch?"

Finch, who maintained a vigil of silence for his murdered twin, smiled hugely. He popped a hand on his waist and whipped out an imaginary fencing sword—jabbing excitedly.

"He says there's nothing like seeing the Berserker in action," Pidge translated. He paused and looked at me, expecting a reply.

"Thank you," I said. Still holding the tray, I cleared my throat and lifted my voice. "Thank you all." Their collected smiles beamed, demanding more. I took a step back and bumped into a maid, then a lab worker. They circled and seemed to breathe down my nape. I caught Covington's eye.

"Okay, people," she said, quickly. "Let's move the party to the Mess Hall."

Martin took the tray and began to herd the crowd away.

I whipped around, glaring at Covington.

"Sorry," she said, sheepishly. She knew I hated surprises; they felt like attacks. "When you didn't come to the Mess Hall for breakfast, they wanted to meet you here."

I moved past her, through the revolving door.

She hurried to keep up, explaining. "And you've been doing so good lately. It's been months since you've had a setback."

I sighed. I'd kept my recent failures private, hoping to turn them around.

"And besides, it was a good surprise, right?" Covington said. "It came with a cake!"

I hushed her as a barrel-bodied courier came to greet us. In addition to the handful that ferried guests across the firewall, three dozen rotund little bots lived with us at the Compound. All were specially programmed and closely monitored by Director Kumar.

"Hello, General Cobane. Hello, Captain Covington. General,

Captain, please extend your hands," the courier said. It wrapped our hands in weightless gloves that would protect the library's extensive collection of paper books. "Thank you," the courier said. "Can I be of service? You can say 'find books', or—"

"We need the repository," I said.

"To access a dedicated study room please provide—"

I interrupted again. "Access number 332875."

The courier recalibrated. It retracted its spindly legs and replaced it with gyrating gusts of air. It led us to an empty corner of the library and asked for the access code again. I gave it and a moment later a ten-by-ten-foot freestanding room blinked then solidified in the open space around us.

As the courier wheeled away, I moved to the far wall of the private room. It was papered with all the evidence we had against Kira Swan. Each thread of research branched out into sub-threads that tangled together endlessly. In the crux of the web was the photo of Kira's English friend, with her severe blonde style. We hadn't identified the woman but each time I looked at her, I knew Kira was no good and my determination to expose her redoubled.

"No new addition?" I said over my shoulder. "I wanted an update on Kira's patrol pack."

Covington came to stand beside me. "Nothing new on my files," she said. "You'll have to ask Martin about Kira. He'll join us as soon as he can."

I sighed and checked my comm-unit. "We're already behind," I said.

Covington shrugged helplessly. "He's helping Walker in the kitchen," she said. It was a lame excuse.

I slumped into a chair, thinking of the night I'd first seen Martin. A red bandanna had been angled rakishly over one of his eyes as he'd argued with a crowd of Loyalists intent on lynching him. He'd been a fierce freedom fighter, but the war had depleted his passion for the cause. Now he hated spying. He wanted nothing more than a home in the Cobane village and, according to Covington, to run a school for Kongo children.

"He's losing faith, like everyone else," I said. "I should have assigned the patrol pack to you."

Covington sat beside me. "Don't say that," she said, gently. "Walker really is swamped. The free market and show are tonight." She rested a hand on my shoulder and squeezed until I looked up. She smiled. I could tell she hoped to encourage me. Give me something to look forward to.

Under the ceasefire, goods and technology from the north flooded in on ships that dared the route across the burning seas. Isolated at the Compound, we'd missed many exciting developments. The market was a showcase of all the free southern territory had to offer. It was a fitting end to our exile, especially since it coincided with the Berserker's triumphant return to her people.

I turned aside, letting Covington's hand drop from my shoulder. "Hurley really pulled it off, then," I said.

"Yes, he did. Three dozen vendors, a dozen more entertainers, and it's all for you."

Her words settled like stones on my shoulders. I pressed my temples where my veins protruded.

She leaned into me, perplexed by my reaction. "Did you forget?" she asked.

Sweat ran down my back. I hadn't forgotten. The idea of an event in my honor terrified me so much, I'd dismissed it outright.

The study room door opened. "Martin," I said, jumping to my feet.

Martin appeared, adjusting his rimmed spectacles. The same piteous look I'd been contending with all day was smeared across his face.

"Let's get started," I said, quickly, forestalling his apology. "Kira's audio?"

Martin sat and pulled the radio he listened to constantly from his bag. It was connected to Kira's patrol pack. He also retrieved a sheaf of papers. "The report's here," he said, handing it to me. I paced back and forth as I flipped through it. "The only notable minute happened this morning," Martin added. He took out two more copies of the file and handed one to Covington. "It's on page thirteen."

We all shuffled the pages.

Martin went on, "She told her assistant to pack a bag before the Council meeting this morning."

"Why?" I demanded. I found the minute and read the entry, twice. There was no other information. "Is she going somewhere?"

Martin ran a palm over his beard. "That information came later," he said. "She's going to pay respect to an ill relative."

"Two days before the murder trial?" Covington asked.

"Attempted murder," I snapped.

Martin shrugged. "Apparently the sickness is bad, and the matter can't wait."

I tilted my head, considering. "This is good," I said, finally. "If she stays even a day, she can't undermine me tomorrow during the workout. What else?"

"Nothing more to report," Martin said. He removed his earpiece and connected the patrol radio to his comm-unit. He circled his finger, turning up the volume on Kira's feed. "This is what I've been listening to all morning," he said.

Silence filled the room. I waited, tilting my head. There was a soft rustle that might have been Covington shifting closer to Martin, then more silence.

"I don't hear anything," I said.

"That's because she's en route," Martin said. "And, as always, she's traveling alone. She sleeps alone. She eats alone. She reads alone. She doesn't have any friends or companions. Sometimes she talks to herself, but that's about it."

Covington snorted. "Sounds like your senior year, Arika." She turned to Martin. "We used to bribe her to come to our parties, and she never did."

I could tell she was teasing me, pushing for a laugh, but I ignored her. "Stay on it," I said, speaking to Martin. "I need to know when to expect her home."

"Will do," Martin said. He focused his scholarly gaze on me. "By the way, General, how did the simulation go?"

"Fine," I said. "We've scheduled another for later today."

"Why?" Covington said. "You—"

I swiped a hand, cutting her off. "We'll discuss it later."

She exchanged a worried look with Martin.

I went on. "Now, the new project. We need to expand the Kumar folder. Specifically, the history of his scientific work. I want more on his mistress, Weka, his adopted son, Lee Ford, and—" I hesitated. "And we need much more on the Kha."

I moved to the far wall and took three images from the accordion folder. The photo of Director Kumar didn't overtly resemble the print of Hosea Khan, but their connection was clear. The photo of Lee highlighted the sharp lines of his face. I attached the photos to the wall.

"This is a major shift," Covington said, looking from the pictures to me. "Why the new interest?"

I met her narrowed gaze. "I'm considering the cure," I said, honestly. "I've already asked that the Director be notified. I have to make sure the workout goes smoothly."

"You sound as if you've already decided," Covington said, glancing at Martin.

"Have you spoken to the Kha about this?" Martin asked. Unlike Covington, he trusted Hosea implicitly.

"Hosea supports my decisions," I said. It was a lie, but I wouldn't divide their loyalty. "Can I count on you, soldiers?"

They looked at each other, then Martin spoke up. "Actually, Arika, there's something we need to tell you."

"What is it, Martin?" I scratched the base of my throat, where the ruby necklace lay.

Before he could answer, Covington placed a hand on his arm and spoke reassuringly. "You can count on us, General," she said. "We'll have more on Kumar, Lee and the Kha by this afternoon."

"And it stays between us?" I asked.

They both nodded.

"Good. Then let's review these too," I said. I dumped the stolen seed files onto the table.

Covington squinted. "Arika, what is this?"

"They're seed files," Martin said. He picked one up and looked at me. "Are the memories yours?"

I ignored his question. I found the *Mother* file and put it into my comm-unit. I'd seen pictures of Weka Vine, but I was curious to see the woman in action. I projected the video into the air between us.

Lee lay on his back, looking up at the sky on a cloudless day. In the middle of the projection the noon sun shimmered like a stoked fire. A baby wailed inconsolably, and a tiny flailing fist flashed at the edge of the scene. The fist was distinctly albino, nearly translucent. The memory, I realized, was from the infant Lee Ford's point of view.

A Kongo woman's face appeared, looking down on Lee and blotting out the sun. Her hair was wrapped around her head like a wreath and her jewelry comprised of precious cockle shells and braided hemp. Despite the title of the seed file, the lines in her face indicated she was too old to be Hosea and Lee's mother, and Kumar's notorious Kongo mistress, Weka. She looked instead like an older version of Weka, and I assumed she was Weka's mother. She scooped Lee into her arms and, cuddled by his grandmother, he stopped crying.

As she walked, the infant looked back over her shoulder. His gaze panned the place he'd been rescued from, a desert clearing piled with rocks. I inhaled, horrified. It was the place babies were left when they were designated worthless from birth.

A sick feeling rolled in my stomach. Hosea had never spoken of his grandmother and I couldn't guess why Lee had mislabeled the memory, but one point was certain: the file was an intimate visual diary—which is why he had hidden it from me.

I turned my back on Covington and Martin and ejected the file, fighting guilt. I reminded myself that Lee, the Director and even Hosea Khan kept secrets from each other and from me. To survive among them, I had to be strategic. The *Mother* file was leverage—nothing more.

"Arika, how did you say you got these?" Martin asked.

I turned to confront him. "That was Lee Ford," I said, defensively. "As the Director's adopted son he's a powerful political player. He's fair game!"

Covington covered her face. "You stole them."

Martin's chest billowed with indignation. "Did you learn nothing from—"

Before he could say more, I held up a finger, warning him. I couldn't have anyone laying into me, not when I was already questioning myself. He would blame me now but thank me later—or so I told myself.

I pressed on. "There are at least ten files here. If both of you work, you can have a report ready by the end of the week. Is that clear—Captains?" I added, ensuring they understood it was an order.

Martin sighed, looking years beyond his age.

Steeling myself, I dared a look at Covington. Her mouth was set in a thin line.

Ducking her gaze, I slipped the accordion folder into my pack and closed the latch. I didn't have the luxury of soft sentiments—children and homes. "I've got to go now," I said. "I've got a book on hold. And I need to review my speech for tomorrow. Cov, you're free to go, but have lunch sent to my room. Martin, keep on Kira."

"I will," Martin said, but he wouldn't meet my gaze.

THE EAGLE

A squawk sounded overhead as I left the west wing, feeling burdened. Covington waited outside, her hip cocked, her arms crossed. The stance reminded me of our childish bouts at the Schoolhouse, which annoyed me. I passed by and started through the mango grove, the most direct path east across the courtyard.

She hurried after me. "Martin didn't want that assignment," she said. "And you knew it. You forced him!"

I kept my gaze on the path. "He's a soldier," I said, flatly. "And I'm the commander of the Kongo militia. I have to issue orders."

"You're not being fair!" Covington said. She took two quick steps and blocked my way.

"Fair?" I said, bewildered. "Fair!?" I held out my empty arms. I opened my mouth, then closed it. If she didn't understand, I couldn't explain. I stepped around her and kept walking.

She stayed close, watching me from the corner of her eye. "You know, you've been off this morning," she said.

I stifled a scoff. In truth, I'd been off for weeks, or years. The squawk came again, and I looked up, following the sound to a brown eagle swooping in the clouds.

Covington caught my arm. "Did something happen in the simulation?"

I glared at her hand. "No," I said.

She squeezed as I pulled away. "How long did you last? Did you have an episode?" she called, talking to my back. "Arika Cobane," she yelled suddenly. "Stop!"

I stopped and turned to face her.

Oriole Cora Covington. My Schoolhouse nemesis and right hand during the rebellion. Her fancy jewelry was gone, along with her brassy hair. And, without them, her character shined. She was wise and intelligent, a trusted advisor and friend.

She came close to touch my shoulder. "What happened in the simulation," she said again. "Let me help."

I covered my face with both hands. She couldn't help, but she wouldn't let it go.

"I was with the Seekers," I said, finally. "After I left Cobane. After Jetson—" I stopped. His name sliced along my tongue like a razor.

"After Jetson was hung," she said.

I winced.

She leaned in. "Go on."

I dropped my hands and looked up. Tree limbs, bowed with fruit, obscured my view. Through them, I kept a keen eye on the eagle rounding carelessly. The bird, sun and sky grounded me and kept the veil at bay. Still, I spoke quickly, relaying the facts of the simulation without emotion.

"And then the man cooked," I said, ending my recitation. "He fried to death, spread-eagled on the wall."

Covington frowned, trying to make sense of it. The scene was grim, but we'd seen worse during the war. "How long did you last?" she asked gently.

"Ten minutes," I said.

She inhaled. I dropped my eyes to my feet, blocking out her disappointment. "Hosea asked me if I knew the Seeker that died," I whispered.

"Well, did you?"

I circled the toe of my moccasin in the dirt, seeing the Seeker's face. Older, like Kiwi. Prone to superstition, like Sky. A smile as constant as a crescent moon on a Kongo night—like Fly Man. I swallowed, but the memory, the one that had resurfaced a week ago, caught in my throat like a fishbone.

•

Voltaire ducked into the opening of my tent, hastily constructed in the field outside of Cobane. She had a missive in her hand.

"What is this?" she said, sharply.

She opened the message and held it close to my nose, but I didn't need to read it. I'd written it that morning in response to her request for a contingent of soldiers. The message was only one word long—*no*.

"I need fifty men, at least," Voltaire said, whipping the missive away. "And I need them now."

Her urgency was understandable. Fly Man had been under strict orders to stay at the oasis, away from the fighting. But, yesterday evening, a message had come from Walker. *Fly Man didn't come to the evening fire. Ain't seen the boy all day.*

An hour later, the Watch had spotted a hundred men heading north with a small Kongo child. We had no doubt their captive was Fly Man.

Voltaire went on. "I'll take Pidge, Finch and Booster's pack. We'll be back before—"

"No," I said, interrupting her.

She glared. "What do you mean, 'no'?"

I rested a hand on my Apex. My leggings were streaked with dirt and my tunic was tattered. I'd slept a handful of hours in four days, as the siege had intensified. Cobane, the diplomats' stronghold, was nearly defeated, and the entire force was gathered at the bottom of the hill, awaiting my command.

Once Cobane fell, the diplomats would run, disorganized and fleeing for their lives. If we were to finish them, now was the time. We were an untrained militia; our strength was in our numbers and our passion. Dividing now and obscuring the goal was not the right call—not even to rescue Fly Man.

"No," I said again, meeting Voltaire's gaze, "I can't spare fifty men."

Her brow wrinkled. "Twenty-five of our *best* will work, but—"

"I can't spare twenty-five," I said.

She stiffened. "How many?"

I filled my chest with air. "You can go, alone, but I advise against it."

I expected an emotional outburst. Or at least a debate. I got neither.

She turned on her heel and left my tent.

I followed her, watching as she mounted her horse and took up the reins.

"Voltaire?" I said, unnerved by her expression.

She looked down at me.

"Where are you going?" I said.

She spurred her horse, calling over her shoulder. "I'm going to get my brother."

That night, as she buried his body, Cobane fell.

Mounted on Mary, waving my Apex, I'd rallied the soldiers. "Find them!" I shouted. "Find their hiding places and leave nothing alive. Advance!"

•

The echo of my own voice faded.

"Was the Seeker a friend?" Covington asked, probing the wound.

A friend. I considered the sentiment. I'd rested with the Seekers for weeks. No commands, no orders. Instead, I'd sat among them and laughed. I'd listened to their stories and, though I could have saved them, I let them race—one by one—chasing a promised land they were never meant to own.

"He was more than a friend," I said, finally. "He was my brother, our brother."

Covington's shoulders slumped. "Oh, Arika," she said. "With that logic you're never going to pass the workout."

My breath hissed from my chest. I'd known she wouldn't understand, but it still hurt.

She held out her palms. "I'm trying to help," she said. "I know how much the demonstration means to you."

I walked away. In truth, she had no idea what the workout meant. Like Hosea Khan, she was more concerned with the trial—with saving my life. She didn't understand that the Kongo *was* my life. That I'd carried it on my back, uphill, for years. That I felt I couldn't put it down.

As we neared the east wing, she closed the gap between us until she was by my side again, so close and quiet I heard her empty stomach growl.

Sweat beaded on my brow as I stopped under a mango tree. The eagle overhead cried out and, suddenly, I wanted to scream too.

I turned to Covington. "You know that I don't have a choice, right?"

She squinted. "What do you mean?"

"I mean that I didn't ask for any of this—I didn't choose to oppress the Kongo. I didn't make the Compromise. I didn't ask to become a Keeper, or fight Jones or lead the rebellion. I didn't want to abandon Robin, or hurt Hannibal or Fount, or my fa—or my fath—" I stopped, swallowing. I hadn't spoken of my papa since the day he died.

Covington looked uncomfortable. "You may not have wanted those things, Arika," she said, "but you *did* choose them. And you keep choosing them. You choose them every day you won't just let the past die."

Her words stung like a slap. I bent over, cried out, then covered my mouth. If I started, I knew I would never stop.

I straightened and ripped the closest mango from its berth, twisting viciously. I squeezed the fruit, popping its perfect skin and digging my fingers into the sun-warmed pulp.

"Arika?" Covington said, stepping back nervously.

Clutching the fruit, I ran, leaving the line of the trees. I ignored the paved path and raced across the herb garden, crushing sage, basil and thyme under my feet. I stopped at the east wing door, panting.

A minute later, Covington joined me. "Are you back?" she said.

I followed her gaze to the mango in my hand. The skin was gone along with the fruit; only the pit remained. I made a fist around it and told myself to be quiet. Instead, like a fool, I tried again.

"Do you see that bird?" I whispered, lifting my face to the sky.

Covington looked up, watching the eagle circle and dip in the sky which was deceptively clear. In truth, a firewall domed over the mouth of the sinkhole.

"The eagle. What about it?" she said.

"It's majestic, isn't it?"

"Sure."

"And you know about the firewall, right?"

She nodded.

"So then, you know that bird is going to die," I caught her eye. "It's going to dip too low and *zap*—" Something metallic congealed in my throat and I paused.

Covington shifted. She knew as well as I that the sinkhole firewall was as deadly as the wall that blocked traffic into the Obi Forest. The Director equipped it with solar mimesis technology which made it indistinguishable from its surroundings.

Together, we looked up, watching the eagle dip lower.

"What if you had the power to warn it? Tell it to turn back. Wouldn't you? Wouldn't you have to?" I said.

She opened her mouth, but I held up a palm, stifling her. "And what if there were thousands of birds to save, Cov— and they're all just as beautiful and the only one that knows about the danger is you? What do you *choose*? What's *fair*?"

I whipped back and threw the pit into the sky, aiming for the bird. The missile fell short, and the eagle continued, unaware. It whizzed beneath the tree line north of the cistern.

It was beyond my sight when a zapping noise punctuated

the ordinary outside sounds. The brief stink of burned flesh and feathers permeated the air.

I looked down at my hands, coated in sticky sweet acidity, then over at Covington.

She put a hand on my shoulder, her eyes wet with tears. And, in that moment, I believed she, at least, felt the sincerity of my pain. Still, I could feel her sadness for me, her disappointment. She wanted me to be different, happier. She didn't realize her hope, kindly meant, mounted inside me like pressure.

We stood for a while, watching the sky, listening to our growling stomachs. Finally, she opened the east wing door. As I went ahead, I wiped my hands on my tunic, in vain. The flesh and pit of the fruit was gone, but the juice had dried and stuck.

•

In my room, I removed my pack and holster and checked the time. Two hours until the rescheduled simulation.

"How do you sleep in this mess?" Covington said, entering behind me.

"I manage," I said, absently.

"I'll check the food I ordered, then I'll go," she said. She picked her way across the disarray to a small side table set with a noon meal. As she inspected it for accuracy, I took out my comm-unit and scrolled through the schematics of the triple-point sword. It was a habit I'd formed in the past days, since we'd got wind of its prowess. Every spare minute, I read and analyzed, searching for its weakness.

With a sigh, I closed my palm as Covington spread the meal before me. A bowl of boiled cassava, yogurt and remnants of the tray I'd sent away earlier. The icing on the yellow cake was cracked and flaking.

As I ate, Covington lingered. She went to the window overlooking the courtyard. "It's really coming together," she said. "You'd like it if you looked." She glanced back at me and held out a hand. I couldn't say no.

I picked up my yogurt and moved to her side. Down below, Hurley led a team of people into the square with crates. Behind them, a trio of couriers wheeled in, dressed in holographic kitchen uniforms. Each carried a mess hall table in their elongated arms.

"They're moving more tables outside," Covington said, explaining the bustle. "With all the vendors, there's not enough room to build the show stage in the Hall."

More couriers came to line the perimeter with the tables, leaving the center bare. Another two robots were building a platform.

Covington went on. "The last group of merchants arrived this morning and their outfits are wild. They're calling it protest fashion. You inspired it, you know." Her eyes twinkled.

"I've heard," I said, flatly. The Director allowed mail in and out, and I received the *Southern Bell* once a month. It leaned conservative, but it covered entertainment and fashion news as well as political happenings. The military and a far-left fringe of society were rallying around me, gearing up for my return.

Covington took a quarter-sheet of stock paper from her tunic and placed it on my palm. The words *You're Invited* had been decoratively handwritten. "I planned this before I knew about the simulation," she said. I turned the invitation over. The other side was blank. "It's a surprise," she explained, smiling. "Just give me two hours before the market."

I let myself smile back, then I looked out again at the rapidly changing space. Hurley unfurled a bright square of cloth, and his kitchen assistants smoothed the peach lace over the raw wood edges of a relocated mess hall table. Others hurried about covering every surface with candles, pots of fresh flowers and platters that would be filled with food. Another pair hoisted a giant sign over the platform in progress. *Welcome Back General Arika Cobane.*

"Come on. Two hours, Arika." Covington prodded. "Just us girls." I blinked, caught on the word *girls*. Covington didn't wait for my answer. "Two hours," she confirmed. "We'll meet outside the west wing after your simulation."

I sighed, but I didn't protest. She kissed my cheek and let herself out. I watched her go, contemplating—*us girls*. We were just twenty years old. Technically, the term applied, but it seemed far off to me, like a dim star, by another Earth, a galaxy away. Maybe on that Earth I was still a girl.

At my desk I put on my holster and packed my sack. Rather than leave early for the simulation, I sat and opened the video we'd secured earlier. It showed the triple point in action.

The sword was a deadly fleur-de-lis; a glowing blade framed by two glowing daggers. The English man wielding it was no more than thirteen. With his immature muscles, the sword looked to outweigh him. And yet, I knew the video went on, uncut, for an hour as the boy whipped the sword around, slicing left and right. He never stopped to rest, drink, or catch his breath, demonstrating the sword's most treacherous danger, its feather weight.

Ten minutes into the video, the solid blade turned to gas, disappeared mid-swing and reappeared a yard away in liquid form—a molten fireball. There was no visible connection between the boy and the ball, but he controlled it with thin silver gloves. When his opponent tried to cut the ball in half, the boy opened his gloved hands and the ball split in two, so the warrior's blade passed between.

At fifty-eight minutes, the boy spread his fingers, creating a dozen molten drops. They flew into his opponent's nose, ears and mouth. When the boy brought his hands together again, in a double fist, the sword solidified and exploded his enemy's head.

The schematic was already making its way around the Kongo and this new, gruesome video would follow. I had to address it in my speech tomorrow—or risk my hold on the military. As I closed the video, the door to my room burst open and smacked against the adjacent wall. I whirled.

"Lee!" I cried out. His mouth was tight, his face red. "What's wrong?" I asked.

He brushed past me and sat down at my desk. Without asking, he picked up the half-full tray and set it on the floor.

I hurried over. "What are you—hey!" He was rummaging through a drawer. "Leave that alone!" I leaned over to close the drawer and he turned his attention to the folders stacked on the corner of my desk. The one on top scattered across the floor. I dropped to my knees and snatched up two fallen pages.

"Where are they?" he demanded.

"What are you talking about?" I hissed, shoving papers back in their place.

"The files you stole. Where are they?"

Realization dawned and I sat back, leaving the mess. Lee opened another drawer and filtered through it. When he reached for my private drawer, I stood. "They're not here, Lee," I said. "Martin has them."

He jumped to his feet. I stepped back. "I'll return them," I said.

He jerked away to prowl like a bobcat. Then he turned, his shoulders rigid, to glare at me. "Did you watch it?" He inhaled and held his breath.

I didn't ask which file he meant. I looked down at my feet.

His slow exhale made a scraping sound in his throat. "So then, you know," he said.

•

We walked in silence from the east wing and across the courtyard. He kept a slow pace, and we were running late. Still, I stayed behind him. As we waited for the lift, I wanted to explain why I'd taken the files, but I couldn't.

At the renovated laboratory, he opened the door a fraction. Then he stopped and whispered. "Mother didn't care where I came from or what I looked like. She birthed Hosea and rescued me, but she didn't have a favorite. She loved me like she loved Hosea. You see?

In the dim, damp tunnel, presented with the wall of his back, I didn't answer. I didn't even breathe.

"It was only Father who ever saw a difference," he said. His left hand jerked up to press his eyes. The heel of a palm in one socket, then the other. He opened the door and walked inside.

THE DIRECTOR

The renovated lab was a soaring warehouse divided into ten neat stations, five on each side of a polished concrete aisle. Each station was devoted to an area of study. The space was bright with crystalights and, ordinarily, it teemed with the Director's staff. Today, it was deserted. The only movement came from a courier near the far wall, which was lined with shelves secured to the mountain rock with heavy bolts and brackets. The robot hustled about, polishing the equipment stacked on the shelves.

Lee guided me down the center aisle. "Where's Hosea Khan?" I asked, warily, looking from side to side.

Lee glanced at my furrowed face and rolled his eyes. "Relax, General," he said. "Master is on his way."

"Hopefully not," a voice said.

We stopped and my gaze flew up to the Director. He stood outside of a second-story loft office space built out from the south wall. An airy flight of stairs connected the office to the ground level.

"But, Lee, do check the feed and make sure," he added. "We need Hosea to stay put." He moved across a short balcony to stand at the stair rail, like an overlord surveying his fiefdom.

Obediently, Lee flipped open his palm and pulled up the live feed he'd shown me earlier. Hosea Khan was at his desk, working. "He's *not* on his way," Lee said.

"And the white girl?" Kumar asked. "Quickly, boy."

Lee checked his palm again. "She looks to be asleep," he said. He switched to another image. "And her vitals confirm it."

"Good, good," Kumar said. He closed the office door.

As he fiddled with the lock, I stifled the urge to ask Lee what was happening. He was still angry about the files, and I knew he wouldn't answer. I looked up, probing his expression. It gave nothing away, but his breath steamed from his nose in puffs. He was as surprised as I was, I guessed. Kumar had ambushed us both.

"Lee Ford, I'm ready," the Director said.

Moving like a courier, Lee took the stairs two at a time and bowed at the top, letting his father hook an elbow around his neck. He wrapped an arm around Kumar's waist and, with their sides sealed together, they descended. At the bottom, the Director adjusted the mandarin collar of his colorful tunic. "My cane," he said.

Lee ran up the stairs and retrieved a hook-necked cane from outside the loft office. He handed it to Kumar who waved impatiently, ordering Lee away. Kumar's knuckles tightened into peaks as he found his balance and came over to me. He held out a large square palm. "Ms. Cobane!" His pleasant tone contrasted with the one he used to address Lee Ford, who stood at attention behind him.

"Why isn't Hosea here?" I demanded, eyeing Kumar. "Did you reschedule the test?"

Kumar's smile didn't waver over his outstretched hand. I looked to Lee, pleading silently. He rolled his eyes then, reluctantly, his red gaze narrowed on the older man's proffered palm. Taking Lee's hint, I acknowledged Kumar's greeting, shaking firmly. As soon as I did, his other palm lifted to sandwich my hand in both of his.

"Good, good," he said. The sound crackled in his throat. He wrapped a heavy arm around my back and pulled me so I faced the far end of the room. He guided me forward as a pair of couriers arrived to arrange a seating area in the center aisle. Kumar gestured for me to sit, and Lee stood beside my chair. When the couriers left, Kumar placed his manicured hands on my shoulders.

I shrugged—breaking his hold on me. "Director, please. Why is Hosea arriving late?" I turned in my chair to meet his gaze.

"He's not here because he received a note from you explaining your plans had changed. Now—"

I stood, interrupting him. "But my plans *haven't* changed," I said. I placed one hand on my holstered boomerang.

Kumar's eyes widened on my weapon. "Disrespectful! Lee, take it away."

"Don't touch me!" I said. I bent defensively as Lee lunged.

I reeled back and Kumar's cane caught my ankle. "Now, boy! Get it!" he shouted.

Lee grabbed my arm and pulled me upright. He yanked me around, so my back butted against his chest. I grunted and kicked backward, trying to catch his knees. I felt his hand at my waist.

"No!" I growled, "Noo!"

Lee lifted the boomerang from its holster. "I've got it, Father," he said. His tone was clinical and, beneath that, satisfied.

Kumar wiped his brow. "Good boy." His cool gaze met mine. "Now, should I tell him to tie you? Or will you sit while I explain."

I swallowed, understanding the score. Kumar would play nice, but he had every advantage. "I'll sit," I said, finally.

Before Lee could release me, I shoved an elbow into his side and twisted away, freeing myself. I turned and glared at him as I sat down.

"Lee," Kumar said. "Hosea Khan will be here in thirty-five minutes. Go set an alarm."

Moving stiffly, Lee tucked my boomerang in the waist of his trousers, climbed the stairs and closed himself in the office.

"That's better," Kumar said. He leaned to collect my hands in his. He chafed warmly. "Don't worry. Hosea will come," he said. "Rest assured, you are my top priority. We'll draw your blood and the cure will be ready tonight. Only," he hesitated, then sighed, "something more important has come up."

"Nothing's more important," I said, firmly.

Lee Ford returned from the loft office as Kumar eyed me over low-hanging brows. "Allow me to convince you otherwise," he said.

He tapped his comm-unit and Obi Solomon appeared behind him in the center aisle. I registered, slowly, that it was only a picture of Obi, frozen in time. The Director had engineered a larger-than-life version of the incriminating photo I'd seen a hundred times before.

"Take a look," Kumar said.

I stood and moved around him to look up at Obi's visage. He sat in a chair somewhere in the Northridge. He wore a collar, black trousers and boots. The hand on his lap, with five perfect fingers, identified him as a traitor.

"I've seen it before," I said. "I think he—"

"I didn't tell you to think, girl," the Director snapped, eyeing me. "*Look* and tell me what you see."

Knowing I had to, I played along. "I see Obi Solomon, the first general of the Kongo," I said, simply.

Kumar paced. "Go on, what else?"

"He's a large man," I said. "His hair is thick, parted and combed. His lips are thin beneath a straight nose. He's older, but he's aged well. High cheek bones. Broad shoulders. A coat with a tail and a ruffled collar. A cummerbund and heeled boots. He's sitting in a high-back, high-gloss chair which fans out behind him. His nails are trimmed and clean. Should I go on?"

"Good, good girl," Kumar said. He was purring again, clicking slowly in the base of his throat. "Now, look for what's trying to hide." He adjusted the image so that it brightened, casting him in shadow.

I looked. In the forefront, grey stones spotted a sparkling layer of snow on the ground. Behind Obi's black chair was a backdrop of dark cloth. "I don't see anything else except—" My breath caught as something new announced itself near the edge of the picture. "Is that—are those eyes?"

"Just eyes?" Kumar said.

I studied the difference between the gaze and the dark surrounding it. Slowly, a figure took shape. "It's a man," I said. "There's a man leaning from behind the curtain. He's staring at Obi like—like a lover," I said finally. There was no better word. The man was enthralled. His lips were pressed tight together. His eyes, wide open, were pinned on Obi like darts on a target. I leaned forward in my chair, finally intrigued. "Who is he?"

Kumar smiled. "His name is Jacamar."

My mind raced. I was familiar with the name. Jacamar was a famed historian, Obi's constant companion during the

Last War and after. I started his catalogue file myself, hoping it would shed light on the Kongo General. To date, the file consisted of passing references, rumors and, conspicuously, not a single picture. Jacamar was more obscure than his treacherous companion. I stared into the dark man's beady eyes. "How do you know it's him?" I asked.

"Well, he fits the descriptions, don't you think?" Kumar said.

I shrugged. "They called him small and dark, but that could fit many men."

Kumar nodded, acknowledging the point. "Well, knowing he was present on this day, I had my team search other images from the same day for his likeness. And they found this." He tapped his comm-unit and another image appeared. A close-up of a highly polished pewter vase. The Director enlarged the image and focused on the bottom curve of the container. He enlarged and focused again, and a human body took form. A pair of eyes in a grey face, magnified by the shape of the vase. My gaze skipped around, making sense of the scene. A man stood in a soaring tent on a bright day, surrounded by English officials. He was slim, dark as a shadow and extremely old. His eyes were wide, dark darts; the same possessive expression as the man behind the curtain in the incriminating picture of Obi. I decided the men were the same. More, I was convinced the man was Jacamar.

"This is invaluable Kongo history," I said. "It needs to be catalogued immediately."

Kumar inclined his head. He tapped his comm-unit again. "I'll send you a copy now."

He waited quietly as I sent the picture to Martin and altered the photo of Obi, circling Jacamar in the background. With a swipe of my hand, I selected Martin's name again and sent out the altered image as well.

I looked up at Kumar. "It's valuable," I said. "But hardly more important than the workout tomorrow."

Kumar stroked his beard like a grandfather, full of secrets. "Tell me what you know of Jacamar's connection to Obi," he said.

I searched my memory. "They were close in life, like brothers. Jacamar designed the library and he built Obi's mausoleum, the Watchtower." I thought a moment, then added, "He was a talented medic and Obi's advisor during the Last War."

Kumar nodded. "Correct. This picture was taken just before they died, two days apart."

I looked again at the man's face, old and frail. He was eighty at least and he looked ill. I frowned suddenly, picturing the watchtower. "Days apart," I said. "So, Jacamar built the mausoleum *before* Obi died?"

"Excellent question," Kumar said.

"There's no question," I insisted. "If they died days apart, then Jacamar would have had to build the entire structure in a matter of hours, which would be impossible."

"Impossible for some," Kumar agreed. "But easy for Jacamar." I leaned in, waiting for him to expound.

"Jacamar wasn't a medic," he said finally. "He was a priest of the Core. A spiritualist, not a medic. More, when Obi died, Jacamar promised to keep the record of Obi's life hidden. The watchtower was integral to him keeping his promise, so Jacamar would have used every bit of his power to see the tower built."

My eyes narrowed. "A record of Obi's life?" I said. "You think Jacamar *wrote down* what Obi told him."

"I do," Kumar said. "Despite his promise, Jacamar, the historian, couldn't let Obi's truth die with him. Jacamar was what you call a Record Keeper."

I nodded slowly. "The first Record Keeper," I whispered.

Lee shifted, catching my attention just as Kumar removed an object from his right breast pocket. Lee's eyes widened and flew to mine. Following Lee's gaze, I saw Kumar was holding the invisibility bracelet Lee had shown me earlier.

I ducked my head to hide my expression.

Kumar scoffed. "No need, girl. Lee doesn't keep secrets from me," he said. "You know what this is—no?"

I lifted my head and met his gaze. Slowly, I nodded.

He held out the bracelet. "Good. Now then, I want you to take it. Keep it," he said.

Keep it? "Why would you give me something so valuable?"

Kumar opened his comm-unit. "Because, dear, you'll need invisibility to enter Hasting undetected." As he spoke, a 3D holograph of the Watchtower sprang up beside us. The building stood tall, indestructible, amid golden flames and smoke. Beside it, Kumar stood with his hands steepled.

As I stared, the pieces of our conversation crystallized in my mind. "You think Jacamar left Obi's confession in the Watchtower," I said, knowing I was right. If Jacamar wanted to protect Obi's truth, it made sense to place the record in a sacred tomb few would enter.

Kumar smiled slyly. He tapped his comm-unit again and an audio of my own voice broke the silence.

"There's only one path forward. We demand entry to the library and to form a coalition of scholars to decipher the records there. We insist on a rigorous investigation of Obi, whatever it

takes, wherever it leads. Brothers and sisters, Councilors, after years of appeasement; upon terror, upon lies—it's time to lay bare the truth. Take raw account of the roots of our oppression; only this will set us free. No truth—"

The Director cut the audio. "No peace!" he said, raising a fist. He smiled indulgently, then sobered. "Do you still want the truth, Ms. Cobane?"

I imagined my triumphant re-entry to society, buttressed by the crown jewel of history: Obi Solomon's confession.

Kumar wet his lips greedily. "Would you say the truth is worth dying for?"

I didn't hesitate. "If I thought it would save the Kongo—yes."

He smiled. "That's what I hoped you'd say. Lee!" he shouted.

I jumped. I'd forgotten Lee's presence entirely. I looked to see his eyes burning red with resentment and glued to his father. As I watched, he took a step forward, encroaching on Kumar's space. The old man didn't seem to notice. He snapped instructions.

"Go watch the feed. If Hosea is to arrive even a minute early, I want to know."

Lee spoke through thin lips. "But, Father—there's an alarm," he said. "We'll know the moment anyone opens the door to leave the infirmary."

Kumar stiffened. He wanted to speak to me in private and he wasn't used to back-talk from his youngest son. "You're not needed, boy," he snapped. "Go watch the feed."

Lee glanced at me, then down at the bracelet in Kumar's hand— months of his work, I realized, taken from him in an instant. He climbed the steps and closed himself in the loft office.

Kumar turned to me. "Here's the deal," he said, speaking quickly. "I'll give you the bracelet. And, in return, *you* will enter the Watchtower and get the truth, agreed?" He dangled the bracelet in the air between us. I looked up at the burning tower. Kumar angled his body, shielding my view. "Don't be afraid, girl. It's not dangerous, not for you. That's why I asked you here, see?"

I shook my head. "If it's safe then—"

"I didn't say it was safe!" he snapped, cutting me off. "I said it's not dangerous *for you*."

I frowned, not understanding.

Kumar sighed and glanced at the time. "To keep his promise while preserving Obi's legacy, Jacamar locked the story behind a curse—death in three days. Once you've seen the truth, the timer starts."

"A curse?" I scoffed. "You can't possibly believe that."

He lifted a slow brow. "I assure you, my dear, I very much do," he said. "Only those willing to die for the truth will live to proliferate it. The curse itself will test your integrity. You, dear, are the only one that has ever fit that description. So, for *you*, the tower is safe."

"I'm the One," I whispered.

Kumar's eyes gleamed. "Now, Ms. Cobane. Do we have a deal?"

I swallowed, mentally scouring his offer for holes. Obi, Jacamar, the Watchtower, the bracelet, the curse, the One. It had all happened so fast.

Kumar waved the bracelet beneath my nose. The design, with its beady-eyed snakes, shook me to my core and I still didn't know why.

Kumar growled. Time was up.

I grabbed the bracelet and shoved it into my sack.

Kumar smiled. "Good!" he said. "Now, my son should be here soon. Perhaps—"

"What do you get out of it?" I said, suddenly. The words popped out of my mouth without warning, forming a question before I'd registered my own curiosity. Now that they were out, I found I stood by them. His generosity didn't sit well. For months he'd focused exclusively on the cure, touting it as mutually beneficial. He *was* a scientist, a truth-seeker in that sense, but I doubted he cared about Kongo history. So, what did he really want?

Kumar looked at me, his mouth puckered. The gold in his pinky ring winked as his hand tightened on his cane.

"You said earlier that something *more important* had come up?" I said, slowly. "Those were your words, *more important*. And, to me, the truth about Obi is vital. But what's in it for you?"

"I'll tell you when you need to know," he said evenly, but I could see he was sweating.

"I need to know now," I said, recklessly, digging in.

Kumar stopped blinking. "I offer your dreams. I give you the key to unlock the tower—and you're making demands?" His head sank to his barrel chest. "Disrespectful," he whispered. His nostrils flared. His cane trembled. He looked up and I jumped back, knocking into the table behind me. His skin was bright red. His left eye ticked. White spit foamed at his mouth.

Eyes wide, I fumbled reflexively for my Apex, finding only an empty holster. I opened my mouth to scream.

Before I could, a high thin wail sounded. A door opened and Lee appeared at the top of the stairs. "Hosea's on his way," he said. He silenced the alarm.

My eyes locked with Kumar's.

"Is there something else in the tower?" I said, urgently. "There is, isn't there? What is it?"

Kumar didn't answer. He produced an embroidered handkerchief and wiped his mouth as the rage drained from his face.

"Tell me, or I won't go," I said.

Kumar continued to stare. I met his gaze and steadied my breath. I lifted my chin and straightened my shoulders, refusing to appear intimidated.

Finally, he nodded thoughtfully. "Bravo, girl," he said. "I see why he chose you."

As Lee came upon us, Kumar swiped a hand, minimizing the projected pictures.

•

As they set up the simulation, I studied the Kumar men. They greeted each other with stiff shoulders, like champions in the old Kongo tournament, touching off on middle ground before the fight.

The Director smiled and chuckled often. He'd transformed so quickly I might have imagined the tyrant he'd been only minutes before. But I hadn't. I was attuned to the man like to a foe in battle, recording every nuance. The sound of the opening door had startled him. He'd whipped around to face the entrance. When Lee called, his shoulders had visibly relaxed.

The Compound was an impenetrable castle, and the firewall an impassable defense, and it was all under Kumar's control. And yet, when he'd thought Hosea had come early, sneaking up on us, he had been worried. Hosea, a peacemaker, posed no physical threat. And yet, Kumar had been afraid.

Two years ago, before I led the Kongo army, this fear would have confused me—but not now. Now, for my people, I'd faced death a thousand times. Now, I saw. Kumar didn't just love Hosea, he worshipped him. I knew such love, and the fear wrapped up in it. It was the fear of loss. It made Kumar dangerous to anyone who came between him and Hosea, his *blood*, his blessed son.

My comm-unit beeped and I pulled my eyes away. I opened my palm to see a message from Director Kumar. *Subject: The Watchtower.* I tapped my palm and an image filled it. The picture was grey and distorted, a small section of the pewter vase from before enlarged to focus on a different part of Jacamar's body. I leaned in, squinting past the distortion to see Jacamar's left arm. I inhaled. Wrapped around it was an invisibility bracelet. His right arm held a second bracelet. There was one around his neck and one more on each wrist. My eyes skipped down to his ankles as I counted. There were seven bracelets in all. On Jacamar's wrists, arms, neck and ankles.

I stared across the room at Lee, recalling our earlier conversation. "Seven," I whispered. Beside Lee, Kumar watched me, waiting for my reaction to the picture. I turned aside, needing to make sense of it all. Lee couldn't reproduce the bracelets, and neither could Kumar, and they were both brilliant scientists. How had Jacamar succeeded in making seven? Jacamar, a historian and Keeper—my eyes narrowed—*and* a priest of the Core. Kumar had mentioned that specifically.

I thought back, recalling the religion well. It was the workers' primary belief system. In the Schoolhouse we'd studied the Second Brothers' culture as part of our effort to control them. I could repeat two dozen myths and tenets on command. Streets of gold, prophets and priests. Soltice was their God and Her right hand, Osa, sat near the gate of their heaven at the center of Earth.

Still, I couldn't guess what the bracelets had to do with the workers' old folktales. There was nothing technological or advanced about the Core. Nothing that would support the state-of-the-art science like invisibility. The Core was a backwards creed, an amalgamation of old-world legends, new-world superstitions and—

"Curses," I breathed. Kumar had seemed to believe that Obi's story was locked behind a curse. The idea was ridiculous, *but*—I turned my mind to examine the fantastical elements of the workers' beliefs. Osa, for example, was legless and blind but, in certain myths, she furnished the dead with a heavenly body with which to travel the Earth and through time, *without being seen*. The workers called these heavenly creatures Invisibles. They were endowed by faith to do what would otherwise be physically impossible. Put another way, the creatures of the Core could bend the laws of physics.

My chest heaved. Had I been thinking about it wrongly? Perhaps Lee hadn't been able to describe the science behind the bracelet because he didn't believe it was science at all. I closed my eyes, recalling exactly what Lee had said.

"Imagine ordering the Council to reject the Accord. Or doing away with the Council entirely."

"Impossible," I said.

"Like magic," Lee agreed.

"Magic?" I said out loud. I shook my head. Everything in me rejected the possibility. I was a scholar, a First Brother, a soldier—I didn't believe in magic! I looked over at the Director—a scientist who said he *did* believe. More, his actions proved the strength of his belief. He'd sent me the enlarged image to explain what he wanted from the Watchtower—the remaining bracelets. A weapon, more powerful than the Helix and triple point combined. He knew where they were, but he hadn't gone for them himself because, right or wrong, he truly feared the curse.

"Arika," Hosea said.

I jumped, looked up.

"It's time," he said.

I cleared my throat. "Coming," I said. I closed my palm.

As I started across the room, I slipped a hand into my bag and touched the bracelet, reviewing my conversation with Kumar. He thought to use me to advance his goals, but Jacamar had left his bracelets to the one willing to die for the truth. He'd left them for *me*. And I'd learned of them just in time. The triple-point sword threatened our freedom, and now I had the means to secure it. I resettled the bracelet into a secret compartment at the base of my sack.

THE WIDOW'S PORTION

EXCERPT FROM, THE CORE: THE ORIGINS OF SOLTICE
AND THE INVISIBLES, CHAPTER ONE

Once there was a clever widow with three children. Two daughters and one son. The youngest of them was Africa. The older children were weak and had bad teeth, but Africa was strong, with a heart like the tusk of an elephant.

One evening, the woman said to her children, "Children, your father is dead, and we are starving. In the morning, before the sun comes up, go to the rich man's onion patch and take seven onions for our dinner."

"Yes, Mother," said the children and they went to lie down.

When everyone was sleeping, a great light slipped under the door of their hut. It passed over the woman and the three children, listening to their hopes and dreams. When it heard enough, the light settled beside the youngest, Africa, and whispered the truth in the tongue of God.

In the morning, the children set off for the onion patch. Before long, their hunger pains began. They sat down to rest, and Africa fell asleep.

"It's no use," the oldest said quietly, so as not to wake the youngest. "I had a dream last night and, in my dream, we did not make it to the onion patch and we did not return alive."

The younger child agreed. "I too had a dream. If we go on, we will not survive."

"We need food and water," they said.

They talked together and determined to turn back. Instead of seven onions, they decided they would slaughter Africa into seven parts for their dinner.

"Because she is our mother," the older said, "we must bring her a portion for dinner. Divide Africa, but let her portion be the last. Do you agree?"

The younger nodded. "And, because you are my brother," the younger said, "you may take the first five parts of Africa for your dinner; only, give me the sixth and Mother the last. Do you agree?"

The oldest nodded.

This is how Africa was divided.

The first portion was tongue.

The second the teeth.

The third was cheek, the next, neck.

Five, eyes.

The sixth, the limbs.

The last, the seventh portion, was the Core.

When the younger laid down her knife, the oldest saw he'd been deceived. Feeling sad, he gathered his five portions in a small bag and left, taking the road to the west.

When he was gone, the younger heaved the last portion onto her back and carried it to her mother.

Seeing Africa was divided, the widow wept bitterly. "Leave and never return," she said.

Feeling sad, the younger called the widow a fool and scorned her. She gathered her portion, the great limbs of Africa, and left, taking the road to the east.

The next morning, the widow went to the medicine man. She showed him her portion of Africa and asked about the future.

The medicine man played a slow sad song on his reed pipe and answered.

"The oldest took five parts of Africa. But the parts are tough, and he has bad teeth. He will long to eat but die hungry. Even so, in the place where he lies, the whole truth will sit—like a rock without merit.

The younger took one part of Africa. But the parts are heavy, and she is weak. She will eat her fill but wither, deceived. Nevertheless, in the place she lies, the whole truth will grow in season—like a vine."

Hearing this, the woman fell to her knees. "Please," she said, "help me put Africa together again."

The medicine man took pity on the woman. "I can return the pieces of Africa home for you to bury," he said, finally. "Or, I can breathe life into the parts, wherever they lay. You must choose. But be warned, whatever you choose, the truth resides in Africa."

The widow thanked the medicine man and left, thinking to herself, "If I bury Africa, I bury the whole truth. But, if Africa lives, divided, the truth will never be wholly known."

The clever widow went back to her hut and, finally, decided. She roasted her portion over the fire and swallowed it without chewing. It took three days and, inside her, the truth produced pain worse than the pain of labor.

On the third night, the widow cried, but in the morning she woke laughing. She clapped her hands, shouting loudly and groaning.

When the villagers heard her, they were cut to the heart. They gathered and said, "The woman lost her husband and her children, and now she is losing her mind." They went to comfort her, bringing figs, roots, meat, milk, onions and every other good food. Soon all the food in the village sat in baskets near the widow's hut.

When dinner came, those who were hungry sat at the widow's window, listening to her shouts as they ate. And so, many years passed, and the people were satisfied: giving all they had, eating only what they needed, and leaving the rest.

When the widow was very old, she opened the door of her hut and said, "I am tired. You have heard the truth for many years and now, you have seen it. Let me die." Then she instructed them, teaching them how to preserve the Core for their children and their children's children for all future generations.

Leaving the village behind, she traveled to the patch of land that had drunk the blood of her youngest, Africa. That evening, she lay down. And, in the morning, she was gone.

When the villagers came to bury her body, they were amazed. They searched far and wide, but there was no body to be found. Where her body should have been, a single drop of red blood flowed, like a river.

The villagers clapped their hands and stomped, shouting loudly and groaning. They fell to their knees and worshiped. Then, they built a well around the drop and said to themselves, "This is the clever widow's river from which no man must drink."

And, from that day, they followed her instruction closely, teaching it to their children and their children's children, preserving the Core for generations to see.

THE THIRD AMYGDALA

Lee Ford's voice spoke into the darkness. "Vitals level," he said. "She'll awaken soon. Do you have the scans?"

"They're printing now," Hosea's voice answered. "Page me when she's lucid." His footsteps moved away.

I opened my eyes. I was on a medical bed in the station across from the loft office of the renovated lab. Lee Ford stood over me in a short lab coat. His red gaze studied a double monitor at the foot of the bed. One screen was paused on an image of Covington's flat, from the simulation I'd just exited.

The test had been seeded from the morning I'd heard the news of Jetson's death. The despair of the moment had instigated my first long episode. The other monitor held an image of my brain. The image was black with a red blotch in the middle that looked ominous.

I moaned and tried to move, but my forearms and legs were fastened to the medical bed.

"Can you hear, General?" Lee said. "The test is over."

"Did I pass?" I whispered.

Lee hesitated. "If you want to pass tomorrow, you'll need the cure."

My throat trembled as I swallowed.

"Don't worry," he said gently. "I'll make sure it's harmless."

I flinched at his tone, so different from the caustic anger of earlier. In my heart, I could still see his retreating back climbing the loft stairs, leaving me alone with Kumar. He would have tied me too, had Kumar issued the order.

I wanted to rail at him, but, as the *pagote* cleared my system, the details of my meeting with the Director returned to me and I knew I had to hold my tongue. Everything I said to Lee would be reported to Kumar—and I had to be careful. We were working together while he secured the cure but, soon after, he would be my enemy. We both wanted the bracelets, and I had no doubt he would kill for them.

Hosea climbed the stairs and went into the second-floor loft.

Lee watched as the door closed, then turned back to me. "I need a blood sample now, as your body is responding to an episode."

"Fine," I said, "but hurry." Hosea would be angry if he knew.

Lee picked up a needle and I felt a sharp sting as he inserted it into a vein on my right wrist. He filled three vials of blood and carefully removed the needle. He pressed on the punctured vein with a cloth and lowered his lips to my ear. "We need to talk," he whispered.

"Just bandage it, Lee," I said.

"It's about the bracelets," he said.

I turned my head away from him.

Keeping pressure on the wound, he moved to the other side of the bed, gearing up to say more.

"No!" I hissed. I looked up at him. "Just stop. You took my weapon and left me alone. We're done."

He met my gaze and saw I meant it. He deflated. I saw he was still angry I'd taken the seed files. But, to his credit, behind his anger was shame.

I looked away, but I could feel his eyes on the side of my face as the loft office door opened and shut. Hosea was on his way down. Kumar moved slowly behind him, clutching the stair rail. Lee slipped the filled vials into his lab coat and spread a clear bandage over the wound just as Hosea and Kumar arrived.

Kumar was wearing protective eyewear that he pushed aside to speak to me. "Hello, dear," he said. His manner was doting, nothing like the despot I had glimpsed earlier. "Here, can you sit up? Lee, boy, unstrap her."

Upright on the edge of the bed, I took the cup of coffee Hosea offered. As I sipped the bitter liquid, hot energy shot through my heavy limbs and revived me. Hosea secured another mug, and I took it gratefully.

"How long did I last?" I asked, loosening the chin strap of the radiological gear.

Hours ago, when Hosea arrived for the rescheduled test, we'd agreed to use Lee's advanced simulation technique. Instead of physically engaging with the memory, I wore a medical imaging helmet and engaged only in my mind, which was sedated with *pagote*.

The helmet, made of tightly woven metallic mesh, was lightweight and sleek. On a still specimen, Lee had explained, it produced a crystal-clear video of brain activity from which still frames could be printed. Hosea peeled the helmet from my head and rested it on a crystal manikin where it shimmered like silk in the light.

"You lasted twenty minutes," he said. "Your vitals tanked again in the middle of the simulation."

"But there's good news," Kumar added. "We were able to watch exactly what your brain was doing as you shifted into and out of the episode. Show her, Lee."

Lee started the simulation video. We watched as Martin struggled to contain me on Covington's bed. My Apex flew in threatening circles around his head.

"Now, look at your brain activity," Hosea said. Lee paused the replay as Hosea tapped the monitor that held the radiological feed of my brain. When my heart rate reached two hundred, the ominous red blotch exploded, doubling in size across the temporal lobe.

"*Obi Solomon*," I said. Without any radiological knowledge, I knew something powerful had happened.

"Here's a still frame of that explosion," Hosea said, holding out an image. "You were at the height of your aggression."

I took the scan from him, running a hand across the enlarged red blotch. "The brain of the Berserker," I said. I returned my attention to the monitor. Lee restarted the simulation replay. I watched myself weaken, stiffen and collapse. The scene faded to black.

"Now, here's a still frame of your brain the moment you fainted," Hosea said. "You were unaware and—"

"Behind the veil," I said. I clasped my hands and looked away, reluctant to see the flat black brain of the Mute.

"Look at the scan, Arika," Hosea said, urgently.

Steeling myself, I took the scan from him and looked down. I gasped. "Obi! How is this possible?" I looked from Hosea to the Director then over at Lee Ford. Finally, I looked back down at the scan in my hand. I scrambled to place the first image beside the second. "They're the same," I said, still struggling to process what I was seeing.

"Nearly identical," Kumar said. His eyes gleamed. "The activity in your brain was the same. And yet, they produce vastly different actions."

"How?" I asked.

"That's precisely the question," Kumar said. "How does fight or flight work, and how is it different in you?" He shooed Lee Ford and Hosea Khan away from my bedside, then assumed a professorial posture. "Do you know what I study, Ms. Cobane?"

I glanced at Lee Ford, and then looked back at Kumar. "Physics," I said.

"Mathematical physics," Kumar corrected. "I established the Orwell lab where we study complex systems. Unlimited and invisible systems." He tangled his fingers together, creating a visual of complexity. "The physics of emotions."

"Are you saying I'm damaged—emotionally?" I said.

"Damaged?" He sounded confused. Then he smiled suddenly, and laughed. "Ms. Cobane. You are not damaged at all; you're one of a kind." He took my shoulders and squeezed. "Your blood can help us isolate the trigger hormone, the chemical that initiates fight or flight."

Kumar waited, eyes bright, for my response.

"Okay?" I said.

"*Okay!?*" He closed his eyes and composed himself. "Ms. Cobane, thousands of us at Orwell have worked to map the chemistry of this one pathway. The trigger has escaped us for a decade. Isolating it is the final step, the missing link!"

Hosea stepped forward. "Be clear, old man. Give her a chance to say no." He turned to me. "Father thinks once he maps the process, he'll be able to control it."

"Mind control? Like the rebirth?" I stood from the bed, shaking my head.

Kumar adjusted his body, shielding Hosea from my view.

"No, no," he said. "At Orwell, we don't toy with selective neuronal deletion, or what you call the rebirth. Thought erasure is old science. At Orwell, we're interested in anticipating neuronal pathways to generate them at will. Not neuronal deletion, but selective neuronal *gestation*."

I pieced his words together. "You want to *generate* thoughts?"

"Exactly," Kumar whispered.

I crossed my arms, considering.

Kumar took my shoulders again and pivoted, so I faced him squarely. "Imagine choosing what you want to think. Seizing a sad thought, setting it aside, resuming it whenever you choose. Complete control of your stress response, no matter the circumstance."

"Complete control," I said. "Impossible."

He squeezed, flexing his knuckles. "Nothing's impossible, Ms. Cobane. The human brain is always collecting new variables, bits of input that alter the system. And you're right, that makes it difficult to anticipate the output. Difficult," he repeated, "but not impossible. Complex, but not chaotic. Does that make sense, Ms. Cobane?"

I nodded, slowly. "I understand the goal, but not how I advance it."

"I'll explain. Son," Kumar said, gesturing to Hosea.

Hosea set an image in my lap. "A scan of your brain from a

slightly different angle," he said, through clenched teeth. I could see he regretted giving his consent to photograph my brain at all. I tore my gaze from him and studied the picture before me.

"Something's wrong," I said, dissecting the image. Kumar grinned. Suddenly the anomaly became clear. "There are three." I touched the two chestnut-shaped nodules located in the center of the brain scan, then the third located above the left nodule.

"Amygdala," the Director supplied. "And yes, instead of two, you have three. I suspected this, but the imagery confirms it."

I tried to make sense of the information I'd gathered. "So, having three means that—" I hesitated. "—I get more emotional than others? Does it explain my episodes?"

"It does," Hosea said. "This third amygdala isn't fully formed and doesn't function like your other two. It might have been there at birth and grown more recently. Perhaps, like a tumor, it developed later, based on environmental factors. We do know that it only secretes the trigger hormone which hijacks your higher thinking ability."

"It *hijacks?*" I repeated, alarmed.

"It's an aggressive word," Hosea said. "But because of how completely the trigger commandeers the brain, the term is appropriate." With open palms, Hosea gestured to the front portion of the brain scan monitor. "In a normal brain, the prefrontal lobe works to analyze concerns," he said. "So, a person comes to logical conclusions about the danger they're in. How immediate is the threat, how ominous—what's the best response? All that happens in the prefrontal region. It wraps around the inner brain and provides reason. Reason that the trigger hormone shuts off." He squeezed his palms together, extinguishing enlightenment.

I frowned. "So, the trigger hormone hijacks the brain," I said. "What does it do once it's in control?"

Hosea looked grim. "That depends on the person, but some responses are predictable. Everyone will display little to no analytical activity and, at the same time, elevated aggression. Pupils dilate, blood flows as energy rushes to the head, feeding the frenzy. The heart rate careens as the muscles tense to battle the threat or escape it."

"Fight or flight," I said, understanding. "And how is my brain different?"

"We don't know," Hosea said, quickly.

Kumar held up a hand. "We aren't sure, but we do have viable theories," he corrected. "Lee, explain."

Lee took a breath. "Without getting too theoretical, your third amygdala cycles the trigger hormone in a self-perpetuating loop. When fight or flight is triggered, the hormone runs through your veins, hits the third amygdala and circles back to fire again until, finally, you overload. So, you can't fight or fly. You see?"

"No, I don't understand," I said. "Speak plainly. What happens?"

"Practically, the process looks like what happened in the simulation," Lee said. "You felt threatened by Martin and Covington, so your body signaled the need for fight or flight. But then, when others would peak and deescalate, your third amygdala continues to pull the trigger, pumping hormone in ever increasing amounts until finally, you short-circuit and enter a stupor state."

"The Mute," I said, understanding.

"Precisely," the Director said. "Your catatonic episodes are an extreme form of self-defense. Not flight or fight, but freeze. Play dead, avoid the threat and hope it goes away."

"So, how do we cure it?" I asked.

Hosea rushed to answer. "You don't have to cure it at all. The threats you're facing aren't real. You're safe from Jones. The war is over. You were never in danger from Covington and Martin."

"Or the dark, or surprises. Even certain words will set me off," I said. I rubbed my hands along my arms, warding off a chill.

Hosea nodded. "Because of your past trauma, you exist in a perpetual state of perceived danger. So, when triggered, your body responds as if old threats are imminent and real."

"They are real, my boy," Kumar said, banging his cane on the ground. "We can isolate and control the chemical responsible for the triggered response. There's little more real than that."

"Control it?" Hosea scoffed, facing Kumar. "If I'm right, then the third amygdala is evidence of trauma and the trigger hormone it produces is pain—liquid pain. You can't control the pain any more than you can erase her past." He turned to me. "You have to break the cycle and root yourself in reality."

Kumar bent forward, slipping between us. "Whose reality, my boy?" he whispered. "You said yourself, history is replaying in her mind. So, for her, it is present."

Hosea swallowed. A muscle bulged in his jaw, but he had no answer. What Kumar said made sense.

"Whether the danger is real or not, it hurts, Hosea," I said, softly. "What's your solution to *that*?"

"Master your emotions," he said. "The aggression will fade, and you'll stop fainting."

I grimaced. It was his typical response. More self-control, more meditation, more acceptance.

"Or," Kumar said, "now that we've isolated the trigger, we can develop a medicine that binds with it in your bloodstream. Using simple medical biochemistry, we can fix you."

"She doesn't need to be fixed," Hosea interrupted. "And he can't perfect the chemistry, Cobane. He doesn't have the technology. The Berserker's aggression will always be there, haunting you."

"Protecting you," Kumar said. "More, with the binder, you'll be free of the Mute forever."

"Forever?" I said, feeling hopeful.

"It's not the Way," Hosea said, aggressively. "The trigger hormone has never been isolated. Any benefit the binder provides will be short term; and a misstep or misuse would be—" He shook his head. "Chaos."

"No! Never chaos!" Kumar said. He limped forward. "There's no such thing. No insanity, only complexity. Mysteries waiting to be solved."

I looked between the two men. They stood on either side of me like stags, one weathered, the other in his prime. This was the heart of their disagreement. The cross of their animosity. This was the science that, Lee said, would inevitably cause Hosea Khan to break with Kumar and leave. I looked at Lee but his face was impassive as his brother and father argued.

"Believe me, girl," Kumar said. "Together we can figure anything out. Death, plague, pleasure. It's all input and output, like couriers." He spoke to me through thin lips, but his gaze was trained on Hosea. "The breath of life itself is a calculation; and we, all of us, can be mathematicians."

"Magicians," Hosea said.

"Gods!" Kumar shouted. "And not the kind that hide up there in the cosmos, afraid to show their faces." He waved his cane towards the ceiling. "We can be real life, visible gods, keeping world order."

Hosea's eyes flashed. He reached out and pulled my arm. He was trying to push me behind him, but I stayed put, blinking up at him instead, fascinated by his response to the notion of world order.

Suddenly an alarm sounded and Lee turned his back. He walked down the center aisle and opened his hand, scanning his palm for information.

"Father," he said, signaling for Director Kumar to join him. They moved to the stairs and climbed up together, closing themselves in the loft office.

I squinted up at Hosea Khan and, for once, I disliked what I saw. He disagreed with his father's science, but at least Kumar was trying. He was testing his theory, unraveling complexities. Hosea, it seemed, was displaying what Lee so often accused him of—fear. He was avoiding something, but what was he afraid of?

"They're distracted," he whispered. "Let's get these scans and leave."

I watched him collect the pages. "I don't understand," I said. "You're a man of strict order. You don't believe in chaos any more than he does." I lifted my chin to the loft where Kumar and Lee stood together.

Hosea settled the images into a stack and slid it into his bag. He scanned the area, ensuring the task was complete.

"See?" I said, gesturing towards him. "A tidy stack, an orderly bag. Checks and balance. He's only seeking a mathematical theory that proves an idea you believe in."

"In the wrong hands, ideas can be dangerous, Arika," he said. He moved down the center aisle, towards the laboratory exit.

I stayed put, eyeing him. It was true. Under the old Compromise, the English never tied our hands; they hadn't had to. By controlling our scholarship, they'd determined our actions more exactly than chains ever could.

"You're right," I called. "Ideas can be dangerous, but what's the threat here? If what he says is true, then why run from it?"

He stopped, turned. He seemed relaxed, but I knew his tells. The tension in his shoulders. His flared nostrils, the pinched corner of his mouth. My question had rattled him.

I gripped the strap of my sack and lifted a brow.

"I don't run from his theories," Hosea said finally. "I just don't embrace them and neither should you."

"Why?"

"Because some truths are better left alone."

"By your father?"

"By mankind!" he snapped. His eyes flashed gold. I felt mine go wide, and suddenly, I thought of the bracelet in my bag, of Jacamar, the Core and the Watchtower.

"How are you doing that?" I said. I leaned in to examine him closer.

He ran a hand over his face, pressing two fingers into his closed lids. "Look, Cobane, there's more to it than I can explain now. Can we talk tonight?"

I straightened, blinked. "You—you still want to train?"

His gaze slid away. "Yes, but *not* in the gazebo."

My heart twisted. "Fine," I whispered. "We'll talk tonight."

If he noted my disappointment, he didn't mention it. He glanced briefly at the loft office, where Lee and Kumar were still huddled, then he continued down the aisle.

Brooding, I followed.

THE LIFT

The renovated lab was twenty-four levels above the place where I was set to meet Covington. I kept my head down, and looked up through my lashes at Hosea Khan, walking beside me.

Yesterday, I would have bet my life on his dedication to me as a friend—and more. Today, his affection seemed muddled. We'd grown so close, I thought. But how much of that closeness did he regret? How much was a *mistake?*

We turned a corner en route to the lift and the bracelet seemed to shift in the bottom of my bag. The truth of its origin, a strange mix of science and magic was, somehow, connected to Obi Solomon and the history of the Kongo. And now I felt certain it was also at the root of Hosea's fight with his father and brother. Yesterday, I would have asked him about it outright, but not today.

For three nights now, our training sessions in the gazebo had led to intimacy. The emotion, always dammed between us, erupted there, and neither of us knew why. I wanted to explore the feeling and he routinely denied it. His resistance triggered in me an equal and opposite reaction—I wanted to trust him, but his mistrust was forcing me away.

"Do you know what I think?" I said. He looked down at me. "I don't think you're rejecting Kumar's science. It's not about science at all—is it?"

Hosea pushed open a barrier door and gestured for me to go ahead of him. I stopped on the door jamb and faced him.

"I think you're afraid of getting too close to anyone. I think you're rejecting love."

He considered me. "I don't love my father any more than he loves me," he said, calmly. "And Dana Alexander Kumar does not love me."

"He *doesn't* love you?" I said, incredulous. I couldn't tell him about my encounter with Kumar but, from it, one thing was clear. The man was infatuated. "How can you say that? He'd give you anything. He bends to everything you say."

Hosea didn't disagree, but he walked around me and continued down the hall. "What you're describing isn't love, Arika," he said.

"Why, because love doesn't give? It doesn't bend—ever?" I said, calling after him. "It never makes mistakes?" I glowered at his stiff back, his upright walk.

"No," he said over his shoulder. "Love is a firm foundation upon which the beloved can stand. It doesn't bend—ever."

His words intrigued me, and, as always, his confidence sent a thrill down my limbs to my toes, despite my anger. I left the door swinging to join him. "You call Lee 'brother,'" I said. "You grew up together. But he barely speaks to you."

"What's your point, Cobane?"

"Surely *that* love has bent over time," I said. "Tell me about that."

At first, I thought he wouldn't answer. Then he shrugged. "What do you want to know?"

"Everything!" I said, quickly.

His mouth twitched with humor and a bit of tension drained from his shoulders. "Well, as boys we were close," he said. "Our home had two rooms. The main one, and one upstairs—so we all lived together. Lee stayed near to the kitchen, with Mother. I spent most of my time in the garden. But we got along. He'd sketch the leaves I collected and trap crickets when they overran the plants. We had five years together before it ended."

"What happened," I said. "Why does he hate you?"

I expected him to deny Lee's dislike, but he didn't. He paused, looking down the hall and into his past. "He hates me because I broke a promise," he said, finally. "One that he very much wanted me to keep."

I pursed my lips. "That's—*mysterious*," I said.

He smiled. We rounded another corner. The lift was ahead.

"I'll tell you this. I should not have promised it in the first place," he said. "And, once I broke it, I should have explained. I suppose I'm used to protecting, not explaining."

"Protecting from what?"

"Knowledge. It's like I tell you. You want so much to know *everything*." He rolled his eyes, mocking me. "But it's best not to know. Knowledge creates responsibility, love creates commitment. Avoiding both is—"

"Lonely?" I said. I thought of his small tent pitched on unclaimed land.

We stopped in front of a pair of sliding doors and he signaled for the lift. He looked down at me. "I do care, you know," he said, stiffly. "I would heal the mistrust between Lee and me. I've tried to explain."

I thought of the seed files Lee had scoffed at and set aside. Hosea didn't know it but, for his brother, his explanation had come too late.

"Why only five years together?" I said, changing the subject. "Why did you separate?"

"Father came to collect us when Lee was five," Hosea said. "He took us to the Kongo Technology Center to train and then—and then Mother died." He slipped his hands into his pockets and looked down, resting his chin against his chest.

Looking back now, I can see his pain. The Kha was still mourning his mother and regretting his role in her death. I should not have pressed the wound. But, in my youth, humility escaped me. I longed for knowledge, having no understanding of its underside—its yoke. I always pressed for more. More knowledge, more of Hosea Khan, more *everything*.

"I saw a picture of your grandmother," I said, thinking of the woman with the braided crown and cockle shell necklace. "She was very beautiful—like your mother. But you never speak of her."

A bell tolled as the glass lift arrived. The doors opened, and he stepped inside. I followed, trying to read his expression. He pressed the button for the lowest level. The lift doors shut.

"Lee doesn't mention her either. Which is odd because she rescued him—right?"

"And Lee told you that?" he said.

My eyes shifted away. "Not exactly."

We stood silent for a long time. "You didn't see a picture of my grandmother, Arika," he said. "There are no pictures of her."

My head snapped up. "No pictures?" I said, reminded of Jacamar and his bracelets. "Not a single one. How do you know that?"

"Where did you see her?" he said, his eyes shined, suddenly, like brass.

I squinted into them. "You did it again." I pointed an accusing finger at his brow. "How are you doing that?" I lunged and swiped a hand over his left bicep. There was nothing there. Quickly, I swiped his other bicep. Empty. He stood still, letting me touch his wrists. I ran my fingers down his throat. I stooped to touch his left ankle, then his right.

"What are you looking for, Cobane?" he said, softly.

I turned away from his knowing stare and looked out at the courtyard. Through the engineered glass of the loft, the gazebo's sloped roof and wide pillars were perfectly visible.

When the lift stopped, I turned to face the door. It was slow to open and each moment—with his eyes on me, on the side of my skull, like the eye of the sun—seemed interminable.

I tapped the crack where the sliding doors met. "Come on," I whispered.

Suddenly Hosea cursed. His hand whipped out to snatch mine from the seal. He lifted my wrist to eye level, studying the clear bandage Lee had placed there earlier. "Oh, Arika," he said. "What have you done?" He'd warned me a dozen times—no blood.

"He needed it for the cure," I said.

"Wrong, Cobane!" He grimaced, squeezing my wrist. "He'll use it for whatever he wants."

Before I could answer, a grinding noise sounded and the lift shook. We braced against the lift wall, but the trembling stopped as abruptly as it had come. *An earthquake?*

Confused, I looked up at Hosea, then through the glass, as a movement in the courtyard caught my eye. It was Lee Ford and Director Kumar. They were clearly visible but, as we were on the opaque side of the glass, they couldn't see us. They'd emerged, it seemed, from the sinkhole wall. Lee went first, his comm-unit open, leading them to a glen not far from the lift.

The grinding and shaking started up again and suddenly I knew its source. I pressed my face against the engineered glass. A rock door was scraping closed over an opening in the sinkhole wall adjacent to the lift.

"Another passage!" I said. "It must lead back to the lab."

Hosea glared at me. "*Another* passage?" he said. "Arika—"

"Hush," I said, tilting my head. Lee Ford's alarm was sounding again, a thin wail that I recognized. The same sound had alerted Kumar that Hosea was on his way. Lee had said it was set to ring whenever the infirmary door opened.

In the glen, Lee pointed north and set out in that direction. Kumar followed, leaning heavily on his cane. They disappeared behind the tree line.

"The only thing that way is the cistern," Hosea said, his brow furrowed. The lift door opened and he made to leave.

"Hosea," I said hesitantly. He stopped on the jamb and looked back.

I couldn't look directly at him. "I can't tell you how I know, but that alarm—I think it means your patient is awake. I think she might have left the infirmary and Kumar is going after—"

Hosea bolted from the lift.

"Hosea!" I ran after him, into the ground level of the west wing and through the exit doors. Outside he stood in the center of the glen that Lee and Kumar had just left. His body was tense, his head tilted up.

I followed his gaze to a person running along the foot trail several levels up from the base of the sinkhole. Pale skin, red hair. "It's her," I said. Then I bit my tongue. Hosea didn't know I had seen his patient.

When Hosea didn't respond, I looked over to see if he'd heard me, but he was gone. My mouth dropped. "Hosea?" I said. I looked left and right. He'd been right beside me, not a foot away.

"Arika!" Covington stepped into the clearing. She smiled and waved. "You're here! I only half-expected you to show—" Her voice died as she noted my expression. "What's wrong?"

I turned in a complete circle then ran past her, into the trees. "Where is he?" I said.

"Who?" Covington asked, running after me.

I ran deeper into the wood. When I stopped abruptly, Covington collided with my back. I regained my balance and moved off the path. I found the tallest mango tree in the vicinity and looked up from its base. There were no low limbs.

"Arika," Covington said. "What are you—"

"Hush," I said. "Help me up."

"Up—up where?"

I pointed to the highest bough of the tree.

"Quickly!" I snapped.

Looking distressed, she bent, and I scrambled onto her shoulders. I leaned as close to the tree as possible and flung myself at the lowest hanging branch. I caught hold and shimmied into the core of the tree. Finding footholds, I climbed up, pushing aside large leaves and fragrant fruit.

At the top, I turned, bracing my back on the trunk. From that vantage point, I saw everything from the market preparations in the courtyard square to the red head of the woman still running along the walkway. I spotted Hosea Khan's head, off the beaten trail. He ran swiftly through the staked tomato vines heading toward the cistern.

A hundred yards north of his position, closer to the cistern, Director Kumar was leaning against a tree. He was waving his hand, encouraging Lee Ford to leave him. Lee continued towards the cistern. When he was yards away, the Director stood and pulled something from the waist of his trousers. His position made it impossible for me to see what it was, but as I watched, he braced his back against the tree and grew very still.

"He's taking aim!" I cried.

Covington's face was lifted towards me. "Who's taking aim? At who?"

I squinted out, triangulating the Director's position. "I think he's aiming for the woman!"

I scanned the trees, looking for Hosea Khan. Before I found him, the woman screamed. My eyes flew to her as she tripped. Something, a missile, had shattered the rock just below her. The Director had missed.

Lee Ford stopped, turned back and ran towards his father.

The woman stumbled into the railing that bordered the walkway and flipped over the side. She screamed again—a call for help pitched with hysteria.

In the courtyard square, those working on the market stopped and every head swiveled, looking for the source of the cry.

It came again, then, at a heartbreaking decibel, it stopped.

THE ENGLISH

"Is everyone accounted for?" a voice said.

"Where's the General?" came another voice.

"I'm here," I called. "Captain Covington is with me."

Ahead of us, huddled together in a squash patch, was the group that had been preparing for the market when the English woman fell. Just before we broke through the line of trees to join them, Covington grabbed my arm.

"You're rubbing that thing again," she said. She indicated my chest where the ruby bauble lay. "And your neck is oozing blood. It needs to be cleaned."

She caught my hand as it dropped from the necklace. "If we leave now, we'll still have most of the two hours you promised me," she said. "We'll get you ready."

Except for scuff marks on her leg and shoulders, from where I'd scrambled up her body to the tree, she was already dressed for a party. "Come on, Martin can handle this," she said, gesturing through the trees.

I looked her up and down. "*I'll* handle it," I said. I moved past her and joined the others. Walker and Hurley were present. Then Martin appeared, with Pidge and Finch.

"What happened?" Martin asked as he embraced Covington. "I heard screaming. It sounded like a woman's voice?"

"It was a woman," Walker confirmed.

"We don't know who," Hurley added.

The English woman's arrival had coincided with the influx of vendors and entertainers for the market. She'd remained unconscious, so none of them knew of her presence at the Compound. Certain Hosea would join us soon, I decided to keep quiet about what I knew. They debated what to do next and determined, correctly, that the sound originated from the north bend of the yard, near the cistern. They started in that direction to investigate.

Ten minutes later, we found the Director and Lee Ford, talking low, their heads bent together. My skin tingled as Kumar looked up and caught my eye. I was certain his shot had caused the woman to fall.

The pair came to stand with us. Before they could explain what they'd seen, Hosea appeared through the line of trees. The group hurried to join him. As we neared, I saw he carried his patient.

Her eyes were closed, and her red hair fell in a tangle from Hosea's arm. Around her neck, on a gold chain, was a small cross, a religious symbol. Other than the lacerations, like whip marks, she appeared unhurt.

Director Kumar stormed forward. "She's alive?" he asked, incredulous.

Hosea nodded, looking grim.

"What happened?" Pidge demanded.

The Director hesitated, his face tight. "She triggered one of Lee's alarms," he said, finally. "We were on our way to investigate when she fell from the railing."

"She didn't fall," Hosea said, meeting Kumar's gaze—and holding it. "She caught on a lower rail and I pulled her to safety."

I eyed Hosea Khan, recalling the exact sequence of events. Lee and the Director had a head start to the cistern. Hosea was five minutes, at least, behind them. When she fell, they were a hundred yards closer to the woman. And yet Hosea Khan claimed he'd gotten to her first. It was highly improbable, unless Lee Ford had stopped running, and let her fall. From the corner of my eye, I noted Lee seemed tense, but he didn't look guilty.

"She's awake," Martin said suddenly.

The woman stirred in Hosea's arms. Her lashes fluttered as he bent, laying her flat on the ground. He checked her pulse.

I stepped closer, examining the web of cuts on her arms and legs. They appeared to cover her whole body. She shifted restlessly and pushed herself up on her elbows. The cross on her chest clung to her moist skin as she began to mutter. I leaned in with the crowd as her eyes flew open, and her mouth moved.

"He arose. He is risen," she said. Her voice was soft, but clear. Her eyes, wild and bright. It was the strangest thing she could have said, and, for a moment, I thought I'd heard wrong. Then she said it again. "He arose. He is risen."

"She's mad," someone called, echoing my own thoughts. The crowd shrank away but I stepped closer and our eyes locked. Hers narrowed with—recognition? Her lips parted and I thought she was going to speak to me. Then she jerked and her eyes rolled.

Hosea bent to catch her head. He took off his brown top shirt and folded it beneath her. He pointed at Pidge and Finch. "You two, get me a stretcher. I'll treat her in the infirmary."

"No!" Kumar said. "Now that she's awake, she's under my purview. She'll need to be erased and observe quarantine."

"She's asleep again," Hosea said. "You said you'd give me until this evening—unless you've changed your mind again." His tone was cold with anger.

I watched Kumar struggle. Clearly he didn't want to upset Hosea Khan, but to him the woman posed an intolerable risk.

To my surprise, Lee stepped forward. "Let Hosea take her to the infirmary, Father," he said. "I'll guard her. I'll perform the complete wipe at six this evening, as you ordered. Or, if she awakens again, I'll see she follows protocol."

The Director mulled this over briefly, and then nodded, mollified. "See that you don't leave her side," he said. "And have her gagged and bound. I don't want her talking in her sleep."

Lee lingered as Director Kumar limped away, and the crowd dispersed. A few minutes later, Pidge and Finch arrived with a stretcher.

"One moment, I'll walk you to the infirmary," Hosea instructed them, then he came over to Covington and me.

I spoke before he could. "How are you doing it? If it's not the bracelets—what's your source?"

"I've told you, Cobane," he said, "alignment with the Will is—"

"Lie," I whispered. "You didn't save that woman by standing on a pillar!"

He met my gaze. "There's more to it," he admitted. "I told you. I'll explain tonight—"

"Now!" I said, my voice louder than I intended.

He ran a hand over his jaw and glanced towards where Pidge and Finch had lifted the woman onto the stretcher and were making her comfortable. Lee Ford was beside them, leaning against a tree. He had his sketch pad out. Hosea eyed him warily.

"It *can't* be now," he said. He lifted a chin to the English woman. "She can't wait."

"Then I'll come with you to the infirmary," I said.

Covington put a hand on my shoulder. "You promised me two hours," she said. "And you need it, now more than ever. Then there's the market and—"

I groaned and turned my back on them. I didn't trust myself to speak without screaming.

Hosea came around to face me. "I'll see you at the market," he said gently. "We'll leave early, okay? In the meantime, take this." He retrieved a sheath from his waistband and held it out to me.

I took it and drew out my ruby knife. I looked up at him. It wasn't the truth, but the weight of a real blade felt good in my hands.

"Until we know what happened to that woman, keep it with you," Hosea said. "Right next to your skin. And stay with Oriole." He nodded to Covington and handed me the slender *bambi* holster that held the knife against my lower leg.

"What about my Apex?" I said.

Hosea held my gaze. "If you still want it after tonight, it's yours," he said. He reached down and took my hand. I could feel his thumb pressed to the bandage on my wrist. "Just trust me," he whispered. "One more night."

My heart cramped in my chest, but I squeezed his palm. "One more night," I said.

He glanced over my head. Pidge and Finch had lifted the stretcher between them. Lee stood close by, protecting Kumar's interest in the woman. Hosea joined them and soon they were out of sight.

THE REPORT

I followed Covington into my room and immediately went to my desk where the couriers had delivered a package. I picked it up, sat and ripped at the binding. The brown paper wrap fell away, revealing *The Core: The Origin of Soltice and the Invisibles*. I'd ordered the book from the library earlier to refresh my memory. The book was short; perhaps I could read it in one sitting, before the market. I went to open it, but Covington placed a hand over mine, halting my progress.

"Put that away," she said.

"In a minute."

"You promised me *two hours*."

She reached for the book, but I waved her away, hugging it to my chest. "This is important."

"And so is this," she returned impatiently. She snatched the book from my grip and went to the door. She opened it, letting a trio of couriers inside. One carried a large tub.

"A bath!" I said, standing. "That's the surprise? I don't have time." I pointed to the closest robot. "Take that tub away!" I reached for the book.

"Pause!" Covington said, contradicting my command.

The courier froze.

I glared at her, releasing my anger. "Do you have any idea what's at stake?"

"Of course I do!" she shouted back. "I fought in the revolution too, remember? I was right beside you. When Booster lost his eye, you hauled him to the medic tent, but *I* held the bloody rag across his cheek. I followed you here because I love you and I've organized your entire defense without any help. So don't talk to me like I don't know what's at stake!"

"Then what are you thinking?" I shouted back. "Surprising me this morning. Bothering me about the market. Dances and dresses? How can you worry about what's on your body when the body itself is at stake?"

She sighed. "I'm thinking of *living*, Arika. Living—despite the past, because of the future." She let the book fall to the ground and cupped her belly with both hands. "Respectfully, General, life is more than duty. How can I dance and talk about music?" Her voice broke. "How can *you* not?"

I took a step back, my eyes glued to her hands clasped low on her midsection.

"I know what's at stake," she said. The tears in her eyes spilled down her cheeks. "So, I have to live. Live, right now, while I can."

I stepped over the book and went to her, wrapped her in my arms. "I see," I said. And, I did see. Not just that her baby was already conceived, but what else Covington carried. And that, despite our differences—her smile and my screaming—we carried it in common.

"I'm sorry," I said, softly. "I'm no one to judge." I thought of the look on Martin's face when she walked into a room. "I—I wish. I wish—"

She stopped me with a kiss on my cheek. Then she wiped

her face and pulled me to the window. "Don't wish, Arika," she said. "The Kongo needs you just as you are. Look here!" She rested her hand on the glass. Below, the courtyard square bustled with activity. "Those people are excited for the first time in months," she said. "They believe in you." She took my shoulders and guided me to the mirror on my wall. "Which is why you can't go to them like this or they'll know something is wrong. And tonight—" She broke off, shaking her head. "We all just need *one* night."

I looked at Covington in the dusty mirror. She wore a traditional aura. It was coal black, slim cut and draped loosely around her body and neck. One leg and the opposite arm were exposed, and both were ladened with bronze rings. Her hair was plaited close to her head in a beautiful design. The ends of the plaits were decorated with wood and metal beads that dangled around the small of her waist.

I bit down on my lower lip. In contrast, I hadn't properly washed in days.

Covington's brow lifted. "Now?" she asked. "Will you let them fill the tub?"

The couriers filed in then out as Covington rubbed ointment beneath the ruby necklace and helped me out of my garments. I stepped into the tub and lowered myself down. The wet warmth wrapped around me and my eyes shut involuntarily, as the heat lulled me towards sleep.

Beside me, Covington perched on a stool. "Are you ready for your real surprise?" she asked.

I popped one eye open to see her sly smile. "I finished the Glosser report," she said.

My mouth fell open.

She grinned. "I knew it was important to you so, when I lucked upon a source, I got to work. I made summary sheets for each major player."

She opened her comm-unit and projected a copy of the report into the air over the tub. Moving too quickly for me to read, she flipped through a series of slides with pictures, dates and names, then she closed it.

"Covington!" I screeched. I picked up the towel slung along the rim of the tub and stood.

"Sit down," she said. "You don't have to read it. I prepared a presentation to brief you. I'll post anything you note in the repository, and I'll send the full report to your comm-unit in case I miss something."

Still on my feet, dripping water, I looked at the piles of unfinished business on my bed and desk. In stacks on my floor. I met Covington's gaze. "A summary presentation," I said, softly. "It's perfect."

She shook her head. "I'm not giving it to you yet," she said. "I have conditions."

I scoffed.

She held up a hand. "I know you, General. If I don't lock you in, you'll be in the bushes before supper. Now, sit down!"

I glared at her.

She closed her comm-unit and made to leave.

I sat.

With a small smile, she eased herself back down onto her stool. Then, she turned and rummaged in her bag. Taking her time, she pulled out a vial of essence from her bag and poured a generous portion into the tub. The smell of coconuts wafted up with the steam. She then produced a vial of oil, a bag of salts and a wooden spoon. She poured in a good amount of oil, a pinch of salt and stirred to combine.

Finally, she spoke. "If we start now, I can finish the presentation before the market, but—you have to soak while I talk. The whole time. Neck deep to activate the ointment."

"Done!" I said. "Let's—"

She held up a pair of fingers. "Condition two—"

I waited.

"You have to let me do your hair."

"My hair?" I touched the asymmetrical mass of my bonsai. "I don't usually do anything to it."

She snorted. "Oh, we *know*."

I squinted and flicked wet fingers in her direction. She shrieked, shielding her perfectly coiffed hair. We both laughed.

"Can I start?" she said, sobering.

I sank further into the water, a heavy feeling in my chest. "Thank you," I said. She nodded. I exhaled and settled down deep in the tub.

•

Thirty minutes later she flipped to the last slide. It was a full-body image of Dana Kumar. His legs were flesh and blood, and I wondered when he'd replaced them with the bionic legs he had presently. Still in the tub, though the water was beginning to cool, I digested the story she'd detailed.

"Go back two slides," I said. Covington complied and a picture of a handsome white man loomed above me. "Enlarge his face." Covington zoomed in as instructed. "That's Marion, Kumar's father?"

"Yes, Marion Glosser, the Duke of the North," Covington confirmed. "Marion's father was dubbed the Marquis. And the grandfather, in his time, was…" She checked her notes. "The Earl."

"A royal family," I murmured. Kumar had lived his life trying to please the duke, and it showed. Though they shared no blood, the two were a matched pair. One dark, one bright, opposites at first blush. But a closer inspection—the tilt of their heads, their dominant posture, the direct bite in their gaze—revealed they were much alike.

Covington minimized the projection. "You're free to stand," she said, smiling. "I'll be right back." She rose from her stool and left the room.

My hair had soaked up water like a sponge. As I stood, the water clung to the coils, lengthening them, so they hung near the middle of my back. I reached for a towel and stepped out of the tub. I patted myself dry, sat on Covington's abandoned stool and smoothed cream over my entire body. Relaxed, I slipped into a robe and moved to my desk.

My comm-unit buzzed. A message from Martin.

The picture was taken on the day the Compromise was signed. Jacamar isn't mentioned in any of the literature surrounding the signing. My guess is he was there unofficially, and didn't realize his picture was taken at all. I've sorted through hundreds of images from that day and I did some triangulation. With some certainty, I believe the image attached is what Jacamar was looking at in the one photo of him that exists.

I opened the images Martin had sent. The first was the one I'd seen before, of Jacamar. He stood in a soaring tent on a sunny day, surrounded by English officials. I noted the bracelets but, this time, I focused on his expression. His dart-like eyes were desirous, but they squinted at the corner, as if he was near tears.

I switched to the next image. It depicted the same sunny winter day, in the same soaring tent. Obi sat at a table with an English man to his left and a Clayskin man, in official-looking garb, to his right. In his hand, Obi had an open scroll of paper. Suddenly I understood what was going on in the scene. My eyes found the picture's caption. "The delegates at the signing ceremony," I read. "This is the moment Obi committed to the rebirth and consigned the Kongo to slavery."

I looked back at the picture of Jacamar, and again struggled to understand his expression. I touched his face, wishing I could see behind his eyes, into his head. One thing was clear: he didn't want Obi to sign, which meant he knew Obi was making a mistake. "Why did he do it?" I whispered, as if Jacamar could hear. "And you! You had all the power in the world, so why didn't you stop him?"

"Ready?" Covington said. She'd returned quietly. I looked up at her. "Oh, Arika," she said. "Are you okay?"

I blinked away tears. She had a basket of hair supplies on her hip. I closed the picture and wiped my eyes. "It's nothing. Here, come sit."

She sat on the chair at my desk and rested the basket of supplies on the floor beside her. At my bed, I pushed aside a mass of papers and picked up two feather-stuffed pillows. I stacked them on the floor and sat down with my back between Covington's knees.

She uncapped a jar, and the room filled with the scent of sweet almonds and fresh aloe.

I inhaled. In my chest I could still feel the dark gape of sadness for my people, for what could have been. But, as I exhaled, the worst of the burn subsided.

Covington parted my hair and set to work, weaving with strength and dexterity. The tight pull of her hands made my scalp tingle to life as my neck stretched from side to side to accommodate her design. I got to my knees as she styled the back and rested my head in her lap as she arranged the sides. She worked silently, only speaking to adjust my position.

"There, now. It's done," she said finally. Her brown fingers and trim nails glistened in the light. "Just one more thing." She dipped her finger into a pot and patted my lower lip. She dabbed a finger in the pot again and smoothed it over both brows. She came back a third time and anointed my upper and lower lashes so they curled lavishly.

She reached around me to pick up a hand mirror. I looked, angling it around. Glossy braids, precise parts and soft edges. My face shone like a jewel, steeped in light. My eyes sparkled, my mouth glowed.

"Oh, Cov!"

She grinned.

I put down the mirror and wrapped her in a hug.

THE MARKET

Hurley had done wonders with the Courtyard Square. The crystalights were powered down in favor of a hundred candelabras and the area glowed against the fading day.

The time was five after six and I wondered, fleetingly, what had become of the English woman. Director Kumar sat like a sultan at the head of a decorated table, but Lee was nowhere in sight. Perhaps he was performing the complete erasure at that very moment. Or maybe Hosea had used his considerable influence to garner a night's reprieve.

Aside from Lee Ford, it seemed every other resident was present. Most were eating or browsing the various stalls, but some, including Hosea Khan, were gathered around an elevated stage, waiting for the night's entertainment to begin. He'd dressed for the occasion in a warm cream tunic and leggings. The garments were embroidered with gold thread and cut on a bias, highlighting the perfection of his shape.

Several musicians formed a semicircle in the corner of the stage around a tall slender Kongo girl, the first entertainer. Her black hair was crinkly and long; she wore it loose except for a pair of pins above each ear. It fell forward across her face as she warmed up for the show.

As we passed the refreshments and moved towards the stalls, I tore my gaze from Hosea and straightened my shirt.

I'd rejected the refined garments Covington had procured, and insisted instead on wearing my training shirt, leggings, vest and high moccasins. All were black and some needed mending. But they were, at least, clean.

"What are you shopping for?" I asked Covington, looping a finger in my thick *bambi* belt.

"A gift for East Keep," Covington said. "She got married."

"Again?" I snorted. We strolled along the perimeter of the space, where the tables were heavy with goods. "Is this her third or fourth husband?"

A vendor beckoned me over for a closer look, but I shook my head, returning my attention to the stage, where Hosea Khan was approaching the slender girl.

Covington followed my gaze and smiled. "Jealous?"

"Of East Keep's fourth marriage?" I asked, incredulous. "No!"

"Then you're not in love?"

I watched Hosea chat with the dark-haired young woman. "Not in a way that can last," I said. "Not like I love the Kongo."

"Marriage can last," Covington pointed out, folding her arms across her chest.

I shrugged. "East Keep's didn't."

"But others do—" she insisted, then stopped, considering. Under the Compromise, Kongo marriage had been prohibited. Now one merely needed to ask and receive an affirmative reply to formalize a union. And dissolving one was just as easy. Marriages were abundant, but they didn't flourish. The nuances of why were routinely the subject of public debate.

"Well, they *can* last," Covington went on. "And I won't give up on the idea."

I frowned, distracted. The girl had removed her flared skirt to reveal a pair of black silk shorts that fluttered loosely around the firm mound of her buttocks. She loosened her top, an intricately wrapped black scarf, and retied it so that it outlined her ribcage and left her arms naked to the warm evening air. She continued to limber up, bending at the waist, showing great flexibility. She stretched her arms over her head and her neck seemed to grow an elegant inch as she smiled at Hosea Khan.

Covington looked at me from the corner of her eye. "No interest at all?" she said, knowingly.

I glanced at her. "I care for him," I said. "Perhaps, if things were different. If we were English and met in the north and our only obstacle was the strength of my affection—maybe then." I shrugged. "But in this reality, I can't reach him. And besides, I'm the Kongo's general. Until they're free, the people look to me."

"A general currently without a country," Covington pointed out. "We'd better discuss the trial."

"Have they all agreed to testify?" I asked, giving her my full attention.

"They have," Covington said, reassuring me. Then she bit her lip. "Everyone except Hannibal."

We figured the prosecution would turn on first-person testimony, and we'd asked the senior students to publicly affirm my character. As eyewitnesses, their opinions were valuable, but each of their testimonies carried a different weight.

East Keep wasn't in the public eye, but she spoke well. She'd be convincing so long as the prosecutor didn't delve into her erratic lifestyle. The twins, thanks to their boutique, were famous—but mostly among the younger set. It was Hannibal, a well-respected and well-spoken journalist, whose testimony would have guaranteed me success.

"She's still in mourning for Jetson," Covington said. "She's not even writing."

A pain shot through my chest. "I understand," I said.

Covington squeezed my shoulder. "The twins will both be there," she said. "They're taking a vacation to come, and they *never* take vacations."

I squinted at the idea of the silly West Keep twins as tireless businesswomen.

"They're as ridiculous as ever," Covington laughed. "They asked for per diems! The nerve. They've amassed a mountain of coin and spend all day amassing more, and for what?"

"At least they're doing well for themselves," I said. "That's good."

Covington raised a brow. "Have you seen the corsets they're peddling?"

I shook my head. "I've seen pictures."

Glad to change the subject, she pulled me to a vending table with a star-spangled sign. *West Keep Boutique. Ready-made old-world English clothes.*

She riffled through the merchandise and pulled out a garment. "Feel this," she said. The metal boning beneath the ivory fabric wasn't soft. "Ridiculous!" Covington said. "But men love it so." She flipped a hand. "Good Kongo women trussed up in printed girdles and tottering around in kitten heels. And in this heat? I could faint for them."

"There *are* a lot of ruffles," I admitted.

"It's lace from the north," Covington said. "They ship it in to make their idiot clothing."

Thinking of Hosea Khan's finery, I took the corset from Covington and pressed it to my chest, imagining it on.

The young woman behind the table cleared her throat.

I tilted my head, taking in her outfit, a prime example of what Covington called 'protest fashion,' streetwear popularized by the political left. According to Covington, they rallied around my cause and questioned everything. Over her lower face, the young clerk wore a tattered muzzle to highlight her full, untethered right to speak. And, instead of a shirt, she wore gold chain mail with loose links that exposed her glossy skin. As I eyed her, she cleared her throat again, reluctant to speak.

"Sorry, General, but we don't allow try-ons." She looked awkwardly at my unkempt clothing.

Covington took the corset from my loose grip. The clerk, on high-tip shoes, was inches taller than either of us. Still, Covington managed to look down on her. She tossed the garment back on the table then looped her arm in mine.

We moved on, passing competing clothiers. Frocks and neckties, feather hats and, finally, a table display of joysticks and dismembered keyboards the size of my forearm.

"'Imitation Wreckage'?" I said, reading the sign.

"Nintendo," the clerk said, gesturing to a gaming console. "Go on, pick it up. They look exactly like real old-world antiques, but they cost half the coin. And look how it shines," he said. The *haute* ink inlays on his center teeth glistened like oil as he handed me a brochure. In it, a man posed with a boxy controller hung from his neck by a chain.

"No, thank you," I said, avoiding the clerk's smile. I returned the advertisement.

Before I could back away, he slipped another item in my hand. "Perhaps you're in the mood for a collar," he said.

I looked down at the crescent-shaped object in my hand. "A collar?" I glanced over my shoulder to see Covington had moved on to a table of sweets.

"Go on, try it!" the clerk said, flashing a smile.

I started to shake my head and, again, the man forestalled me. He picked up another crescent collar and replaced the one he wore around his own neck. He adjusted a switch on its base and his head disappeared in a bright sun.

I inhaled. "Amazing."

"I like this one because you can change it," the clerk said, speaking from behind the illusion. He adjusted the switch again and the bright sun disappeared. His own face flashed then disappeared again, replaced by a flurry of monarch butterflies whirling in a globe shape.

I reached out to touch them and instead grazed the clerk's face. I snatched my hand back. "How many changes?"

"There are thirty helmets in that collar, sixty in this one," he said, picking up another.

It had a sleek square design that appealed to me.

The clerk came around the table and I let him fasten the collar around my neck, holding the ruby necklace aside as he adjusted the switch.

I heard and felt nothing. But, when he pulled me to the edge of his vendor table and stood me in front of a mirror, I saw, in place of my head, a pink sun, the fading moon and a dozen yellow stars stuck in orbit sat on my shoulders.

I scooted closer to the mirror taking in all the details. I found the switch and adjusted it, flipping between an alpha lion's head and a billowing smokestack. I settled on a basic distortion. My own visage with a black crow perched on my shoulder.

"She'll take it!" Covington said. She'd come up behind me with a feathery bouquet of dandelion seeds.

"General?" the clerk said, waggling his gelled brows.

"I'll take it," I confirmed.

As I paid the clerk, Covington popped a white fluffy flower head into her mouth. "Engineered sugarcane!" she exclaimed in delight. "East Keep will love it, don't you think?"

She offered me the bouquet, and I took a stem and held it close to my nose. It smelled pungent, like a common weed. Somewhat hesitant, I rested the puff on my tongue and laughed. It melted deliciously, as light as air and sweet as table sugar.

"Want another?" Covington asked, holding out a stem.

Feeling light and young, I took it immediately. As it melted, I completed the transaction, taking my change and accepting my new collar in a brown paper bag. I slipped the purchase in my sack and saw the back of my hand was lit blue.

As Covington chatted, I flicked my wrist to open my comm-unit. At the top of my palm was a message from Lee Ford. *Subject: The Cure.* The message inside was brief: *22:00 top level lab.*

Covington quieted and touched my shoulder. "What is it?" she asked, reading my expression. "The entertainment's about to start but, if it's important…" her voice trailed off.

I looked across the way to Hosea Khan.

"Arika?" Covington prodded.

"It's nothing important, Cov," I said, finally. I snapped my palm shut. "For a few more hours, nothing is more important than this." I looked around the square, took her hand and squeezed. "Let's grab a seat."

Hosea saw us coming and waved us over. "Oriole, Arika—here. I saved seats."

We sat just as the lights darkened. The slender young woman with crinkly hair moved to the center of the stage where a wooden chair had been placed. She was barefoot and had a bundle in her arms. As the crowd hushed, caught by her beauty, she held out her hands to reveal a pair of shoes.

They weren't like any shoes I'd seen. They were dainty and brown with a long, thick toe box and wide brown straps sewn into either side. She sat and placed her right foot in one shoe and adjusted it so that it covered her heel. Then she laced up the straps to secure the slipper to her foot. The inside ribbon came across the top and around her ankle, the outer ribbon wrapped the other way, so the ribbons crossed over at the top. She tied the straps together in a neat knot then tucked the ends in. The shoe left the top of her foot bare.

She made a slow show of encasing her other foot and displaying both feet neatly wrapped in the shoes. The unusual taper of her slippers elongated the lines of her legs, accenting their tone and strength. Finally, she stood and nodded to the musicians. The music started. Slow and mysterious. The fiddler pushed his bow forward and pulled it back, forward and back. Forward and back. The woman began to sway.

"She's going to dance," I whispered, finally realizing.

Hosea bent to speak in my ear. "It's called the hiplet," he said. "It's twenty-first-century African American culture."

"Fascinating," I said.

The woman seemed to be hypnotized by the slow strum of the music. The toe of her right shoe pulled forward and her slender calf followed. Her heel lifted and her ankle turned out, exposing the flesh of her firm inner thigh. She pulled her leg back then pushed it forward again, following the music.

As it quickened, so did she. Her arms joined her leg motions, out and in, until, on a breath, she rose. She was so graceful it took a second for me to confirm that she had not, in truth, left the ground. Instead, two inches of the tapered peak of her shoes rested flat against the stage flooring as she balanced on the point of her toes. The cords of her ankles and feet trembled as she shimmered forward. Her arms moved around her as she danced, striking elegant lines and angles. She beat her legs together, dipping and flicking. Stretching but never straining. Her scant clothing left every muscle in her body, taut and supple, on display.

Suddenly the music changed. Instead of sliding his bow, the musician used it to chop at the strings closest to his chin. The dancer's tempo adjusted. She flung her arms forward and her back arched like a panther. Then, she threw her shoulders and arms back and tilted her chin to the ceiling. She performed the same move again, hunching forward and bursting back. Her fingers splayed, and her mouth gaped as she laughed silently.

Someone began to clap along. Someone else began to stomp a bassline and others pounded the nearest flat surface. Untutored, we created a wild syncopated rhythm and the dancer gyrated accordingly, flinging her hair, thrusting her hips and clutching at her heart and stomach as if something inside her—something winged—wanted out. She pulsed and shivered, leaping from toe to toe around the stage. She leapt up from the stage onto a table, lifted up on the point of her shoes then opened her legs and bent into an earthy squat. She straightened and leapt back again to float across the stage like a mirage.

Finally, as the beat of the crowd reached a fever pitch, she began to turn. Balanced on one toe, she whipped her free leg in and out. Its momentum pulled her around and around. The audience beat faster. Covington and I exchanged an ecstatic glance. Hosea, beside me, stomped rhythmically. The dancer kicked and whipped until the lines of her body blurred. She was movement, enchanted smoke, a pure black gust.

THE ROCK, THE RIVER AND THE VINE

Hosea took my hand after the first act, just as the sun shifted towards the horizon. Hours of entertainment remained, and, after the entertainment, the food, drink and shopping would continue late into the night. As he stood, I rose with him, and we left the revelry behind.

The lampposts that ordinarily illuminated the courtyard at night were unlit on account of the market, so we walked in the dark. He led me to a break in a row of tall evergreen bushes. Inside, the bushes formed a fence around a sizable square of grass. The space gave me pause. Its lack of privacy meant Hosea was not yet consigned to our agreement.

"You want to *talk* here?" I asked.

He turned to confront me. "I agreed to talk, and we will. But my hope is that you'll train first."

"That wasn't the agreement," I said. I stepped back, ready to leave.

He caught my hand. "Please," he said. "Once more. Give yourself one more chance to see the Way."

It was no use, I knew. But he wanted it badly, and I found I couldn't say no. "This time, don't dictate," I said. "Speak with me; explain the harm in the cure."

He tossed a crystalight and began warming up in the center of the knoll. I joined him, pressing my limbs into various positions of offense and defense. Like two halves, we moved as one. Squatting, plunging, rising and lunging—exchanging air. Pivoting in and out. Hard and soft, slow, then darting. Inhale, exhale, repeat.

The series ended and he gestured for me to move aside. "I'll explain this time," he said. "Just watch."

I stepped back to observe.

"The Forty-Second Way," he announced. He progressed through a series of twenty-five movements that mirrored itself in a perfect palindrome. Then he spoke. "The harm is in the imbalance. Inside you, the trigger hormone exists in harmony with every other part of the body. Way Sixty-Three." He began another symmetrical series, speaking as he moved. "Everything seen and unseen is by design," he said, shifting smoothly. "And its design is *exactly* what it does—nothing more, or less. Disrupting that design is not the Way."

I stepped into the square. "Way Nine," I announced. I began an aggressive series of offensive movements and sudden turns. "Not every way is balanced, or even. Some things are just odd." I performed the next position, a closed-fist strike and pivot. "These episodes come in random fits. So maybe the solution is just as chaotic." I ended with a swan kick and let my foot dangle awkwardly, at an asymmetrical angle. "I'm right," I said, moving to stand in front of him.

He shook his head.

I switched tactics. "And what if *I'm* the anomaly," I said. "Have you thought of that? Anatomically, I'm incorrect—three amygdala. In that sense, Kumar's binder will restore the balance."

"But anomalies aren't wrong," he said, leaning in. "They're not imbalanced."

"How can you say that? Three amygdala. Three is *exactly* odd. Two on one side, one on the other. If that's not imbalanced, what is it?"

"It's evidence," he whispered. "Now you know. There are some balances you can't understand." His gaze traveled over my face. "You can't see it. You can't feel it. But, if you let it be, you'll find it's the most beautiful thing."

We were chest to chest, taking and discarding the same air, and I realized, suddenly, I could smell his sweat. He cupped my chin, bent his head, and pressed his mouth to mine.

I let him kiss me, balancing on my toes and pressing my body to his. But, in my heart, I knew it was time to move on. At long length, I turned and covered my mouth, sealing in the moment. I was trembling all over, searching the knoll, struggling to catch a single breath that wasn't composed of *him*. I thought of the Kongo. Fount, Kiwi, William. Slowly, my heart regained a steady beat. "It's time to keep your promise, Hosea," I said. "Will you?"

I could see he didn't want to, but he nodded. "Ask me anything," he said.

I went to my sack and took out the bracelet. He looked at it without blinking. "I know you know what this is," I said. I sat at his feet, expecting him to join me.

Instead, he stepped back and crossed his arms. "What's your question, Cobane?"

I held the bracelet up on a flat palm. "Did Jacamar make it?"

"No," he said.

I hid my surprise. "Then who did?"

His hands clenched. "It was made by my grandmother."

"How?"

"I don't know."

My eyes narrowed."*I don't know*," he said again. "Next question."

I sighed. "The bracelets. I assume you know there are seven in all?"

He said nothing.

I went on. "Is their power scientific? Or, Lee said I could change the Council's mind like—like magic."

Hosea stared, but remained silent, forcing me to press him.

"Are they science or magic?"

"Yes," he said.

"That's not an answer!"

He met my eyes. "Next question."

I moaned and covered my head. I was exhausted. Tired of begging him and fumbling in the dark. I reached up, catching his hand. "Please, Hosea. Please let me in."

He held my gaze a few moments longer, then deflated. "It's both, Cobane," he said. "It's both science and magic. You're going to regret this, but—" He sighed and sat down.

Legs crossed, we faced each other as we had many times in the gazebo. He was, once again, my friend. Devoid of censure, ready to explain, so everything made sense.

"Breath is everything unseen," he began. "And we cling to it for moments at a time. That's how we humans, ideally, connect to truth—to God." He inhaled and exhaled slowly, demonstrating the Way.

I nodded impatiently. He'd explained this before on a dozen occasions. It was why we practiced the Ways. To teach ourselves to move in concert with the ultimate Will.

Hosea went on. "We can't hold even a single breath. But, in our pride, like fools, we longed to," he said. "And so, a great wind came to mankind and whispered the truth."

"The Widow's Portion!" I said, recalling the myth. "'A great wind came and whispered the truth to Africa, in the tongue of God,'" I recited.

Hosea nodded. "The truth was whispered into the heart of Africa," he said. "But then Africa was divided."

"Murdered!" I said, recalling the gruesome story. "Slaughtered and scattered across the nations. But—but that wasn't the end of the story. The truth survived, didn't it?"

"It did, in a way," Hosea said. "According to the Core, when Africa was divided, the truth divided too. Some say it was more than divided; that it broke, so we'll never understand it."

"Obi," I said, imagining the possibility.

He went on, choosing his words carefully. "Others, including myself, are hopeful. We believe that the truth continues to thrive in the scattered pieces of Africa."

I thought back to the myth, trying to recall where the siblings took their portions. "East and west is all it said."

"And that's all we know," Hosea said. "That somewhere on Earth there is a rock that sits, a river that flows, and a vine that grows with the truth. They're called 'Perfections'— breath embodied."

I inhaled, leaning in. "I—"

"Shh. Don't talk. Listen first," he said, cutting me off. He rested an open palm on each knee. "Way Seventy-Seven."

I held my breath, watching the rise and fall of his chest. A minute passed. I closed my eyes and assumed the first position, resting my hands on my knees and closing my eyes—

waiting for the power to start. I looked around in the dark, then deeper, searching my heart. I shook my head.

"Nothing's happening," I said, impatiently. "I don't hear anything. Just explain it."

"I can't explain it, Arika," Hosea said. "If I could, it wouldn't be worth explaining."

I picked up the bracelet and turned it over in my hand. "You say it's breath and body. Magic *and* science. Science *can* be explained. So, explain that!"

His mouth thinned and I knew he didn't want to tell me. But, again, he gave in. "I've told you, humans, by nature, can't hold the breath. But that doesn't stop us from trying. The fountain of youth, the tree of life, the holy grail. We've been trying forever. Some have successfully used one of the three Perfections—the rock, the river and the vine—to make objects for human use. Magical things—like that bracelet. My father has made a scientific study of identifying the mechanics of that process in order to clone perfection. He believes it's the final frontier in physics."

"The science of magic," I said, slowly. "Fascinating."

Hosea's face darkened. "You really don't get it."

I pulled back, not understanding his anger.

"Magic attempts to control what will be, Arika. If Father succeeds in cloning it, anyone with the algorithm will be able to play God." He took my shoulders, looked up at the sky and down at the earth. "And *Gods* don't like that."

A chill quaked down my spine.

He went on, his mouth tight. "More, humans are supposed to breathe in and out." He inhaled and blew a warm breath of air. "We're meant to observe perfection, submit to the

Will. We aren't designed to hold it. So, the better the magic, the more corrosive. It makes good men bad and turns bad men into devils. Devils with the power to bend the laws of the physical world. So, the bracelets you're talking about aren't to be touched, let alone held. Jacamar learned that the hard way."

I frowned. He spoke as if power itself was bad—but that wasn't true. With power, I would do good. I would save the Kongo. "You say Jacamar learned," I said. "But, before, you said Jacamar didn't make the bracelets."

"I said he didn't make *that* bracelet." He pointed to the one in my hand.

Moving quickly, I opened my comm-unit and pulled up the picture of Jacamar with his seven bracelets. "But see, he's wearing it."

Hosea glanced at the picture. "He's wearing the seven Principles. The seven aren't the same as what you've got there."

I looked between the picture and the bracelet in my hand. "I can't make out every detail," I said, "but they look identical."

"And they nearly are," Hosea said. "Grandmother did a good job. But nearly is not enough. When it comes to the truth, there's perfection." He sliced a hand, dividing the air in two. "And everything less than that."

I traced the snake pattern with one finger then I squinted at the picture. "What do the patterns mean?"

"They're the fingerprint of perfection. Those snakes are a distortion of the true print, which means they're less perfect. And so, that bracelet, while formidable, isn't as powerful or as dangerous as the seven."

"You called them Principles."

Hosea nodded. "That's what Jacamar called them. We know he used the seven to bolster the Kongo army in the Last War. And, at least once, he saved Obi from a deadly infection. Their origin is unknown, but my guess is that he got hold of one of the three perfections, and used it to make the seven. So, even they aren't perfect—but, together, they're a very good imitation."

"What did your grandmother use to make this?" I asked, holding up the bracelet.

"I told you, I don't know," Hosea said. "But the snakes indicate a serious departure from the truth. If the whole truth is present, the magical object will imitate the perfection used to make it, so the imprint will resemble one of the three. A rock, a river or—"

I inhaled sharply. "A vine!"

The world around me darkened as space and time collapsed and memories surfaced. When I could see again, I knew exactly why the snake pattern bothered me. It was similar to the etching on the red leather journal I'd gotten from the Schoolhouse supply room in my senior year. The pass I'd used to acquire it had been a gift from Jones, a token for obedience to the Compromise. I'd brought it with me to the Compound and it was, even now, stowed away in the private drawer of my desk.

I envisioned the etched cover of the journal. Spiked vines and berries. More, in the center of the journal was a maroon oval, the shape of an egg and the size of a fingerprint. It begged to be touched and, when I did, it grew warm, then hot. At my request, Covington had put her finger on the oval but she hadn't felt the heat—neither had Walker or Martin. After that, I'd researched the journal's technology in vain. The genius behind it had remained a mystery—until now.

"Cobane, what is it?" Hosea said.

I contemplated telling him about the journal. Something stopped me. "It's nothing." I looked down at my hands, knowing he didn't believe me. I could feel his eyes on the top of my skull, searching my thoughts.

Lee had told me wielding Jacamar's bracelets took skill. But according to Hosea Khan, wielding them also took a toll. Before I retrieved the bracelets, I had to know how to stop their corrosive effect, or else I wouldn't hold them long.

"Hosea," I said, "if the bracelets can't be held, how did Jacamar do it?"

Hosea swallowed. I could see the question in his gaze—*why do you want to know?* I ignored this and begged him, silently, to answer.

"Jacamar was fifty-three years old when he acquired the Principles," Hosea said. "He was fifty-eight when he died."

I gasped, thinking of the withered old man in the photo. Fifty-eight, the same age Obi had been when they died days apart. "So, he died young."

"Young in years," Hosea said. "But destroyed by the Principles."

"Why didn't he take them off?"

"He couldn't. Once they're on, they're yours for life—however short that is. As your life force drains, so will your ability to hold and use them. Jacamar's term lasted five years. He turned the tide of the Last War but, in the end, he realized what power does to a man. So upon his death, he made sure the bracelets were in a place no one can reach them."

I nodded, slowly—but I disagreed. Jacamar had left his bracelets in the tower for the one that *could* reach them. I wouldn't wield them foolishly, to travel through time or, as he had, to save a treacherous man. I'd use them honorably; to free my people and preserve our land.

Hosea touched my knee. I looked up at him and my thoughts stalled. His eyes were gorgeous, brown and gray. And, for once, they were wide open. I saw the tenderness shuttered inside him. I saw friendship, hearth and home. And, of course, I wanted to taste all of it—*everything*—if only for a night.

I stood and backed away, aiming for the opening of the knoll. "Where—where are you going?" he said.

I smiled. "To the gazebo." I turned and passed through the exit. By light of the moon, I wove through the ackee trees, bypassing the square. The east wing doors slid open as I approached. I entered and made my way to the lift. It didn't take long to arrive; everyone was at the market. Inside, I pressed the button for the top level and waited as it ascended.

I stifled the urge to look out of the engineered glass. I wanted Hosea to follow me, badly. But either way, I couldn't turn back.

In the gazebo, I stared out at the forest trees. I heard his footsteps before I saw him. I turned my head to the sound and, slowly, his form took shape.

He was bare from the waist up. Long and broad. His legs and thighs, like scepters. His arms, like bronze. His hair lay in soft ropes around shoulders as straight and strong as a throne. My gaze found the tattoo over his heart, a snake wrapped around a winged staff. It glowed like lava in the moonlight.

I took off the ruby necklace and slipped it into my pocket. Then I fingered the bottom seam of my shirt and pulled it over my head. Hosea inhaled. From him, it was a novel sound, a sign of passion that thrilled me. My shirt fell to the ground.

I tugged at the knotted scarf around my chest and unwrapped it. The last layer clung as I peeled it away. My gaze, suddenly shy, followed the scarf down to the pile it made with my shirt. I sucked in, lengthening my torso to push my leggings off, taking my undershorts with them. I stepped out of the pool they made at my feet.

Hosea stared.

•

Later, his finger caressed my cheek. His chin tucked in as he studied me, with bright eyes. The great breath of his body curved like a nest around mine and a pulse kicked in the base of his throat.

"You're breathing. Your heart's beating," I said.

He grinned.

I stuttered. "I mean, I can see you breathing. It's not— hidden away."

"I understand," he said.

Before I could answer, a crack sounded. We turned together and saw a shadow retreat. Something had been there watching us.

When Hosea sat up to investigate, I threw my arms around his neck. "Don't go," I said.

He reached back with one hand and broke my hold on him.

"No!" I said, but it was too late. He unfolded and stood. Cool air rushed between us. As he squinted, searching the dark for an intruder, I searched for the pulse in his neck. It was gone, back under his control.

He pulled on his clothes and sat, crossing his legs. Unashamed, I sat up and mirrored him, crossing my bare legs so our knees touched.

"Remember the day you volunteered to tutor me?" he said.

I nodded. "You came just weeks before the final exam. If I'm honest, I didn't intend to raise my hand. I sort of hated you." I shrugged one shoulder.

He laughed. "I figured that out quickly. I thought you were weird and smart," he said. "And so beautiful."

I looked down at my hands.

He went on. "Well, after you volunteered, I stopped at your desk. I don't know what I expected. But I stopped and looked down."

"And I looked at Jones," I said, joining him in the memory. "I looked up, over at you and back down at my notes."

It was a blink of an eye. A flutter too fleeting to remember, and yet we did with crystal clarity and laughter. We spoke together in the open-air gazebo, a boy and a girl. A man and a woman. Lovers.

"I think that was the moment I went wrong," Hosea mused.

I winced. "Another mistake?"

He inclined his head and I held my breath, dreading whatever he would say.

"I think, if I hadn't stopped," he said, finally. "If I'd kept to myself as I intended. Maybe then, I wouldn't have fallen so completely in love."

I exhaled. "But you *did* fall?" I said.

He nodded. "And I've fought it every day since."

"But I love you too, surely you know that. I love you so much I—"

He covered my mouth. "And that was my second failing. Not convincing you to fight it too."

I turned my head, freeing my mouth. "Believe me, I tried," I said. "But why do we have to fight it?"

Hosea looked away for a long moment, then back at me. "Because I'm afraid, Arika. I'm not who you think I am."

I let out a huff of laughter, but the dark planes of his face didn't soften. "You—you mean it," I said.

"I do."

My mouth gaped. I pulled in my knees and hugged them close to my chest. "Then who are you?"

He stood and walked to the far edge of the gazebo, resting one shoulder on a concrete pillar. He stared over the bramble bush where the strange trees colluded in the valley. He fell quiet and, for a terrible moment, I thought he wasn't going to explain.

Then, he did. In a rough whisper, he told me the story his grandmother had told him—the same story every night, for five years. In it, the hero killed his mother, followed his father and saved the world.

I stood and turned my back, considering the story as I dressed. It sounded like a myth. Something the workers told themselves to explain what they didn't understand. Finally, I turned to him. "It's a terrible story," I said, flatly. "Why would she tell you that? And, every night!? What does it even mean?"

Hosea rolled his shoulders. "I don't know," he said. "I don't know that I'm *meant* to know. When I was a kid, before I grasped that *I* was the hero, it was just a story. But, over time—"

"Hold on!" I buckled my holster and moved to stand in front of him. "You think it's about you? You—you think it's true?"

Hosea set his jaw. "I do."

I scoffed. "But you didn't kill your mother."

He met my gaze.

"Did—did you?"

"She died in the desert," he said. "They never found her body."

"Then it could have been anything," I said. "Heat, thirst—a gust."

"It's not what in the desert killed her that bothers me, but why she was there in the first place. She should have been home in the Vine tending her garden, practicing medicine. And instead, she was running away, Arika," he covered his face. "She was running away from *him*, because of me."

I bit my tongue, unsure of what to say. I gave him time.

Under cover of his palms, he inhaled and released the breath in a heavy sigh. He dropped his hands and looked up at the stars.

"The lore of the Core is riddled with prophecy," he said. "You know that." He paused and looked down at me, expecting an answer.

"Yes, I know," I said. In the Core, prophecies were pieces of future events. A word, a riddle or rhyme. They were usually given by medicine men or priests. But, in some stories, mules, chickens or vegetation—a sentient fig—had a piece of the puzzle.

Across the universe of Core mythology, prophecies were traded back and forth like commodities on an open market— the goal of each trader being to collect and arrange the pieces into a plausible future event.

I bit my lip and closed my eyes. "Hosea," I whispered. "Are you saying you believe your grandmother was a prophet?"

"More," he said. "I think she knew the future because— because she'd been there."

"A time traveler! Like an Invisible?" I shook my head.

"Something like that." He swallowed. "And by the time I realized it, she was gone."

I held my temples and looked up at the night sky, considering the breath of stories in Core mythology. In the past day, the folktales had sprung from the pages, forcing me to question their substance and my faith.

The bracelets, the perfections and now, a real-life mythical sage. It was all so fantastical. Logically impossible, but if Lee, Kumar and Hosea Khan were right—then it was true? All the myths were true. My thoughts turned to the Kongo.

I looked over at Hosea Khan. "Let's assume she *was* magical. What do you think the last part means. Kill your mother, follow your father…"

"Save the world," Hosea said. He bowed his head. "I told you. I don't know what it means."

"Well surely you've thought about it," I said, incredulous.

He turned aside. "I try not to."

I scoffed. "Hosea Khan Vine!"

"Why should I!?" he snapped. "There are trillions of variables." He bent and picked up a loose stone near the gazebo. "Even something as small as this rock could change everything." He turned, and tossed the stone north, so it landed on the other side of the platform. "My father has spent his life trying to influence fate. But, in truth, we'll never understand what they're doing up there and why. So it's better that I accept it. That's the point of every lesson on prophecy."

He was right. Whenever the hero character encountered a message from the Invisibles, a lesson regarding the foolishness of arrogant assumptions followed, as humans unerringly misinterpreted, and paid a price.

I moved to the rock he'd thrown, picked it up, flipped it over. There was nothing special about it. Still, I was careful to return it to its original spot.

As I stood, brushing my hands, Hosea slammed a fist into the concrete pillar. I jumped.

"I won't be like him, Arika," he whispered.

He was speaking of Kumar. I rushed over to cup the sides of his face. I forced him to look at me. "Of course you won't!" I said.

A muscle ticked beneath his eye. "You don't know that," He whispered. "When I think about what he did to Mother and Lee Ford, I want to kill him. I want to strangle the life from his body. And, I almost do."

I inhaled and turned away, shocked. I recovered quickly. "Well, your father is a difficult man," I said. "There's no fault in—"

"Don't say it."

"It has to be said, Hosea. We all have dark thoughts—"

"No!" he roared, cutting me off. "I'm not going to kill my father!" He bared his teeth and took a step towards me, forcing me back. "Don't you see? Killing my father is just what my father would do!"

I stared. In that moment, he looked exactly like Director Kumar.

"I won't follow him, Arika," he said. "I can't." His chin dropped to his chest, and he turned away from me. "If I give in. Do what I feel, what I want. I could lose control—"

He sealed his mouth, but I saw what he couldn't say. It went back to the story. To sleep at night, he needed to reject his father and, therefore, not be responsible for Weka's death. Or the fate of the world.

I wanted to reassure him, but how could I? I knew about responsibility, the weight of it. The burden of every single life and each terrible death. There was nothing I could say. But only allow him to carry it however he could.

"Way Twenty-Seven," he announced.

I gathered myself and stepped aside, making room. With his arms at his sides, he bent his knees and straightened. He bent again, centering his weight. He held for a moment then bound up and flipped backward, landing on both feet, knees bent, balanced. He bent and flipped again, and again, drawing a straight line across the gazebo.

"A wise man prepares himself to accept the Will and the Way," he whispered.

The anguish radiating from him forced me to his side. I touched his chest and rested my head over his heart. As I listened to its beat, I felt steady and strong. My mind eased and my thoughts turned to the past.

When we were students, he'd had a dozen budding plants on the windowsill of his dorm. He must have planted those seeds of life as soon as he arrived at the Schoolhouse. And in the Cobane village, he'd worked tirelessly, healing as many as possible. And last year, on our way to the oasis, he'd moved like lightning to save a scorpion I intended to kill—the least of creatures, a pest. He collected daily for his medicinal anthology, but he never pulled samples from the limb. He limited himself to fallen foliage, to do the least harm. He never abandoned a patient or used his Helix without just cause. He was dedicated to healing and protecting. Sustaining life on Earth, no matter how insignificant. He was the Kha—the sound the birds make when they call for help.

"I don't know how your mother died," I whispered. "Or what *follow him* means. But you're nothing like Kumar, Hosea Khan. Whatever decision you make will be for the good of the most. That's who you are and who you've always been." I ran my tongue across my mouth, wetting my lips. "So, if you *are* meant to save the world, that's why you were chosen. You just have to trust yourself."

When he didn't respond, I looked up and sighed. He was gone. He stared out, composed. His breath, even. His pulse, at ease. His back, strong and straight. Unbending. He was completely in control.

Or was he?

THE FILTER

In his room, Hosea closed the door and tossed a crystalight. He moved to the trunk at the base of his bed and retrieved a metal box with half a dozen dials. He set the machine on the edge of the bed and gestured for me to sit beside it. I lifted a brow.

"I've been working on it, off and on, for a year," he said. He adjusted dials and the machine made a swooshing noise. It hiccuped, then changed pitch. Hosea reached around me and took a wooden cup from his bedside table. He placed the cup in my hand and positioned it under the machine. It gurgled and burped then a spout popped out. A thick stream of liquid flowed into the cup. "Drink it," he said.

I put the cup to my mouth and took a sip. It was water, cool and refreshing. "Amazing."

He smiled. "Water produced from the moisture present in thin air. I call it an *aerofilter*."

I cupped my hand in the clear stream as it overflowed the cup and spilled onto the floor.

"It's part of why I agreed to come to the Compound. I had to perfect it, just in case," he said.

I glanced at him. "In case of what?"

"In case I couldn't bring myself to leave you behind."

I sat back, letting the water spill. I looked around, noticing details I hadn't seen before. His room was devoid of personal effects.

"You're leaving the Compound," I said.

He took a piece of paper from his shirt pocket and unfolded it, spreading it on my lap. It was the map he'd been working on when Lee and I had spied on him. Now, the altered landscape was even more apparent. Rivers had shifted course and mountains had unfamiliar silhouettes. Some were missing altogether. To the left of the American continent were the boiling seas, but Hosea had added a narrow strip of land, a way through the sea that connected to another mainland. The new continent was labeled *West*.

"Obi, you're leaving the country," I whispered, suddenly understanding.

His silence confirmed my suspicion. He turned off the *aerofilter*, retrieved a cloth from his wardrobe and stooped to mop up the spilled water. He folded the cloth and laid it along the back of his desk chair. He turned to me and lifted his chin to the map, still spread on my thighs.

"I'm leaving after the workout," he said. "I believe there are underground rivers the whole way. But, given the quaking, nothing is concrete. That map is just my current projection." He came to sit beside me and went on. "I didn't mind the risk myself, but I couldn't lead you into the unknown without water."

I stood. "You want to take me from the Kongo?"

"I can't stay, Arika."

"Why? Because of that story? You're afraid of your father!"

He reached for my hand. "Trust me."

"You trust *me*! I will never leave the Kongo."

"There's nothing for you here." His mouth was tight. "You want to grow fake food, play politics?"

"It's more than that! There's freedom at stake. Secession and another war!"

"A war is coming, but not one you're prepared for," he whispered, his eyes darting around the room.

I shivered. His words. His expression, as if we weren't alone. Adrenaline shot through me. "How would you know what I'm prepared for?" A knot tightened in my throat. My fists clenched. "Is there another weapon? Another schematic—what?"

I saw he wanted to speak but held back.

"Hosea, if you know of something that will help the Kongo win, then—"

"I don't know about weapons, Cobane." He shook his head. "And I wouldn't tell you if I did."

I flinched and backed away. I went to the window.

He followed. "You fight, defend, attack. You treat every minute like you're in a corner facing Jones. Another weapon won't help that."

I whipped around, pointing. "Ah! So there *is* a weapon!"

My eyes squinted. His were wide.

He lifted a hand and wrapped it around my finger, hard against his chest. He pressed down.

I glared. "That's not an answer, Hosea! You see? You see how you never answer. You still don't trust me! You don't!"

He stared back and didn't deny it.

I watched him find the fallen map. He folded it and put it back in his pocket. I drifted back to his bed. I'd anticipated our physical joining for months. I'd fantasized, and hoped, believing it would establish a union between us.

"You ask me to leave my country and home to be with you out there." I nodded west. "But I'm not even with you here."

He sat with me and pressed his mouth to the side of my head. My eyes filled with tears and, sobbing, I leaned into his arms.

•

Thirty minutes later, I slipped out of bed and dressed. It was nearly ten p.m.—time to meet Kumar and acquire the cure. I looked around quickly and found the box that contained my Helix in Hosea's wardrobe. I opened the lid and called my weapon home. I was at the door when he called.

"Arika?"

I stopped.

He cleared his throat. "I'll be at the workout tomorrow, as planned."

I understood he wanted to reassure me that nothing had changed between us. I looked back. He sat up in bed, the covers at his waist, his chest bared.

I don't know if he would have said more. I didn't wait. I opened the door and let myself out. I took one step, then another away from Hosea Khan, feeling my heart rip from my chest. I turned the corner and ran, slow at first, then sprinting. As my pace increased, the pain in my heart subsided. Or so I told myself.

THE BINDER

I rapped on the renovated lab door. Lee Ford opened it. His face was blank and white as he looked me over, pausing for a moment on my rumpled hair, then stepped aside. Smoothing my braids, I looked past him into the room.

"Ms. Cobane, you've arrived!" the Director said. He looked giddy, as if tonight solidified our friendship, when I knew I was no more than a pawn he needed to retrieve the bracelets.

I forced myself to step inside. And, when he held out a hand to greet me, I took it and shook, letting his warm palm engulf mine. "Are you certain this will work?" I asked. I turned back to Lee, hoping he would answer.

He closed the door and moved to a station equipped like a private room in the infirmary. He removed a syringe from a cabinet in the station and positioned himself by a medical bed.

"Are you ready, girl?" Kumar demanded.

I tore my gaze from Lee. "You didn't answer my question."

Kumar's smile froze. "Nothing is definite, Ms. Cobane. We'll know more after a simulation. Lee designed a test especially for this occasion." He moved to the bed, brushed Lee aside, and pressed a button to recline the mattress. "Now, come sit," he said.

I tried to catch Lee's eye as I moved to the medical bed and rested back. I cleared my throat, but Lee never looked up. Without warning, I felt a sharp pain in my arm. I gasped and looked down. Lee had jabbed me with the needle. Avoiding my gaze, he drew blood into a small tube. When it was full, he removed the tube and began filling another.

"Easy, General," Kumar said, as Lee switched the tube again. He filled five in total. "That was the hard part. Once the hormone is isolated, we'll have a mold to work from. Binding it will be like fitting a puzzle piece." He smiled.

I nodded, watching Lee take the newly drawn blood to an ice unit. He put four tubes inside the unit: the fifth he took to a small machine.

The Director leaned in intimately. "What you see there is a specialized centrifuge," he said, indicating the machine. "It's already loaded with the blood of the Mute, taken after your last simulation."

I watched Lee load the fifth tube as the Director went on. "In a minute we'll know the difference between the two samples. And, with a few calculations, I'll be able to approximate which hormone enjoys *unusual concentration* in your blood. We'll use that calculation to produce the cure."

•

The whole process took less than an hour. Once Lee had isolated the trigger hormone, he designed a simple compound to target and bind the trigger, limiting its effectiveness in my body.

Once it was ready, he filled a syringe with the binder and squeezed two drops onto a patch that would attach to my skin.

"Lee will put the patch on your neck for rapid transmission," Kumar said.

Lee stopped at my bedside. He shifted my braided hair to reveal my nape. As he wiped a pad of alcohol across my skin, his breath caressed my ear. He held up the medicinal patch, and paused, awaiting his father's instruction.

"Once Lee administers the binder, we'll do the special simulation—to see how effective it is," Kumar said. "Are you ready?"

I eyed the Director. He smiled.

I looked back at Lee Ford, begging him, silently, to soften. Director Kumar had explained the process, but Lee, as usual, had executed the task with remarkable knowhow. I'd spurned his promise to ensure the cure was harmless, but now I wanted his reassurance. "What do you think, Lee? Am I ready?" I said softly.

Finally, he met my gaze. "I don't think you have a choice," he said. He reached around and secured the patch to my skin.

THE WORKOUT

"You heard her. On your feet!" Covington said. She glared around the testing room. The senior students, Martin and Condor, stood as she flipped over a desk. She kicked the desk leg so it cracked, splintering to a point. She yanked it off and held the club out to Jetson. "A weapon in case Jones wakes."

Teacher Jones was prostrate on the floor. She looked peaceful. Except for her eye, and the awkward bend of her leg, she might have been sleeping. Something wasn't right. With a hand on my weapon, I took a step closer to examine her injuries.

Covington rested a hand on my shoulder, stopping me before I got too close. "Arika," she said. "We're ready."

I tore my eyes from Jones. "Let's go."

We moved from the testing room. Everyone sympathetic to the English was in the arena, enjoying the opening ceremony of the Joust. Still, my gut rumbled nervously. I checked each hall before allowing the group to follow.

At the end of the girls' hall, I ran a hand along the wainscoting. I found a crevice the size of my first two fingers and lifted. A door opened in the wall, revealing a landing and staircase.

"This passage leads to the kitchen," I said. "Wait for me at the bottom."

The group filed in. Covington didn't follow the others down. She waited for me just inside the door. Martin was the last to go. "After you, General."

As I joined Covington, something in the rafters caught my eye. I turned to face it and shrank back, horrified. *No! It couldn't be her.* I shook my head and squinted up again. *But it was her!* She swung from her neck, a scarf tangled at her throat.

"Robin!" I whispered.

Covington reached for me. I shook her off, pointing. "Robin! It is! It's Robin!"

"There's nothing there, General!" Covington said. She forced me to look away. When I looked back, Robin was gone.

"She was there! I saw her. Something's wrong."

"Don't worry," Martin said. "The people are waiting. You're to meet Voltaire in the oasis."

I looked sharply at him. I'd only just decided to meet Voltaire myself. "How do you know that?"

Martin fumbled, speechless. I whipped around. Covington looked guilty. I pointed. "You! You're working with Jones?"

She cringed, eyes wide. "Of course not! Jones fell in the testing suite—remember?"

"No," I said. "She's not dead!" And, suddenly, I knew what was wrong. I'd made a grave mistake. "I should never have left her alive," I whispered.

"Arika, no!" Covington said.

I reared backward, knocking down Martin. I leapt over his body, racing back the way we'd come.

I threw open the door to the testing suite. "Alice," I said.

Startled, Jones got to her feet, shouting, "Stay where you are!"

I continued, unafraid. Jones bared her teeth, like a trapped animal. She charged. I stepped aside and hooked the back of her knee, jerking her off balance. She landed on her back.

I squatted over her. "Do you know the stench of death?" I asked.

"Please—" Jones said.

"How it sits in your chest?" I went on. "You run, but it seeps into your mind. Until you can't tell up from down." I put one knee on her chest, gripping the necklace at my throat. I shoved the bauble into her face, and her visage collapsed inward. "I do know the stench," I said, unfazed by the dent in her face. "I won't ever forget it."

Jones whimpered. "Please, General—"

I cut her off. "I should have killed you when I had the chance." A tight thrill rippled along my ribcage. I'd wanted to say that for months. I slid my ruby knife from its sheath at my ankle.

From the arena, I heard shouts.

"That's a real blade!"

"Obi Solomon!"

"Remember, she's disarmed. Cobane!"

I hesitated. That last was Hosea's voice. Before he could interfere, I brought the knife down.

"Arika, no!" Hosea shouted. He appeared beside me. His grip halted the blade an inch from Jones's neck.

I glared at him. "Let go of me!"

"She's disarmed," he said.

The bauble around my neck quivered, itching and burning. The knife sank another inch.

"Look at me," Hosea said.

I closed my eyes, blocking his words. Jones jerked beneath me. She drove a fist into my temple then jumped to her feet and ran.

"Alice!" I shrieked, shaking blood from my head. "She's getting away!"

Hosea held me so I couldn't follow. He said something, but a blast from the arena overshadowed his words. Another blast sounded and Jones cowered, covering her head.

Covington drew her sword. "What's happening?"

Another blast came, louder, closer.

Martin took Covington's hand and they positioned themselves back-to-back, ready to battle whatever came.

A final blast shook the room as the east wall exploded. My Helix emerged from the crash, a spinning sickle.

With a silent command, I sent it to Jones, aiming for her head.

Hosea crossed the room like a zip of lightning. He drew his bow and, in the same motion, shot an arrow that intercepted the arc of my Apex.

"Impossible!" I lunged for my downed knife, scrambling towards Jones. My temple throbbed and lights flashed in my eyes.

"Kha!" Jones shouted, calling for help.

Hosea gripped my ankle and tugged me back. Then he pulled my wrists behind my back. With his other hand, he exposed my nape and removed the medicinal patches stuck there.

He rolled me over. "Arika, breathe," he mouthed silently. His face blurred at the edges. His nose ballooned, covering his mouth. Suddenly, I heard him. "A simulation, Cobane, do you understand? Can you hear me? Look!"

He pushed aside Jones's crisp collar, took the heavy flesh of her neck in a fist and pulled her face off.

I shrank away as Jones unzipped her gray uniform. It fell away, taking her thick arms and legs with it.

A weak-chinned man in britches remained. He stepped from the crumple of Jones's body and kicked it away.

The simulation dissolved as the players gathered around me.

Condor had lost his bulk and the twins' wooden expressions were too identical, like marionettes. East Keep was taller than in the flesh and Jetson, my brother, was alive. The gravity of my mistake exploded in my mind, and there was no taking it back. At my demand, the workout was being broadcast across the Kongo. Above me was a holograph of the Council. Senator Osprey's eyes were wide and bright.

I looked at Lee Ford. His face was beet red. His hands were hidden at the small of his back, but the wings of his forearms, visible at either side of his body, bulged with tension.

Director Kumar leaned on his cane beside the holograph of Osprey. His smile scrubbed the years from his face. He'd changed his official record to reflect the break from his past but, with the crystalights shining like stars in his eyes, I saw a vital part of him would always be an orphaned English boy named Glosser.

The pain in my head exploded and I collapsed.

PART SIX

THE NEW
METROPOLIS

THE COURT TRANSCRIPTS

Character Witness I

Covington:	State your name?
Twin 1:	We're the West Keeps. Of West Keep Boutique.
Twin 2:	You've probably shopped there.
Covington:	No, actually I haven't. How do you know the defendant?
Twin 1:	Well, you must have heard of us. Unless you live under a rock.
Twin 2:	(Snickering)
Covington:	I live in the Compound.
Twin 2:	Is that by the mall?
Covington:	No, it's under a rock.
Twin 1:	Oh, Cov, that's tragic.
Covington:	Ladies, please! How did you meet the defendant and come to know her character?
Twin 1:	Oh, yes. The defendant is innocent, your honors. Jones fell and bumped her head; Arika had nothing to do with it. She would never. She—
Covington:	Slow down, ladies. Tell us first how you're drawing an opinion. Is it from the time you spent with the defendant at the Schoolhouse?

Twins:	Oh, yes.
Covington:	Good. And the Schoolhouse, is that where you met?
Twins:	Yes.
Covington:	And were you there last spring during the final exam?
Twins:	We were.
Covington:	So, you remember it enough to give an account.
Twin 1:	We remember the day quite clearly.
Twin 2:	It was the day we conceived of the West Keep Boutique.
Covington:	*Now,* go ahead and tell us what happened.
Twin 1:	Well, when we woke up that morning—
Covington:	Stop! I'll rephrase. What happened to Teacher Jones during the exam?
Twin 1:	Oh, yes. She fell down and bumped her own head, your honors. Arika had nothing to do with it.
Twin 2:	She would never! Her character wouldn't allow it.
Covington:	Thank you! Nothing more.
Prosecutor:	Objection!
Senator Osprey:	On what grounds?
Prosecutor:	They're lying!
Covington:	And your proof?
Prosecutor:	This is ridiculous.
Osprey:	Sir?
Prosecutor:	Fine. Withdrawn.
Osprey:	Your witness, sir.

Prosecutor:	Ladies, we've heard your account. And we know General Cobane is a friend of yours. But please do consider the moment and weigh the cost of that bond. The fate of the Kongo might very well rest on your testimony. In light of that serious responsibility, do you have anything else to add?
Twin 1:	Yes, sir.
Prosecutor:	Okay—go on!
Twin 2:	We want to add that we *just* opened our third boutique and it's wildly convenient.
Twin 1:	Wildly! A short orbit from the crystal station at the perimeter. Then a quick jog to the top of the Cobane Metropolitan Mall.
Twin 2:	And, thanks to our newest boutique booties, *Level-ups*, you won't even have to sit.
Twin 1:	The heels lock right into the crystalrail. Maximum comfort.
Twin 2:	Supreme comfort—all without unhooking your corset!
Prosecutor:	Is that *all*?
Twin 1:	Yes, that's all.
Twin 2:	Oh, and no try-ons.
Prosecutor:	You're dismissed.

Character Witness II

Covington:	Name?
East Keep:	My married name is Lady Elizabeth Swallow.
Covington:	And the name you went by when you knew the defendant?

East Keep:	She called me East Keep.
Covington:	And how do you know the defendant?
East Keep:	Well, she used to strut around the Schoolhouse like some untouchable ice queen. She thought she was better than everyone. Not anymore. (Snickering.)
Covington:	And were you there last spring on the day of the final exam?
East Keep:	I was there and, before you ask, I remember exactly what happened. It was right after we turned in our final papers. That snob, Arika—
Covington:	Let me remind you, Mrs. Swallow. Not all of us got to turn in our papers. Some of us had our papers stolen and would have died if not for General Cobane's press for freedom. Do you recall that?
East Keep:	I suppose.
Covington:	You suppose?
East Keep:	Fine, fine. Yes, I recall.
Covington:	Good. Now then, go on. What happened that day?
East Keep:	The defendant is innocent, your honors. Jones fell and hit her head; Arika had nothing to do with it. She would never! Her character wouldn't allow it.
Covington:	Thank you. Nothing more. Your witness, sir.
Prosecutor:	You do realize your testimony is word for word what the twins testified, which is, in turn, exactly what Captain and Counsel Covington testified earlier today?

East Keep:	I do.
Prosecutor:	And you have nothing more to add?
East Keep:	I guess not.

THE THIRD WITNESS

A spotlight blared to life in front of me, calling me to consciousness.

"We know you're awake, General," a voice said.

Tentatively, I squinted ahead. Then I slammed my eyes shut. The light was excruciating.

"When we have verbal confirmation of your cooperation, we'll turn off the light," another voice said. It came from the same direction as the first voice and belonged to Senator Osprey.

I cleared my throat. "I'll cooperate."

The spotlight fizzled and my senses rebounded. I blinked, looking around. I was in a warehouse in the west wing of the Compound. The sinkhole staff and courier crew had arranged the expansive room into a temporary courthouse. There was a witness stand and a guardrail separating the audience from the defendants' table, where I sat in an upright chair. Covington sat with me.

I tried to move but restraints dug into my wrists. I looked down to see that my arms and chest were tied to my chair. I craned my neck and saw a detail of the Director's security force stood behind me. Further back, in even rows of benches, every occupant of the Compound—except Hosea Khan— appeared to have gathered to view my trial.

Front and center was a life-sized holograph of the Kongo Council in the permanent courtroom at Cobane.

"Go ahead, Captain," Senator Osprey said, speaking from the chair of the head. Kira Swan wasn't present, but Osprey had a gavel before her. On her head, the raw bone crown of Council came to a point over her pierced nose. Its Corsican horns framed her face with shadows.

"What day is it?" I asked, directing my question at Senator Osprey. "Who's the acting head? Where is Senator Swan?"

"The defendant will remain silent," Osprey said. She lifted her chin at Covington. "Captain, are there any more witnesses?"

Covington stood. "No, Senator," she said. "The defense rests." She took her seat and spoke in my ear. "Don't fret, General. Only a few more minutes now."

"How long have I been out?"

"Twenty-four hours."

"And the trial is over?" I hissed. "I didn't even testify!"

Covington shrugged sympathetically. "Osprey expedited the proceeding, but I've handled everything," she said. "Our witnesses confirmed your account of the incident and their only witness, Jones, refused to appear in person. She claimed you'd harm her."

I scoffed.

Covington went on, warily. "The Council approved the request."

"Kira!" I snarled. I glared at her empty seat.

Covington grabbed my hand. "Keep your voice down," she said. "And it wasn't Kira. Apparently her relative is near death and she's still on leave. Honestly, it's been a boon. Without her, the prosecution was dismal. Jones wrote her testimony in lieu of appearing and the prosecutor let the court reporter read it for the record."

She nodded to the holograph of an older Kongo man in robes. In Swan's absence, he'd been appointed to prove I was guilty. I opened my mouth to ask a question.

Covington hushed me. "More on that later," she said. "Osprey wants you awake for the verdict. So just stay quiet and I think all will go well. Okay?"

I squeezed her hand and nodded as the prosecutor stood. "Permission to add a witness," he said.

Covington clutched my leg under the table. "A surprise witness. This is bad," she murmured.

Her tension made my heart throb as Osprey paused the projection. The Council holograph froze in place. But I knew in the court in Cobane, the members were huddled together to discuss the prosecutor's request.

After a moment, Senator Osprey jerked to life. "Motion granted," she said. "Sir, you may call the witness."

Covington cursed. Her hand slipped into mine as we waited for the surprise witness to appear.

"The state calls Ms. Dovie Hannibal," the prosecutor said, triumphant.

Covington groaned. The Council members shifted, their brows lifted. Behind us the crowd muttered, then roared as Hannibal appeared in holograph. Her dark garments hung lifelessly as she limped slowly to the witness stand.

"What's she going to say?" I asked Covington, struggling to speak over the noise of the crowd.

"I don't know," Covington said.

Senator Osprey got to her feet. "Order!" She banged her gavel. "Order!"

As the room quieted, the prosecutor approached Hannibal. "Name," he said, his tone formal but gentle.

"Dovie Hannibal," Hannibal said, lifting her chin. She looked like a widow determined to avenge herself.

"How do you know the defendant?"

"We went to school together for ten years."

"And were you there last spring? On the day of the final exam?"

"Yes. It was the day after my release from the Pit. I was to take the final exam and then return to the school nurse. She was treating my legs."

"Given your injuries, do you remember the day enough to give an account?"

"I remember," Hannibal whispered.

I couldn't tell if her voice seethed with anger or pain. Either way, she hated me.

"You have the floor," the prosecutor said. He stepped aside, looking confident.

"I remember the injury most," Hannibal said. "I was in pain. My legs were twisted beneath me in the Pit and my circulation failed. The feeling eventually came back to my limbs, but I lost the toes of my right foot. And on the day of the exam, I was only partly recovered from the surgery. I couldn't get out of bed. It was Jetson who came to help me." A long tear rolled down her cheek and under her chin. "He carried me to the testing suite. Arika was there and, at first, we were all angry at her."

"Why were you angry?" the Prosecutor asked.

"Because she was the reason I was in the Pit," Hannibal said, clearly.

"So, she betrayed you?"

"She was trying to help."

"She told Teacher Jones that you were stealing newspapers to fuel the rebellion. Is that right?"

"Yes."

"And that is the reason you were in the Pit. The reason you'll walk with a limp for the rest of your life."

"Yes."

"Go on."

Hannibal took a breath. "Jetson was the one who convinced us to set aside our anger. He explained what he knew about Arika and why, eventually, she would lead us to freedom, if we stood with her."

"And what was the secret he knew about General Cobane?" the prosecutor asked, smoothly.

"It's no secret," Hannibal said. "While we all studied the Compromise, Jetson studied Arika. So, he merely saw the truth before the rest of us. He knew Arika loved the Kongo and he believed her love would save us."

My head bowed beneath the tide of grief that peaked inside me. I lifted my chin, and caught my breath. Tears poured down Hannibal's cheeks.

The prosecutor handed her a handkerchief. "Ms. Hannibal, why are you wearing black?" he asked.

Hannibal hiccupped. "I'm in mourning," she managed.

"To clarify, you're mourning the death of Jetson."

"He was my friend."

"But you wanted more."

Hannibal hesitated. "He was my friend," she said again.

The prosecutor took an aggressive stance. "Your friend who was hung by the neck?"

"Yes."

"And Arika, the one he loved, killed him."

Covington turned to confront the Prosecutor. "Objection!"

"She sent him to his death."

"Objection!"

"She ordered him to steal from a Kongo official and left him to bear the consequences alone."

"Objection," Covington declared again. "Captain Jetson repeatedly denied the General's involvement in his plot. She's been cleared of those charges."

The Council paused to deliberate. When they returned, Senator Osprey's eyes were triumphant. "If Hannibal has an opinion, the Council would like to hear it. Overruled."

I slumped.

"Do you think Jetson was following orders?" the prosecutor asked.

"I believe Jetson always followed his heart," Hannibal said.

"Why are you crying, Dovie?"

"Because you're right about one thing," Hannibal said. "I loved him. And he loved her. And I hate her for that."

The room erupted.

"Order, order!" Osprey shouted. The gold tassels on the horns of her headdress sparkled as she whipped her head from side to side. Slowly the room settled down.

"I have one more question, Council," the prosecutor said. He took his time moving to the center of the room. He struck a dramatic pose and pointed to Hannibal. "Now, Ms. Dovie

Hannibal, in light of your expert knowledge of the defendant and your eyewitness perspective, tell us what happened to Teacher Jones on the day of the final exam."

For the first time, Hannibal looked directly at me. "The defendant is innocent, your honors," she said. "Jones fell and bumped her head; Arika had nothing to do with it. She would never. Her character wouldn't allow it."

The room burst with shouts. Covington collapsed forward with relief. Hannibal stood and moved as though to leave.

The prosecutor cursed. "No! Dammit. Wait, where are you going? I'm not finished with you."

Osprey rapped her gavel. "Order, order! Hannibal, please return to the witness stand."

But Hannibal was gone.

•

Ten minutes later, a sharp bell tolled in the courtroom. We all stopped and looked up. The Council had adopted the Assembly's emergency broadcast system, which worked like a comm-unit: translating radio signals into interactive holographs.

I craned my neck, imagining Kongo people across the territory and the English at Hasting, doing the same. When the bell stopped, a forty-foot, three-dimensional live holograph of Senator Osprey soared to the top of the warehouse. She cleared her throat and began reading the verdict.

I heard only one line. *Guilty*, she said. *Guilty as charged.*

THE VERDICT

Later, I learned the Council deliberated for six minutes before convicting me, not of maiming Jones, but of conduct unbecoming to an officer. To that charge, my service in the military, my time on the Council, the testimonies in my defense didn't matter. According to the sentencing notes, I'd *shown my true colors* in the simulation.

Tomorrow, after my replacement was elected, I was free to return to the Kongo. I could work, travel and marry. Anything except hold public office. From that, I was barred for life.

When the holograph disappeared, the residents filed slowly from the rows of benches. They formed a line and took turns praising my victory.

Congratulations, General.

Your life is spared.

I never doubted.

Magnificent defense.

I sat at the defense table, untied and free to go, as the room emptied.

When Covington sat with me, I looked over at her. "Why is everyone carrying luggage?" I said, gesturing to the last person exiting. Like many of the spectators, he was dressed for a journey. He had a pack on his shoulders and a long bag in each hand.

"They're returning to the Kongo," Covington said. "The Council announced they were expanding the arena, building a road north, and improving communication infrastructure around the territory. They're offering parcels of the land around Cobane in payment to anyone willing to do the work."

I stood and moved to the window overlooking the courtyard. Not everyone had waited for the verdict. There was already a line of people boarding one of Kumar's programmed exit vehicles.

"Expanding the arena," I said.

Covington came to rest a hand on my shoulder. "For an inter-territorial conference," she whispered. "They're preparing for a signing ceremony. To ratify the Accord."

"And surrender arms," I said. I pressed a fist into my stomach and turned from the window. I wove around the benches to the door and left the warehouse, vaguely aware that Covington had followed.

We met Martin in the Courtyard. He started to speak, but his words seemed to me like gibberish.

"Not now, Martin," I said.

He gave me a strange look and huddled with Covington. I kept walking, leaving their whispers behind.

In my room, I sat at my desk. On top of the mess scattered across it was my Apex and a tin pillbox. I opened the tin. Inside were stacks of medicinal patches identical to the one I wore on my neck. I'd placed it the morning of the workout, carefully cleaning the swath of skin with alcohol beforehand. The patch had done its work: I had not fainted in my attempt to kill Jones. I closed the tin and picked up my Apex.

I'd been as surprised as anyone when the wall of the room exploded during the workout. My will had formed the weapon into a sickle from a thousand yards through solid rock—a feat I'd thought was impossible. But, without the Mute, the Berserker inside me had wound to ever increasing heights and my Apex, energized by emotion, had responded in force.

There was a knock and Covington entered with a tray of food. I ate mechanically, just enough to silence the growl in my stomach.

When I set my fork down, Covington sighed. "Come on, Arika. You said you wanted to return to the Kongo, and you achieved that."

"Pyrrhic," I said. I pushed the tray away. "I'm no longer their general."

"But you're free! Another milestone." She pulled up a chair and sat with me. "If you look at that. Just that part. Are you not glad?"

I stood, hitting the chair with the back of my knees. It skidded across the floor and tipped over. I moved to the window overlooking the courtyard. The line to leave the Compound was backed up. The prospect of land combined with the desire to vote on the next Council member, my replacement, had created a surge.

"Remember the charge over River Run?" I said, softly.

"You killed three dozen men. It was a pivotal victory," Covington said.

I looked back at her. "They carried me from the field with honor."

I turned aside and scratched at my throat. "Glad," I said, tasting the word. "Glad to live in a land I'll have no hand in shaping? To forsake the promise of the Kongo of which I've dreamed. For which I've lost my mother, my father and brother. Glad?" I wrapped the ruby necklace around my hand. "Nothing could be further from the truth. No,

Captain. This land I've spilled my blood to enrich is mine. And I will not *gladly* relinquish it."

Covington's head hung. "I hoped you'd feel differently. But I'm not surprised." She stood. "There's something I have to tell you."

She paused for so long, I turned to look at her. Her expression was tight with fear.

"Martin asked me not to tell you, but—"

I squinted. "What is it?"

She took a radio from her sack and settled it on my desktop.

"This was broadcast live two days ago," she said. "It's from the audio patrols we have on Kira Swan."

She connected it to her comm-unit. I moved toward her.

"Martin got behind on account of the market," she explained. "But he caught up yesterday."

"Just turn it up," I said.

She fumbled with the volume on her comm-unit, and a voice projected.

"My name is Alice Jones," it said.

My heart stalled. "Stop the recording!"

Covington obeyed.

My skin rippled as an echo of Jones's barking tone returned to me. My eyes skipped back and forth, needing to be sure before I said anything. "That's not Jones," I said, with certainty. "It's similar but, believe me, I know Jones's voice. Whose voice is that?"

Covington started the recording again.

"I've served my country faithfully for thirty years, first as a Teacher and then as Headmistress of the Schoolhouse at the Cobane Plantation. In my time in the southern territory, I discharged my duties with the utmost integrity and the testimony I give today, by proxy, is an accurate account of the happenings directly preceding the violence notoriously referred to as the Kongo Rebellion."

"That's Kira Swan's voice," I said. It was not the same as Jones's memorable bark, but still deep and gruff—like a growl.

"She's reading the testimony Jones gave, by proxy, at your trial."

"The trial was yesterday. One day. How did Kira read the testimony before Jones gave it?"

"Martin thinks she got hold of it early to prepare the prosecution," Covington said.

I inhaled. "She cheated!"

"She did," Covington said. "But I don't think exposing this will change the verdict. Every eyewitness confirmed your account, and you were still demoted."

I chewed the inside of my cheek. She was right. The game was political. I couldn't expect fair play. Going directly to the Council was the wrong move.

"Keep listening," Covington said. She played the audio and Kira read slowly, lingering over every word. Jones cataloged my anger. She spoke for a whole minute about how I'd kicked her knee and where and how I'd done it again and again.

"It was one kick!" I protested.

Covington hushed me.

Kira went on, articulating Jones's version of events. Towards the end, Kira's voice thickened with emotion. "I was never one to catch the eye, to be sure—that was my sister's charm. Still, I like to think I had a little piece of beauty before the Berserker attacked me. When I look at myself now, with one eye—crippled and half blind after that girl's brutality—I know I am grotesque." Kira sniffed, seeming to shed a tear for Jones's plight.

"Oh please," I huffed. "Jones was born grotesque from the inside out. She—"

"Listen!" Covington threw a hand over my mouth. But whatever Kira said next was drowned by the sound of horses, a shout and a squeal that sent the patrols groaning.

"I missed it," I said.

Covington shook her head. "You didn't."

"All I heard was a horse and a squeal," I said.

"Yes, a horse. Think about it," Covington said. "Kira Swan is a Councilwoman. She has a multi-passenger hovercraft on reserve. Why is she taking a horse and cart when she could travel to her destination in half the time?"

I tilted my head. Some Kongos were still highly suspicious of technology. Along with the new seed, they eschewed solar-powered advancements, preferring instead to live life the old way. Kira Swan, however, was not an old-timer.

"Vehicles require registration," I said, recalling my escape from the basement of the library. "So, they can be traced. She wanted to hide where she was going!"

"That's what I thought," Covington said. "And it could be innocent. She's a public figure trying to live a private part of her life. But then there's that squeal." She replayed that portion of the audio. "It took me a dozen listens to realize it wasn't a horse. That was the sound of a hundred ropes tightening, unwinding from a giant spool."

She looked at me pointedly. "A giant spool that's turning to lower a drawbridge so Kira Swan can travel over the moat."

I gasped. "Hasting! The only moat in the Kongo is the one the diplomats dug at Hasting. Kira Swan isn't visiting a sick relative. She's at Hasting leaking information to the English."

Covington nodded. "You were right," she said. "You were right about her all along."

My heart pounded. "Is she still there, at Hasting?"

"We think so."

I moved to my bed, knelt and pulled out my large pack.

Covington watched me warily. "Are you going to the Council?"

I stood and began filling my pack with personal items. "No," I said. "You said it yourself, every witness confirmed my account, and I still lost. Even with Kira gone, every ruling comes out against me. Allowing a surprise witness, a unanimous vote to indict me—the Council is compromised."

"So, you're going to Hasting."

I could tell from her expression that she already knew my answer. "She has allies on the Council. Or spies," I said. "If I catch her in the act, I can bypass the Council and appeal to the people directly."

"And if they believe you over their elected government, then what? Another coup?" Covington sat and covered her face. "This is what Martin was afraid of. A civil war will only weaken us, and we can't afford to be weak—not at this juncture."

"What are you saying?"

She looked up. "I think we should report Kira to the Council today and hope for the best."

"And Martin agrees?" They were two of my highest ranking, most loyal soldiers. Their resistance signaled a shift in the ranks. "I've lost his trust entirely, haven't I?" I whispered, sitting beside her.

Covington swallowed. "He's been different since he saw the triple point in action," she said. "He thinks the English have the advantage. Once they've stockpiled the swords, they'll

233

fight for everything—then we won't even have the Accord."
She waited, letting that sink in. "So, he thinks we should
bury the news about Kira, and support the Council as is."

"As is!?" I shouted. "As is!" I stood. "The Council is
compromised!"

"Lower your voice!" She was on her feet too. In my face.
"The Kongo is in pieces, including the militia. The election
to replace you has all but destroyed us. We can't take another
split, another betrayal, another faction. And if we can't hold
it together, we'll be back under the English thumb in weeks,
fighting a war that you and I both know we can't win! So
yes, Arika, now is the time to *compromise*." She moved to the
window and looked out, composing herself.

I wanted to reassure her, but everything she'd said was
true. I scratched my neck. The plan had been to secure the
bracelets after the trial. As a Councilwoman, I would have
had access to a team of researchers and the Kongo militia
to shield me from Kumar as I learned to use them. Now,
there wasn't time. I needed someone who knew the bracelets
inside and out, who had studied them for years, to teach me.
I opened my palm and sent a message.

"What are you planning?" Covington said. I looked up to
see her searching eyes on me.

I hadn't told her about the bracelet and, for now, it was
too much to explain. I paced, considering what to say. "I
found a weapon," I said eventually. "I think, with it, I can
unite the Kongo."

"You're going to expose the Council." She looked afraid.

"No, you and Martin are right about that," I said. "No
more infighting. And I can't expose it; Kira's proven to be

too good. She's infiltrated the Council, and it's no longer a reflection of the people."

"So—?"

"So, I'm going to disband it entirely."

Covington's eyes went wide. I held up a hand before she could speak. "If you want to help, pack a bag. We leave within the hour."

THE CAKE

As Covington left, I sent another urgent message to Lee. When he didn't respond, I closed my palm and cursed softly. I would have to find him and plead—or bargain—in person.

I continued to prepare for travel. I bathed in cold water and filled my pack with as much as I could carry. At last, I went to my desk, opened the bottom left drawer and removed the leather journal.

After the war, Walker and Hurley closed the camp they'd established for those too young to join the militia. They'd found me and relayed William's last request: that they pass on the stories he'd told around the fire in the oasis. Since then, the pair had followed me like mother hens, all the way from Cobane and into the sinkhole. When they'd first come to the Compound, I'd carried the journal with me everywhere. And I knew they assumed I'd recorded William's adventures in it. In truth, the journal remained empty.

Checking the time, I pulled out the desk chair and sat with the journal in my lap. Looking now, with my knowledge of the Core, I saw the design indicated it was very close to a perfection. Still, I couldn't bring myself to press my finger to the egg shape in its center—not tonight. I retrieved a small waterproof bag and tucked the journal inside, then I pushed the whole thing down towards the base of my pack for safe keeping. I removed the invisibility bracelet from the secret compartment and slipped it on my arm. I activated the bracelet and left my room, my pack on my back.

•

When I reached the Mess Hall, I stood and waited by the swinging door to the kitchen. A maid with a load of dishes bumped the door open with her hip and I slipped in behind her.

In the pantry, I filled my sack with food for three days for two people. After, I moved to the kitchen door and waited for it to open again. Moments later, Martin's slender physique burst through. Walker followed after him. They turned my way and I lunged back, narrowly avoiding a collision.

"She'll come. She's got to," Martin said, speaking to Walker. "She agreed to meet me for supper."

Walker took a sheet cake from a cooling rack. "Hope so," he said. "This cake won't last another refusal, and I used real flour." He set the cake down and picked up a large kitchen knife. "Question is, is Hurley ready? You know how he snores off."

"I'll check!" Martin said. He moved back to the door and stuck his head out. "Hurley!"

Hurley appeared a minute later, wiping his nose with a handkerchief. "Music's cued up, ready for the big surprise," he said.

"Good," Martin said. He rubbed his palms together and rolled his shoulders.

"One question," Hurley said, looking sheepish.

"What do we play if she says no again?"

Martin froze. Walker shook the large kitchen knife in Hurley's direction. "Of all the idiotic—boy, get outta here!"

Hurley sneezed and hurried away.

As the door closed behind him, Martin looked sick. Walker moved over to squeeze his shoulder. "The General's trial is over. Covington is free and she loves you. You got nothing to worry about."

I went to the counter as Walker returned to work, adding final touches. I leaned over his shoulder to read the message on the cake knowing, in my heart, what I would find.

Walker's neat lettering confirmed it. *Will you marry me?*

THE CUFF

I left the kitchen with the invisibility bracelet still activated. As I approached Covington's room, her door opened and she bent forward, peering into the hall. She looked left, then right and closed the door. I pressed my ear to the wood as her footsteps retreated. She crossed the room, paused, and crossed back. She was not on her way to the Mess Hall to accept Martin's proposal, as he hoped. Instead, she awaited my instructions.

Through the door, I heard her gasp. Her feet rushed closer and, before I could back away, she was in the opening again. Her face was an inch from mine as she listened for my approach.

Up close, I saw she was tired. A dark line creased the skin between her eyes. Her bottom lip was raw where she'd bitten it and her once bushy hair was limp and dull. I'd carried the Kongo and she, my comrade, had carried me.

After a minute, she stepped back and closed the door again.

I continued down the hall without knocking. I took a dripping side tunnel to my own room and locked the door behind me. I deactivated the invisibility bracelet and pulled up my comm-unit. I perched on the edge of my bed and typed quickly, so I wouldn't lose courage.

I changed my mind, Captain. I don't want your help.

She wrote immediately. *What? Why?*

I considered the response Covington needed as she continued to write.

Where are you?

You don't seem well.

You shouldn't be alone.

If she thought I was in danger, she would never give up. I typed: *I'm fine. I just don't need your help.*

She replied: *My bag is packed. Tell me where you are.*

I bit my lip and sent my last message to Covington. *I'm in the kitchen.* Blinking back tears, I turned off my comm-unit.

Martin loved her, and she loved him—desperately. If she went to the kitchen, he would convince her to stay. I looked down at my palms and consoled myself, picturing Covington's unborn baby. Its tiny heart. Its future. I took a shaky breath. I had to ensure that future was more free than our past.

"Interesting conversation," Lee Ford said.

I leapt to my feet, wiping my wet face. "Lee!"

He pointed at my comm-unit. He'd been reading over my shoulder. "I presume you see her future is with Martin."

"How did you get in here?" I demanded.

"Same way you did. But, tell me, why push Covington away?" He moved around my bed to confront me.

Keeping space between us, I went to the door and confirmed that it was locked. "You have a key!" I accused.

"Kumar does, I don't. But then I didn't need one; you let me in. Now, *General*, stop changing the subject. Why the sudden distance towards the Captain? Why not release her months ago when Martin first proposed?"

I considered his explanation: I would have noticed him enter behind me.

Before I could speak, he went on, his head tilted thoughtfully. "Is it possible? Did you *not know* she's refused twice now?" I deflated onto the bed, covering my face. "*Poor* General," Lee said, his tone mocking my disappointment. "And now that you know, your tender heart is exposed. And here, I thought you were a survivor."

I felt his weight beside me on the bed. I pressed my eyes and dropped my hands to my lap. I looked over at him. Despite his tone I could see his sympathy was, for once, sincere.

"Did you get my messages?" I asked.

He tapped a finger to his mouth, telling me to be quiet. Then, leaning forward, he took a curved sliver of mirror from a side pocket of his pack and angled it around. He removed his jacket, went to the door, knelt, and wedged the jacket in the space between the base of the door and the floor, sealing it closed. Using the same sliver of mirror, he checked again for patrols.

I frowned. "Kumar has charge of all the patrols. You think your father is spying on you?"

"Not me—you," Lee said, his eyes on the reflection. "Now, take off your comm-unit."

"What for?"

"Do you want my help or not?" He slipped the mirror into his back pocket and came to stand in front of me. I handed him my unit.

"I'm turning off the signal," he said. "You won't get calls or messages, but Kumar's patrols won't be able to track us."

Track us? My eyes shifted from the barricaded door to his dress. He wore a grey shirt and English-style hiking boots laced over his ankles. On his back, a large pack was secured over his shoulders. "You're leaving and Kumar doesn't know." Lee nodded once. "What about the firewall?"

"There's another way out," Lee said. "And the English woman knows the way."

"I knew it." I stood up. "He tried to kill her that night she escaped."

"He panicked," Lee said. "He thinks she remembers how she got here, and I'm betting he's right. Which is why I didn't perform the wipe."

My eyes widened. "You didn't perform the wipe?"

"Once I realized her value, I couldn't. I gave her a sleeping draught instead and I've compiled all the Compound blueprints. I'll wake her and we'll leave tonight. Between the blueprints and her guidance, we should make it through the tunnels by morning."

"What if there's a quake?" I said. "The tunnels could collapse."

Lee set his jaw. He was going to risk it.

"You're mad!" I said. "Programmed crafts leave every day. Why risk an alternate route when Kumar isn't keeping anyone against their will?"

"He'll let me *leave*," Lee said. "But, if I want to come back, I need a route that doesn't require his permission."

I inhaled, seeing clearly. "You're planning a coup."

Lee turned and paced in front of my bed. "I came here when I was thirteen," he said. "This Compound is my life's work. My work, my mind."

"Your empire," I whispered.

Lee's eyes glowed red. He folded up the sleeve of his shirt. "You said you wanted to know when I was more than close." He rolled the material past his elbow. "I'm more than close. I've done it." He pushed up the remaining fabric to reveal the invisibility bracelet on his bicep.

I gasped. I touched my arm to ensure my own bracelet was still in place. "That's how you followed me in. You replicated the bracelet." I leaned in to examine the pattern of Lee's bracelet, knowing it would tell me about its origin.

The design was identical to the bracelet I wore, except for the snakes. On Lee's bracelet, their bodies were poorly formed, like squiggled lines with dots in place of circles for eyes. More, the shape of his band was uneven. Wider than mine on his outer arm and very narrow on the inner, like a cuff.

I pulled my eyes from it and met Lee's gaze.

"Not perfect, but only because I used an inferior template," he said. "I know the process. And Jacamar's bracelets will provide a better template—seven of them."

I frowned. "So, you want the bracelets for yourself."

"To study," he said, quickly. "Not to wear."

"But why, when you know how to wield them?"

"That doesn't make wearing them safe. Once you put them on, you can't take them off. And they will bleed you in time, like leeches."

"Well, time is all *I* need," I said. "Jacamar had five years."

"And in exchange he gave his life."

I thought of the Kongo, the triple-point sword, and the English. "I don't see that I have a choice," I said, firmly. I want the Principles. But if I go to Hasting in one of Kumar's crafts, he'll take them from me."

"I can escort you to the tower, outside of his control."

"And will you teach me to wield them?" I pressed.

He hesitated, searching my face. "I can only teach you what I know. But if, when we get there, you still want to wear them—then, yes."

THE McCORMICK

Once Hosea had left, Kumar had directed the white woman be quarantined to ensure the wipe he'd ordered was effective. Her unconscious body had been wheeled to a stuffy room in the west wing and she hadn't been bathed since. With her wrists bound and the lines of her face distorted by a gag, she was as helpless as she appeared.

She was ghostly white, except for her red hair, which was piled under her head, like a pillow. Its mound was the only soft-looking thing in the bed she slept in. Even the covers, pulled to her chin, seemed hard and heavy. She faded beneath them to such a degree that, at first, I didn't see her. It wasn't until Lee brushed past me to gaze down at the white bed with the scarlet pillow that I realized a human lay there. I blinked, looked again, and she took shape.

Lee gently lifted her arm and removed a medicinal patch from a shaved spot of skin in her armpit. "Sleeping serum," he explained, holding up the patch. It was the same material he'd used to staunch the flow after drawing my blood. Matted and clear and, like the white woman, invisible if you weren't looking for it.

He tossed the patch in the trash, and then took a tin from his pack and withdrew a bandage, some tape and a vial of medication. He set these on the bedside table, which was already lined with bottles of nutrition pills, left over from Hosea's careful attention. They had traveled with her from the infirmary and sat, collecting dust. Working quickly, Lee prepared another medicinal patch and attached it to the woman's upper arm. "This will wake her," he said.

Twenty minutes later, he checked the patch, pressing with two fingers to ensure its seal.

"What's wrong?" I asked.

"Unclear," he murmured.

I paced to the door, listening for sounds in the hall. We were in the same corridor as the Director's suite of rooms. He was possibly just a few dozen yards away.

"Relax," Lee said, still hovering over the bed. "He's trusted me for thirteen years."

"You've obeyed him for just as long," I said. "And look at you."

Lee straightened and peered around the room as if seeing it for the first time. He picked up the trash bin and set it on the edge of the bed to search inside. His hand reappeared with the medicinal patch he'd discarded. He tossed a crystalight and examined the patch more closely. He sniffed it, then he aimed the light at the woman and bent close, studying the skin where the patch had been attached.

"Lee?" I said.

He hushed me and continued his examination, pushing back the bed covers, checking behind her knees and along the soles of her feet. The skin between her first two toes.

He adjusted her clothes to check more covered areas, stopping short of examining private parts. He moved to her ears and massaged her scalp. When he lifted her hair, he stiffened. There were two patches attached to the back of her neck.

The first, he set carefully on the nightstand. "That's sleep serum," he said. He peeled off the second patch and cursed.

I leaned in to see a white powder still visible on her skin.

He touched the powder and brought it to his lips. He spit immediately.

"What is it?" I asked.

"A chemical we engineered a few years ago," he said. With a jerky motion, he used a bedsheet to wipe off the powder. "Father must have placed it."

"Is it harmful?" I asked.

"Yes, when ingested." He brushed past me and rummaged through the nightstand for a small medical machine. He used it to scan the woman's vitals. "It's usually in pill form. He must have ground a pill onto the patch." He continued scanning. Then the machine beeped and he studied the results.

His shoulders relaxed. "I don't think much entered her system. It wasn't designed to penetrate the skin."

"So, she'll wake?" I glanced outside. The sun was nearly set.

"She'll be up soon." Lee took a presoaked alcohol pad from his tin and wiped her nape. When he pressed another cooling pad to her temples, she stirred.

She moved her legs, shrugged her shoulders, and then opened her eyes. They immediately found mine. She blinked, looked at Lee, then at me again, staring solemnly.

Unnerved, I unsheathed my Apex. "Do you know where you are?" I said.

She nodded.

"Do you remember the way out?" Lee asked.

Slowly, she nodded.

"Good," I said. "We'll free you, if you'll show us."

She sat up, showing more energy. She held out her tied wrists. I looked at Lee Ford.

"Do it," he said.

I resheathed my Apex, and then moved forward and cut through her bind with my ruby knife. She rubbed her wrists and flexed her fingers, eyeing me steadily. I remembered the glimmer of recognition I'd seen the day she'd tried to escape and the small cross she'd worn. It was still there, clinging to her neck, signifying her religion.

"Can you stand?" Lee said.

Two days had passed since her flight from the infirmary and she shifted stiffly to the edge of the bed. Lee Ford took her arm and helped her up.

Her dark blue dress hung and pooled at her feet. The laceration marks on her face and neck disappeared into the round collar of the dress then continued, seeping out of her sleeves to mar her thin hands and red knuckles.

When Lee Ford released her, she swayed then steadied herself with a hand on the bed post. She took a few breaths, then released the post and straightened to catch my eye again. She thrust out her chin and made a chirping noise, asking if she could remove her gag.

I hesitated, searching her solemn face. Then I untied the *bambi* thong that held her gag in place. "I'll tie you again if you scream," I said.

She leaned forward to clear her mouth. "No need, General, I'll take you wherever you want to go."

I drew back. "So, you *do* know who I am?"

"Of course, General, you're the Berserker," she said. She straightened her narrow shoulders. "I am The McCormick."

"*The* McCormick?" Lee asked, his eyes narrowed.

She nodded, her chin tilted proudly. "The leader of the Sisters to the North." She turned to me. "We are your white allies in the Great Rebellion. We salute you!" With a thin arm, she performed the first half of the worker's salute. Touching her hand to her heart and holding her fist out at an angle.

I batted her fist away and glared at her sallow face. "I don't care who you are. You're English, you've no right to that salute."

She closed her mouth, bobbing her head. "Yes, General."

I squinted at her tangled hair. "And don't call me General. Guide us to the Compound exit and we'll go our separate ways."

"Yes." She kept her head bowed so low that knotted chunks of her hair hung forward, obscuring her face. In an English woman, her meekness rang false, which annoyed me.

"We need to take these with us," Lee said, indicating the dozen pill bottles on her nightstand.

"Why?" I said. The pills were available all over the Kongo.

"She's weak. She'll need extra strength for the journey."

I realized he was thinking about the white poison. He'd said nothing was ingested but I could see now he doubted his assessment.

The English woman ducked her head, silently thanking Lee for his kindness. She smiled sweetly my way, and bobbed her head again, showing gratitude.

I took a step back. "You'll have to carry them yourself," I said, gruffly.

She nodded humbly, then she bent and scooped up the bottom of her dress. She turned her back and lifted the hem to her teeth. She bit until a small piece frayed then she ripped, coming away with a length of fabric. She made some knots and ripped more, forming a sling bag. At her nightstand, she swiped a hand so the nutrient pills and vials of medication fell into her sling. She wrapped the bag over her shoulder, so it sat crosswise along her body.

She glanced at me then moved to the engineered window and pointed. "The exit is that way," she said.

We came to stand beside her. She was pointing at the cistern.

THE CISTERN

Lee explained the plan to us as he took the cuff from his arm. When he described its purpose, the English woman's mouth dropped. She looked afraid and glanced between us, then finally, she nodded—letting him slip the cuff onto her right arm. Lee took a length of rope from his pack and tied her left wrist to mine. Glaring at the connection, I moved my ruby dagger from my ankle to my hip in case I needed to reach for it.

With the cuff and bracelet activated, the English woman and I disappeared. Lee, in a hood, was a shadow before us. We followed him out into the dark evening and traveled around the top level of the Compound. The silence was punctuated by the woman's wheezing breaths. They whined in my ear, despite our slow pace.

When we passed the place where she'd fallen over the railing, her breath caught, and she stumbled. I steadied her, my mind filling with thoughts of Hosea Khan—who'd rescued her before.

Lee stopped behind the railing directly in front of the cistern. He turned in a complete circle, looked up and down, then knelt to press a hand against the stone pathway.

"I don't feel anything," he said.

I glared into the empty space beside me and shook my

arm, jerking the woman's wrist. "Where is the mouth of the exit?" I said.

She gasped with pain. "It's right there!" she said, quickly.

"Don't point, woman, we can't see you," I said. "Speak! Left or right?"

She hesitated. "It's in that tower there, to the left of the albino."

"It's *in* the cistern?" Lee said, looking up. The structure soared above our heads. Its side curved twenty feet from the edge of the railing.

"You came through water?" I said, baffled.

"Water, no," she said. She described a ladder leading to the top of the cistern and back down to its base.

"I've not heard of this ladder or seen it used," I said.

"It's covered in vines," she said, "thick enough to hide it from view."

"Lee?"

He glowered in the woman's direction. "You're certain you're telling the truth, McCormick?"

The woman didn't hesitate. "I was running for my life," she said, solemnly. "I'll not forget, ever."

"Then let's go." Lee adjusted his hood and turned from us, instantly blending in with the night. He led us to the gazebo then on, around to the grand stone staircase. With the dark obscuring the steep grey steps, and the bracelets hiding our feet, the way down was treacherous. The English woman stumbled constantly, pulling me off balance.

"Just stop," I hissed.

She obeyed, breathing like a congested power fan. I fumbled blindly with the tie that joined our wrists. When it gave way, I wrapped my arm around her waist, and continued down the stairs, supporting her weight. At the bottom, I tapped my invisibility bracelet and signaled to Lee. "We have to break," I said.

Lee flipped open his palm to check the time. He looked worried, and I understood why. We'd been lucky so far. The people still in residence after the trial and exodus were likely still celebrating the wedding in the Mess Hall; so the Courtyard was deserted. However, our luck wouldn't hold. As the party wound down, the guests were bound to venture out to enjoy the night.

"Ten minutes to rest," Lee said. He looked around and lifted his chin. "There's a secluded spot up ahead." He led us to the same grassy square that Hosea and I had trained in the night of the market. Lee stayed close to the opening in the coiffed bushes to keep watch.

I dragged the invisible English woman with me to the center of the knoll and deactivated her cuff. The tall bushes filtered out ambient light from nearby lampposts. Still, I could see she was unwell. Her red face dripped with sweat and she shook like a blade of grass. I handed her a skin of water. "Sit down before you fall," I muttered.

She collapsed and drank thirstily. Her hair was dirty, and her legs were skinny beneath her threadbare dress. The bones of her face jutted forward unnaturally. She'd been starved.

"You need strength for this journey," I said, inexplicably bothered by her frailty.

She looked up at me. "Where I come from, food is scarce. I'll take what you can spare, and gladly."

I opened my sack and took out one of Walker's energy bars—oats, seeds and nuts rolled together with honey. She took it and folded all five inches into her mouth.

I looked at her from the corner of my eye and sighed. "Give me your bag," I said. Without hesitating, she pulled it over her head and handed it to me. I rummaged through it and removed a container of nutrient pills. I shook several into my hand and gave them to her.

She took them eagerly, and swallowed them with more water.

"You know what those are?" I said, watching her gulp another handful. I'd heard of the famine, but, I realized, I'd never pictured the reality of an English person without enough to eat. It didn't seem possible. But the English people I knew had been diplomats, teachers and overseers—the privileged class of the north.

She nodded. "Many times, these were all we had." Holding my gaze, she took another long drink of water and wiped a hand across her mouth. She smiled gently. "I'm staring," she said, apologetically. "I can scarcely believe it's you in the flesh. General Arika Cobane."

Feeling uneasy, I tossed two more bars on the ground and stepped back, discouraging conversation. She brushed the dirt off the bars before devouring them. When she'd finished, she shook the crumbs from her dirty dress and stood.

"Let's go," Lee said. He hesitated, then added, "This place is deserted. Let's leave off the bracelets, for now. We'll move faster without them."

We stopped again when we arrived at the base of the cistern.

"Okay, where is the ladder?" I demanded.

"This way," she said. She started to the left. As we followed, she spoke softly over her shoulder. "I'll never forget. We were running from the Dark Guard that followed us from High

Bend. They chased us to a cliff overlooking a rapid. We leapt in because we had no choice."

She walked around one of Director Kumar's *No Trespass* signs and went on, her lilting accent strengthening as she warmed to the story. "I was lucky, I was, to miss the rocks jutting up from the glen. When I surfaced, the guards never found me. Holding on to a rock, I was. The others, those that weren't dead from the fall, floated downstream. Each one hit the great wall and burned."

"The firewall," I said, then bit my tongue. I'd intended to ignore the woman, but the words were out of my mouth before I could stop them. She turned and smiled at me. I looked away. "The river you jumped into must have led to the firewall."

"Aye," she said. "I saw my friends burn so I swam upstream, fighting the rapids, gripping rocks to pull me along. But I was weak. I grew weary and drifted downriver to die."

She stopped suddenly and stiffened. Alarmed, I stopped beside her. An ethereal look softened her face, and she closed her eyes. She touched her forehead, her sternum, her left shoulder then her right. She opened her bright blue eyes and fixed them on me.

"Wha—what is it?" I said.

"If I told you how I survived the water, you wouldn't believe."

I looked at Lee. He shrugged, clearly not believing a word.

"Go on then," I said.

"It was the arm of our Lord, Jesus the Christ, that pulled me from the rapids." Quickly, she performed the same ritual as before. She tapped her forehead, her dangling cross, and both shoulders, "He arose!" she whispered.

"Arose?" My mouth slanted. The English at Hasting had taken to this old-world God. And, under the ceasefire, missionaries roamed the Kongo clutching specially issued visitor passes. Still, I'd never personally encountered a devotee. "What did the arm look like?"

Her eyes burned. "Thick as a man's thigh and black as night, pulsing with the ruddy blood of life."

"Black as night," I said. "So, your Jesus is—Kongo?"

She tilted her head, considering. "I suppose so. I awakened in a small puddle of water in a dark tunnel. I followed it down to a circular room with soaring walls—just like that." She pointed at the cistern.

I looked at her, then at Lee, then up at the cistern. I scoffed. "You're right, white, I don't believe you."

"Okay now, we've got to move," Lee said. He marched past both of us and continued around the cistern.

Before I could follow, the English woman gripped my arm, her thin hand like a vice. "He's come back," she hissed. "The end is nigh." Her gaze was ecstatic; the pupils pierced like nails.

"You're mad," I said. I jerked my arm away and pushed her forward.

Within minutes, we came upon the workman's ladder just as the English woman had described. It was rusted and covered with vines, so it blended into the curved side of the cistern.

"You go first," Lee said, pointing at the woman.

She gathered her strength and began to climb. When she was several feet in the air, I reached for the ladder. Lee stopped me with a hand on my arm. He eyed the woman, pale on the rising rungs. "I've seen Nicky McCormick," he whispered. "The woman is not who she claims."

I hid my surprise and bared my teeth. "The English never are," I said, bitterly. She'd almost gotten to me with her wide-open gaze. My hand shifted to my Apex. "Should I get the truth from her?"

Lee rested a cautioning hand on my shoulder. "We can't scare her off," he said. "Not yet. I'll play the friend, for now. When the time is right, you do what it takes to get what we need. She knows you as the Berserker—use that."

I met Lee's gaze and nodded.

The climb was slow and difficult. The thin slats of the ladder bit into my palms and, despite my disdain for her, I considered the English woman's fleshless hands. Without padding, the rusted metal would scrape against her skin and bones. We stopped five times before we reached the top. By then the woman was struggling to remain steady. I braced myself, gripped her ankle and pushed up, helping her onto the narrow landing space at the top of the ladder.

She lay there gasping, glowing with sweat. As Lee and I completed the climb, she stood cautiously, to look down into the cistern. She gasped. I moved to stand beside her and followed her gaze. The cistern was full of water.

I glared at her and hissed, "And how did you stand at the bottom of a cistern full of water? Did Black Jesus breathe air into your lungs?"

"No, General," she said, guileless. "Christ appeared only the one time."

"You liar!" I grabbed her matted hair and dragged her to her knees. I forced my Apex into a dagger at her throat.

She arched away and reached to put her hand in the water. She rolled her eyes pointedly, begging me to look. I followed her gaze and jerked with shock. The water blinked as it recalibrated around her pale hand. I sheathed my Apex then plunged both arms in the pool. I touched my face. My hands were as dry as a bone.

"A holograph," Lee said from beside me, his face slack with surprise.

The woman regained her footing and pushed her hair back. "Yes, a holograph," she said, solemnly. She dipped her hand back in the water and felt around. She smiled suddenly as her hand touched something out of view. "And here, feel this."

Lee and I reached together. Just beneath the false waterline was the ladder down.

I was the first to climb from the cistern wall to the surface of the earth, lit with thin strains of moonlight. From inside, the cistern was exactly as she described, a circular room with soaring walls.

The English woman climbed down after me. She looked around, straining to see in the dark. "There!" She pointed to a manhole with a stone lid in the middle of the cistern. "Down there is a way not five yards wide. The ground is prickly rock and drowned with water. That is the way out."

I ran to the manhole cover just as Lee stepped from the ladder. I waved him over. "It's heavy, get that end," I ordered. "I'll lift from this side."

The cover had been bolted down, but the ground around it was cracked. Lee gripped and, together, we lifted it away. I swung my legs around to lower myself into the hole.

Lee's hand stopped me. "Let me go first," he said. He climbed down and tossed a crystalight. The English woman followed, and I brought up the rear, dropping beside them. My moccasins splashed into the three inches of water that covered the floor of the tunnel, which was about five yards wide—exactly as the woman had described. Through my shoes, I felt the sharp rock beneath my feet and water droplets seeped into the fabric of my leggings, chilling my calves.

Lee removed the rolled blueprints from a pocket sewn into the lining of his jacket. He moved beneath the crystalight and flattened the papers just above a horizontal crack in the tunnel wall.

As he studied the map, the English woman moved to his side and felt along the crack. As I watched, she closed her eyes and pressed her fingertips into the opening, testing its depth.

"How long before we reach the entrance you took?" I asked.

The woman opened her eyes. "I don't know, exactly," she said.

I asked more questions and learned she also had no recollection of how she'd gotten the marks that covered her body.

"Did you stop to rest?" Lee asked.

"I don't think so," she said. She bent to look inside of the opening.

"To relieve yourself?" he asked. "Anything that would help you gauge the time?"

She hesitated, thinking. "Not that I recall," she said, finally.

"What *do* you recall?" I snapped.

She took her hand from the crack and stood, pointing into the darkness ahead. "This crack runs along the stretch of tunnel that I walked. It's wider in some places, deeper in others. I think I'll remember the feel of the tunnel walls where I woke up. I remember thinking—this is the *wall* of heaven."

I sighed. She was useless.

Lee, playing the friend, consoled her with a hand on her shoulder. "No time to waste," he said. "Let's go."

He climbed back up the ladder and replaced the manhole cover. When he came down, we started out, three abreast, with the English woman closest to the tunnel wall.

We walked quickly on jagged rocks and in silence punctuated by the sound of water splashing beneath us. Our only good fortune was that the tunnel flowed southeast, directly towards our destination.

Before twenty minutes had passed, the woman suddenly stopped and pointed to the left. "I awakened here," she said.

Lee Ford tossed another light and we scanned the rock wall, looking for a break big enough to fit an adult woman. There wasn't one.

"Look over there," the English woman said, pointing right. "Perhaps I got myself turned around."

We walked back the way we had come, this time scanning the right face of the tunnel.

"Nothing," I said, my dread mounting.

"Let me," the woman said. She plucked a crystalight from the air and went right up to the wall, scanning and banging every inch within reach. "Perhaps it's another holograph?"

Lee and I joined her, searching with our hands. Ten minutes later, Lee was ready to give up.

"It's here. It has to be," the woman insisted. As her emotions intensified, the lilt of her accent thickened again. She closed her eyes, pressing the sensitive tips of her fingers into her temple. "I awakened on my side. Me right side." She took her bag from her body and handed it to me, then she knelt in the cold water, which was deeper in this part of the tunnel. "I remember me right ear being numb. I couldna hear a thing for hours. It was black as night and the water came up to me chin."

Light in hand, she lifted a finger to press her chin. "A sound woke me, a gristly grinding and I rolled onto me back, listening, wondering what it could be." She rested the crystalight on her chest as she laid down. The water covered half of her face, leaving her nose above the waterline, but her ears beneath. A second later, she sat up, gasping. "I heard it—I did!"

I started towards her just as Lee Ford shouted. I looked back at him. His eyes were wide, his mouth open on a silent cry. I followed his gaze down and cried out myself. The crystalight had rolled from the woman's chest to illuminate the ground beneath the water. It was covered with bones.

THE VARIANT

"Obi Solomon," I whispered.

The English woman jumped up, shrieking. "Jesus in heaven!"

"Give me the light!" Lee said.

She retrieved the crystal, slapping at her hair and neck. Lee held it in the water near his feet. He bent and plucked a bone from the water. "Fish bone," he said. He looked around and identified another tiny bone. "Frog." He gathered a handful to examine; all belonged to small land or sea creatures.

"Where did they come from?" I said, stooping down.

"The rapids were jumping with life," the woman offered.

"But how did they get *here*?" I said, pointing to the ground of the tunnel.

"Same way I did?" the woman suggested.

"That makes sense," I agreed, for a moment forgetting my disdain. "There has to be an underwater hole that leads here. They wander into the hole and can't get out, so they die trapped up here without nourishment. What do you think, Lee?"

On his knees in the cold water, Lee picked up another bone and held it to his nose. "Most of that sounds accurate. Except, these animals didn't die here. The smell of rotting flesh would be pervasive."

He had a point. I walked over to him. "With all these bones, where else could they have died?" I asked.

Lee pointed towards the ground.

"In the rock?" I said.

"Hold this," he said, handing me the crystalight. He took a sheath from his pack and drew out a wicked-looking knife. He lifted it high and drove it into the water. The ground made a hissing noise and recoiled from the blade. I leapt backward.

The English woman rushed forward, eyes wide. "It's not rock," she whispered.

"No, it's not. I believe you called it the arm of Christ," Lee said. With effort, he pulled up his knife.

Getting hold of myself, I crept forward. The ground shifted back together, closing the cut he'd made. Tentatively, I plunged my hand in the water and ran my fingertips over the now invisible seam, feeling a slippery substance. I held my fingers beneath the light and saw they were smeared with red.

"The very blood!" the woman breathed, touching her necklace.

"You should rinse that off," Lee said, nodding at the red on my hand.

I dipped my hand in the water and wiped it dry on the front of my shirt. "What's going on, Lee?" I asked.

He took the crystalight and shined it so he could see clearly. "If I'm not mistaken, these are infant vines of Variant R-14, the species that dominates the Obi Forest." He spoke in a hushed tone, as if not to disturb the ground. "I've read descriptions of the plant in notes left by the original scientists."

"You have access to those notes?" the woman said. She sounded surprised.

I looked between them. "Is the information not public?"

"The notes are a national treasure," she said. "They're sealed and under guard in a vault at the Assembly Library." She was looking at Lee with a new, shrewd interest.

Lee's eyes lingered on her, then he turned to me and explained. "The original scientists studied at the Compound for years. When they abandoned their work, they fled with some of their materials. That's what's in the Assembly vault. They left the bulk of their reports behind. When Kumar won the bid to research the Obi Forest, we found the abandoned documents and reviewed them, *privately.*"

"You mean you did it without permission," I said.

"Not exactly," Lee said. "There's a branch of the Assembly that isn't publicly known. It's funded with quasi-public money and composed of a few very powerful people."

"Dorian Glosser?" I asked.

"Yes, my uncle is one of them. It was the branch that permitted our research." Lee knelt, careful to stay clear of the red-tinged water. "We never learned the exact evolution of the variant. The notes towards the end were brief and unfinished. I've seen the mature variant from over the wall— but never up close."

I knelt beside him, examining. Beneath the bones, hundreds of tiny vines clumped together, tangled over and under. Each of the tiny vines had a red vein running down the center that pulsed, as if it were pumping blood.

"I can't believe it," the woman said. She squatted beside me. "The arm of Christ drove out and snatched me from the rapids. A tree canna do that."

"Shut up about that, will you?" I snapped, touching a blood-red artery. "Apparently trees *can* reach."

"In the old world, trees were highly specialized," Lee said. "They could talk, move, hunt, listen, respond. No one species could do all of those. But during the Last War, the original scientists stockpiled plant samples from around the world. They used those samples in their post-war efforts to manufacture vegetation that could withstand the harsh new world environment."

"They experimented here, in the Obi Forest," I said, recalling my training. "First, they tried to revive the land, then they turned to altering plants. And when that failed, they withdrew from the forest entirely."

"They fled their own creation," Lee Ford said. "But they left behind both natural and synthetic plants in an environment so hostile, nothing was supposed to survive."

"But Variant R-14 did," I guessed.

"Right. Well, that's what Father and I think it is. The scientists manufactured dozens of species. R-14 is the one that most closely resembles the trees in the forest and this arm of Christ. Only, its struggle to survive made it advanced, stronger—intelligent."

"Clever trees," the woman said. "Remarkable."

"About a decade later, we think, R-14 began to choose its features to maximize its ability to thrive. You've heard of grafting—where two plants, joined together, begin to grow together, mingling attributes."

"Something like that," I said.

"Well, there you have it," Lee said. "Imagine what our top scientists could do with DNA from the most intelligent humans that ever lived. If they could isolate and splice."

I nodded. "A superhuman."

"A league of them," Lee said.

"It's no wonder the scientists fled," the woman said.

Lee stood and dried his hands. "We think most of the R-14's key advances came through trial and error," he said "But the plants did better than anyone expected, so there's no guarantee. For all we know, they could be self-aware. Their vines move like arms—only each tree has a hundred arms. And they're poly-meristematic."

"Poly-what?" I asked.

"Many meristems," the English woman explained. "They're the growing cells of a plant."

I eyed her and gripped the sling bag I carried for her, pulling it over my head. "How do you know that?" I demanded.

"I studied in an agriculture megatech lab until I was seventeen," she explained.

"I thought you were a soldier." I shoved the bag towards her. "The *McCormick*—right? And you're clearly a religious fanatic. And now you're a scientist? Which is it, English? Are all whites liars?"

She took her bag and ducked her head.

Lee looked between us. "In any case, she's right," he said. "Watch this." He placed a crystalight above the water. With his knife, he hacked out a chunk of the plant. The gash spurted red liquid. A second later, the wound scabbed over. "Because R-14 vines are made entirely of meristem cells, when a vine is cut off, it regenerates." The plant was already restoring the gash.

"Remarkable," the woman said.

"And dangerous, especially to humans," Lee said. "When they realized what they'd done, the original scientists tried to destroy the trees. It didn't work. The only thing that works is containment."

"The firewall!" I said. "Its purpose isn't to keep humans out, but to keep the trees in."

"Until they learn how to uproot and get around it," Lee said.

My eyes narrowed. "Is that possible?"

Lee didn't answer. He took a square cloth from his pocket, wet it and wiped off his knife. The red liquid had a stench and the woman wrinkled her nose as she took in the stained cloth.

"It's digestive fluid," Lee explained. "I believe the two of you were right about how the bones got here. The vines at the north end of the forest must have worked their way through the sediment rock into this tunnel and out that way, to the Clayskin River." He pointed to his left.

"It bypassed the firewall," I said.

"Likely in search of space—or food."

"They eat meat!" the woman said, her mouth twisted.

Lee shrugged. "They're carnivores. Still, I do wonder how you came out alive. Rightly, you should be a pile of bones."

The woman whimpered and rubbed her hands along her arms.

I considered the matter. "You said they were young plants, saplings," I said. "Maybe they couldn't handle a meal her size."

"True," Lee said. He handed the wet cloth to me and gestured to my forehead. "You have some digestive fluid there," he said. "Wipe it off, or you'll have a scar."

The woman gasped. We turned to her. She lifted her skirt, showing her right thigh laced with thin red lines. "I awakened with these," she said. "They're much worse on my right side."

"The side you woke up on," I said, seeing her reason. "So, the plants did try to digest you."

"But you overwhelmed their system," Lee added. "So, they released you here."

"Which means there isn't a hole in the vines," I said, deflated. "And we can't get past the firewall unless we risk being digested."

"We're stuck," the woman said. She looked over her shoulder. "Unless there's another entrance." She stepped further into the tunnel. "It makes sense, no? They created an algorithmic entry, why not preserve a physical path too—a tunnel in?"

While her back was turned, Lee nodded to me. It was time to get the whole truth.

Lee shined his light down on the English woman. "I think there's something you're not telling us," he said, gently.

She squinted, shielding her eyes. "I know nothing more than what I've said."

I snorted. "Liar."

Lee held up his hand, stifling me. "Please, woman. Don't make us hurt you. I don't hate English people, not like the Berserker, but even I'm losing patience." His voice was kind, but steady.

I growled, slapping aside his hand. "Enough of this." I grabbed the English woman by the neck and squeezed. She croaked.

"Careful," Lee said.

I continued to apply pressure. "If she can't tell us about the exit, she's worthless to us."

Lee stepped forward. "Arika! Let me!"

The woman's face paled, her eyes bulged.

I nodded to Lee. "Ask your questions."

"You say you're the McCormick?" Lee said. "The leader of the Sisters to the North?"

I relaxed my fingers enough for her to nod. Lee grimaced.

"Lie!" I snapped. She gasped as I tightened again.

"Nicky McCormick is a covert insurrectionist," Lee said. "Kumar made a point to know her well—in case she succeeded. I gathered intelligence on the Sisters on his behalf. I've seen Nicole McCormick's likeness and you are not her. *Who are you?*"

I relaxed my hand. She gasped, clawing at her neck. I tightened again, viciously.

"Stop fighting. Use your breath to answer," I instructed. After a long minute, I relaxed again.

"Not Nicky," she gasped, immediately.

I tightened. "He knows that, white. *Who are you?*"

Her skin tinged blue as her oxygen depleted. "My name—is Anna—McCormick."

I looked at Lee. He nodded, accepting the answer. I released her and the woman—Anna—collapsed at my feet, splashing into the water. She coughed and sputtered, dragging herself away. I stopped her progress with a foot and flipped her onto her back. Snagging the crystalights, I threw them to shine in her face. Slowly, the blue faded and she regained her sallow color.

"Why are you pretending to be *The* McCormick?" Lee asked. "Take your time."

The woman panted and cleared her throat. "Nicky was my wife," she whispered. "I became the McCormick after her death. I do lead the Sisters." She bowed her head. "Only I am the last of our tribe."

"I heard the river story, but I don't believe it," Lee said. His tone was resolute, but he knelt beside her, ready to listen. "Nicky was a big strong woman. How do you explain her drowning when you were strong enough to escape?"

"Inexplicable," I snapped.

"Nicky didn't drown," Anna said. She scooted away from me, one hand on her rib cage just over her heart. "My Nicky never made it to the river. She died hunting in the woods at

High Bend. And still, we dinna have enough food. When her horse brought back her body, we had a choice—either run or stay and die slowly. We ran."

"What is High Bend?" I asked, recalling she had mentioned it before.

She rubbed her neck, where bruises formed. "I was seventeen when my parents realized I was different. They'd chosen a man for me but—but I wouldn't marry him. So they sent me to the High Bend for treatment. And, when the treatment didn't fix me, they wouldn't take me back. I had nowhere else to go. So, I stayed at the convent and trained as a nurse. I cared for anyone who came to us for asylum. Nicky was in my care."

Lee nodded. "High Bend is a convent near the Clayskin border," he explained. "It's run by nuns, English diplomats to the Clayskin territory." He turned to me. "This story makes sense. When the riots were quelled, the Sisters to the North were rounded up and sent to convents for—" He looked with compassion at Anna. "They might have called it treatment," he said. "But it was torture." He took Anna's hand and pulled her to her feet. "I assume you're a nun."

"A novice," she said. "And a nurse. I was assigned to Nicky, to try to change her. She converted me instead. I accept who I am now; I accept that I loved her." She bowed her head to her wet chest and tears dropped from her eyes. "I should have told you everything from the beginning. You were right not to trust me."

Lee put a hand on her trembling shoulder. I took Lee's arm and pulled him a few feet away. "You heard her; she doesn't know anything more. We'll rely on the blueprints going forward," I said. "Let's turn her back towards the Compound and be done with her."

Lee shook his head. "Father would kill her. And besides, if we send her back, she could talk and ruin our plans." He didn't wait for me to answer. He took a spare shirt from his pack and went to the woman. He wrapped the warmth around her thin, wet shoulders.

A queasy feeling rolled in my stomach as I stared at them, their bright heads bent together. Lee was right. I'd told her I'd free her if she showed us the way out but doing so would jeopardize our mission. Eventually, a choice would have to be made.

In the crystalights, her wet hair glowed bright red—like raspberries. Against my will, I was reminded of another red-haired English woman—Teacher Saxon. She'd taken pity and tutored me, securing for me the protection of the top of the class. In the brutal world of the Schoolhouse, she'd been kind.

Just then, Anna started coughing. The coughs shook her frame, depleting her already dwindled energy.

"You need food and rest," Lee said.

I started to protest, but Anna brushed off Lee's concern. "I'm fine," she said.

Lee lifted a brow. "Are you certain?"

Anna nodded, stifling a cough.

As we started off, Lee handed her a waterskin and I shoved my remaining nut bars into her hands. She ate more nutrient pills. They seemed to revive her, and we continued at a steady clip, moving faster as Anna's strength returned. Lee drifted to walk beside her.

Eventually Anna broke the silence, asking Lee about his blueprints. After that, they chatted; stilted at first, then with more ease. They exchanged stories. He spoke of his scientific work and the future of agriculture. She was an avid gardener and trained as an agricultural engineer from a young age.

"In the north, they dinna ask us what we want to do with our lives," she said. "We take a test that sorts us, and they set us on that path."

"Sounds stifling," Lee said, pensively.

"Yes," Anna said. "But the Lord provided." She smiled softly and performed her now familiar ritual.

We walked for two hours before Lee called for another break. I could hear Anna panting as she moved away, looking for privacy.

Lee bent to my ear. "There are dry spots around here where we can sit and eat."

I glared at him. "I don't need to sit. I don't need to eat."

"Anna does," Lee pointed out.

"I can see that, but we can't afford to care, right, Lee? The Kongo, the empire," I reminded him. "You're aiding the enemy."

He swallowed. "You heard her story. She's one of us."

"She's white!" I hissed.

"Her *skin* is white," he said, shrugging. "Who am I to judge that?" He walked off, taking the crystalight, as the English woman returned.

I stayed in the dark, listening as they decided, without me, to make camp. I found a dry patch and sat down, seething with dislike. Just the sight of her blue-veined skin was triggering. It reminded me of Jones and the violence I'd suffered at white hands. And here Lee was, smiling at her, softening.

He waved a hand, catching my attention. "Food, General?" he asked.

I refused, gruffly. He gave my portion to the woman.

"Thank you, albino," she said. She took the dried meat from his hand and bit off a corner.

Lee shifted, so both of their backs rested against the tunnel wall. "I'm sorry for your loss. Nicky was a great woman," he said.

Anna nodded. "Thank you, albino."

"You can call me Lee."

She smiled and coughed, rubbing her throat. "I guess you'll call me whatever you like," she said.

Chuckling, Lee held out a handful of dried fruit. She took it gratefully.

Their conversation grated. I turned my back to them but couldn't avoid hearing it.

"Tell me about the riots," Lee said. "I hear you destroyed a soup kitchen."

Anna cleared her throat. "It was Nicky that started it," she said. "Just before the Great Kongo Rebellion, there was famine. Nicky and a friend were waiting in the rations line—with money to pay. But, when the portions ran low, a member of the Dark Guard began splitting the line."

When she paused, I shifted to gauge her expression. Her eyes were narrowed, shrewd. She went on. "Nicky, her friend and every other sister, all of them friends—we stick together up north—were moved to the second line."

"Did the lines go to the same place?" he asked.

Anna looked up at him through brown lashes. "Does it matter?"

He blinked, slowly, shook his head. "No," he said, finally. "It doesn't."

Anna relaxed. She blew warmth into her hands and rubbed her bare toes. "Nicky was the first to sit that day," she said, "to protest the segregation. Three others followed and then another two, a pair of brothers. They would not get up, no matter what. Then Nicky started the chanting, and the riots began."

Anna scratched her red head and smiled thoughtfully. "Nicky McCormick never could hold her tongue. Not like I could." Her head hung, exposing a knotty spine and dirty collar. The freckles along her cheek stuck out like flea bites. "I was always a coward," she whispered.

A feeling tightened in my chest and I looked away, quickly—fighting it. I removed another trigger patch from my sack, lifted my braided hair and pressed it to the back of my neck.

THE CLIMB

Hours later, we broke camp, feeling hopeful. We worked out that the distance and direction we'd walked had put us past the firewall, which meant the tunnel had bypassed its threat. With every step, we were closer to Cobane, albeit underground. We just needed an exit to the surface. We studied the blueprint and took a path that inclined. The water beneath us thinned until eventually we walked on dry ground.

After food and rest, Anna seemed revitalized but, a few minutes later, she collapsed. Lee helped her to her feet but, from then on, she declined, shaking feverishly and barely keeping pace. She coughed and sipped water to soothe her throat, which forced us to stop often as she relieved herself.

Lee shortened his step to match hers and checked her vitals. A precaution, he said. But, as he checked the results, his face was grim. When she yet again signaled a stop, I sighed. She moved off for privacy and Lee grabbed my arm.

"Change of plans," he said. "We have to go directly to Cobane." I frowned. "Why?"

"It wasn't just a chemical," he said under his breath.

"You mean the patch you removed. The powder. What was it?"

"It's a virus." He hung his head, rubbing a hand over his nape. "I engineered two vehicles to disguise its danger. The powder you saw is the first vehicle. And I was wrong about its ability to transmit through skin. Or, perhaps her skin was compromised because of the lacerations."

I looked over at Anna. "So, she's not tired, she's sick."

"She's dying," Lee whispered. His pupils dilated, engulfing his gaze. "I engineered the virus, but I also made a cure. An infirmary should have the medicine Anna needs."

Or, I thought, *we could leave her here.* It would solve a handful of problems: she was weak, she was English and the promise I'd made her, in the end, had to be broken. From the corner of my eye, I watched her sit and gnaw another length from her dress. She ripped it in half and wrapped each foot. She tested the binds and nodded up at us.

"I'll move faster now," she vowed.

I avoided her gaze as Lee helped her to her feet.

When the tunnel forked, we went right, moving south up a steeper incline.

"We're moving towards the surface," I announced. We slowed our pace and floated our lights overhead, in search of another manhole.

Twenty minutes later, both crystalights began to flicker; their solar power was running low. We exchanged worried glances and put one light away, to use later. We pressed on, ascending into darkness.

The incline transitioned into steps with large rectangular levels. We changed formation to climb three abreast. Each step was steeper than the last, and soon Anna collapsed again. Lee plunged to one knee to catch her. He held a water skin to her lips and tilted her head back, letting the liquid slosh into her mouth. She wheezed, spitting it up.

"We've got to move," I said, touching the pair of patches on my neck. Despite them, the darkness was getting to me. I could feel my heart rate increase as panic crept in.

"Give her a minute," Lee said.

I moved past them, mounting the next step, and the next. As I left Lee's light behind, I took another binder patch from my pocket and added it to the two already on my neck. I secured the remaining patches in my breast pocket and climbed the next step—and the next, trying to control my breathing.

The way darkened to pitch black. I tossed my dimming crystalight—our last—and kept climbing. Again and again. When the crystal stuttered and failed, I closed my eyes and pictured the sun. I felt my way forward with my hands and pressed on.

I didn't sense Lee until he was beside me, breathing heavily. I opened my eyes and in the dim light from his remaining crystalight I saw Anna clung to him like a child. His pack was on his chest and her face peeked over his shoulder.

Anna scrambled down. "Let me try again," she said. "I won't hold us back, General, not this time."

She struggled on for a few minutes, then Lee and I took turns hoisting her onto the next platform. Finally, she shuddered and sank to her knees. "I'm sorry, General. I canna go on," she said. "Leave me."

I wrapped a hand around her arm. I pulled her over to the next step and climbed up. On my knees, I reached down to drag her with me. She was a dead weight. Her stomach scraped the rough step and she whelped like a new pup. Finally, I let go and slumped back into Lee's arms.

"It can't be long now," I said, though I had no way of knowing. "Stay here. I'll come back for you." Before they could protest,

I turned and climbed. Up, up. My muscles cramped and my chest caught fire. In the dark, I grew disoriented. I imagined wings and a cool wind at my back. I saw what looked like a twinkling star in the stark night sky. It called me forward. My thighs trembled as the starlight held steady, then grew.

I froze, realizing my eyes were open.

"Lee!" I shouted over my shoulder. "I see light! There's a light!" I pressed forward, pushing the limits of my strength. When my pack weighed on me, I took it off, letting it clatter to the ground. I climbed—jumping for the next level, landing on my stomach and scrambling up.

My gaze fixed on the star, and it brightened, slowly. Finally, the dark gave way. At the top of the last step, I pressed both hands to the manhole cover. A significant crack along its edge provided the beacon of light that had called me forward. I bowed my head, gathered my strength, and pushed against it. A scuffle sounded and I turned as Lee mounted the last step. He pulled Anna, barely conscious, up behind him. She crumpled to the rock floor and Lee came to help me.

Side by side, we pushed the heavy cover from its perch and climbed into the Kongo.

THE ROAD TO COBANE

After resting for a few minutes, I retrieved my pack. I then sealed the tunnel and joined Lee Ford on a wide rock ledge where he sat with Anna, supporting her weight.

The climb had ripped the nail from his thumb and the bed oozed blood as he shifted to rest a hand on her chest.

"How long does she have?" I asked softly.

"She's barely breathing," he said. "My guess—hours."

"Hours?" I was shocked. Minutes before her first collapse, she'd been laughing. "But she said she was feeling better."

"That's part of the viral design. It lays in wait, to mitigate concern while the virus replicates."

"So, the infected person won't seek help, because they won't know they're sick," I said, feeling queasy. "You did that on purpose."

The cords in Lee's throat stood out in stark relief as he nodded. "Arika," he said, suddenly. "We'll move as fast as we can, but I don't want to alarm her. The symptoms will wax and wane, then at some point, she'll go to sleep and we won't be able to wake her. It will be better for her if she doesn't know what's coming."

Anna shuddered. His eyes dropped to fix on her chest. When her sternum lifted, filling with her breath, he exhaled. He pointed over his head, towards higher ground. "Find out where we are."

Gritting against the pain in my own hands, I climbed ten feet up to survey the landscape. It was very early morning, and still dark. We were on the side of a rocky hill overlooking a green oasis and sizable peak. The Obi Forest was behind us and the nearest crust of civilization was south.

When I came back down, Anna sat on her own, drinking the last of the water. "I'm feeling much better, General." She coughed, feebly and smiled.

I ignored her and glanced at Lee. A pulse ticked in his jaw. "We're about fifteen miles from Cobane. The road is south," I said. "If we leave now, we'll be on the road before dawn."

"I don't think I'll make it fifteen miles without more food," Anna said.

I looked at Lee. His eyes were squeezed closed, but he nodded.

"The stream pools about a hundred yards out from the base of this hill," I said. "We can rest there."

Lee and I cleared sticks, rocks and insects for a campsite. Anna insisted on helping. We off-loaded our packs then went for water and kindling. I carried the empty skins and Anna led us, setting a pace she could keep.

We found the stream and a flat rock formation that jutted into the flow like a pier. At the edge, Lee waded into the water, his head bent, looking for fish. Thinking to join him, I removed my knife and sat to remove my shoes. Anna, barefoot, lay on her belly with a water skin, holding the mouth to the current and letting it fill. Her other hand trickled in the water.

In the shallows, Lee arranged a trap with stones and caught a large fish. I used my knife to gut and clean it in the running water.

Anna finished filling the skins and laid back on the rock. Her feet had borne the worst of our trek through the tunnel.

They were dirty and bleeding, but she didn't seem to notice the pain and she said, again, that she was feeling better.

A pearl of pity made me splash some water her way. "You should care for those cuts," I said.

She sat up. The fading moon reflected off the water, highlighting the dark circles under her eyes. "What's that, General?"

I nodded towards her feet. "You don't want an infection."

"You're right, General." She scooted towards the water and hummed as she washed. At the chorus, she broke into song.

On a bonny eddy wafting
Waft a fairy the stream
bonny fairy she was longing
for her bonny Charlie king.

She hummed again, then launched into the second verse.

"Enough!" Lee hissed, cutting her off.

I looked over my shoulder at him, then back at Anna. Moisture beaded in the dip beneath her nose. We watched Lee trudge upstream and climb onto the bank. He disappeared into the tree-line.

I looked back at Anna and saw her confusion. I watched her wince as she swallowed it. "He's just hurt," I said, surprising myself.

"What's that, General?" She spoke softly, staring after him, plotting how to make it better. She didn't know *she* wasn't the cause—that *he* was. She didn't know she was dying.

I didn't want to lie, but I couldn't confess Lee's guilt to her wide-open gaze. "It's not you," I said, finally. "He struggles with his brother. He always has." After I said it, I realized it was true. Lee had made the virus to fulfill his imperative, to be the better son. It had more to do with Hosea Khan than Kumar.

Anna nodded. "Like Cain," she whispered, understanding. She touched her cross and went back to washing her feet.

We gathered the full containers and the fish and started back. We found Lee back at the encampment, sketching impatiently in his pad, and we agreed, silently, to ignore the trouble that haunted us.

Lee roasted the fish on a small fire. He gave half his portion to Anna, and I watched him watching her eat from the corner of his eye. When we burned the bones, he added fuel to hasten the process. Anna sat beside him, passing kindling. She stood to fetch water to douse the flame and, on her way back, her knees buckled. She sank down and slumped onto her side.

Lee jumped to his feet and ran to her. He grabbed her shoulders. She was unconscious and panting and she didn't wake when we shook her.

Working together, we found two fallen branches and collected our excess clothing. We ripped and made knots, piecing together a makeshift litter. We installed Anna's sleeping form and placed other travel gear—a waterskin, both bed rolls and Lee's pack—on the litter around her body. We attached the bracelet to her arm, so, as we left camp, we appeared to be carrying our belongings between us. I found the collar I'd bought at the market and chose a distortion—a harvest moon and crown—to hide my identity.

We journeyed down the hill and south to catch the main road, which wound southeast to Cobane. The road was crowded with travelers. They marched, walked and cycled. Country people with traditional head scarfs, old folks in carts and buggies, single men on horses and mules, just in from the field. In clumps among them were soldiers, set apart by their sleeves of *haute* tattoos. They were on their way to vote in the Council election, set to replace me.

I was content to be among them and surreptitiously counted my constituents. Lee, with his white skin, height and hurry, drew curious looks that he didn't notice. His gaze circled between Anna's bed, the time and the road ahead. A few hours later, City One was in view.

THE CITY

The new metropolis imposed rudely on the old Cobane village. Huts with thatch roofs and wax-paper windows squatted below crystalways that curved like limbs around hastily stacked high rises. Every other structure was a brand-new store with a front designed to outshine the one next door. And in between these were platform way stations and triple-decker eateries stuffed with food. Towering in the center of the city was the new Grand Canal Station, which impressed from every angle, its walls of water sparkling like a freshwater stream.

At midday, Lee and I moved with a swell of people through the city gates. Inside, the streets were roughly hewn and heavily trafficked. People on every corner argued about the election and shouted support for their preferred candidate. My sentence and the Council's refusal to include me on the ballot was, it seemed, a source of strife on the left, which was dominated by career soldiers loyal to their general.

"We need to rearrange," Lee said, shielding Anna with his body.

"Over there," I said, pointing to a less populated plaza.

Hoisting the litter between us, we hurried over and rearranged our load. As we merged back into the bustle, Lee carried Anna strapped to his back and I carried both our packs. When we bumped into a man handing out pamphlets of city sites, Lee took a tri-folded paper and hastily opened it.

As he studied the map, I wandered to the next street corner where a woman stood on an overturned barrel. She was explaining to a crowd how to vote for me by write-in. The crowd paid rapt attention. They figured the Council had applied my sentence and, given pressure, they would amend it. They hadn't yet guessed that the Council was compromised. As more people stopped to listen, the woman on the barrel bent at the waist, nearly toppling from her platform in her effort to reach them.

Lee tapped my shoulder. "There's an inn this way," he said.

"An inn?" I repeated.

"You'll stay with Anna while I get the medicine," he said.

"Why stop at all? We can go to an infirmary now and be on our way within the hour."

Lee ignored my question. When I dipped my head to probe his gaze, he moved off quickly in the direction of the inn. Frowning, I hitched our packs higher on my shoulders and followed.

Our rented room was small, but neat. A queen bed with a nightstand dominated the space. The nightstand was set with a menu, and an old model lamp and landcom. Its solar battery pack buzzed noisily. Along one wall was a double desk with a pin-cushion chair beneath. In the corner, a shelf with water for washing sat below an ornate mirror. The mirror was angled to reflect a holographic art piece that hung over the bed, a kaleidoscope of red dwarf and supernova stars.

Lee removed the invisibility bracelet from Anna's arm and lifted her onto the mattress. Her limp frame made a shallow impression. She stirred and coughed, opening her eyes.

Lee called over his shoulder, "Water."

I moved to hand him a waterskin. She drank thirstily then sank back.

"I'm leaving now," Lee said. "The sooner she takes the medicine, the better."

"Lee, wait—" I said, too late. He was gone.

I adjusted my collar, changing the illusion to a burning bush, then secured Anna to the bed and hurried after him. He kept a quick pace, but I stayed close to his back, dodging people left and right. When he paused on a bustling street, I waited by a lamppost nearby, watching. He flagged a couple walking hand in hand. "Can you point me to the closest infirmary?" he said.

"Sorry, friend, we're just visiting," the woman replied. "But, if you don't mind a walk, we saw one at the Schoolhouse when we voted."

At the corner, Lee flagged a taxi and leapt inside.

I took the next taxi available. "Schoolhouse," I said. I reached around to close the door.

The taxi driver shook his head. "They don't let buggies round there on election days. Road's too narrow."

"I need the infirmary," I said.

The driver shrugged. "I'll get you as close as I can."

I sat back as he pulled off, navigating the streets. He stopped in front of the Grand Canal Station a few minutes later. He pointed over the passenger seat. "Go to the top of the station, buy a ticket and take the south box or, if you're in a hurry, ride the rails. The last stop is the Schoolhouse."

On the ground level of the station, I angled a hand on my forehead and stared up. I'd read about the canal's ingenious engineering. The walls were made of water. It shot up from the center and powerful jets angled the flow just so, creating the barrel shape of the building. The water refracted the sun shining through, so it scattered rainbows on every surface.

Lee's white head, bobbing on the looping incline that led to the top of the station, was easy to spot. As I followed him, I observed the people around me. On the ramp down, a young man's bonsai rose at an angle and rounded at the end like a fist. His shirt read 'Free Cobane'. Beside him, a woman's bonsai hung left over a gauged ear. The end had been gelled to a point like a sickle and from it hung small gold lettering: 'Where's Voltaire?' Further along a woman came towards me wearing red make-up and aggressively spiked jewelry. Another, close behind her, wore a long printed skirt and shirtwaist. As she came closer, I saw a pair of simple navy waves over her left brow, a quiet nod to the changing tide of democracy.

I closed in on Lee as he made his way to the ticket counter and greeted the clerk.

"A ticket to the Schoolhouse," he said.

"Two, please," I said, stepping out from behind him.

He jerked, glared, then sighed, resigned. "Two tickets," he said.

The clerk nodded. His hair, a celebratory neon green, was braided to the scalp and shaved at the sides, revealing inked scarifications. He took a ticket from a stack beside a portable clock on his counter. He jotted information on one side, then the other, glancing between me and Lee. He leaned forward and spoke in confidence. "You two look smart," he said. "You writing in for the General?"

"Perhaps," Lee said. He looked at me, then glanced at the portable clock impatiently. "The tickets?" he prodded.

The man went on. "Word is, they're closing the poll station at fifteen hundred. Too many votes for the General, eh?" He winked and slid the tickets across the counter. "Better cast yours while you can. Here you go—two two-way tickets!"

Lee picked up the slips. The man's joints popped as he got up from his stool, came around the counter and beckoned Lee closer. He pointed at a golden gate on the other side of the level. "The entrance is through that gate and right." He winked.

We rode down from the station in a large translucent boxcar hung from a clear wire. Around us, the high-top *level-up* shoes, invented by the West Keep twins, were on full display. Young Kongos, with their sleek kicks locked into transparent rails, surfed by us, their glorious bonsais holding steady in the wind.

Our progress in the boxcar, by comparison, was strategically slow—affording passengers time to spend more coin. As Lee moved down the aisle in search of a seat I followed, passing a barber shop. A hairdresser with clicking scissors stood behind a young woman getting her bonsai shaped-up. Beside them, a clerk bustled behind a small cart, helping patrons try on brightly printed neckcloths in all shapes and sizes.

Eventually, we got off at the Schoolhouse station, the official seat of the Kongo Council. Dozens of elaborate fountains testified to the wealth the Kongo had amassed since the rebellion. Career soldiers, decked out in raw *bambi* camouflage and Helixes formed into sickles, patrolled the limestone halls. Council members, officials and family group representatives from around the Kongo went about in their upper-crust finery: robes with puffed sleeves, close-cut tuxedos with capes, ruffled tights and corsets, all paired with minimal jewelry and elaborately styled hair.

The clinic was inside the old reel room. As we entered, Lee greeted the woman behind the sleek white counter.

"Can I help you?" she said.

"I'd like three doses of Hydraphagia, please."

The woman inhaled quickly. She opened her desk drawer and removed a medical-grade face mask, hastily placing it over her mouth and nose.

"Are you having symptoms? Coughing, runny nose, sore throat, fever?" she asked.

"No," Lee said.

"Have you been exposed to anyone with the fever?" She checked a schedule. "A medicine woman can see you in under an hour."

"No appointment," Lee said. "Just the medication."

She looked doubtful, but she went away and came back obediently. I stifled a surprised noise when I saw the pill pack in her hand. It held a series of three purple tablets well-known for treating the mysterious fever that had plagued the Kongo before the rebellion.

THE SECOND VEHICLE

We left the Schoolhouse the way we'd come and took a taxi from the rail station back to the inn.

In our room, Lee sat next to Anna on the bed and gathered her upper body in his arms. He opened the pill packet and administered the medication, levering her mouth open and placing one tablet beneath her tongue.

From experience, I knew the purple pill fizzled on contact and dissolved instantly. So the patient didn't have to be conscious to take it. Lee cocked a hand beneath Anna's neck, forcing her chin up and her head back, then he gently placed the covers around her. He checked the time and made a note. The tablets were to be given an hour apart. He closed his palm and, finally, joined me at the foot of the bed.

"You," I said, quietly.

Lee sighed. "The original vehicle was perfect," he said. "A white pill disguised to look like an analgesic. But Father said we couldn't rely on it. So, I designed another. It didn't provide as clean a hit. The symptoms were obvious and, eventually, caused respiratory failure. But Father didn't care. Later, I realized why. He was targeting the Kongo. Only, no medicine man would offer a white pill, and no Kongo would take it. That's why he insisted the second vehicle be one of the only treatments the medicine man would prescribe: liquor, a spoonful of salt or—"

"Hash," I said. "It was the hash that spread the fever." My mind worked, connecting the pieces of information I had and seeing how it all fit together. I stared sadly at Lee.

"He told me it would be a weapon of war," Lee said. "I didn't know he'd use it on innocent people. I informed Hosea Khan when I knew. But thousands were gone already and I'm responsible." His cheeks were wet.

"You didn't know, Lee," I said.

He winced. "Please, don't make excuses."

When I touched his wrist, he growled and snatched his hand away. He stood and grabbed his pack. From it, he took his sketch pad. "You might as well see this," he said. He handed it to me. "Open it."

The pad was square, filled with manila paper. My eyes darted over a picture near the front, taking in the scene. At a training session, I commanded a dozen soldiers, my brows pulled low over my nose. I recognized a soldier in the front row and Hosea beside me. Hosea's eyes were too small and slanted. The black ropes of his hair fell too long, almost to his waist. His undersized body was rendered in angry lines.

"This was months ago," I whispered. "I remember."

"So do I," Lee said. "Kumar had me follow from time to time—to keep tabs. I was there when you made that trainee cry—and I was there after and—*after*."

He reached over and ripped out the page. He crumpled it and pointed at the next picture, watching for my response. The caption read: *After the training, she returns near midnight.* I stood at the door of my quarters in the east wing of the Compound, shoulders slumped. The vantage point was head-on, implying Lee had been inside my room, invisible, when I entered. I shivered and turned the page. My blood ran cold. Covington sat on a stool beside me, attending—as I took a bath.

I slammed the pad shut. "I don't want to see any more," I said.

"Well, I've seen," he whispered. "I've seen everything."

I jerked, whipped back and hurled the sketch pad. It struck his chest and fell to the floor.

"I deserve that, and more," he said.

I glared up at him.

"That's right, Arika. Don't excuse me; hate me." He spread his palms at his sides, creating an easy target. "I've been following you for months." I covered my ears, but he went on, listing violations. "In the mess hall, you barely eat. You sleep with a rock by your pillow. The repository, access number 332875—"

"Shut up, Lee!"

"Your secret wall, your shrine to Kira Swan, I've seen it— and more. Last week, behind the bramble bush, in the gazebo. I saw *everything*."

My stomach lurched. I looked at him. His face was red. His body rigid with pain. He nodded, confirming my suspicion. I squeezed my eyes shut, but the image was there, still—in charcoal. Me, Hosea—and Lee Ford hovering in the background. My breath hissed from my chest, and I jumped up. I lowered my head and charged.

My shoulder collided with his middle and we stumbled across the room, slamming into the desk. I pinned him to the far wall, pounding with both fists. My knuckles cracked along his rib cage, hurting me more than him. But he fell anyway, finally moved to defend himself.

On his knees in front of me he pleaded. "Hate me! Hate me, but understand, I had to survive!" He looked up, his eyes bright. "You're a soldier. You give orders. You see? I *had* my *orders*."

"You're not a soldier," I sneered. "You're a snake. Sneaking around in secret. A henchman!"

He jumped to his feet, suddenly defensive. "If I'm a henchman to the father, you're a whore to the son! We've both been used. Come on, admit it. There's no difference!"

"You!" I jabbed a finger in his face. "I'm nothing like *you*! I would never—"

"Meh!" he bleated, sounding like a stuck goat. "*You* would *never*? Never just means you haven't had to yet. But you're young still, General. Give it time." His eyes thinned into slits.

Gorge rose in my throat, and I opened my mouth, then covered it, realizing, suddenly, he wasn't wrong. I stumbled back until my knees knocked the bed frame. I sat, reviewing what I'd done to survive in the Schoolhouse and save the Kongo. Cheat, steal, maim. If someone had told me a year ago I would sacrifice Jetson, reject Hosea Khan and lose my place in the Kongo, I would have called them a liar. And yet, here I was. And *damn him*, but he *wasn't* wrong.

Our eyes locked. Mine ached. His were like bleeding wounds. His mouth, white at the edge, reminded me of a tiny fist, tender and flailing. My shoulders slumped and, all at once, my anger dissolved. "You're young too, Lee," I said, finally. "You can still do what's right."

He blinked, then stared strangely at me for a long time. A knock sounded at the door. Lee tore his gaze from mine and moved to answer it.

At Anna's bedside, I checked her temperature. She was warm, but she breathed easier. Behind me, Lee Ford spoke softly to the clerk, then shut the door. I checked Anna's temperature again, and wet a cloth with cool water.

"The washing facility is down the hall," Lee said. "We have the room for three more hours. He says there's plenty of hot water, but you should get in line now."

I folded the cloth and centered it on Anna's forehead. Finally, I turned to Lee.

He looked like a caricature of himself, chalk on canvas. His arms, bent at the elbow, held a pair of folded towels, delivered by the clerk. He walked to the side of the bed, bent his knees and sat, staring down at the towels, as if he didn't know where he was or how he'd got there.

•

When I came back from the washroom, he sat in the pincushion chair at the desk. His palm was open and a scene hovered above it.

I stood, watching it from across the room. I saw a pair of hands, then the grandmother standing on the stairs. She looked tense but satisfied. Then I saw Weka Vine. Her face was torn and bleeding. Her eyes, swollen.

Disturbed, I closed the door with a click. Lee stopped the projection and twisted in the chair to look at me. I shifted under his gaze.

"I'm going to call the valet now," I said.

He nodded, turned, and started the projection again—minimized in the palm of his hand. I craned my neck to see he'd rewound the seed file. The same pair of hands filled the scene, then the grandmother, then Weka. This time, I was close enough to hear Weka scream Hosea's name.

•

Fifteen minutes later, I hung up the cone-shaped landcom receiver. "The vehicle will be here in an hour," I said. "I've rented it for three hours and I chose an automatic pick-up. So we'll just leave it when we reach Hasting." Lee didn't seem to hear.

I walked over to the desk, catching a glimpse of the scene he watched. It was a new file. I saw a garden and heard laughter. Someone called his name.

"Lee?" I said. "I'm going to get food. Do you want anything?"

He looked up. His eyes had a soft sheen I'd never seen before; his mouth was pulled back in a half-smile. "Nothing for me," he said. "Get a take-away meal for Anna."

•

An hour later we checked out of our room and met the valet runner on the roof deck of the inn. The young woman explained the pick-up procedure, handed over control of the multi-passenger hovercraft and flew away on a slim board.

The craft was a new, open-air model. There were no doors. Its rugged pipe frame was attached to crystal flooring. Its four fly tires gyrated powerful gusts of air so the streaks of dirt whirling in their midst made complete circles.

I stepped closer, looking for the solar tiles that I knew fueled the vehicle. They were nearly invisible. I moved to examine the exposed engine, which was intricately woven and worked silently. It seemed impossible that an engine so small could power such a large craft.

I stowed our packs and climbed in, watching Lee manipulate Anna's invisible, sleeping form. He'd given her another tablet before leaving the room.

"Is she going to be okay?" I asked, gently.

"I'll know more when she wakes. But, yes, I think she's out of danger."

Still, guilt hung over him, casting shadows on his face. He'd watched a handful of seed files, then drifted into heavy silence before watching the same files again.

When Anna was buckled in, he moved to the driver's seat. He went to start the vehicle, then hesitated. He shifted onto one hip and took a seed file from his pocket. He held it up between us; it was unmarked. He pressed it between his forefinger and thumb, then flipped it over his first knuckle.

"I watched Hosea Khan's seed files," he said. He rolled the file back, then over his knuckle again. "The ones he's been wanting me to see for—months. There's something I want you to see."

I wet my mouth, waited. He put the file in his comm-unit and projected the scene.

THE AX IN THE BACK

"Lee, come boy. Your father is almost here."

Lee's small legs beat like hummingbirds as he hurried across the field towards Weka Vine, who stood at the door of a village hut. She wore her hair braided just like her mother and her cockle shell jewelry was also familiar. She was looking in the wrong direction. She cupped her hands at her mouth and shouted again. "Lee!"

"I'm packed, Mother!" Lee said, coming into her line of sight. His cheeks were red, his hair a sunny yellow color.

Lee walked into the house and the scene changed to a view of the sparsely furnished interior of the hut. He stood beside a small trunk and Weka knelt before him, holding his cheeks.

Director Kumar appeared in the doorway, young and muscular, his legs flesh and blood. He went immediately to Weka, bent and kissed her lightly. He glanced at Lee, then around the small space. "Where is the boy?" he demanded.

Weka stood. Her smile was wide but stiff. "He's right here," she said, touching Lee's bright head.

"Don't be obtuse, Weka," Kumar said.

"Hosea is with his grandmother, Dana," she said. "He's going to stay here and complete his study of medicine."

"I told you to have him ready," Kumar said.

"Lee will go with you instead." Weka pushed Lee forward, a hand on his back.

Kumar's face darkened. "Bring me my son."

Weka covered Lee's ears. "Lee is our son," she whispered.

Kumar ground his teeth. "Weka. Why do you do this? Why do you always choose what's hard? I warned you. Guard!"

A trio of Kongo Guards entered the hut.

"Search everywhere," Kumar ordered. "Find him."

The guards started up the stairs. Lee sat down on a cushion by the fireplace, his eyes wide.

Kumar began pacing in front of the door, mumbling. "I pulled you from nowhere, taught you everything. I trusted you," he turned on a heel. "Then she comes and you quit the lab. Now this?"

"She knows things, Dana," Weka said. "And she brought proof. She knows what we've been working on and why."

"Because she's a spy!" he said. "She's working for Dorian."

"She knows things about me," Weka said. "Things I haven't told anyone. Things about the future!"

"She's lying!"

Weka pinched the bridge of her nose, exhausted. "Well, I believe her," she said. "If we do what she says, follow her plan, Hosea will—"

"*We* have a plan," he shouted. "You've had him seven years, now it's my turn."

Weka ignored him. Her eyes moved to the stairs.

A few minutes later, the guards filed back downstairs, alone.

Kumar pinned Weka with his gaze. "Please, Weka. Where is my son?!"

Weka shook her head. "I don't know—"

"Where is he?" Kumar roared.

Weka lifted her chin and sealed her mouth.

For a second, Kumar's face broke—exposing deep love for her. Then he clenched a fist. "You fool." He turned to the guards. "Get her." He waved a hand towards her obstinate pose and the guards came forward.

Weka stood tall but Lee, on his pillow by the fire, shrank. He curled himself in a dark corner of the room and covered his face. A guard took each of Weka's arms and the third positioned himself in front of her.

"Last chance, Weka," Kumar said, pleading.

Wetness flooded her eyes, a tear slipped down her cheek.

When the first blow fell, Weka jerked with its weight, but it was Lee who screamed.

Kumar turned his back on the scene, his jaw tight. "Again." The muscular guard landed another open-handed blow. Weka jerked, Lee covered his face and ears and cried.

"Again," Kumar ordered. Weka whimpered; Lee howled. Kumar, clearly distressed, lifted his face to the ceiling. "It doesn't have to be this way, Weka. Give me the boy as we agreed, and I'll go. I'll be good to him. I'll teach him to fight. Make him a king."

Weka spit. "I tell you, Dana. You can't have him. She says our plan will ruin him. She says—"

"Lies!" The Director spun and took three quick steps to Weka's side. "He's my child. *My* blood. I'll do what I want with him!" Before Weka could respond, he signaled the guard. "Again!" he roared.

The beating progressed from harsh slaps to brutal fists. When the guard grew tired, Kumar rolled up his sleeves and began landing body blows. He was red-faced and sweating, spitting as he shouted, "Where is he?"

Finally, Weka seemed to lose consciousness. The guards let her drop to the floor. Lee, sobbing, scurried from his corner. When he reached her, Weka's eyes went wide, as if she'd forgotten his presence. She rose on an elbow and pushed him away, pointing to the stairs. "Run, baby! Find grandma!"

Lee stood and raced to the stairs.

Kumar caught him by the neck.

"No!" Weka screeched, but it was too late. Seeing her weakness, Kumar turned the beating on Lee. After one blow, Weka's resolve shattered. She was sobbing, begging Kumar to stop.

"My son!" Kumar demanded.

"Dana, please. I don't know where he is, I swear. She wouldn't tell me. We haven't seen them for days—"

"Witch!" Kumar shouted, aiming his voice at the staircase. "Witch, I know you're here!" he screamed at the top of his lungs. Furious, he turned back to Lee, venting his rage in a flurry of blows.

The beating continued until, suddenly, the three guards, one after another, jerked and collapsed onto their backs, bleeding from their heads. Director Kumar froze, his fist raised, his eyes wide. The young Lee barely avoided being crushed by his father's body as Kumar fell, an ax protruding from his back.

Weka was on the ground, close to the prone guards. Lee's body was swollen and bruised, his eyes shut. Just then, fingers and palms filled the scene as the author of the memory focused on his hands, still flexed from throwing the ax.

He looked left and up, to the top of the staircase. The grandmother stood there, looking down on him, her brown gaze satisfied—almost triumphant. Then she jerked and hurried down the stairs.

"Hosea, baby!" Weka said, identifying the author of the seed. She tore her eyes from Hosea and struggled to reach Lee. He was unconscious, but she gathered him in her arms.

The older woman brushed past Hosea Khan and stepped over Lee and Weka. She checked Kumar's neck. "Alive, barely," she said. She sounded relieved. "I'll get my bag." She rose quickly. At the stairs, she glanced warily at Weka.

The woman cradled Lee, but she glared at Kumar with hatred.

"Watch her," the grandmother said. "And remember the story. He's more work to do. "

As she climbed the stairs, Hosea looked down at his hands again. They were trembling. He clenched them into fists.

He looked up as Weka shifted Lee from her lap. She carefully arranged his limbs, then got to her feet and went to the hearth, returning with a knife in her hand. She moved back to Kumar, knelt and took his hair in one hand. She lifted the knife to his throat.

"Mother, stop!" Hosea said.

Weka froze at the command. She looked up. "We can end it now," she said.

A long pause followed. "I think he—he has to live," Hosea said.

"And me?" Weka hissed. "And your brother?"

"I'll go," Hosea said. "He won't hurt you if I go."

THE NUCLEAR VOTE

As the scene faded, I sat in silence, stunned.

"The next morning, the guards came to escort us to the Kongo Technology Center to begin training," Lee said. "I was only five but, even then, I knew my worth. I was only welcome there, only alive so he could control Hosea Khan."

"But Hosea had already agreed to come," I said.

"To *come*, yes," Lee said. "Kumar took me to ensure Hosea would stay. The plan was to transfer from the KTC to the forest when the Compound was complete. Father was a harsh teacher, but Hosea was like a shield. When he did what he was told, life with Father was—manageable, for all of us." Lee hesitated. "Hosea promised me he would come to the Compound, for my sake and Mother's. He told Father he'd go, too. And we all believed him. So, when he didn't—"

I shuddered, imagining Lee enduring Kumar's anger alone. "It must have been terrible, Lee," I said.

Lee shook his head. "I don't remember most of it. I've tried but I *can't* remember." His eyes lost focus as he manipulated the file, flipping it again and again, staring into the past.

"I understand," I said. And I did. Lee had the ability to mine his memories and examine them from a safe place. He left these particular memories in the past because pain that couldn't be borne was better forgotten.

"Since then, Hosea Khan's not stayed any place too long," Lee said, thoughtfully. "Mother left Kumar's *protection*, but she didn't live long. And I never tried."

He opened his mouth to continue, hesitated, and closed it again, flipping the file.

I didn't push him to reveal whatever he was holding back.

He glanced at the back seat. Anna hadn't made a noise. "Let's get out of here," he said.

•

In the late afternoon we landed in an oasis close to Hasting.

Night fell quickly and Lee sat beside Anna, who was still unconscious. He took her vitals.

"How is she?"

"Her numbers are good but she's not waking." He hung his head then met my gaze with the same pregnant expression he'd leveled at me since we made camp.

"Lee, what is it?"

He took a breath. "I've been thinking about why Hosea gave me that memory," he said. "Why the moment he made the promise that he broke?"

"It's what caused the rift between you," I said, seeing his point. If the goal was to heal the relationship, why remind Lee that he'd lied?

Before he could answer, a sharp bell tolled.

"An announcement," I said. I looked across the oasis we'd stopped in. It was deserted and sparsely packed with trees that blocked our view of the sky. The toll came from the south, however, which meant the closest projection would be at Hasting.

I got to my feet and ran to the southern trees. Lee followed to stand beside me.

When the bell stopped, a visual of Senator Osprey in front of a noisy gathering in Cobane appeared in the sky over the castle. We had an unobstructed view, and clear audio. Osprey called for the crowd to quiet. When the people calmed, she cleared her throat and read from a prepared speech.

"Good evening. This is Senator Osprey speaking on behalf of the Kongo Council, with a live special announcement on this election night." The image blinked and the sound fizzled as a hydroplane, as flat and round as a disc, flew through her middle, separating her torso from her hips. It flew on, and the image came back together as Senator Osprey continued. "The election votes have all been cast and counted. I'm pleased to announce that General Arika Cobane, by write-in, has preserved her seat on the Kongo Council." Raucous cheering erupted through the audio. "The people have spoken," she said, firmly. "And we, your Council, hear you. We've amended the sentence and reinstated the General's full legal status, that she might, henceforth, hold public office."

I inhaled, meeting Lee Ford's gaze.

"Congratulations, Arika," he said. He rested a hand on my shoulder, but I shook him off.

"I don't trust it," I said. "Kira is still on the Council. If they've reinstated me, it's for a reason."

A hydroplane began to rain, losing fat drops over Cobane. Osprey lifted a cloak over her head to shield herself. She went on, "The new Council quorum is already at work, securing safety for the Kongo people," she said. "We've agreed with boisterous consent, and one abstention, on our first matter of order."

"Abstention?" I hissed. "I didn't abstain!"

Osprey announced the subject and outcome of the first official vote, but her voice was drowned out by the cheers of the crowd. They shouted my name and screamed their support of unity in the Kongo.

She waited for a lull and spoke quickly. "Again, by nearly unanimous vote, Councilwoman Voltaire's status has changed. After much consideration, the Council has determined to presume her dead."

The crowd hushed and I pressed a fist to my middle. Voltaire was a much-loved public figure. For months now, I had counted on her staying away, but I never doubted her loyalty and never once, in all that time, had I wished her dead. I stiffened as another thought occurred to me. "Obi," I whispered.

Lee looked down at me. "What is it?"

I held up a trembling hand, mentally filtering through the law I, myself, had written.

"Arika, calm down," Lee said. "You're shaking."

I clenched a fist, staring up at Osprey as the Council's true purpose took shape. "Declaring Voltaire dead leaves them free to fill the seat for the remainder of Voltaire's tenure."

Lee's eyes narrowed. "They *fill* it. There's not a vote?"

"'The replacement is to be appointed by a quorum of Council,'" I quoted. "That's it. That's why they wanted me reinstated, so that they can name a new member—and give them my tacit approval."

A crack of thunder sounded from Cobane and the rain redoubled. This time it was natural rain, from the storm clouds that had gathered there earlier.

Osprey called over the tamed crowd, "In light of that declaration, I'm proud to announce we've appointed an official to serve out the rest of Councilwoman Voltaire's time in office. Please welcome our newest Council member, Director Dana Kumar."

My heart slammed into my chest. The crowd cried and called out, a mix of cheers and hisses, but I didn't hear it; every noise was crushed by the sound of red-hot blood rushing to my head.

THE RUNAWAY

"Wake up!" Lee said.

I opened my eyes to find Lee squatting over me. I scratched my neck where the ruby necklace chafed and sat up. I recalled Osprey's announcement, but I pushed it to the back of my exhausted mind. "What happened?" I said.

He held up my brown medicinal patches. "You collapsed, which means your levels are up. You've got to keep at least three of these on at all times. Understand?"

I touched the nape of my neck, feeling four patches. I checked my comm-unit and stood, realizing hours had passed. "The tower. It's near dawn!"

"There's something else," Lee said.

I shook my head. "We've got to get to the tower."

"Anna's gone," Lee said quickly, over my protest.

I paused. "Gone? Gone where?"

"She must have left during the announcement."

I went to the place we'd laid Anna to rest and rummaged around. The bed roll was cold. "She's a fool," I said. "The desert isn't kind to wanderers and we don't have time to look for her. Pack up, I'll be back." I moved toward a dense patch of trees to relieve myself.

"She took a map, water and her medications," he called after me. "She must have heard us talking about the fever."

I found a spot and raised my voice to Lee. "I told you the English aren't to be trusted. She's probably been spying the whole time. They're hypocrites, liars, and thieves—" I froze in the act of pulling up my undergarments. I straightened and ran back to the camp, sliding to a stop at my pack.

"Arika?" Lee said, concerned.

Ignoring him, I pulled everything out and opened the secret container at the bottom. The scarf I'd wrapped the bracelet in had been folded neatly. But the bracelet itself was gone. I slumped over, making a noise like a wounded animal.

Lee knelt. "Are you hurt?" He tugged at my shoulders, forcing me to straighten. "Are you having an episode?" He lifted my hair to ensure the medicinal patches were secure. "General, can you hear me?"

"She took the bracelet," I said, finally. Lee's hand flew to my upper arm. I cleared my throat, where a hard lump had formed. "I took it from her when we made camp here. I thought she was sleeping." I shook my head. "I actually felt bad for her." I looked down at my hands and balled them into fists. "She waited until I let down my guard and took what was mine. Just like the English always do."

Lee shook my bag out, searching in vain. "She's not safe in the Kongo or the north," he said at last. "She needs it."

"I need it!" I said. "Me and you. We need it!" When he opened his mouth to respond, I cut him off. "Save your breath, Lee." I stood. "You'll need it for the walk to Hasting."

"It's over, Arika," he said, rising to stand beside me.

I glared at him. He was concerned but not angry at Anna's betrayal. "You want it to be over," I said. "Why?"

"Hasting is under armed guard," he said. "Without invisibility, we'll be walking into certain death."

"We still have the cuff," I said. "If you carry me, it should cover me just as it does your pack when it's on your back."

He opened his mouth and closed it, seeing I was right. "What about our belongings?" he said.

"We'll come back for them."

He fell silent. I faced him squarely. He'd changed. Something about those seed files had changed him; he no longer had the same determination. He seemed defeated.

"Lee," I whispered. "At least keep your part. Show me how to wield them. Then we'll go our separate ways." I could see he didn't want to. And he wasn't ready to tell me why. But, finally, he nodded.

I repacked my bag, taking only the necessities.

•

When we reached the edge of the oasis, I wrapped my small pack around my body and climbed onto Lee Ford's back. When every part of my body touched some part of his, I tapped his shoulder. "Activate the cuff," I said.

He did. I looked down at our joined bodies, fighting the dizzying feeling of being both on his back and invisible.

"It worked," I said, relieved. "The watch won't see us coming."

He bent and set me back on my feet, then he deactivated the bracelet. He stood for a long time, his arms crossed. "Fine," he said, finally. "But first, we eat and drink—both of us. We need fuel for the journey."

"Done," I said.

Thirty minutes later, we started toward Hasting.

THE PUSH TO HASTING

Hasting had suffered during the rebellion. As the seat of the old Kongo government, we battered it in our campaign to force the Keepers who lived there to our side. And when the diplomats fled to its walls for safety, we'd laid siege to it.

Fear of reprisal had fueled the diplomats' repair efforts early on. Once Nicky McCormick was captured, however, their fervor slackened. In the nine months of my absence, restoration had nearly come to a halt. The cement blocks of the outer wall skirted only three quarters of the keep. Through it, the ruined inner curtain was visible. Even from a distance, I saw its ancient limestone boulders were weathered and crumbling.

The moat they had dug was deep but drained, ostensibly to facilitate repairs. Lee and I approached from the north and walked down to the dry base of the moat. We crossed, unbothered, except by the jagged rubble that littered the ground and slowed our progress.

We walked around to the front gate, reaching it just as the drawbridge creaked and lowered. Lee stopped as a dozen Kongos, a remnant of the Guard, pooled out of the castle. Following them, an English diplomat dressed like a captain of the Guard appeared. He gave instructions, and they scattered to various parts of the bridge and outer curtain.

I leaned forward, so my mouth brushed Lee Ford's ear. "Repairs," I whispered. "They aren't looking for us."

"Agreed," Lee said. Avoiding the workers, he moved around to the part of the inner wall near the front of the tower and prepared to climb.

He released my legs, and I tightened my grip on his shoulders and waist. Below me, a flexible length of wire attached to a metal anchor appeared. It whizzed above my head then flew up to curve around the top surface of the wall. It blended in perfectly.

I heard Lee prepare his hands and felt his arms move to grip the wire; he took a deep breath. "Hold tight. It's extremely windy," he whispered.

Twenty minutes later, dripping sweat and shaking with the effort, he pulled us to a standing position on the crest of the wall. Bracing against the wind, which battered our tired bodies relentlessly, he turned to collect the wire. As he leaned forward, I craned my neck, analyzing our view, squinting in the weak early light.

The fortress courtyard was a patchwork of cultivated earth and abandoned projects. Most of the neat green plots were close to the castle where the diplomats slept, ate and worked. Further out, the land was tilled, but unplanted.

I recognized the remains of the Kongo library and felt nausea swirl in my stomach as I contemplated all that had been lost when it burned. I thought of Kira Swan: if she wasn't nearby in the diplomats' keep, she'd just left. What had she felt at the sight of so many lost souls and stories? Did they cry out to her as they cried out to me? *Did they even give you pause, Swan, as you betrayed your people?* My throat burned and I swallowed, hard. When I returned to power, I wouldn't hesitate: She would be the first to die.

In the middle of the sooty ruin, our destination, the watchtower, sat like an overgrown mushroom. Red clay over brick and mortar, topped by a glass dome. Its face was unremarkable, except for its pristine condition. Every other part of the castle appeared ragged, or in recent repair, but the war had spared Obi's mausoleum. A chill swept down my neck as I considered why: Jacamar. He was protecting Obi's secrets from the grave.

My eye caught on a small shelter next to the tower. It was shabby, surrounded by a hastily made fence, a stark contrast to its neighboring tower of strength.

"What's that shack?" I whispered. I felt Lee's head turn to look. The wood cabin had a thatch roof, overshadowed by the tower. "It's new," I said. "Built sometime after the fire."

"A dorm for servants?" Lee guessed.

"Perhaps," I said. But I wondered why, then, they'd put the house so far from the rest of their shelter. As I watched, a white woman with a kitchen apron around her waist and a medical mask on her face opened the gate. Balancing a serving tray, she delicately picked past the overgrown garden surrounding the hut. At the door, she set the tray down on a small table that seemed placed outside for that purpose. She knocked and hurried away. As she fidgeted with the gate of the rickety fence, I noticed she wore gloves.

My eyes skipped around, noting the flow of foot traffic in the courtyard. While it was never deserted, those who did venture out stayed mostly in the cultivated garden close to the keep and no one else visited the watchtower or the nearby house.

"We can descend on that side of the wall, behind the tower," I said.

"Agreed," Lee said.

His feet touched the ground a few minutes later, the descent fortunately quicker than the climb. With me still on his back, we walked over sun-scorched vegetation to the watchtower and opened the door. It creaked and a musty stench wafted out. I sneezed and squinted around the dust that billowed. Inside, I inhaled. I'd seen pictures of the tower interior, but none had done justice to the sight of the mausoleum at dawn. The sun shining through the glass dome made pictures on the smooth clay walls and stone floor and on the spiral steps that soared up to a platform near the glass dome.

"Put me down," I said to Lee.

Lee hesitated then bent down. I reappeared as soon as my feet touched the floor. I moved to the base of the staircase and took the first step. Lee turned off the cuff and followed me. The staircase was sturdy wrought iron and had a low handrail. The ledges were narrow and shallow, which forced me to balance my weight on the ball of my foot. I leaned forward as we climbed, anticipating the next level. The spiral tightened with each step until, around the last bend, I felt a wave of dizziness. I gripped the rail to steady myself as I made the circular landing and turned sideways to make room for Lee. He pressed his front to my back and squeezed onto the platform.

His breath sounded in my ear as I stared at the glass dome that surrounded us. With each passing minute, as the morning brightened, expelling the early mist, more shapes and pictures appeared on the walls and on our bodies. I held both arms over the rail, palms up, catching the images. "Stunning," I breathed.

When Lee didn't respond, I twisted to look back at him. My heart stalled. Beneath the tattoo of pictures, his face was ashen and sweaty. His eyes darted, jumping from wall to wall, and he trembled.

"Lee, what is it?" He opened his mouth and huffed, then closed it.

I grabbed his shoulders and shook. "Lee!"

He blinked. "We've got to leave," he whispered.

"But the bracelets—"

He shook his head. "I don't think the bracelets are here."

"What—why?"

He started down the stairs.

"Lee, wait!"

He kept moving, taking the steps two at a time. "The symbols on the wall," he said over his shoulder. "It's writing. It's the tongue of God."

I grabbed his arm, forcing him to stop or pull me down. He looked up at me.

"The tongue from the myth?" I said. "It's a language."

He nodded. "Grandmother was the last person alive who could speak it."

"And she taught you?"

"No. She studied it around me as a kid, and, like I've said, I studied my memories. I taught myself. It was necessary for reproducing the bracelet."

I looked again at the tower walls and, eerily, I felt them looking back. "What does it say?" I said.

"It's an obituary to Obi Solomon. A list of his feats in battle and after. And a warning about the curse." He pointed to the left. "This says, 'If Obi's spirit chooses to speak to you, you won't live past three days.' So, we need to get out of here in case he decides to speak."

"What does it say about the bracelets?"

"That's just it, General. It doesn't mention the bracelets at all. And that's what I'm afraid of. I've been thinking about Father and the past. About why Hosea Khan gave me that file. The moment he made the promise that he then broke. Why remind me? What was he trying to show me?"

"I—I don't know."

"Neither do I. But it's had me thinking about Father. And the more I think, the more certain I am. Father didn't send you here for the Principles. Why would he?"

"Because he can't get them himself," I said. "Because *I'm the one*."

Lee scoffed. "Flattery. That's how he operates. He smiles, tells you what you want to hear, so you're never looking at what's not being said. There's nothing written here about 'the one' or loyalty to the Kongo."

I wet my mouth, examining his logic.

He flung out an arm to point at the wall to his left. "Why didn't Jacamar mention the bracelets?"

I shook my head. "I don't know. To keep them secret?"

"Maybe, but tell me this," Lee said. "Kumar has to know we're gone by now, that we left together. And he knows that I know how to wield the bracelets. So, why are we still alive? Why is he angling for power on the Kongo Council when he knows you and I are about to unleash the most powerful weapon on the world?"

I bit my lip. "Then he sent me here to die?"

"Negative." Lee stared, waiting for me to catch on. Finally, he whispered, "He came up with the scheme to send you here right after he saw Hosea's map."

"The map of the west," I said, still confused.

"Right," Lee said. "I sent it to Father and, right after, he suddenly decides to give you the bracelet—why?" This time he didn't wait for me to answer. "General, I think he's after what he's always after. You saw him in that seed. He's hoping his real son, his blood, will be lured back home to save you."

I squinted, picturing Kumar's shrieking visage—the madness, the possession, the fear. My face grew warm, then hot. "I'm the bait," I said slowly. He wanted to send me so Hosea Khan would follow.

"Father has always maneuvered to control Hosea, but nothing works. He lives in the woods. He keeps to himself. He's impossible to bribe because he hasn't cared about anything since Mother—until you."

I could feel Lee's gaze on me, probing. I turned away, and my knees buckled beneath me. I sat on the iron step.

"What are you doing?" Lee hissed. "We have to leave!"

"You leave," I said, my heart in my throat. "I have to stay."

"Oh, give up, General," Lee said, exasperated. "Hosea's not the prince Father wants him to be or the hero you think he is. He's not coming to save you!"

"I know that, Lee," I said. I squeezed my eyes shut, blocking the pain of the admission. "But I have to stay," I whispered.

"To die!?"

I looked up. "To bring the truth to the Kongo," I said. "For me, the bracelets were only part of the mission. This mystery has haunted us—haunted *me*, for years. Why did Obi betray us and why did we follow him? What did he love more than the Kongo? We need to know. *I* need to know. Once I do, I'll have three days to share it and maybe it'll make a difference—maybe they'll see."

"It isn't worth your life," Lee said. He knelt on the iron step below me. When we were eye level, he took my hand. "I love you," he said.

It was an argument. A last push to persuade me to run, though I saw he believed it. I smiled sadly, and squeezed his hand. Like everyone, he didn't understand. He couldn't see that my heart belonged to the Kongo. To the rich earth that nurtured me and never let go. I blinked, releasing a stream of tears as I watched him go.

•

When he was out of sight, I climbed the stairs to the platform and lifted my face to the dome. I raised both arms and shouted.

"I am the one. I have come. Now, speak!"

A soft breeze blew as my tongue formed around the last word. It tickled the hair on my neck and dried the sweat that cooled in the pits of my upraised arms. I breathed in and out as the breeze grew stronger. It curved around my body like an arm and tightened around my waist. It whirled, thickened, lengthening to encompass my thighs and calves. It lifted me off my feet and snuggled under, so my whole form hung in the crown of the dome. Then, it rose over my chest, my shoulders. It crept up over my neck and swallowed me whole.

I felt no fear in the dome of the tower—only love. I was a bird and I flew with a flock. We formed an arrow in the sky, calling—ready, ready, set, set, go. We flew back down to the earth, pierced the ground and burrowed down through the crust and the mantle to the core.

There, I broke formation. I fell and landed, gently, in a breeze. The time was many years ago, in a place I'd never been.

My arms and legs were human again, but invisible. And I was not only myself; I was more. Dark and countless. All-knowing and ever-present.

I stood, turned and opened our eye.

THE TRUTH ABOUT OBI

Obi Solomon sat half-dressed on a desk in a large tent. He rubbed his cheek with a square hand up and down, digging his fingers in the stiff bristles of his mutton-chop beard. With a quick motion, he opened the desk drawer and lifted out a sheet of paper with a billowing quill resting, ready, on top. He picked up the quill in a fist, revealing the page beneath. It was covered in angry fits of ink.

Obi turned the page over, revealing the clean back half. I moved closer to look over his shoulder. The page was printed with neat rows of signature lines with the words *Kongo Delegate* written underneath. Taking a deep breath, Obi dipped the quill in ink and adjusted his fist, so the tip hovered over the first signature. He lowered his hand and scratched the name *Obi Smolon*.

He lifted his hand, and we examined his work. The letters were wobbly, the S looked wrong, but I could tell he didn't know why. I could feel Obi's frustration as if it were my own. Our skin burned and our blood ran hot. Then, with a grunt he told himself to remain calm and try again. *Oib Snolmon*. The B was backward. He shook his head, and we tried again. We failed. We were shaking all over now, besieged by impending doom. We stood up, looking left and right. We had to escape.

Someone behind us cleared their throat.

Obi turned. "Jacamar," he said, his voice unsteady.

Jacamar's face was lined with sympathy. "It is time, Obi," he said. "We must go."

Obi bowed our head; a pulse pumped at our temple. "Master," he breathed, trembling. "What am I to do?"

"I've tried," Jacamar said, sadly. "The Will will not be moved, and I have no strength to fight it. The people will suffer, but you won't be to blame, and they will know it. Now—come."

Obediently, Obi stood. He picked up an armful of belongings and left the tent. I hurried after him.

"Eh, Obi!"

Obi stopped and turned, dropping his things on a nearby work bench. He wore no shirt. His feet were bare, and his head ached from too much drink the night before. The sun at his back cast a long shadow so the boy who'd hailed him disappeared into it. Obi squinted, but it was no use. The boy was a shadow, a worshipful smile in the dark.

"What is it, boy?" Obi said.

The boy grinned, showing all his teeth. "I hear you papa was a quarter god and you ma was a fairy princess."

Obi sighed. He fitted a belt around his waist and sheathed his danomite sword. He was not in the mood to think about his father, a man his mother had called 'the Pirate.'

The boy went on. "I hear you papa carried a trident and swam in the sea."

Obi grimaced. He'd made up a relatively simple lie about his father, whom he'd never met, telling anyone who would listen that he was the son of the old-world Congo's greatest king.

In truth, he'd made up the lie long before he'd become the General of the Kongo Army. When he was a boy with a wild imagination, tickling fish in backwater streams of Botswana. His real father, a man his mother could barely remember, had been a traveler.

After the Last War had taken his mother and decimated his native country, the lie had sprung easily, again and again, to Obi's lips. Actual Congolese survivors had laughed at his stories of his father king, not bothering to call him a liar. As the Last War had raged on, however, erasing order, along with most of Africa, he'd met less opposition to his tale. Now, fifty years after the first earth-destroyer attack, no one contradicted him. Instead, they embellished his basic tale and worshiped him with unnerving faithfulness.

The boy clicked his teeth with glee and gushed on. "I hear you ma birthed you in a volcano that was blowing its horn and that's how come you pitch black. I hear you fought a lion that had ten heads and a tiger with a forked tongue. And you bested them with your bare hands and only one leg."

Obi frowned. At some point the embellishment had become ridiculous. He supposed his rule against letters had done its job too well. Few in the Kongo could read the handful of history books they had left. Consequently, no one could unravel the image he'd created for them. He'd done it for the people's own good, he told himself. The remnants of Africa would never have survived the Last War without unchallenged loyalty to their leader. The Great Obi Solomon, by design, was worth following. No one laughed at him, no one told him to shut up. No one questioned him.

On the other hand, because it wasn't written down, no one could keep the story straight. As he'd told it, the last Congo king had married the only living daughter of Emperor Mbutu, the Lion-Hearted. He, Obi, was their issue. As bare as a babe, he'd spilled his first blood in battle off the coast of the Zambezi River—a devil with a forked tongue and a French accent. He'd slain his foe and injured his heel, not his leg, in the scuffle. The story had been so butchered over the years, he no longer bothered to correct the inconsistencies. Though, these days, they were increasingly tiresome to hear.

The boy continued eagerly. "I hear you fed ten thousand starving Kongos with but two fish and five loaves."

Obi balked. "That's impossible!"

The boy scratched his chin. "I hear nothing is impossible for you. Is it true you're leaving today to torture the English general? I bet he will bow to you and the whole world will be ours!"

Obi shifted uncomfortably. He'd been in peace negotiations with the English for weeks and the committee was set to make the Compromise public any day. From the start, he realized he was in over his head. Page after page of English documents had passed by him, but he was not a lettered man. He was a soldier, a leader, a god on Earth—not a professor.

Not wanting to appear weak, he had pretended to read the papers. But the day of reckoning was coming. When the agreement was ratified, his people would know that he was not the one to deliver them. Their faith would break. And, without faith, nothing was possible.

Obi felt an overwhelming urge to come clean. "I am not the one you speak of," he said, suddenly. The boy started. He looked confused. Then, slowly, the light in his eyes faded. His shoulders slumped. His head lowered. Obi couldn't stand it. He couldn't disappoint. "I am not the one," he said, quickly. "But one is coming—mightier than I."

The boy's head came up. A huge grin spread across his face. "A one greater than you, the great Obi Solomon? Now I know you are jesting."

Obi sighed. Jacamar's strength was waning now, so he had no idea of the future—except that it looked bleak. The light of faith was back in the boy's eye, however, and—for now—he didn't dare disturb it. The people wanted to believe in him; they needed to.

He would sign the papers, as Jacamar commanded, and make the best of whatever came. When their faith flickered, he would find a hill somewhere. And when the night came, he would take his own life before all the faith in the Kongo died. He turned away as the boy trotted off.

He took a dry cloth and spot cleaned his left hand—a gift from the English general's wife, who fancied him. The prosthetic was a near perfect replica of his right hand but the brown flesh, a prototype, tended to gather dust. When the hand was suitably clean, he donned his English clothes and the rest of his armor.

At the docking pole he paused and looked back over the encampment. For their sake, he hoped he was right, that there was one coming: a savior of real substance and not—he admitted—the lies of a lonely Botswanan boy. Someone who would stand up for the people. He thought of the legends he'd worshiped as a child. Someone who would live and die for them. A man of unusual strength and intellect, a warrior born of a virgin—a true hero. Obi smiled at his own fancy—or heroine. Shaking his head, he mounted his horse and turned its head to the north.

THE TRUTH ABOUT KIRA SWAN

Obi's image faded as I fell from the center of the dome. I landed on the iron staircase and crumpled to my knees—reeling. Beams of daylight blinded me and the blare of a siren assaulted my ears.

"Arika!" Lee shouted from the bottom of the stairs. "They know we're here. Come now!" His voice was hoarse as if he'd been shouting a while.

When I tried to respond, I toppled over, disoriented. The scene, the light, the siren. How long had I been up here?

"Arika!" Lee called again. "They're coming, Arika. We've got to go!"

I pushed to my feet and bent over the railing. "Lee!" He didn't hear; he was halfway to the exit. I turned and stumbled down the steps. I reached the bottom just as Lee touched the cuff on his arm and dashed into the courtyard. I ran to the door and peeked outside.

"Lee Ford," I whispered, hoping he was close by. "Lee!" I slipped out, circled the tower and darted to the inner wall. I cupped a hand around my mouth. "Lee!" I hissed, but there was no reply.

The sound of marching footsteps undercut the pitch of the siren. A handful of guards were coming my way to secure the tower.

Ducking, I ran to the nearest shelter. I hurdled the fence of the dilapidated shack, crossed the backyard and flattened myself against the wood siding. My heart pounded. It was only a matter of time before they rounded the watchtower and saw me. I needed a place to hide. On my hands and knees, I moved to a back window. It was crusted with filth. I couldn't see inside, but I had no choice. With a hand on my Helix, I opened the door a crack and slid inside.

Oppressive heat and the stench of alcohol greeted me. The air was stale, as if the hut had been shut tight for weeks. I moved through a small washroom and crept into the main space, then crouched with my back against the clay wall to assess my surroundings. It was furnished like an infirmary. A four-post canopy bed was centered, facing away from me. Beside it were medical machines with tubes running to and from the dingy sheets. Near the foot of the bed was a freestanding hearth with a low fire glowing inside.

Straightening, I skirted an unsealed oak desk and chair, then edged around to view the headboard. There was a person beneath the sheets, engulfed in a fluff of covers and pillows. Her eyes were closed and she lay as if sleeping, despite the low moan of the siren. She was no threat. I spotted a wooden wardrobe, the perfect place to hide.

I was in the center of the room, halfway to the wardrobe, when a hoarse whisper stopped me.

"Girl."

I froze. That voice. It came from the woman on the bed. Slowly, I turned my head. She wasn't sleeping, as I'd supposed. She was old and the skin of her brows hung loose over her red, watery gaze.

I squinted, and caught my breath. "Teacher?"

Jones' eyes flashed at the sound of that name. My hand flew to my throat and gripped the ruby necklace as I moved closer. Her body, once thickly muscled and well marbled, was diminished, barely a swell in the blanket. An ugly face, a sunken mouth, skin on bone.

At the bedside, a strange elation seized me. How many times had I imagined coming upon her like this? Small, helpless, in need—as I'd been that day by the Schoolhouse window. How many times had I pictured standing over her, like she'd stood over me, smiling down, perfecting my shame?

"Girl," she whispered, through stiff lips.

I met her cold gaze, still sharp and full of hatred. Beneath it, I felt transported back in time and an old fear peeled down my spine. I retreated a step, defensively.

Glad to have scared me, she wheezed happily, and a coughing fit seized her. She sounded congested, like a sticky substance coated her throat and lungs. When the spell passed, she continued to heckle. "Girrrl. Heh, heh."

My eyes narrowed. The sound was feeble. And her lips were split and flecked with spittle. My shoulders relaxed. "What's that, Jones?" I returned to the bed, rank with the smell of illness and decay. I bent, lending an ear as she whimpered, trying to intimidate me. "Spit it out," I whispered, snidely. Pain stung my face and I shrieked. "You bit me?!"

My hand zipped out to slap her withered cheek. Her neck snapped left and, for moment, I thought I'd killed her. Then her head turned slowly back to me. Her eyes twinkled and a barking sound erupted from her throat. She was laughing!

"Shut up! Shut up!" I ripped my ruby knife from my ankle. I pressed it close to her throat. "Shut up!"

She quieted, but her eyes gleamed still—with hatred, pride, fond memories. She was not beaten. She was not afraid. I tried to hold her gaze, match her disgust but, to my horror, tears stung my eyes. I shifted my knife and dashed them away.

"I did nothing to you," I said, my chin on my chest. "I was just a little girl." I swallowed, realizing, foolishly, I wanted her to admit it. To acknowledge the truth. I had done nothing, and she had tortured a little girl.

I looked down at my knife and, slowly, sheathed it.

Her arms flailed suddenly, trying to catch me defenseless. I reared, taking a corner of her cover with me. It slipped from the bed, revealing her body to the waist.

I gasped. "Oh!" I gagged and leaned away. Scarlet boils and dark gray lesions covered her torso. A ghastly smell, like rotting flesh, wafted from the sores.

She gurgled and my gaze flew to her face. I froze at the emotion there. She'd tucked her chin and curled up, pressing into her pillows to avoid exposure. But it was too late, and she knew it. A fleshy vulnerability flared around her nostrils.

Instinctually, I looked away from her nakedness. I bent to pick up the fallen blanket and leaned forward to cover her body. She hissed and clawed at me, bursting a boil close to her left breast. Liquid oozed down her side. Still, she swatted. I stepped back, easily avoiding her reach. And, for the first time, I saw Alice Jones. Her hatred, anger, pain—like poison. I saw how it festered and spread. Biting at others, little girls, then turning on her to eat her alive.

"You're dead, Jones," I said. And she had been for years. I lowered my eyes and turned my back on her.

A loud crash sounded. I jumped and looked over my shoulder. One of the bedside tables teetered, then toppled. Tubes popped and bottles clattered. As they settled, a faint *click* reached my ears. My eyes flew to identify the sound. I gasped when I found it.

Jones, propped on one elbow, looked satisfied. Her mangled fingers were wrapped around an old-world gun. It was pointed at my heart.

My stomach dropped. Old-world guns had been outlawed since the Last War. The one she held was wreckage. Still, one shot, I knew, would end me. Hosea Khan crossed my mind. His face floated before me as he'd been the last night we were together.

"Bitch," Jones whispered. Her finger tightened on the trigger.

I closed my eyes, not wanting her smile to be the last thing I saw.

"Auntie, no!" came a voice.

My eyes opened. Jones, startled, fumbled the gun once, twice. Kira Swan darted like a hawk from the corner of the room. She was going for the gun, but Jones managed to steady it again, on me.

I looked from her to Jones then back again as months of questions fell neatly into place. It was Kira's voice that had cried 'Auntie.' *Aunt?* I blinked. In my mind, the picture of the beautiful blonde woman collided with Jones's image, as she'd looked in her formal school picture, hung with the others in the Teachers' Hall. All their poses identical. Sitting, gazing out over her left shoulder, facing the camera, cropped from just above the name tag and title. The two women melded together. A lovely, sweet visage covered in heavy slabs of fat as hard as muscle. Beautiful and thick. Strong and serene. A queen. Together they were the image of Kira Swan, minus her dark skin.

"*She's* your aunt!" I said, my voice shaking. "*She's* your 'sick relative.'"

Kira nodded calmly. "My mother's sister."

It had all been right there. Why Jones had favored her. Why she had a birth certificate. They weren't issued in the Kongo. But Kira Swan had been born in the north where, undoubtedly, her mother had fled to avoid whatever illicit relationship she'd had with one of the Kongo workers. No doubt a man with jet-black skin, like Kira Swan's. No name, no house. But was she still Jones's political ally?

Kira answered the question herself. With her hands resting calmly at her sides, she continued closer, placing her body between Jones's bullet and me.

"Don't do this, Auntie," she said. Her tone was evenly pitched, tranquil, soothing. "I believe in you. I believe in the Accord. Think of my mother. Remember how—"

Jones cut her off. "Your mother was a whore," she said, and she pulled the trigger.

I shouted as Kira Swan collapsed. I caught her body before it hit the floor. My hands flooded with blood.

"You shot her!" I yelled.

Holding Kira tight, I eased her onto the ground, half aware of Jones rummaging through her nightstand with one hand. I bit a strip of cloth from my shirt and began to tie it around Kira Swan's wounded neck. The blood came more slowly, and I used both hands to staunch the flow, slowing it to a trickle.

Finally, Jones found another bullet and jerkily loaded the gun. I ducked, covering Kira Swan, just as the shot rang out.

THE BRIDGE

With the blast of the gun still ringing in my ears, I looked down at my body then Kira's. No new blood. No pain either. Keeping a tight grip on her wound, I flexed my arms and legs to be sure.

Jones howled from the bed. She'd collapsed to one side and her arm dangled awkwardly beside her. Where her hand should have been was a bloody stump.

She howled again and lurched forward, suddenly strong in the grip of death. "Come here, girl! Come here and get what's coming to you. Get over here! I'll kill you, bitch. Rip the flesh from your bones!"

She threw herself from the bed, taking the sheets with her and knocking into a vial-filled tray. The tray flipped, its contents flew into the hearth and there was a sound of cracking glass as the vials exploded one by one. I hunkered down, trying to protect Kira, as sparks flew, flying backward and blowing fire.

Jones flailed on the floor as the bedding burst into flames, fueled by wood and alcohol. Moments later, the bed frame caught and the nightstand, the desk and chair, the wardrobe, and then the ceiling. The entire room was on fire. The front door burst open, reviving the siren. It wailed, echoing the roar of the fire.

Lee Ford was beside me, one arm across his mouth and nose. "Arika! God, is that Swan?"

"Lee!" I gasped, struggling to speak as the smoke burned my lungs. "You came back!"

"I saw you from the wall," he said quickly. "I realized something. We've got to talk—"

A chunk of flaming wood fell from the roof. We both ducked. Lee glanced up then took my arm. "Come on."

"No!" I said, indicating Kira, lying in my arms. "I can't leave her—not here."

He followed my gaze. "The entire castle's looking for an intruder. I can't carry you both."

"Take her then," I said. "I'll go out the back." He coughed. There wasn't time to argue: the roof would fall soon, and trap us in the burning building.

Lee took my face in his hands and kissed me. "You fool!" he said. He took the cuff from his bicep and wrapped it around mine. He initiated invisibility then ripped Kira Swan from my arms. Her blood flowed for a moment then he replaced my hands with his. "Go to the bridge," he said, nudging me. "I have a plan. If it works, I'll be right behind you."

When he prodded me again, I stood and ran to the back door. I waited there, coughing and wheezing as Lee got to his feet. He took off his jacket, covered Kira and hefted her onto his shoulder. I turned and ran, aiming for the keep and the drawbridge exit.

The scene in the yard was chaos. The wind was high, so the fire was spreading quickly, feeding on plants, the wooden fence and garden tools. People scrambled to put out the flames, calling directions over the wail of the siren.

I took the most discreet route, looking back over my shoulder to see that Lee was still with me. With his white skin and his head down, he might have been a diplomat. Kira's height and weight, covered in his arms, might have been an injured Kongo guard. We found the bridge without incident, but it was raised.

"Dammit!" I said.

"We'll turn back and hide," Lee said.

I shook my head. "She needs medical care now. Leave her in sight, on the bridge. I'll let it down; you run." I grasped the crank of the drawbridge and pulled it around, unwinding the rope. The bridge creaked; the rope whined. My hand cramped around the crank.

The task was nearly done when a shout rang out behind us. Guards. Lee ran onto the bridge, Kira steady on his shoulder. He placed her gently on her side, then he jumped down into the dry moat. A dozen guards were close behind. One stopped and knelt beside Kira Swan.

"It's Councilwoman Swan!" he cried. "Come quick. Bring a medic."

Invisible, I ran down the bridge and jumped into the moat, following Lee and the guards that chased him. There was hope. Lee was fast and I saw the guards were tiring. Then a volley of arrows rained from the sky. I looked up to the ramparts. A handful of soldiers were shootingg into the moat.

"No!" I shouted. I doubled my speed. The guards were reckless, missing their target and instead piercing the men following Lee. Sprinting, I hurdled their bodies until, finally, I was right behind Lee Ford. I shouted his name as a pain stabbed near my shoulder blade.

His stride faltered and five arrows found their mark in his back and sides. He bellowed, limped. Another handful of arrows landed, one in his neck. He groaned and collapsed.

Behind him, I couldn't stop in time; I tripped over his body and flew into the air. I landed a few feet away, cracking my head on something hard in the ground. Stunned, my vision blurred and my arms and legs went numb.

A whoop of triumph rang from the guards on the ramparts, and those on the ground stopped to congratulate themselves, standing over Lee's still, bleeding form.

"Lee," I whispered.

He opened his eyes and searched the air in my direction.

The guards, still bleating, didn't notice.

When I whispered again, Lee's gaze settled on a spot just over my head, then his mouth worked, as he tried to speak. "Hosea, tower," he said. Blood trickled from his lips. He grunted and tried again. "Hosea—is—watchtower."

Tears leaked from his eyes, ran across the bridge of his nose and settled in the sand. Then Lee Ford took his last breath and closed his eyes.

My mouth stretched on a silent cry. Something burst in my head and my vision darkened.

·

When I woke, I tried to stand but couldn't. The arrow lodged in my back had twisted out as I'd fallen, and I felt blood flowing from the wound. In a last effort, I pulled myself along with my elbows, dragging my legs, but the pain in my head was blinding. I collapsed and rolled onto my back, my eyes wide open.

I lay there for hours, aware but unable to move. I couldn't feel my legs or my arms. I saw the drawbridge lift back up as the castle settled for the night and I wondered about Lee and Kira. Were they now, as I feared, both buried? I shivered in the cool evening breeze then shook as the wind pushed the sand over my body, covering my legs, my torso and, finally, my face. I blinked, feeling the sand scratch my eyes. It filled my nose and ears. I managed to turn my head, and tears of pain and regret washed the dirt away. But the sand kept coming the next day. And the next.

On the evening of the third day, every inch of me was covered. My throat and mouth filled and before the sun dropped behind the west horizon, I died.

PART SEVEN

THE

COTTAGE

When we drop fear, we can draw nearer to people,
we can draw nearer to the earth, we can draw nearer
to all the heavenly creatures that surround us.
BELL HOOKS

THE WOMAN, THE MAID AND THE LARK

For years, I pitied the workers' erasures. In diagrams and lectures, I offered proof to any loyalist who would listen, arguing that the *Animus Rasa*, the low spirit, destroyed the man. It left the workers vulnerable, shunning technology, worshiping Earth, faithful to superstitions.

Now, in spirit form, hovering inside my dead body, I was forced to admit the workers had been right. Despite the rebirth, or maybe because of it, the Second Brother had understood great things—invisible creatures, gods—better than the First.

I could hear Kiwi's voice in my ear—*see?* And finally— though, not fully—I did.

According to Core mythology, an Invisible of Soltice would come and collect my body. And so, being newly converted, I was not surprised when, on the morning of the fourth day, the earth began to quake and an aperture formed beside me. A ray of light, brighter than the sun, broke through the hole and flashed rhythmically, making shapes that shot into the ozone. From Lee, I knew the geometric light was the tongue of God proclaiming, and I wished I could read it.

When the light dimmed, a fiery wind blew, shifting sand from my body and face, so that I might have been able to breathe again, if I had been alive. When the wind hushed, a pillar of molten lava swelled out of the opening. The lava grew tall and slender, taking a human form. Flecks of black ash on its surface thickened into skin and the shape narrowed at the waist. Breasts pushed out from the chest. Lips, eyes and ears formed.

As the shape cooled, it became a woman with medium-brown skin and soft tufts of black hair. Her brows were thick ropes over expressive eyes. Her features were even and full, her neck long and strong. A snakeskin sheath covered the length of her body, except for the stomach, where the sheath cut away in a circle displaying her scars. Thick and thin, concave and raised, puckers and twines. They gathered over her navel and stretched in every direction. Twin canals beamed up. A serpent coiled to one side, a wild mane thrashed across the other. Through the center, a shiny black keloid plunged, like a broad sword.

Fully formed, she stepped from the hole. When her foot touched the ground, she changed. The brown woman, an Invisible, was gone, replaced by a little girl who knelt beside me.

"You!" I gasped. The little kitchen maid bowed her shorn head. Other than when her memory had visited me in the veil, I hadn't seen her since the night she'd told me Robin was dead. She'd bathed me, then I'd given her food and tied a handkerchief around her head. We'd spent the night talking. I'd fallen asleep only to find she'd disappeared the next morning.

She reached out and took my spirit hand. Hers was boiling hot but it didn't hurt. I lifted the palm to my cheek and closed my eyes. She smiled and pulled me to a seated position. I felt a ripping sensation and looked behind me. I'd separated from my body again. I looked back at the kitchen maid.

"Are you Osa?" I asked, full of awe.

She looked amused. "Not nearly. Osa would be offended at the suggestion."

"Then who are you?"

"My name is Mother Lark," she said. "Mother Lark Paradise."

I repeated her name. It was, somehow, familiar to me. "Do I know you?"

She nodded.

"Are you my mother?"

She shook her head.

"Then who?"

Looking sympathetic, she shook her head again.

I grimaced. "What *can* you tell me?"

She thought for a moment and smiled coyly. She placed the tip of her middle finger on my temple and my vision cleared. The world vanished and I floated up in the air, to look down at a tapestry in a frame. A second later, she removed her finger, and I fell to the ground, into the tapestry. As my vision clouded again, I flailed and gasped, terrified and excited by what I'd seen: a long loom with wide warps and a thousand yarns. Some yarns were thick with a billion threads, or more. All the yarns were in various states of crossing to the far end of the loom. Only one yarn, heavy and frayed, was close to the end.

"What happens at the end?" I said, gripping her hand.

She squeezed my fingers. "Something good," she said. "Or so we hope."

I thought of the yarns and threads and, deeper still, the fibers, infinitesimal, clinging together, jittering in the wind. And, I knew, for my whole life, I had been one of them.

"Show me more," I said. "Take me with you."

"Not yet, dear one. You've more work to do."

"Here?" I looked down at my body. Lee Ford's inferior bracelet was wrapped around my arm but, with my spirit eyes,

I could see myself despite it. My skin had darkened in the sun and my legs, slender and strong, were bent at right angles. "But I've died," I said.

She nodded. "Which is why I've called someone to rescue you." She gave my hand another squeeze then stood and stepped back into the hole. Instantly the little girl was gone, replaced by the Invisible. "Stay strong. We'll do what we can for you." Her little girl voice had gone, along with the body, and her Invisible voice was like nothing I've heard before: sparkling brown and deep, like a djembe drum. And, even though she spoke in the tongue of God, I understood.

Her skin showed cracks. The cracks widened. I had a million questions. I opened my mouth to beg her to stay, but she was gone. Her features disappeared, then her form. She was a pillar of lava as she sank back into the ground.

THE SAVIORS

When I woke next, I was in a room lit by early natural light. I opened my eyes but the light hurt and I shut them again. A figure leaned over me, making a dark shape in the bright red world behind my closed lids.

"Eat up, General," said a voice. The words chimed up and down in a way that was familiar.

My stomach growled. I was starving. I opened my mouth. Food filled it. A cool finger touched my chin. "Chew now, General." I chewed. "Open up." Eyes still closed, I opened my mouth, accepting another bite. And, as before, the command came: *chew*. When my belly felt full, the voice quieted, and I slept.

I woke next to a hand cupped gently around my skull.

"Drink up, General." My mouth flooded with cold liquid. I jerked away, but the hand tightened. Another hand encroached to massage my throat, forcing me to swallow. The water washed down to splash in my belly. Finally, the hands released me, and I sank back into darkness.

•

When I woke again, I was in a bed in the same bright place. I blinked, raising my lids halfway. Light from the windows in front of me filled the space. There were two windows on one side of a door, and two on the other. The windows were decorated with green curtains that were presently drawn back and tied with a matching sash.

Squinting to block the light, I tried to see out of the windows. Hoping for a better view, I struggled to sit up, grimacing. Nausea cramped in my belly and a sharp pain shot down my neck. I lifted my chin and twisted left then right. My neck cracked in both directions, giving some relief, but my stomach heaved. I sat still for a moment, letting the queasy wave pass. Then I lifted my arms and rolled my shoulders, wincing with pain. Every movement produced a faint popping as my bones and joints adjusted.

"She's awake!" a voice called. I looked up and saw Anna walking towards me.

"You!" I said. She waved with one hand, the other held a bunch of fresh-cut violets. She laid them on a square dining table and came to perch on the edge of my bed. Reaching around, she fluffed the pillow behind me. She took my shoulders and gently pressed me back into the soft mound of covered cotton. She smelled like sweet green grass. Without dirt weighing it down, her red hair curled in tight spirals to her waist.

"Vee, do you hear me?" she called over her shoulder. "She's awake."

I followed her gaze to a desk and chair in the corner of the room. It was positioned directly in front of the window on the other side of the cabin door. It took a moment for my eyes to adjust. Slowly, a small black figure took shape in the chair. She twisted around to face the bed, and I gasped.

"Voltaire!"

Voltaire ignored me, and addressed Anna. "Good. Now she can leave. You have three days, princess."

Anna laughed. "Don't be daft. We said a week, and you affirmed it."

"I said that when I thought she'd die," Voltaire replied. "Now that I see she won't, I've changed my mind." Voltaire stood and strode across the room to stand beside Anna. She didn't look at me.

"Seven days, Vee," Anna said. "And that doesn't include today."

I looked between them. Voltaire wore a pair of wire glasses that I didn't remember. Leaf-shaped earrings dangled around her chin. Her hair was shaved low to her scalp and, despite her rumored illness, she looked healthy.

"Fine, a week, but we're counting today," she said.

Anna laughed again. She leaned over and, with one pale hand, caressed Voltaire's dark cheek, which was full and round. The sight of such obvious affection between people from such disparate times in my life overwhelmed my psyche. I lifted a hand to my head and fell back.

•

When I woke next, I looked around without sitting up.

The green curtains were drawn but the windows were open, emitting a breeze. Voltaire and Anna were eating at the square table. Beside it sat a potbelly stove. The smell of fish and leeks drifted from their bowls and their heads inclined together as they talked quietly.

I sat up slowly. I pushed back the covers, looked down at my body and touched my head. I wore a loosely wrapped lilac aura and my hair was stretched into an oval topknot. I shifted to place my feet on the ground and the wooden floorboards shot pins and needles through my soles. I wiggled my toes, forcing the blood to flow evenly. When the pain passed, I stood on wobbly legs. The spun material of my gown drifted like petals around me as I walked to the dinner table.

Voltaire looked up, harrumphed and turned back to her meal.

Anna bound to her feet. "General!" She ran to put an arm around me, helping me to an empty chair at the table. She sat at my feet and motioned to Voltaire, who moved reluctantly. She dipped from a copper pot on the stove and brought me a small bowl of fish broth.

"Thank you," I said. I put it to my lips and ate hungrily. When the bowl was empty, I set it down. "Where am I?" I asked. "I can't remember."

"You're here at our home in the east of Hasting," Anna said.

"They call it the haunted oasis," Voltaire clarified. "I've had it to myself for over a year."

"What do you remember?" Anna asked.

I gazed into the fire. "The watchtower," I said. "And you— you escaped!"

"Lee Ford released me," Anna corrected. "He gave me the bracelet and medicine and pointed me to the east. I walked all night and Voltaire found me in the morning. She looked lovingly at Voltaire. "The pair of them saved my life."

"I set traps to scare travelers away," Voltaire added, gruffly. "But when I saw her, I made an exception." She covered Anna's hand. "Had I known she came with *you*—" She shrugged.

Anna laughed as if Voltaire had made a great joke. Then she sobered. "I've been afraid to ask, General," she said. "But where is Lee Ford? He wasn't in the moat where I found you and I searched all over. That was four months ago."

"Four months!" The shock faded slowly. Then sadness swelled as I recalled Lee's last day.

"General?" Anna asked.

"He—he's dead." Tears ran down my face. "He took ten arrows, but he wasn't in pain for long. It—it was my fault." I covered my face.

"No surprise!" Voltaire announced. "Death follows you wherever you go. Death for others, that is. But you? You just keep *living* and *living*." Her lip curled.

I wiped my face, unable to deny the accusation. She hadn't mentioned Fly Man, but a pit widened in my stomach. "What about Kira Swan?" I said. "She was wounded, shot in the neck. Has there been any word?"

"Senator Swan is dead," Voltaire said, flatly.

I bit the knuckles of my fist, drawing blood. "Jones," I whispered.

"Yes, she died too," Anna said.

"Did you kill her?" Voltaire asked.

I stiffened. "No! Is that what they're saying?" I shook my head. "She died in the fire. She killed Kira Swan—her niece."

Voltaire's eyes widened, and she momentarily forgot her hostility towards me, suddenly hanging on my every word. "Who killed who and how is all anyone's talking about. When Kira Swan didn't return to Cobane, the Council offered a thousand-coin reward for information on her whereabouts. People went mad looking. After my disappearance and your lunacy, Kira's death was the last straw. Everything political has come to a halt."

Anna nodded. "When Hasting admitted to having her body, the people were convinced the diplomats killed her.

They rioted in the north and south. They forced the Council to hold off on the Accord vote. It's been chaos. We need to know how Kira came to be at Hasting and how she died. The fate of the nation rests on the current investigation, and no one is owning up to anything—but you. You say Kira died in a murder-suicide? You saw it with your own eyes?"

I nodded. "But not a suicide."

"Then an accident," Voltaire said.

"Not that either." I began to shiver. My heart rate tripled. Blood rushed to my face and my palms began to sweat. Desperately, instinctively, I reached for my Apex. A spark jolted the air and my Apex clattered through an open window.

"Arika!" Voltaire commanded. "Stop!"

I got to my feet, panting—looking left and right. Then I collapsed to the ground.

Voltaire was in front of Anna, her Helix drawn, ready to ward me off.

"I'm sorry," I said. I closed my eyes. "I—can't help it."

They blinked at me. Then Anna came around Voltaire and helped me back into my chair.

Voltaire snatched up my Helix. "I'm burying this again," she said. "If I see it out of the ground before I say you can have it, I'll kill you myself." She stomped outside.

Anna brought me a cup of tea and I sipped gratefully.

When Voltaire returned, her brows dropped low over her nose; she had a metal box in her hands. "You can have these too," she said. "We want nothing to do with them."

She tossed the box at me, and it opened in my lap. Inside was Kumar's bracelet and Lee's cuff. I set my teacup aside and examined the trinkets. I slipped both on my arm. Nothing happened. I took them off, examined them and put them back on my arm. They sat like two cold stone rings. My mind raced, sorting and patching details. "They need a charge," I said, finally, recalling the charging station Lee had revealed in the empire lab.

"They've been in the sun for months," Anna said, confused.

"They're not solar powered," I said. "They're powered with old-world electric cords."

Her eyes widened. "How?"

"I don't know," I said. Lee hadn't told me enough about the duplicate bracelets to even guess. And now he was gone.

Voltaire pulled up a chair and leaned forward. "So, if it wasn't an accident, then Jones killed herself on purpose?"

"Sort of," I said, frowning. "Kira was Jones's niece. When Jones tried to kill me, Kira sought to protect me. Jones shot Kira then tried to shoot me, but the gun misfired."

"Gun?" Anna said, shocked.

"A relic," I said. "It fired backward and shot off her hand. She fell and started a fire."

Voltaire looked skeptical. "A surprise niece, an old-world gun, a fire? Do you have any proof?"

"Ignore her," Anna said, rubbing my knee. "To answer your question, no one thinks you killed Jones. The people don't even know you're missing. We haven't told a soul that we found you."

"You say I was in the moat at Hasting," I said. "I remember! But how did you know I was there?"

Anna nodded. "I had a dream just after I met Vee," she said. "A wee bird, like a sparrow, but black, perched on my chest and told me—*Anna, fetch the General*. The sparrow told us where to look and we followed."

Voltaire finished the story. "Anna was still on the mend. I wore the bracelet and carried her. I stepped on *you* in the moat. *Pure* ill luck," Voltaire added, shaking her head.

Anna nodded excitedly. "It was a miracle, General. You were invisible and weak as a lamb. That was four months ago."

"I believe you, Anna," I said. "The diplomats shot me in the back and I couldn't move."

I didn't tell her that, in keeping with the curse, I had died three days after learning Obi's secret. I didn't tell her that it wasn't a bird, but a brown woman, Mother Lark Paradise, who brought me back to life and sent her to rescue me. That the lark was a creature of the Core—and that hundreds or thousands of other invisible creatures were, even now, listening in on us, conducting and shaping.

Anna went on. "The back wound was in a bad state. But the sore here was worse." She touched the base of my neck, where the ruby necklace had clung. "Full of pus and infection. It took weeks to close. And even then, you didn't wake. That's when I knew something more was wrong."

I touched my nape where the medicinal patches had clung. I ran a hand down my throat, thinking of the ruby necklace. "I've been sick for a while," I confessed.

"Well, we wondered if you'd awaken at all. It took two of us to move your legs and arms, to keep you strong. And, of course, we had to get you to eat for the bairn."

"You have a baby?" I said, looking between them.

Anna glanced at Voltaire, her eyes wide. Voltaire laughed snidely. "No, *we* don't have a baby, you fool."

Anna gave her a cold look, then turned back to me. "General," she said, slowly. "When you came here, you were with child."

I scoffed. "No, I wasn't."

She nodded. "Yes, General, you were. You are."

"That's impossible. I—" I broke off, realizing it wasn't impossible at all. Blood drained from my head and the room tilted. The last thing I heard, as my body struck the ground, was Voltaire's snickering laughter.

THE NEXT SEVEN DAYS

The next day I woke and immediately remembered Anna's news. I touched my stomach. It was full, perhaps, but flat. I closed my eyes, deciding she'd been mistaken.

"She's not our responsibility!" Voltaire said, from somewhere beyond the darkness. I knew she was talking about me, but I didn't care. I rolled over, pulling the covers up to my chin. I stuffed a corner into my mouth, gagged and vomited. My stomach clenching as it ejected last night's fish broth.

Over the next few days, my heart froze. I stared vacantly as Anna leaned over and pressed food to my mouth. "You've got to eat for the bairn," she said.

I pushed her hand away. "There is no baby." Anna gasped.

"Do you hear that?" Voltaire snapped. "That's what I'm talking about. She cares for no one and nothing but herself."

I burrowed beneath the pillow and held my breath, managing to pass out.

When I woke next, it was night again. I could hear Anna and Voltaire arguing again. I ignored them. On the nightstand beside me was a tray of food and a set of utensils. I picked up a small eating dagger and pressed the tip to my forefinger, considering.

Before dawn, Voltaire was shaking my arm.

I opened my eyes. "What is it?" I asked, groggily

Voltaire snorted. "Day seven, princess. Now get up," she said.

"What—why?"

"Time's up, queen."

"Wait!"

She took a handful of my hair and yanked me to the ground. I screamed.

Behind her, Anna shouted, "Careful, Vee!" She wrung her hands, looking apologetic.

Voltaire adjusted her grip and dragged me through the door by my arm into the pre-dawn chill. A few yards from the house, I stopped struggling. *What did it matter?* Thorns cut my bare calves and my heels tangled in passing vines. A cruel rock jabbed my hip and I hissed but said nothing. Voltaire didn't slow. She dragged me up the hill away from the cottage and toward a thick line of trees.

Anna, once again, came to my rescue. "Leave her alone!" she shouted. She tripped Voltaire and took my other arm in her hands.

"I'll not have her in my house," Voltaire screamed. Yanking me her way.

"She won't be in your bloody house, you cruel bitch," Anna shouted, pulling me back.

"She's not wanted!" Voltaire let go and crossed her arms on her puffed-up chest.

"*I* want her!" Anna said, but I was too heavy for her to hold alone. I fell to the forest floor, and she propped her hands on her hips as their argument continued, back and forth.

Finally, it was decided that I could sleep in the garden, which was technically Anna's domain, since she tended it and did all the cooking while, it seemed, Voltaire sat about brooding all day.

With that settled, Voltaire dragged me back through the trees and down the hillside. We reached the garden in front of their cabin just as dawn broke the horizon. She stood over me for a bit, glaring, then left me in the vegetable patch. I listened to them eat breakfast, rolled over and fell asleep.

THE GARDEN

I woke up soaking wet. It was raining. I curled into myself and buried my face in the ground, waiting for sleep to return. Having gone with little food for days, it should have been easy. Instead, the rain kept me conscious, dribbling into my ears and nose. I lifted an arm and swatted at the sky. Then, finally, I sat up.

Voltaire stood over me, a sprinkling can in her hand.

I sputtered. "Just leave me alone."

"This is my house, princess." She held the water directly on my face. "I built it with my own hands, and I won't have you here another minute."

"Anna said I could live in the garden."

"Anna's gone on one of her Christian missions. She won't be back until tomorrow. And by then you'll be gone." She emptied the can onto my head and went back inside for more.

She came back and resumed her attack.

I growled. "Just let me die in peace!"

"You're taking too long, and besides, you're with child. I can't have a baby dying in the garden. Anna would never forgive herself, and she's had a hard-enough life. I won't have you causing her more pain. You're not worth it."

Her words struck me. "So, you're just going to annoy me until I leave so I can die in the desert where Anna can't see me?"

"Exactly." She dumped the watering can over my head.

I screeched and struggled to my feet. I tried to stomp away, but my legs wouldn't hold me. I got a yard out before I fell, hard, onto my side.

Voltaire followed me and resumed her attack. She adjusted herself so the worst of the sun beat down on my face and continued sprinkling me.

I lay on my back, wide awake and frustrated. Finally, I got to my hands and knees and crawled back to the garden, determined to stay alive long enough to make Voltaire regret not letting me die. Soaking wet, I glared at the vegetation around me and yanked at a carrot top; it came up easily in my fist.

I lifted it to Voltaire. "Cheers," I sneered, then I put the carrot to my mouth.

I froze as it touched my lips. It wasn't one-tenth the size of a full-grown carrot. The flesh was skinless, tender looking. It was a baby. A baby and I'd almost eaten it. I burst into tears. Uncontrollable sobs tore from my chest and my fingers trembled as I clawed up the closest bit of earth and stuffed the baby carrot inside. Using one hand to hold it upright, I packed dirt around the pale orange root, muttering to myself.

"You're okay, baby," I murmured, shaking feebly. When it was back in the earth, I laid my cheek down on the ground beside its green sprouted top and continued to sob, resting a hand on my belly. "I'm sorry. I'll not leave you. I'll never leave you," I choked between sobs.

"Will you feed it?" Voltaire asked.

I nodded, pressing my face in the dirt.

"Give it water?"

"Yes, yes!"

"It's not a new seed carrot. This is the old, difficult kind. And the dirt is dry. It'll need constant care," Voltaire warned.

I shook my head. It didn't matter. I would tend it day and night. "Forever," I whispered.

Voltaire harrumphed and tossed the sprinkling can at me. It collided with my bowed head. "You can't use the water barrel in the cottage," she said, gruffly. "The stream is uphill, that way." She pointed.

I nodded and pulled myself to my feet.

•

That first trek to the brook was the longest of my life. At the foot of the hill, I fell to my knees and pulled myself up with my elbows. In the woods, I collapsed onto a bed of mushrooms. Sobbing, I bent my head to graze, staving off the pain of hunger.

At the stream, I plunged my head and opened my mouth, letting the water flow into my throat and belly. After I'd had my fill, I dipped the watering can and started back immediately, aware the baby carrots were even more thirsty.

Just uphill of the cottage, I lost consciousness. My strength gave out and I slid on my back the rest of the way downhill.

When I woke, the sprinkling can sat upright on my chest. Filled, the small can held about a quart of water. After my tumble, about half was left.

Grateful, I pulled my way to the vegetable patch and carefully emptied the cool water on my replanted baby carrot.

The rest of the plants cried out to me, and I knew they would need water too. "Mommy's here," I whispered. Then I laid prostrate in the dirt and fell asleep.

Anna nudged my shoulder gently. I opened my eyes. On her knees beside me, she held out a bowl, encouraging me to take it.

"What is it?" I asked.

"Porridge, queen!" Voltaire shouted. She stood behind Anna. "It's what the workers ate under the old Compromise. It's good enough for you. If you tend Anna's garden, you'll be fed three times a day. Just stay out of the house and fetch your own water." She nodded to a large barrel with a tin pail beside it.

Tears sprang to my eyes and I moved a hand to cup my stomach protectively. I would be able to feed my baby.

"What do you say," Voltaire asked. "Yes, or no?"

"Yes," I said quickly. "And—thank you."

I finished the porridge without a spoon. No spoon was provided. I used my finger to scoop the last sticky bits of oat that clung to the side. After, I was still ravenous. Nevertheless, I crawled to the stream. I left the bucket; it would be too heavy once full. I opted instead to refill the watering can. On my return trip, I had another bad tumble, but I managed to fall strategically, protecting my belly. I brought back one cup of water—less than half of the can—but I felt good.

With Anna's porridge padding my bones, my strength came back, slow and steady. I took naps every hour that first week. But, by the end of the following month, I slept with the sun and rose at dawn, ready to work. If the summer days were too warm, I can't remember. My only concern was tending the garden.

Voltaire hadn't exaggerated its state. The soil was rocky and dry. The sun scorched the tender shoots and bugs and animals plagued me day and night. I shooed raccoons, caught crickets and composted their bodies in an epic battle to protect the crop. "My babies!" was my constant refrain.

I slept with the broad beans under the moon in the cool night air, and I didn't bother bathing, relishing the dirt. Mixed with water, it formed a fine crust over my skin that kept the biting insects at bay. In time, the plants grew under my care. Their foliage reached for the sky, creeping along the ground and stretching at the sound of my voice.

I thought of nothing but their needs and, in quiet moments, warmed by the sun, with the eddies upstream babbling, I found earth, that black boss, was the best of company.

•

Some weeks after I had taken charge of the garden, as summer began to turn to fall, Anna came with my bowl just before dusk. As always, she knelt, met my eyes and smiled as she handed it over. "General," she said. We were both keenly aware of Voltaire's watchful eye. I was a worker and Anna was not to treat me kindly.

According to our routine, I smiled up into Anna's ivory visage. "Thank you," I said. When she made to rise, I gave in to an impulse. "Anna," I said, quietly, breaking script. She stopped. Voltaire, at her desk by the far window, poked her head out to glare at us. I could feel her ears straining to hear. I ignored her.

"I'm sorry about your wife. Or, your first wife," I said.

She tilted her head, taken aback. "Thank you," she said.

"And I'm sorry I didn't give you shoes in the tunnel from the sinkhole. I keep seeing your bare feet." I swallowed. "You were so cold, and I should have given you shoes." She nodded, accepting my apology. "You saved my life, make my food and treat me kindly. And I don't deserve it," I said, plainly. She opened her mouth, but I laid a hand on her knee, quieting her. "It's because you're a kind person that, just now, you were going to make an excuse for me," I said. "And I thank you for that. But I want you to know that *I* know how I treated you was inexcusable, and I'm sorry."

For a while we sat in comfortable silence, and then I spoke again. "In the Kongo there were two lines too. First and Second Brothers. The lines ended in disparate places." I hesitated. "And—I was a coward, too."

Her head came up. She pressed her lips together and lowered her eyes. When she stood to leave again, I watched her go. Voltaire's head receded into the cottage.

•

That night Voltaire opened the window overlooking the garden, so when she read out loud, as she always did after dinner, I was able to rest my back against the cottage, my hands cupping my gently swelling belly, and listen.

"'Adam made love to his wife Eve,'" Voltaire read. "'And Eve became pregnant and gave birth to Cain. Then Eve said, "With the help of the Lord I have brought forth a man."'" Voltaire groaned loudly. "Another man?!"

"Hush, Voltaire," Anna said. "Keep reading."

Voltaire sighed. She turned the page and read on.

THE STORY

The next morning, nestled between the peas and beets, I found the pack I'd prepared the night I'd left the sinkhole. I'd abandoned it in the valley close to Hasting. Anna, bless her, must have retrieved it.

I opened the pack and took out the leather journal. I looked over the back and sides ensuring it hadn't been damaged. Then I turned it over to examine the cover.

Vines, leaves and berries. The thickness of the vines waxed and waned, like hand lettering.

When I looked closer, holding the book to my nose, the berries swung around like eyeballs to study me and, I realized, all the vines were connected. Each one wound its way to the center, and the center itself was a thousand circling vines.

I pressed my finger to the egg at the heart of the vortex and, as always, it grew warm. But then, as it got too hot to touch, the egg dipped and pushed back, like a beating heart.

I whipped my hand away. I looked at the pad of my finger, then down at the nappy foliage—the mark of perfection.

Holding my breath, I traced the embossment, following a branch which thinned as it descended to a line that ended in the circle. At random, I picked another branch, and followed it to the center, the core. I picked another point and followed it, too.

I circled the pad of my finger around and around as the center egg again grew warm then hot. And when the circle pressed back, pumping like a heart, I pressed harder and the book began to quake.

Terrified, I yanked my hand back as the vines on the cover adjusted, scrambling like moss in the wind. When they settled again, the vines were arranged in a title: *Narrative of the Life of William Cobane, an American Slave, 177 A.E.*

I read the title twice, then the book moved again. The sheets fluttered open to a page as if bookmarked for me, for just this moment. The page was near the middle of the book. Nevertheless, it contained the first line of my father's story.

My birth was long and so, I came, as tall as a crane.

My eyes brimmed with tears, making it impossible to read on. I slammed the book shut and stuffed it away. Sniffling, I watered and weeded my garden.

Later, I pulled out the book and performed the same ritual. I read the first line again and again. And then, when my tears eased, I read on—remembering my papa. As the memories flowed, the pain in my heart burst open, drained and eased.

The sun sank behind the trees as I turned the last page. I closed the book, fell back and slept.

The crying began that night. I awoke, curled on my side and wailing, bloating the earth with an unnamed and unknowable pain.

Near dawn, I thought of the Kongos gone before me and a new wave of pain descended. Their stories had lived in the library the English burned down. Their lives were gone for good, unnamed and unknowable. How many thousands of my ancestors bloated the earth? I looked up at the sky. As many as the stars, I wondered. More? I felt a mass grave open beneath me and, in my grief, I began counting.

The next morning passed over me and the evening too, as I lay, choking on groans and counting. How many thousand? Untouched, my porridge dried and my garden lay suffering.

As my dinner bowl gathered dew the next morning, Voltaire stomped from the cottage. She took me by the shoulders. "You have to eat!" she said.

I nodded obediently and, with one finger, scooped a bite into my mouth. A sob erupted from my chest and I gagged.

Voltaire jumped backward, cursing. "Anna's out being Christian," she said. "A family down the way lost their mother and she's tending the body. She went for three days and returns tomorrow."

I nodded, hiccupping. "Good for her," I managed.

Voltaire rolled her eyes. "Her only instruction was to see that you fare well in her absence. If she comes back and finds you ill, she'll think I mistreated you, and she'll leave."

"So—you need my help," I said. The notion struck me as hilarious and I bowed over with laughter.

"Shut up," Voltaire snarled. "I don't need your help. Cry yourself to death." She marched back to the cottage and hesitated. She turned, looking afraid. "But when you're finished—do eat?"

I cackled and fell to my side where I laughed until my back ached. Then, after a brief moment, my humor passed, and I sobbed again.

A sigh reached my ears and I looked up to see Voltaire had moved her desk to face the window overlooking the garden. Her glasses were perched on the end of her nose and she had a book, *Candide*, open before her, but her attention was on me.

She propped an elbow on the windowsill and cupped her chin in her hands. "What's wrong?" she said.

My brow furrowed at the look on her face. It was soft, welcoming almost—concerned. I sniffed, distracted from my misery. "Excuse me?"

"Why are you counting?!" Voltaire snapped. She took a breath and spoke more gently. "Maybe I can help."

I blinked. "Why would you do that?"

Voltaire considered, then shrugged, unable to ascertain a reason.

I wiped my face with the dirty hem of my skirt. "What's wrong?" I said, repeating her question. I closed my eyes and looked inside. I saw an ocean with a ship sunk to the bottom. I saw a mother in a bed of blood. I opened my eyes, my fists clenched. "I wish I'd told Sky her eyes were blue," I said. "I should never have shaved Kiwi's hair. I should have written down Fount's song—because now, no one remembers it."

The tears slipped down my cheeks and I lay face down sobbing—adding salt to the sea of ancestral pain. At some point, Voltaire sat beside me in the dirt. I buried my face and continued to cry. Only, with her hand patting the space between my shoulders, my tears came easier. After a while, they slowed and ceased. And still, Voltaire didn't leave. She rested her back against the cottage wall and I slept.

When I woke in the afternoon, she had a hot bowl of porridge ready. She lifted it up, offering me a spoon. I took it and ate.

When I was finished, she took the bowl and returned to the cottage. At her desk, with her glasses perched on her nose, she continued reading *Candide*. She was very near the end.

With a full belly, I went back to tending my neglected garden.

At dinnertime, instead of porridge, Voltaire set a bowl of rabbit stew on the sill.

"Why are you doing this?" I asked.

She looked down at her own bowl, resting on her desk. "Because you helped me answer a question I've been pondering for some time."

I took a bite. "And what's that?"

"Yes," she said. "The answer is: yes, you are. We all are, actually, each other. We eat from the earth and return to it, nourishing the land from which, one day, our children will harvest. So, we've got to keep—keep—" She looked at the half-circle moon in the sky.

"Voltaire?"

She lifted a hand. Her eyes closed.

I stopped.

"I always thought I'd lead the Kongo from captivity," she said, quickly. "I prepared for it my whole life. But now that it's all over, I see. I see what it took to win. And I'm glad it was you. You made decisions I couldn't have made. And they were right." Finally, she opened her eyes and looked at me. She nodded. "You made the right decision, General."

I clasped my hands and bowed my head.

We didn't speak anymore. We ate by the light of the stove. And when the stove died, we finished beneath the constant smile of the bright half-moon. And, when the wind blew a cloud to cover the moon, like a small hand in the sky, we cried, together, for Fly Man.

"Do you want to sleep inside tonight?" Voltaire asked, after a while.

I declined. She closed the window and curtain and I settled back in my okra patch.

Sometime that night, unable to sleep, I tossed a crystalight and took out the leather journal again. I pressed a finger into the center. It pressed back and a new title emerged. *Remarkable Incidents in the Life of Mother Lark Paradise, South Carolina Bay Colony, 1739 A.D.*

A chill ran down my spine. The cover flipped back, revealing the first line.

I was born at dawn in mourning, killing my mother, Lark.

In awe, I read that story and ten more like it that night. Finally, towards dawn, I closed my eyes and lay back down in the dirt.

THE ANSWER

When Anna returned I sat cross-legged on the floor, eating my porridge by the stove. Voltaire was reading at her desk by the far window.

"I see you've made peace," Anna said. She took off her light scarf, laying it on the dining-room table. She had a package and a rolled scroll of paper under her arm. She handed me the package. "I got these for you, General," she said, looking gladly between Voltaire and me. Then she crossed the room and put the scroll into Voltaire's hand.

I opened the package to see two identical grey books inside. They were filled with empty sheets of lined paper.

"Oh—thank you," I said, flipping slowly through the clean sheets.

Anna smiled. "I had a feeling you'd need them."

Voltaire set her book aside and unrolled the scroll. Anna touched the cross on the cover of the book Voltaire had discarded. "Oh, Vee!" she said, delighted. "You're trying again!" Anna looked at me conspiratorially. "She couldn't get past the fourth chapter."

"It made no sense," Voltaire explained, glancing up from the letter. "What kind of story raises questions it doesn't answer?"

Anna smiled indulgently at Voltaire. "And now, what? You like mysteries?"

Voltaire removed her glasses. "No, your good book is maddening still. Poorly written and vague." She looked at me thoughtfully. "Nevertheless, I found, when I looked more carefully, there were answers." She put her spectacles back on her nose.

Anna smiled and embraced Voltaire affectionately. She leaned away and her smile dimmed. "Did you read it?" she asked.

Voltaire sighed.

"What is it?" I said.

Anna glanced over her shoulder. "A notice from Hasting; they're putting us on the grid."

Voltaire tossed the scroll onto the table. "When I first built here, you couldn't get a signal for miles. Now the Council has mandated communication antennae all over the Kongo. Their workers will be in these parts tomorrow morning."

Anna took her colorful scarf from the table and hung it on a hook in the closet. "There won't be a single mile they can't reach in minutes," she said. "It'll be like the Northridge—completely ruined."

"How is the family you visited?" Voltaire asked.

Anna moved to the kitchen and filled a pot of water for tea. "They'll survive, but barely." She glanced at me. "A sweet family," she explained. "And the mom caught a fever."

"I'm sorry," I said, sincerely.

"Any news from Cobane?" Voltaire asked.

I tensed, continuing to eat though the porridge was sand in my dry mouth. I'd avoided political talk for months.

Anna hooked the teapot over the hearth, then faced the room. "They're done with the inquiry into Kira's murder—they ruled it a suicide. And Dana Kumar's been named the new Head of Council, seeing as how he patched things up between the territories."

I looked up from my bowl. Anna went on. "They're moving on with Kira's Accord. Only now, Kumar's in charge." I chewed slowly.

"What do you think about that?" Voltaire asked, lifting her voice to reach me.

I took a breath. "About what?" I said, avoiding her gaze.

"Director Kumar is leading the Kongo towards the Accord with America," she repeated. I looked back down at my bowl. Voltaire leaned forward, eyeing me. "*We* don't trust Kumar," she said. "But we've got no proof."

"Nonetheless, we do trust the Council," Anna said, patting Voltaire's shoulder. "Senator Osprey nominated Kumar as head. She wouldn't do that without good reason."

My fingers tightened, threatening to crack the enamel of the bowl. As I'd gained strength, my mind had begun tinkering with old problems, just like it used to, digging up swatches of logic anyone else would have forgotten and piecing them together until a picture emerged.

Without my bias against Kira Swan tainting my view, I could see Senator Osprey was a bad actor. "Osprey and Kumar are in league," I said, quietly.

"Do you have any proof?" Voltaire asked.

"No proof," I said, "but they *are* working together, and it has nothing to do with peace."

I longed to put the matter aside, but my mind worked, unbidden, as automatically I started eating again.

That night I washed and Anna made a bed for me in the corner of the cottage. I went to it after dinner. I sat by the windowsill and took a pen from my sack. I picked up one of the notebooks Anna had gifted me, knowing she'd been right. My own story quivered inside me, wanting out. Resting my back against the wall, I began writing.

I sang a song as I sprang from the womb—which is not unusual.

THE RECORD KEEPER

I wrote all night and into the next morning, detailing my life like an epic tale of fiction. I closed my eyes and imagined your face, dear reader. Sometimes you are Kongo, sometimes Clayskin. Sometimes you're old and often you're young and, because of my budding admiration for Anna, at times you're English.

Despite my tiny writing, the pages filled fast. I finished the last page and closed the first notebook, breaking the tale on a high note—after my Schoolhouse battle with Jones and before the rebellion.

I took the second journal from my sack, opened it to the first page—and hesitated, unsure how to continue. I began the next chapter again and again, reviewing what had happened since the war and following the thread back to a pivotal decision. The decision had led to many deaths, including my own. By any estimation, it was regrettable. But did I regret it?

Outside, dawn peaked and the Council workers broke earth on the new antenna. With my pen poised, I watched them clear the land. They cut down a tree and it fell away from the cottage. It lay on its side, so I could see its core of a thousand concentric rings.

The workers cut the tree into logs, then dug around the stump to sumptuous roots that channeled in every direction. There was no way of knowing where the threads would end. Even so, the workers set off into the wood, following the veins.

I looked down at the book again and a certain peace came over me. I started to write plainly, admitting the facts, hoping for the best. When the noise of the workers' efforts assaulted my concentration, I closed the window and continued the final chapters. I pored over the lines about Hosea Khan, recalling every word, every gesture. I put down my pen, touched my stomach and sighed, missing him, wondering where he was.

When the desert sun was high in the sky, I closed the book. I would return to write the ending later. For now, my plants cried out to me for water. As I left the cottage, I saw the Council workers walking in a line. Realizing their work was finished, I rested a hand on my belly and ducked back inside as they passed the cottage door. They spoke loudly, making plans to camp for the night near their next destination.

When they were far off, I stepped outside and found the sprinkling can. Instead of filling it from the barrel, I rolled up my sleeves and headed uphill to the stream. I made three trips. On my third trip downhill, I shaded my eyes and looked up, searching for the antenna the workers had installed. When I spotted it, my heart dropped into my stomach. It was narrow and cylindrical, a canister in the sky.

I'd seen it before.

I ran up the pebbled walkway and into the cottage. I slammed the door.

"It's not an antenna," I said.

THE OPTIMIST

Voltaire stood from her desk. Anna turned off the stove. We all moved to stand in the center of the room.

"You mean the tower they built. It isn't for a signal?" Voltaire asked.

"No. It's called an aerator," I said. "It turns liquid into breathable mist."

Voltaire moved to the window and looked out.

I went on. "I trained with it at the Compound. It's one of the Director's inventions."

"How does it work?" Anna asked, urgently.

I moved to the open window, to stand beside Voltaire. "See that?" I pointed to the top of the structure. "That piece of the canister recedes and mist sprays from the hollow, so you breathe it in."

Anna came to stand with us, her eyes wide as she looked up, tracking the upward angle of my finger.

"There's a nerve," I said. I tapped one nostril and followed the cartilage up to the center of my forehead, recalling exactly how Lee had explained it. "It's a specialized nerve that runs from your nose to your brain. It's why, when you smell something, you remember exactly where you were and what you were doing the last time you smelled it. It transports you. It alters your mind. Like the smell of burning bodies," I whispered, recalling the stench that had haunted me.

"All right, let's stay calm," Anna said, but her voice trembled. "So, you think Director Kumar is planning on spraying the people—all of us?"

"If those antennae are all over the Kongo, then yes," I said.

Voltaire cleared her throat. "Why? What for?"

"I don't know," I said, biting my lip. I moved from the window and paced to my corner of the room. I picked up the notebook Anna had given me and sat at the square table. I flipped back through the pages of my own tiny writing, skimming for details.

Beside me, I heard the chairs sliding across the floorboards as Anna and Voltaire joined me. I slowed, reading about the time the Director had attended my simulation. He and Hosea Khan had been at odds, arguing.

"The Director had a thousand scientists working for a decade on the most complex systems—the ones that control our emotions," I said, flipping the page. "He wanted to isolate the hormone that initiates the fight or flight response."

Anna started. "I've heard of that!" While I read, she explained the basics to Voltaire.

"I gave him the hormone needed to complete and control the pathway," I said. I turned the pages and found the exact phrase Kumar had used. "Selective neuronal *gestation*." I emphasized the last word.

"Neuronal gestation?" Anna gasped. "Do you mean creating thoughts?"

"Creating thoughts *and* emotions," I added. "Choosing what we think, what we feel. Complete control of our stress response, no matter the *trigger*."

I stood, letting the book drop from my hand. Hosea Khan had said it. He'd tried to warn me. A misstep or misuse would be— "Chaos," I said. "The trigger. The Director is going to trigger fight or flight in the people!"

Eyes wide, I looked between Voltaire and Anna. "Every man, woman and child running on pure aggression. No logic, just fear. A nation of berserkers."

Voltaire rubbed the low fade of her hair. "That sounds right," she said. "When I led the rebels, Kumar funded our raids. I'm sure he did the same for the White-Face army. He was after violence."

Anna spoke up. "Lee told me the Director spread the fever I contracted. It plagued the Kongo last year, killing thousands. Violence, and sickness, aggression and fear—they all create instability."

I thought of Lee. In his last hours on Earth, he wondered why Kumar angled for power on the Council. Given their plans for an independent empire, it hadn't made sense. Unless Kumar didn't want independence or an empire. Unless, instead—

"He wants a kingdom," I said, thinking of Covington's report. "He wants to start a war, destroy America and build his kingdom on the ruins."

Suddenly it all made sense. "His whole life, he's wanted to outdo his stepfather. What's bigger than the Duke of the North?"

"King of the World," Voltaire said.

Anna crossed herself. "Do we warn the Council?"

"The Council?" Voltaire said. "We're talking World War Four. I say we pack our bags and get back off the grid!"

Anna reached for Voltaire's hand and held tight. Voltaire kissed their woven fingers and looked up at me, waiting.

"General?" Anna said.

I moved back to the window, my heart in my throat. A cool breeze came through the open curtain to graze my neck. I still bore a scar from the infected rash I'd developed at the place the ruby necklace had hung for over a year.

I crossed my forearms, letting my hands warm the skin where the invisibility bracelet had sat. The first time I'd put it on, the power that surged through me had been terrifying. I'd wanted to rip it off and run away and yet, I'd suppressed the feeling. I had the same feeling now. I loved the Kongo more than ever. But I knew I wasn't meant to save it.

I lifted my face to the wind drifting through the open window. "Which way?" I whispered, inquiring of the open air, the Earth and the ancestors.

I lifted a hand and let the breeze play in my fingers and, suddenly, I knew what I needed to do. Only, the knowledge didn't make me feel any better.

"Arika!" Voltaire said anxiously, demanding my attention.

I turned, looked at her. "Have you seen the shovel?"

Voltaire stared at me as if I'd lost my mind.

I addressed Anna. "The shovel? It was in the garden by the barrel, but I haven't seen it in days."

"Sure, wait here," Anna said, glancing at Voltaire. Moving stiffly, she went outside, returning a moment later, shovel in hand.

I took it, nodding my thanks. I then left the cottage and started towards the hill.

"Where are you going?" Voltaire shouted.

"To the stream," I called over my shoulder.

"What for?" Voltaire demanded.

"Way Seventy-Seven," I replied. I picked up my pace so I couldn't hear her response. I wasn't able to explain. I knew, even if I tried, she wouldn't understand.

I held my belly as I walked uphill to the water. When I reached the bubbling creek, I sat and listened to its babble. I watched a leaf tumble into the water and move with the current.

A tiny foot pressed below my ribs. I closed my eyes, and caressed its heel, longing for Hosea Khan.

When a branch cracked behind me, I raised my head from my contemplation of the stream and looked around.

"You didn't eat," Anna said, holding out a plate.

I lifted the fork to my mouth and ate a bite of food. It tasted like ash. Still, when she sat beside me, I forced myself to eat the entire plate of nourishment. Satisfied, the baby inside me seemed to sleep. "Thank you, Anna," I said.

She stood to leave.

"Anna?"

She turned back.

I cleared my throat. "Will you sit with me?" I managed.

She sat close and took my hand in hers.

I worked the rest of that day digging an irrigation system. I ate little dinner, just enough to keep strong for the baby. I kept a calm façade but, as I chewed, I went through every turn and nuance and, again, came to the same answer. Way Seventy-Seven.

•

Voltaire and Anna talked over breakfast the next day.

"The ceremony is taking place in two weeks," Anna said, passing the *Southern Bell* across the table.

Voltaire read the article. "People from all over America are coming to trade in their arms for *peace*," Voltaire said. "They think they're coming to honor Kira Swan and celebrate the Accord."

"I've seen the new stadium in Cobane," Anna said. "It's twenty times the size of the last arena. Big enough to hold the beginning of the end of the world as we know it."

"It's a three-day ceremony," Voltaire said. "I bet he'll release the trigger hormone on the last day."

"Way Seventy-Seven," I said, muttering to myself. I was worried but resolute. I stood from the table and went to the garden. I took the shovel to the ground near the peppers, lengthening the irrigation trench.

Through the window, I heard Voltaire whisper, "Way what? Is she counting again?"

I didn't hear Anna's reply. But, a few minutes later, she came to sit beside me in the dirt. She had a pick and a rake. Without a word, she began pulling weeds and tilling the soil.

A few minutes later, I heard Voltaire gasp as she took in the scene in the garden. Her entire torso stuck out from the window in her effort to eavesdrop on our companionship. Her book, *Candide: or, the Optimist,* fell from the sill. She snatched it up and stuck her nose in the middle, as we worked.

That afternoon, before lunch, the window closed and the cottage door opened.

Anna and I looked up.

Voltaire stood there. She had my Helix and a trowel in her hand. She gave me my Helix, knelt and dug in, widening the trench.

THE COMING

For the next two weeks we fortified our sanctuary, relishing every luxury: mushrooms, greens, poetry, earth, streams and sky.

We dined on roast duck and fish seasoned with herbs and garnished with turnips and carrots from the vegetable patch. We mashed yams and roasted cassava in the fire. We procured real sugar for rock candy and tinted it with berry juice. We boiled ginger tea that tickled the baby, so she moved beneath our palms.

On the last night, Voltaire cut each of us a piece of cornbread, and the moon was big and bright. Anna had come home that morning with red wine and news: the roads near us bustled with Kongo travelers heading north to witness the signing of the Accord. Rumor had it every roadway was just as packed.

The Assembly commissioned ferries to run between the northern territories and the Kongo, day and night, bypassing the Obi Forest. They estimated millions of attendees. No one wanted to miss the beginning of the new world order.

The ceremony was set for the next morning. The Kongo Council, as host, would preside over the formalities, and Director Kumar himself would give a speech.

The surrender of arms was no longer voluntary; every governing body, North and South, had ordered all weapons—relics and otherwise—be destroyed on the first day of the festivities.

They would come for our weapons within the hour—or so we suspected. Our bags were packed but we hadn't determined whether to run or surrender our Helixes.

We ate, cleared the table and moved close to the fire, as was our custom. I lay on a rug, one hand behind my head and one cupping my now-prominent belly. Voltaire settled in a high-back chair. And Anna bustled about, wiping the table and sweeping the floor.

"Perhaps we should close the windows tonight," she said, as she settled on a padded stool close to Voltaire's feet.

We took turns holding the torch of optimism over the dark doubt that threatened to overtake our home. It was Voltaire's turn. "They stay open," she said, firmly.

Anna nodded and looked over her shoulder. "Which book tonight?" she asked.

Voltaire moved to her desk and removed the black book with a small cross from her drawer. She sat down to read. A minute later, a whistle interrupted her.

The three of us exchanged looks.

"The wind," I declared.

Voltaire cleared her throat and bent to the page. Another whine sounded.

Anna inhaled sharply. She crossed herself and looked fretfully out of the window. "That was not the wind," she said.

"Keep reading, Voltaire," I said. My voice was calm. My Helix, however, unsheathed itself and circled my head.

I stood, opened the door and looked out. The trees stood in ranks, like an army of giants with spring leaves whispering in the breeze.

I forced my Helix into two knives that spun above my knuckles as I listened and watching.

Anna tended the fire then took a heavy frying pan in hand. She stood by the window overlooking the garden. "They're coming!" she said.

Voltaire jumped to her feet, catching the holy book before it slid to the floor. Helix in hand, she moved to the far window.

Silence fell in the cottage as a horse approached at a gallop. As it came close, I saw the rider and stopped breathing.

The rider shouted, "General Cobane, come out, girl. The workers saw you. I know you're there. Come out or I'm coming in."

It was the Head of Council, Director Dana Kumar.

He'd found us.

THE WEKAS

I closed the cottage door and turned to my companions. "I need the bracelet," I whispered.

"Your invisibility bracelet?" Anna asked.

I hadn't explained the bracelet's origin and there wasn't time now. "Yes," I said briefly. "Only it's rightfully Kumar's and it can be weaponized. I think he's here to retrieve it."

Anna's face looked ashen.

I turned from her to Voltaire. "If we give it to him now, without a fight, he might leave us *our* weapons, and we'll need them in the days to come." I cupped both hands around my belly.

"You want to go out there?" Voltaire said.

"To give him a weapon!" Anna added. "General!"

I hesitated, searching for another way. "Lock the windows and draw the curtains," I said, finally. "I have to go."

Reluctantly, they moved to the windows as I went to my bedroll and opened my sack. I shifted Lee's inferior cuff aside and retrieved Kumar's bracelet.

I stood, deactivated my Helix and slipped it into the waist of my skirt. I squeezed Anna's hand and nodded once at Voltaire; then I left the cottage and shut the door behind me.

I stopped in the middle of the yard as Kumar dismounted and moved closer, balancing on the toes of new prosthetic limbs. They attached to his thighs and flowed smoothly into legs, hinged like the hind legs of a cheetah.

I loosened the cinch of the small *bambi* bag I carried, and held up the bracelet it contained. I closed the bag, pulled back and threw it to Kumar.

He caught it and looked inside.

"It's real," I assured him, nervously. "It only needs a charge."

He removed the bracelet and traced the cold snake design with a fingertip. "As I expected," he said.

He brought the bracelet to his lips and whispered, "Goodbye, my love."

He returned the bracelet to the bag, anchored the tie of the bag on one knuckle and shifted his finger, so the bag clocked back and forth like a pendulum. Back and forth, higher and higher, until, with a jerk, it looped over his hand.

Unnerved, I leaned in, peering through the dark. He looked strange. His eyes were bloodshot and his hair disheveled. His collar hung, unbuttoned and wrinkled, as he watched the bag tick.

"We made it in a time when electricity was readily available," he said.

We? The question drifted through my mind. Before it fully formed, his hand stretched out over the path and tipped so the bag dropped to the ground. One of his legs, covered in brown flesh, shifted forward to pin the bag beneath the ball of his foot. He twisted his foot at the ankle, and the bracelet made a *crunch* sound as it gave way.

He went on twisting, slow and violent, crushing the pieces into bits and grinding the bits to sand. Finally, he picked up the bag, cupped it between his palms and moved my way.

I stumbled back, but he wasn't coming for me. He pivoted in the opposite direction. His silhouette stretched on the bright green curtains as he fell to his knees in our vegetable garden.

Behind me, the curtains slid open. I glanced back. Voltaire and Anna's expressions mirrored my confusion and their necks craned to see what bizarre thing Kumar would do next.

I looked. He was digging a hole. Ruining my plants! "Director Kumar, what—" I shut my mouth as he opened the cinch of the bag and held it aloft, towards the full moon.

He tilted the bag so the sands of the bracelet poured, in a measured stream, into the hole he'd dug. When the bag was empty, he replaced a handful of dirt—burying the bracelet's remains.

He hung his head for a long while, then cleared his throat. "I did care for her," he said. "They'll say I didn't, but a great tree will grow here!" He set a fist on the ground where he'd buried the bracelet. "Timeless and magnificent. Young people will sit in its shade and their children will swing in the branches and grow. And I'll know the truth of what nurtured it," he looked back at me, "and you'll know it too," he said.

I should have told him to leave. I should have locked myself in the house and prepared for a fight—but I didn't. I moved closer. "And what's the truth?" I said. "What will I know?"

"You'll know it was the time that killed her, not our love." He looked back at the garden, at the bracelet. "In another time our love nurtured life, limbs, Hosea Khan." His voice broke. "In another time, he didn't run from me. And we were kings." He bowed his head, and his shoulders shook.

Realizing he spoke of Weka, I leaned in. Suddenly he threw his head back and howled, shrill, pitiful—like a bitten dingo.

He bared his teeth and, in a fit, mangled the ground, throwing earth left and right, exposing roots and muttering.

"They say we threatened the world, but the world worshiped us," he said. "The truth is, our love threatened the gods! And that's why they killed it." He rose on the caps of his knees and raised a fist so his complaint registered in the trees, around the oasis and up to the sky.

He fell back and swiped a forearm over his eyes, then he blinked down and carefully rearranged the earth, filling every hole and pressing it gently into place.

He twisted around, to pin me with his gaze. "But you know, and I know, right?" He nodded. "And anyone who sits here will know—in another time, before God damned it—it grew."

"In another time," I said, after a while. "You don't mean the past, do you?"

His thighs flexed as he shifted in my direction. "No, I don't mean the past," he said. "Time is an element, Ms. Cobane. Like silver or mercury, it can be manipulated and brought under control." He eased himself to his feet and brushed his hands off. "So, yes, in another time, when electricity wasn't outlawed, Weka and I isolated the god gene, the DNA of perfection. We used it to make a clone of Jacamar's first Principle."

"And the gods didn't like that," I said, recalling my conversation with Hosea Khan.

"We got too close," Kumar said. "We began to understand what the hell game they have us playing down here. Free will," he scoffed. He turned to me. "The moment Weka and I got our hands on it—they sent *her* here to destroy us."

"Her?"

"Her—her!" he shouted. "The witch!"

I recognized the tone in his voice. "You're talking about the grandmother!"

"She wasn't their grandmother. She was Weka, older and *holy*." He spit. "Changed! She was sent here to stop us from cloning the bracelet, stop us from building our kingdom. She got to my Weka first and got in her head. Weka was turning our son—my son—against me. So, you see?" he said. His voice whined. "She *had* to die." His eyes were dark, haunted. "Oh, Weka," he moaned. He covered his face.

"You killed her," I whispered.

His eyes bulged. "No! No! *They* killed her." He pointed up to the sky, his finger black with dirt.

I nodded, finally understanding.

He turned on a heel and pawed back and forth, like a caged bear, troubled and hungry.

"Director Kumar," I said.

He didn't seem to hear me. He glared, turned and padded back a few feet.

"Dana," I said.

Finally, he looked at me.

I lifted a chin to the aerator towering over us. "You don't have to do it."

His mouth bent angrily. "Have you heard anything I've said!?"

"It won't bring her back," I said. "Or erase what happened in any time."

He glared. "There are powerful invisible creatures toying with us because they can. And you think we should let them win?"

I thought of Lark, the loom and the threads weaving their way toward the far end of the frame. "What if winning's not the point," I said, suddenly. "What if—if...oh, I don't know, sir. There's so much we don't understand."

"Because they won't let us," he hissed.

He held up a hand, dismissing the conversation. "My blood *will* sit on the throne," he said, finally.

"But Lee is dead," I said. "Hosea is gone. He never came to save me."

Kumar nodded. "Yes, he's even stronger than we'd hoped. And still a fool. I've laid a kingdom at his feet, but he won't take it." His eyes gleamed as he pivoted towards me. "Which is why I'm here." He took something from his breast pocket.

I flinched and armed my Helix. A pair of daggers swirled around my hands. "Stay where you are," I said.

Ignoring the blades, he brushed lint from the object he'd retrieved from his pocket and held it up for my inspection.

It was a metal sphere, like a small old-world bomb with a hoop protruding from its side. He pulled the hoop from the ball, revealing the pin attached. He tossed the pin aside. "There now," he proffered the ball again, "I can see you don't know what this is."

"Drop it!" I said, edging back to the cottage door.

He chuckled, merrily, his eyes too bright, as if the sound parts of him had unraveled. Then, suddenly, the smile dropped from his face. "Stop moving!" he snapped.

I froze.

"Smart girl." He extended the metal sphere. "Now, this is a no-lead hand grenade. If dropped, it will kill you and me. Anything in a five-yard radius—give or take." He smiled again and took a small sheath from his breast pocket. He tossed it to me. "Please, disarm the Helix."

Tears burned my eyes, as I slid my Helix into the sheath, cutting off my connection. I threw it back so it landed between us.

When he kicked it aside, a chill slipped around my neck. "What do you want?" I said.

"Is it not clear, dear? The workers *saw* you." His eyes narrowed sharply on my middle. "I'm here for my blood."

"No!"

He scoffed. "It wasn't a question. I've brought equipment and attendants." He nodded back the way he'd come. "I've set up a tent. I'll take it from here."

My mouth gaped. "Take—it?"

"The baby," he said. "The female womb is a complex system. It required detailed programming, but I have just the courier to nurture my blood. Hey, now, don't cry. He'll be fine," he said, softly. "I'll make him a king."

I shuddered and looked behind me, left and right.

Kumar brandished the grenade. "Come here, girl."

I stumbled back. We were a yard apart. I wouldn't make it out of range.

"Come on, now. Come!"

I eased back further.

"Stop moving!" Kumar snapped. He turned his head to the darkness. "Guards," he said. "Get her!"

The cottage door flew open behind me. Kumar jumped, looked up. I didn't hesitate. I leapt back then launched myself up and away.

Bang!

I was airborne when the ball of fire grew from the ground. The blast hit like a fist, forcing my body up and around. I curled over my middle, flipped and began to fall, bracing for impact. It never came.

A soft wind, twisting like a gust, caught me a foot from the ground. It wrapped around my limbs, and slowly lifted me up. My hair whirled in orbit around me and through its haze I saw Hosea Khan appear.

He flew in from the darkness and with a mighty shout, opened his mouth and consumed the swell of fire. It streamed into his nose and mouth, filling his throat and chest. An orange ball gathered in his middle then exploded out. He jerked as the force extended down his limbs, lighting him from the inside out, so his entire body glowed, except for his neck. There was a dark band there that the light couldn't penetrate. There was another band on his left arm and another on his right. My eyes skipped down: bands on his wrists and ankles. Seven in all.

I looked past Hosea Khan to Kumar. He was on his knees with his head tilted back and his face up, reflecting the light that shined from Hosea Khan, his blood, his dear son.

THE WATCHTOWER

Voltaire and Anna's rescue attempt was what startled Kumar and triggered the explosion. The blast drove them back into the cottage, so they missed Hosea's astounding entry.

When they opened the door again, Hosea and I were on the doorstep. With cold fingers, I slipped my Apex into my waistband as he ushered me inside. He left without a word. Through the closed door, we heard him move down the paved way to speak in low tones to Kumar.

Voltaire helped me to the table while Anna brewed tea. She set a cup before me then took Voltaire's arm and pulled her to the second room in the cottage. I heard them talking—wondering if I was okay. Voltaire wanted to ask me. Anna told her to give me space.

I looked down at my ginger tea. Was I okay? My Apex unsheathed itself to fly around my head in oblong patterns. The baby inside me was sleeping, at least. I flexed my arms and legs. I rolled my neck. I was uninjured, fine except for the disturbing image flickering behind my eyes.

Slowly, my mind turned and brought the image into focus: Lee Ford, with an arrow in his neck, struggling to explain what he'd realized in the seconds before his death.

Hosea is watchtower.

In retrospect, the truth made sense. Jacamar knew the

power of the bracelets. That people would kill and die for just a moment of supremacy. So, it seemed plain now that he would not have left them in a building. That, instead, he would have left them with some*one* who would watch over them. A sentry. A man just like Hosea Khan: immovable, unbending, unreachable—a tower in his own right.

Hosea is watchtower.

Slowly, I got to my feet and moved to the window. Hosea stood in the ruined garden speaking with Kumar who, for once, seemed old and feeble. I thought of his earlier despair and confession. He'd murdered Weka and tortured Lee—horrible acts of madness—and yet, a part of me ached for him. He was a fiber in a thread in a tapestry. An infinitesimal, jittering. Making his peace, finding his piece, his place. I looked up at the sky and down at my vegetable garden. I was no one to judge.

In their room, Voltaire and Anna still argued, so they didn't hear Hosea enter the cottage. He took my hand and we moved to sit at the square table.

"Arika?"

I looked up at him. "Hosea is watchtower," I said.

He frowned.

"Those were Lee's last words."

Hosea's eyes widened. "So, he understood why I left?"

"I think so," I whispered.

A muscle in Hosea's forehead tightened and released.

I went on, thinking of the pregnant expression on Lee's face before our trek to Hasting. "What I can't figure out is how he knew. It has something to do with the seed files you sent him. After he watched them, he changed. He kept thinking about them.

Hosea waited, holding my hand as I worked it out.

I thought back to the file Lee had shown me. To the sequence at the end that he'd watched again and again: Hosea looking down at his hands, having just thrown the ax, looking left to his grandmother on the stairs, then Weka screaming—*Hosea baby!*—identifying the author of the seed.

I shook my head, studying the details. I was missing something. Then suddenly it came to me. "The guards didn't find her," I said. I searched Hosea's face for confirmation. "There were three guards," I said. "And your home was small. You all shared an upstairs room." I turned in my chair, looking around Voltaire's two-room cottage. There were not many places a grown woman could hide. "They would have found her unless—"

"She had a bracelet," Hosea said.

"And you had one too," I added. "That's how you watched the scene undetected. One of you had the clone bracelet your mother and father made. But that means one of you had to have the Principles."

"She got them from Jacamar," Hosea said. "Then she came here—"

"To our time?" I said, confirming the truth.

Hosea nodded. "First, she rescued Lee. She knew he would be important. She brought him to our home in the Vine and stayed, teaching me and waiting for me to grow up.

"For five years, she carried the Principles around, in secret. Then, four days before Father came to collect us, she gave them to me."

My heart ached, recalling his hands, so small, in the seed file. "Wait," I said suddenly. I calculated quickly. "You're saying you've had them twenty years? Impossible."

Hosea nodded. "It's why Lee had to see the file for himself. I wanted to explain my motivation all these years and I don't think he would have believed me if I'd told him outright."

I leaned forward. "Hosea, how have you done it?"

"The Way," he said, emphatically. "Restraint and self-control. Alignment with the Will *is* strength."

I nodded, finally understanding. "You don't use them and that's why they haven't destroyed you. All the power in the world and you still bow to the Will."

Hosea sat back, crossing his arms on his chest. "No one was supposed to know I had them," he said. "The plan was always to leave. To go west, over the sea. Grandmother warned me they were indestructible. But, I hoped, if I kept them hidden and died alone in an unknown, unreachable place—"

"They would, in essence, die with you."

He nodded. I stared at the top of his head as another piece of his mystery fell into place. His meditation, hours on end spent in solitude, standing on pillars, apart from society, aloof. He'd been preparing himself to leave us—to save us from the tyranny of any one person with that much power.

"So, what stopped you?" I asked.

"Love," he said, meeting my gaze. "Weakness? The plan was doomed from the moment I threw the ax." He stood abruptly and paced to the window.

When he spoke again, his voice was gruff. "On the night she gave me the Principles, she came to my bedroll. She told me the story, the prophecy, and when she finished, she locked the fifth Principle around my neck."

I gasped and stood from the table. "She didn't ask you? Let you decide?"

Hosea rested a fist on the windowsill and looked out into the night. "At first I was confused," he said. "I knew of the clone bracelet, the one she wore. But the Principles, to me at the time, were a myth. And the training she put me through—she told me they were *games*."

He touched his nape, where the bracelet rested beneath his skin. "Once I understood it was all true. That mankind really had been given the power to destroy itself and demolish Earth—I knew the right thing to do was disappear and do no harm.

"Grandmother didn't want me to leave, but she gave me the idea. She was here five years and the villagers never coveted her power, because they were blind to it. She made them blind by remaining invisible. And if I had just done that—" He bowed his head.

My knees felt weak and I let myself slide down into the chair. I knew the next part of the story. Four days later, Kumar had come to collect him; and Hosea, to protect his mother and brother, had shown himself and made the promise to go with Kumar.

Hosea went on. "I tried to leave again eight years later. Lee refused to come. He wanted me to keep my promise, but I had to go. Every time I saw Father, I could feel my anger growing out of my control. So, I left Lee to go his own way and I ran from the KTC. When Father couldn't find me, he went after Mother."

"And she fled into the desert," I said, quietly. Finally understanding his guilt.

"When she died, I was free."

"No attachments," I said. "So, then?"

He shrugged. "I disappeared. I studied medicine and practiced when I could, mostly on animals. I lived with the trees. It was that way for ten years. Living with people but not touching, trying not to feel. If I did, if I cared too much, any one of them could be used to control me and I couldn't let that happen again. I knew I would eventually make my way out west. I had maps, plans. When the fever broke out, I thought I could help and then disappear again." He paused for a long time staring out of the window, then he turned and looked at me. "But then I met you."

I stood and went to his side.

"I thought maybe the trial would loosen the Kongo's hold on you. You'd see that they didn't deserve you any more than I did. But your love for the Kongo is like nothing I've ever seen. And I realized I'd never convince you."

His eyes were wet, and I blinked, releasing a tear as we remembered the night.

Hosea went on. "Father sent me a hologram after I left. He told me about the verdict. That you'd left with Lee to—to get the bracelets. I came back, to see what happened and—Oh god, Arika!" He pressed his face to my neck. "Seeing, but knowing I couldn't save you was..."

"Shh. I'm okay," I said.

He was trembling as he moved back to the square table and sat. He cleared his throat. "I saw that you lived. I saw—" He looked at my belly. "I saw you were happy," he said. "And so I left for the west."

My mouth dropped. "You left?"

He nodded.

I came back to the table and sat in front of him. "You mean, you made it west with the bracelets and you—came back? Why?! Why would you come back?"

He swallowed. "I can't explain how lifeless it was in the west," he said. "There was nothing there, Arika. Nothing. No food, no water. The air burns your lungs. I ran the aerofilter constantly. Scorched earth and lava geysers. They shoot hundreds of feet into the sky. Canyons of magma, acid rain."

I sat back. "It sounds terrible."

"It was torture!"

"You couldn't endure it," I said, understanding.

He stilled. "No, It's not that. I've trained so that I *could* endure it. And I always thought I was meant to remove the bracelets from the face of the Earth, to keep people in their place. But now—now I think doing so would be a mistake. When I saw the fire out there, I knew— I know." He lowered his head, struggling for words. He looked up at me. "I couldn't let you die again, like that," he said.

My heart stalled. "What do you mean?"

"Variant R-14," he said. "It's coming. Now, today."

"The arm of Christ," Anna said.

We turned to see her and Voltaire standing in the bedroom doorway, their faces tense. They'd been listening.

Hosea stood. "You know about the variant?"

"Lee Ford explained it," Anna said.

"We came across the vines when we left the Compound," I added.

Voltaire stepped forward into the room. "What do you mean, they're coming?"

"I've been studying the trees," Hosea said. "Listening."

"Listening?" Voltaire said. "You're saying you can understand trees?" She sounded as if she wanted to scoff at the possibility but couldn't.

"I don't understand perfectly," Hosea said. "The language is complex. But I've heard enough to know that we're no longer the dominant species on Earth. Or the most intelligent. And they want to secure their place in the food chain."

"The apex predator," Voltaire said.

Hosea nodded. "They're planning to strike. Now, today."

"Strike—at us?" I said. "At the Kongo?"

"At mankind, Arika," he said. "The Variant has been on the move for a year, positioning itself around our cities north and south. The fault line is what alerted me. It was a mistake on their part. They usually move covertly underground, closer to the magma layer. They can withstand extremely high temperatures. When they're ready, the strike will come from below." He bent his elbow and cut upwards, explaining how the branches would attack and break the ground.

"They'll destabilize the crust layer, and all of this we've worked so hard to salvage will look like the west."

I shivered, but kept my eyes trained on Hosea Khan. His face gave nothing away, but his eyes were dark.

"I've honored the Will in everything," he said, his jaw clenched. "I left my mother to die, and endured years of my brother's hatred because I knew he wouldn't accept the imperative. I watched my love get buried alive and die with our child inside her. I've honored the Will in everything, hoping that the things I can't see are good."

I shivered, thinking of Lark and the loom. "Are they not good?" I said.

Hosea paced. "Perhaps. Only, now I don't think it matters. I think the end has come and they want us gone."

"Destroyed by fire," Anna said, crossing herself.

"No!" Voltaire said. "We've been warned, we can run."

Hosea rested a hand on Anna's trembling shoulder. I saw the mission in his eyes before he spoke. I inhaled. "But you didn't come back to warn us, did you?" I said, knowing I was right.

My eyes shifted, examining the past year. I saw the grandmother running to save Kumar's life; he still had *work to do*. I saw Kumar, his arms outstretched, his face pulled as he pleaded with Hosea Khan—*I did the work; I gathered the world*. Kumar's fear, his deference. He'd believed in the truth of Hosea's purpose, and he'd forged it into being.

"You came back to follow your father," I whispered. "To sit on the throne. There's going to be a war, and you're to lead us."

"King Kha," Anna said. Her voice rang out.

Voltaire bowed her head. "The King."

Hosea looked from Voltaire's awe to Anna's trembling and, finally—to me. A bright gold light shone in his gaze, but it didn't flash. He didn't try to hide it. And when he took my hand, so I flanked his right, it rose to burn between us with the eternal and unknowable force of fate.

THE ASCENSION

We traveled throughout the night and neared City One early the next morning. We stopped to water the horse on a high hill overlooking the arena.

The venue was open to the air and, as promised, over a million people were present. They were packed into tiered platforms that curved around a smooth stone wall. Just inside the bounds of the wall, on white sand flooring, officials from every territory sat in gilded chairs. The Kongo Council, the day's host, sat front and center.

The program started with a large speaker chiming over the crowd. As it quieted, a quartet of musicians filed onto a circular platform that rose and rotated as the singers crooned in memory of Senator Kira Swan.

The platform lowered then rose again as a Clayskin governor read Swan's obituary. After, a Councilwoman revealed a statue of Kira's likeness.

The tribute ended with several long minutes of applause.

When the bell chimed again, demanding quiet, the official signing ceremony commenced. Director Kumar stood to address the crowd.

He was dressed in silver and gold and the horns of his headdress proclaimed him the new Head of Council. He came around the long table of Councilors and nodded to Senator

Osprey as he passed her seat. He started across the sand to the platform, where a pair of groundsmen positioned a podium.

Beside me, Hosea Khan waited quietly. "It's near time," he said. He squinted out at the holographic projection of the event then back down at me.

Avoiding his gaze, I turned aside and opened the sack slung across my body. I removed Lee's inferior cuff and stared at it.

"Arika? What's wrong?"

"I've been thinking about time," I said. I took a leather thong from my bag and tied it to the cuff.

Hosea peered over my shoulder. "What's that you've got?" he asked.

I turned and showed him. "Lee made it."

When Hosea reached for the cuff, I pulled back protectively. "He gave it to *me*," I said.

I fit the thong around my neck and tied the ends, so the cuff fell to the center of my chest. It felt warm there and, somehow, gave me confidence. "Your father spoke about it too. About time," I said.

Hosea nodded. "He's troubled by the idea. He doesn't understand how Grandmother got here."

"Because he thinks she traveled here from the future," I said, eyeing him. He hesitated then nodded his agreement. "And that's what has *me* troubled," I said. I bit my lip.

"There are things we're not meant to understand, Cobane. How Grandmother got here is one of them."

"I don't care *how*, that's just mechanics," I said. "What's bothering me is that Kumar was ranting about time when he destroyed the bracelet."

Hosea shrugged. "Good riddance."

I faced him. "You're not hearing. *He* destroyed the bracelet. The bracelet he was supposed to make with your mother, in the future. The bracelet that never gets made," I said. "*He* destroyed it."

Hosea tilted his head, finally understanding. Regardless of how she'd traveled through time, the bracelet should have ceased to exist in the moment Weka died. In the moment it became impossible for her future self and Kumar to create it.

"Did she duplicate the science?" I asked. "Make another bracelet once she got here?"

"In the parochial south?" he said, shaking his head. "In what lab, with what equipment? Not the KTC; Father hated her."

"So then, she didn't come from our future," I said. "She brought the bracelet here from—*another time*!" My mind raced, sorting and figuring parallel timelines, like threads on a loom!

"Arika?" Hosea said.

Our eyes locked, but I couldn't speak as my thoughts drove, mining the next conclusion. I'd seen thousands of unfinished threads. But my focus circled on the largest, most frayed thread that was nearest the end. And suddenly, I knew.

"You said you think the end has come," I whispered. "I think you're right."

The stadium roared, capturing our attention. Kumar's speech had ended.

I looked back at Hosea. His gaze had shifted back to the arena. His face gave nothing away, but I knew he watched his father.

I followed his gaze. Kumar, in his madness, had said *they* were toying with us, playing a game. And now I believed him. Lark was one of them, and Weka too. They were with us—guiding us to save humanity. So then, who of them was against us?

I looked around the deserted hillside, down at my feet then up into thin air. The fine hairs on my body rippled to life.

Hosea grabbed a tuft of Cumin's mane and swung up. "Are you ready?" he said. He lowered a hand. I touched the cuff around my neck and thought of Lee. *Ready or dead.*

I swung up behind Hosea Khan so the mound of my belly rested safely between us. I wrapped an arm around his shoulders, fitting my fingers in the opening of his shirt, against the dark skin of his chest. His heart beat strong and steady in my palm.

He kicked Cumin's side and we raced down the steep, bareback. The wind lifted his hair to mingle with mine like a black flag in our wake. As we closed in, he let go of the mane and took up his Helix. Following his lead, I gripped his waist with my thighs, unsheathed my weapon and held it ready, low on the pony's flank.

Hosea took aim and loosed the first arrow. It soared into the sky at an angle. When it disappeared, a crackle of gold light scattered and burst, raining down over the earth. Every head in the arena lifted, searching the skyline.

We were close. I could see the look on Kumar's face—it shined with love. We reached the stadium, and, with a giant leap streaked with lightning, we hurdled the arena wall.

"Father!" Hosea shouted. The sound ripped the air like a rooster declaring a new day.

Kumar stumbled back from the podium, turned and abdicated. He moved fast, like a cheetah, his hinged legs blurring beneath him. We reached the center of the arena, as Kumar leapt over the far edge. With a heave, Hosea dismounted. He flew into the air, pressed his Helix into a staff. Blue fire smoked on his skin, as he came down on one knee, driving the tip of the staff a foot into the earth. The ground beneath it puckered like a boil, then came alive, driving like a snake directly at Kumar. The snake reached the stadium wall, and stone and mortar exploded into the air.

Several hundred yards away, debris pummeled Kumar's back. He cried out, breaking stride and stumbling to a stop. He turned and raised a hand to his son, saying goodbye, passing the kingdom. Hosea got to his feet and raised a hand.

A second later, the snake reached Kumar, tossing him a hundred yards into the air.

I placed a hand on Hosea's back, offering my support, knowing what he had to do next. He looked down at me. Then, moving faster than the speed of light, he notched an arrow and sent it flying directly into his father's heart.

Kumar's lifeless body fell slowly, like a feather, back towards the earth. When he was still ten yards above the ground, the snake shot up like a cobra. It opened its mouth, flashed a red light, and swallowed the Director whole.

Quiet followed. Every eye in the stadium focused on Hosea Khan and me, wrapped together, as one. His hand in mine around his waist as the dust of the southern desert settled over us, sticking to the sweat on our skin. Pale, bright, dark, red and brown; they were, all of them, stunned, hushed by the force of our entry. Our summary slaying of their leader lent authority to our claim.

We stood tall, back-to-back. A king and queen by right of fight, demanding allegiance and awaiting a challenger. I gazed out at the spectrum, forcing my heart to acknowledge what my eyes saw clearly—the breadth of the us. The balance of tint and tone. The shade and the day, a perfect palindrome. My people.

Hosea shifted behind me and I pulled my gaze from them. I followed his to the horizon and froze, fear in my heart. He'd warned me, but I was unprepared as I watched one mountain peak drop from the skyline and another crumple like clay.

The tremors were small at first, then unmistakable. The people looked around wondering; then, finally, they looked to us.

As one, we forced our Helixes into points, encouraging them to follow suit. Slowly they obeyed that first order, opening their sacks and withdrawing the weapons they'd come to surrender.

Just before the trees attacked, a holy silence descended, surrounding the world like a breath, blessing us with a second of peace, perfect unity under one head, with all authority.

Then, with a mighty crash, the sand beneath us cracked in two, and a root came through, toppling a quarter of mankind.

The fourth war—the Earth War—began.

EPILOGUE

I squeezed Arika's hand, stood and stepped into the transport that hovered over the aperture in the crust layer of the Earth. As the transport closed over me, my immortal form lost its feminine shape and a strange feeling, like blood swelling a wound, consumed me. When the swelling stopped, I had no eyes, no ears, no body. I was molten Earth, a soul prepared to journey.

I sank into the ground, conscious of myself and aware of the individuals, also in soul form, swirling around me like magma. They zoomed by in hot gold streaks, processing their last life and waiting for their next permutation to begin.

The transport was programmed so my trip took less than a minute. I traveled through the middle layer of Earth to Eternity, an office in the core, where I, and the other Invisibles, lived and worked.

At the Eternal Gate, I stopped and felt my face cool as my eyes formed. I looked down and watched the remainder of my immortal body coalesce around my molten soul. My face shrank, my neck narrowed. I felt my waist and mouth recede. As soon as I could, I spoke, shouting to be heard outside of the transport. "Did it work?" I said. "What's the Count?"

Osa, who managed the gate, was adjusting levers at her workstation a few yards away.

I lifted a partly cooled hand and banged on the clear transport siding.

She looked up. "It worked, alright," she said, her tone droll. "And, yes, the Count is up."

"Aha!" I threw a fist, still glowing, into the air.

"Pipe down," Osa said.

"Pipe down?" I shouted. I glared at her. "The mission was successful!"

The smooth skin where her immortal eyes should have been wrinkled derisively. "If you'll recall, it was a *covert* assignment, Lieutenant." The tan pants wrapped around her thin, bent legs flapped as she wheeled towards me. She came to a stop and pointed a body scanner at my head. She slowly scanned down as she spoke. "No one knows you left, and the Warden wants to keep it that way."

I lowered my fist, understanding the need for secrecy. The rest of the Eternal workforce was wary of direct intervention in the human thread. The mission I'd been on had been risky, at best. I sighed. "They may not have approved before, but surely they will now!" I said, pointing behind her where a live image of the current human thread hung over her desk. Beside it was a black and white number ticker, the Count. Identical tickers hung in prominent places around Eternity and the workforce watched them compulsively. "They've got to know something big happened if the Count's up," I said.

Moving slowly, Osa placed the scanner in a compartment on her wheeled chair. She picked up another machine and began making notes.

"So?" I said.

She looked up.

"Where's the celebration!?" I demanded.

She shrugged. "Conference room A?" She checked her notes. "The Warden is scheduled to make an announcement right about now."

My heart throbbed. The announcement of the millennium, Earth time, and I was missing it. I looked down, impatient, as the black specks of cooling lava solidified into smooth skin. When my dark brown legs formed, I pulled the exit lever that opened the transport door, jumped from the clear tube and off the platform. I started in the direction of the conference room.

"Wait!" Osa said, rolling towards me.

I dodged her wheeled chair and hurried on.

"Lieutenant! We need to talk. There's something else. She told me to give it to you!"

I hurried on, calling over my shoulder. "I'll come back for it!"

I left the gate running flat out. I sprinted left, through the low ceilings of the Accounting Department, then took a shortcut through the training center and break room. Conference room A, our largest meeting space, was on the other side.

I grasped the door handle then stopped, sensing something was wrong. I released the door and pressed my back against the adjacent wall, trying to pinpoint what it was. It occurred to me suddenly. The room was too quiet.

The conference room door had a narrow, inset window and I leaned over to peer through it. The room was packed with workers—seated around an oval table, standing shoulder to shoulder, and leaning against the room's four dingy white walls.

Every eye was trained on the Warden, who sat beside an overhead projector. She was supposedly announcing that my mission had worked. That humanity was united and on the

405

brink of the Earth War that would, ultimately, usher in what we'd all been waiting in Eternity for—peace on Earth.

Only, no one was cheering. No one was laughing. No one was smiling.

The lights were dimmed, but I knew the room well. It doubled as a tactical briefing center. Of the eighty-nine missions I'd completed, eighty-eight had been assigned to me while sitting at the large oval table inside. Only one mission, my last mission, had been given to me in the privacy of the Warden's office.

•

I'd been asked to come early, and I did so, knocking discreetly on her partially opened door.

The Warden looked up. "Lieutenant, come in, close the door."

I stepped inside and shut the door behind me. "If this is about my last assignment, I can explain—"

She held up a hand. "It's not that," she said.

I waited, dropping my eyes to her desk. Front and center was a long wooden bar with her name etched on it: Weka Vine, Warden.

The bar didn't say it, but she was the tenth Warden of Eternity. There'd been nine before her. Their names and the missions they oversaw were easily accessible, filed chronologically in Accounting—but we didn't speak of them or the fact that, ultimately, they had failed. One by one, all nine had chosen to rescind their immortal form contracts and return to the magma.

As a workforce we agreed to focus, instead, on the positive: that under the tenth Warden, Warden Vine, humanity had made it farther than ever before. That, in fact, at their current pace, there were fewer than a hundred years, Earth time, until the end.

One hundred years. I found, if I thought on it hard enough, it felt like a ray of light burning in my chest. And if I closed my eyes and whispered it—*one hundred years*—I remembered how it felt to be human and sit in the sun.

The Warden shifted, regaining my attention. She took a folder from her top drawer and placed it on her desk. It looked like a standard issue assignment folder. Only, instead of brown, it was bright blue. She moved again and rested something on top of the folder.

I looked closer and my mouth dropped. The object was a small stone shaped like a half-moon. I hadn't seen it since my human death over six hundred years ago, Earth time.

"Do you remember how to use it?" the Warden said.

I blinked. Of course I remembered. "I used it last in 1739 Anno Domini," I said. *The last time I'd seen my Cato.*

"Good," the Warden said. "Here's your next assignment." She pushed the stone and folder across the desk.

I hesitated, eyeing the rock. If I'd learned anything at all in Eternity, guiding humanity, it was to fear God in any manifestation.

"Lieutenant!"

I jumped, reached out and snatched up the half-moon, one of the three living perfections. I slipped it into the slot of my snakeskin sheath.

The Warden cleared her throat and lifted her chin, indicating the blue assignment folder.

I slid it from the desk and opened it: *Mission: Warrior line one. Subject: Arika Cobane, circa 179 A.E.*

•

Outside Conference Room A, I stared down at the Eternal flooring. It was stained and worn, as tired as the stoic room of workers just inside. I bent to look in the window again—*why weren't they celebrating?*

A soft rattle reached my ears and I turned to look down the hall. Osa was wheeling towards me. She was waving a folder—I inhaled. The folder was bright blue.

By the time she reached me she was huffing and livid. She spouted off, but I ignored her, eyeing the folder. "What is that?" I said.

She pinned me with her sightless eyes. "It's your next assignment."

"Mine?" I said, touching my chest, certain I'd heard wrong. Breaks from Eternity, even for a minute, were coveted. The workers fought over the chance to return to Earth as a wind, a shadow, a whisper. "There are higher ranking officers," I said. "Better workers. Why is she sending me again?"

Osa smiled sympathetically. "You know the answer to that."

The half-moon perfection shifted in the hidden slot of my suit. Its power had made direct intervention in Arika's life possible—though no less risky.

"It's another intervention," I whispered.

Osa glanced at the conference door, then nodded. "And you're to leave immediately." She turned her wheeled chair around and started down the hall.

At the gate, Osa prepared for the launch. I moved to the platform and stepped into the transport, gazing at the Count behind her desk. When it reached zero, the current human thread would die and join the dark matter of other threads that had died over the course of time. Mankind would, once again, return to the beginning of the loom: accretion, primordial juice, evolution—and *another* dark age. I shivered.

We knew what we'd signed up for when we accepted passage from the magma. Eternity was, by definition, time without end. Every worker, to a soul, arrived hopeful. But, as the Count declined, along with the possibility of us guiding humanity to peace on Earth, more of us were accepting passage back. Our numbers were in decline. And, recently, the Eternal halls felt like everlasting torment, quiet wailing, gnashing teeth. We didn't just hope this current thread made it to the end—we needed it to.

"The program is complete," Osa said.

I nodded listlessly.

"Lieutenant, you can't take the folder with you," she said. She bent her head to catch my eye. "Lark?"

"Oh—yes, of course not." I cleared my throat, straightened my shoulders. I opened the folder in my hand. *Mission: Warrior line two. Subject: Starla Brown, circa 1919 A.D*^{2}. I skimmed the details once, then again—I had an excellent memory. I closed the folder and tossed it so it landed smoothly on Osa's flat lap.

I pulled the lever and the transport closed.

"Good luck," Osa said. She gave me a rare, reassuring smile. "In three, two, one—"

ABOUT THE AUTHOR

Agnes Gomillion is a speaker and writer based in Atlanta, Georgia, where she lives with her husband and two children. Homegrown in the Sunshine State, Agnes studied English Literature at the University of Florida before transitioning to Levin College of Law, where she earned both a Juris Doctorate and Legal Master degree. She's a voracious reader of the African-American literary canon and a dedicated advocate for marginalized people everywhere. Follow her on social media @agnesgomillion